John Steele was born and raise
In 1995, at the age of twenty-two F
and has since lived and worked o.

thirteen-year spell in Japan. Among past jobs he has been a
drummer in a rock band, an illustrator, a truck driver and a
teacher of English. He now lives in England with his wife and
daughter. He began writing short stories, selling them to North
American magazines and fiction digests. He has published four
previous novels: *Ravenhill*, *Seven Skins*, *Dry River* and *Rat
Island*, the first of which was longlisted for a CWA Debut Dagger
award. John's books have been described as 'remarkable' by the
Sunday Times, 'dark and thrilling' by Claire McGowan, and 'spec-
tacular' by Tony Parsons. The *Irish Independent* called John 'a
writer of huge promise' and Gary Donnelly appointed him 'the
undisputed champion of the modern metropolitan thriller'.

THE SKY TURNED BLACK

John Steele

SILVERTAIL BOOKS • *London*

For my family, near and far, especially Hana and Tomoe
who will always be my greatest adventure.

New York City
1997

One

Callum Burke listened to the end of the joke and thought of smacking Gerry Martin with the stock of the Mossberg shotgun wedged between his knees.

Martin said, 'So the lady cop, she says, "Sir, where's this guy with the toothache?"' The tall, thin Martin, folded in his bench seat in the back of the NYPD van like a lawnchair, cracked a huge grin.

Callum sighed and shot a glance of solidarity at Georgina Ruiz sitting up front. She was turned back toward them but didn't catch the look, busying herself with her Kevlar vest.

Martin heard the sigh and grunted, satisfied he'd pushed some buttons.

'What,' he said, 'you pissed I offended your little chiquita, Cal?'

Before Callum could answer, Georgie said, '*Qué vaina!* Gold star, Gerry: you just used a couple words with more than two syllables.'

'Pity his dick is still shorter in inches,' said Callum.

Georgie gave him a smile for that one. For a moment, he enjoyed the light in her eyes.

Martin spat, 'Fuck you, Burke,' and hunched up tight, like a mean dog snapping at the alpha male in the pack, then slinked back, scared of the consequences.

The windowless Prisoner Van sat a couple of blocks from the projects, out back of a Russian church off Surf Avenue, Coney Island. Callum could see one of the taller amusement park attractions spearing an overcast late April sky a block away by the boardwalk.

As the only cop in the unit who hadn't yet made detective grade, he could have minded his Ps and Qs with the ranking Gerry Martin. But the asshole had been riding him since day one of his time with Brooklyn South Narcotics Division, and if he didn't stand up, the others would eat him alive. He knew Martin was a little frightened of him, of his reputation, and enjoyed it. And he sympathized with Georgie, one of two women on their team, who had been working narcotics for just over a year to Callum's three months. They had good history together and he knew she'd been gritting her teeth throughout a chunk of her career thanks to assholes like Martin.

Today's target location – the *set* – was a housing authority complex bisected by West 23rd Street running north to south. Two massive slabs of concrete studded with windows formed an almost semi-circle, facing each other across West 23rd. On the second floor of the eastern block two drug dealers, Charles Beresford and Willie Mayhew, would be busy cutting, apportioning and packaging 8 ounces of heroin.

Callum heard the piercing scream of gulls. Coney Island Beach and the water of the Atlantic were a short walk to the south. Beyond lay Ireland, land of his birth.

A garbled squawk blasted from Georgie's radio. The message came through that the Criminal Informant who had given the tip about the heroin had reported she wasn't sure if the dealers' dogs were asleep yet. One of the mutts had barked about ten minutes ago. They had to wait a little longer for the "Go".

Detective Angel Patrosi, in the command car with their sergeant, was the cop "getting on" today. It was his CI who was loitering in the hallway outside Beresford and Mayhew's apartment. According to the CI, Willie Mayhew got headaches from the constant barking of the guard dogs, two pitbulls named Bert and Ernie. Mayhew had confided to the CI that he laced the dogs' lunch with triazolam to knock them out for a couple of hours in the afternoon. The CI was going to knock on the dealers' door and ask to borrow money for cigarettes. If the dogs stayed silent, the CI would call from a payphone in the courtyard of the building and the bust was on.

'Fuckin' dogs,' said Martin. 'Why they always got dogs?'

Callum said, 'Because candy-asses like you are afraid of them.'

The bust would get each cop on the team up to five hours of overtime. Problem was, they'd have preferred going in heavier. They could use the ESU tactical unit, but that meant a methodical forced entry. Narcotics cops could get in faster to root out the stash before it was flushed or dumped, so the team had opted to keep it in the family.

The family, thought Callum. And am I a paid-up member?

The others had done their time on patrol, building arrests, amassing the points for a shot at an investigative unit and a detective's shield. Georgie had been on the Job seven years before she hit the numbers, Angel Patrosi six. Rumor was Gerry Martin spent more than ten Christmases in uniform before he got a shot.

And Callum? Just thirteen months at the 6th Precinct: then the round-robin, the oral board interview and the nod for Narcotics. He'd known by the sour-lemon pout on a couple of supervisors' faces at the interview that they didn't like him cutting in line. He saw it everyday on the Job. Martin was the guy in his face but Callum would notice a hushed word between colleagues, a brusque answer; hell, he was always last in line for a slice when they worked late and ordered in pizza. Only Georgie treated him as a true equal.

Only she knew the whole story of why he'd risen so fast. Why a Triad Dragon Head godfather was making license plates at the NCI in Somers. Why Jimmy Mulligan, scourge of the New York Irish mob, got his jaw busted and a skull fracture. Thanks to his undercover work on a multi-agency task force busting the big names, Callum had caught the eye and earned the gratitude of now-Inspector Bochinni. Bochinni had become his rabbi – a powerful ally, like a sponsor, within the department.

Callum caught Georgie's eye and she offered a wink.

Martin was bitching and moaning.

'Sarge notifies Communications that we're working in the Six-Oh to hit an apartment,' he said, 'the Six-Oh's desk officer offers to give us an RMP with two uniforms, and he turns it down?'

Georgie spoke slow, like she was talking to a kid. 'C'mon Ger, a marked patrol car just sounds the alarm for the street dealers, you know that.'

'All I know is, I'm too young for an inspector's funeral. Sarge is gettin' loose, man. I hope to God he remembers to turn off the radios when we hit the set.'

'The sarge is just fine,' said Callum. 'Patrosi, too. Your balls just gotta drop.'

'It's the Guinea factor, what it is. We're workin' off Patrosi's tip. Sarge is Italian. It's like the Sicilians' shit.'

Georgie laughed, a sound as bleak as the gray Atlantic a block away.

'You think that compares with your green mafia in the department, Gerry?'

'Sister's got a point,' said Callum. 'The Irish still got a lot of the Job sewn up.'

Martin went red. 'You're Irish,' he said.

'I can self-reflect,' said Callum, 'and Patrosi threw the racket for Nowak when his old lady got sick. Raised four thousand dollars for hospital bills from that party.'

'Yeah, Patrosi's alright,' said Georgie.

'We should have more firepower on this,' said Martin.

Callum kept his eyes on the street through the windshield. 'Ten cops in this team with three Mossbergs and a handgun each against two assholes and a couple of puppies: those odds ain't good enough for you?'

'It's the project full of negroes I'm worried about.'

'Negroes?' said Georgie. 'Jesus, listen to yourself.'

'S'what they are, Chiquita, look it up in the dictionary. Better than the other "n" word.'

'Alexander's black.'

'Trish Alexander's a cop. Ain't the same thing.'

Callum checked his watch. It was almost 1400.

The van was warmer than the cool day outside: come June, it would be a sweatbox.

Georgie stopped fussing with her vest and smoothed her hair, scraped back from her forehead and tied in a tight bun. Martin scratched at a patch of dry skin between his eyebrows and bounced his left foot on the floor of the van. Callum gripped the shotgun and played a song over in his head. He tried not to think about the pack of Camels in his pocket.

They were all wired, all waiting for the word to hook up with the rest of the team spread across three cars in addition to the van. One vehicle would double as the hospital car if anyone were hurt on the bust, although the 60th Precinct was less than 10 minutes' drive away.

A crackle like gunfire filled the van and Georgie leaned in to her radio, straining to hear through the static. After a couple of moments she nodded and gunned the engine. They hit Mermaid Avenue, drove three blocks west then turned south on West 22nd and pulled up twenty yards from the huge concrete facade of the rear of the east housing block in the project. A massive annex jutted from the center of the rear of the block, a stairwell and apartments stacked seventeen floors high.

Georgie, Martin and Callum clambered out of the van onto the empty sidewalk. They strode toward a break in the railings surrounding the project, on the northeast corner, and a narrow path laid in the lawn snaking around the building.

A blue Ford pulled up and more narcotics cops joined them.

Callum felt his guts hollow out a little, his arms beginning to buzz as they walked. Martin scratched the back of his head and Callum wondered if the asshole ever washed his greasy-ass hair.

Some cops peeled off the path and ran at a crouch to the stairwell entrance at the foot of the block's annex, hunkering down by a row of trash cans to act as rear security.

Callum and the rest rounded the end of the block and Callum saw Sarge, Angel Patrosi and Trish Alexander stride across the lawn of the courtyard that stretched from West 23rd. The sarge and Patrosi were breathing hard with the shared weight of the battering ram; their car was parked up on the curb. The matching apartment block sat, huge and brooding, on the other side of the street. A pack of teenagers by the Jungle Gym on the lawn ahead started whistling to warn low-level street dealers the cops were here.

People stooped their heads; youths glared hatred. A guy in a filthy hooded sweatshirt spat and muttered. A couple of women with kids hurried them away toward West 23rd.

A rangy kid took off like he was in the first race at the dog track. They ignored him. No one was falling for a decoy today. Patrosi fell into step beside Callum. Two young white boys jogged off to north and south, customers who didn't want mom and pop out in Riverdale or Mount Pleasant to know they'd been busted buying dope in Coney. Callum could've sworn one of them with choirboy looks gave him a wink as he passed. He could have sworn the kid was wearing eyeshadow.

Trish Alexander saw him watching the youth and said, 'Hey, you wanna' ask him for a date, wait 'til we're done here.'

Callum caught the ghost of a smile on her lips. He pulled his badge out from his hockey top and let it hang on its chain in front of his vest. Alexander and the rest of the team followed suit with their shields. They sprinted the last couple of yards to the first entrance of the block frontage and hugged the wall,

Sarge and Patrosi grunting with the weight of the ram. No airmail: rocks from above, bottles, appliances.

The plan was the three cops with the ram ride the elevator, the rest take the stairs.

Through the door, they saw the elevator was out of service. They all groaned and hit the stairs, taking turns with the ram. Callum saw the outline of Alexander's note pad and pen against the ass of her jeans as they climbed.

He gave Georgie the shotgun and took the ram for the second flight, feeling its weight as he lugged it up the steps with Sarge. He and Sarge sounded like they'd run a four-minute mile when they reached the second floor. They all scuttled down the corridor to door 247. The place smelt of bleach and dope, and a kid was screaming somewhere.

Always a screaming kid, thought Callum. It's like they choreograph this shit.

His back hit the wall. Georgie shoved the Mossberg back in his hands then drew her Glock. They fanned to either side of the door, guns drawn and sweating, breathing heavy. Alexander was close to Callum on his right, her body hot and hard against his hip, Glock in a two-handed grip by her crotch. Callum knew what came next – the ram swinging and battering, swinging and battering, the shouts of *Police!*, over and over, the sound of a toilet flushing as the dealers tried to lose the drugs, until the hinge finally gave way and they busted into the chaos of a raid.

Martin was straining, eyes popping, mouth pinched as he swung the ram back. It seemed to hang in the air for a second. Callum heard Trish Alexander pant softly by his ear.

There was a moment of quiet. Callum realised they were all so hopped up on adrenaline they forgot to try the goddamn door handle first.

The ram hit home.

The impact on the door was a detonation in the bare corridor.

'Police search warrant! Open the door!'

Martin cried out in surprise.

Patrosi was first to realise the door gave on the first try and pivoted around the frame, pistol out and shouting a warning. Martin yelled as he pitched forward and let go of the ram, losing it with the momentum of the swing through the open doorway. The steel ram caught Patrosi on the leg and something seemed to pop under his jeans as he went down on one knee. Callum was after him, shotgun to shoulder, screaming.

'Policedon'tmovedon'tfuckin'movefuckyou!'

The fetid smell hit him like a wall.

He eyeballed something red and furry and wet. Then he saw Charles Beresford, the man's eyes like glass marbles, his carob skin fouled by the blood slathered across his neck and shoulders. He had a small crater the size of a dime in the center of his forehead, another under his left eye. A knife was buried in his gut. The man kneeling by Beresford's body was reaching for a revolver on the floor by the far wall, growling an obscenity.

Something hard and narrow punched Callum in the back. He pitched forward, calling out, the shotgun still pointed at shoulder height. The muzzle cracked the killer across the jaw. The man dropped his head to the left. Callum's knee hit the nose with a sound like a baseball bat on a pumpkin. He barrelled over the man and turned as he fell. He landed by someone's head and saw Willie Mayhew staring up at the ceiling and the heavens beyond, a tight grouping of bulletholes in his naked chest. His stomach had been opened and a large combat knife lay by his body. The sarge was kicking another man in the face and bellowing nonsense. Gerry Martin ran over and started pounding on the guy with his fists while Alexander covered him with her Glock. The man Callum dropped was on the floor face first, Georgie standing over him with her gun at his back, yelling at Callum to get his cuffs. The world was all sound and fury.

Callum struggled to his feet and felt his body recenter. The fall had knocked some of the buzz from him. The door hung off one of its hinges, leading to the living space where they all stood. He saw the butchered dogs lying in a corner. He took in the two white men on the floor. He fiddled with his cuffs and got the man covered by Georgie in bracelets. Both men had skewed noses, one a split lip. Their hands were gloved and their arms slathered in blood up to their elbows. Charles Beresford and Willie Mayhew had fatal gunshot wounds to the face and chest. Beresford's neck was a mess and blood had formed a pool shaped like a kidney bean by his head. Both dealers had been opened from sternum to groin. A couple of revolvers, a semi-automatic pistol with a suppressor, and a selection of knives lay on the floor by the wall. A cushion on the floor had been blown open by a bullet, blood smeared on one side.

Patrosi had got his ass up and sat propped against the shattered door frame. His right leg lay at an obscene angle and his face was dirty-ashtray gray.

The rear security team popped into the doorway. A cop said, 'What the fuck?'

Sarge barked over his shoulder, 'Call a *bus* for Patrosi.' They couldn't move him with his busted leg so he'd need an ambulance. Georgie knelt by him to do what she could in the meantime.

Everyone breathed hard. Trish Alexander stared at the blood on her hands and dry heaved. Callum looked away when she caught his eye.

Sarge knelt by one of the gunmen on the floor and tapped him on the shoulder. He pointed to the semi-automatic lying by the wall.

'What kinda' gun is that?'

'Fuck you.' The accent was heavy Slavic.

'Yo, Drac, what kinda' pistol you got?'

'Ivan,' said Martin.

Sarge said, 'What?'

'Ivan, not Drac. Dracula was Transylvanian: that's in Romania – this guy's Russian.'

'How the fuck do you know?'

'History channel.'

'The gun is Russian,' said Callum. 'A Makarov. I saw them back home in Belfast.' He coughed hard and thought of the Camels in his pocket again.

The man on the floor looked up at him, sneered and spat an obscenity that none of them could begin to understand.

Two

Callum lit up a cigarette, tilted his head back to a Brooklyn sky of hammered tin and exhaled. His smoke drifted heavenward like a torn rag of cloud crossing above the Coney Island Wonder Wheel in the distance by the boardwalk.

So close to the water, he thought, and he couldn't smell any salt in the air.

Just the abbatoir reek of the apartment on the second floor clinging to his nostrils.

Callum stood with his back to the wall of the apartment block. George Ruiz was a couple of yards away at a payphone with her hand over her left ear. The earpiece was clamped over her right and she was firing rapid bursts of Spanish at her husband on the end of the line, shouting to compete with a burping siren as another RMP arrived on the sprawling housing project court-yard. There were Radio Mobile Patrol cars scattered across the space. Tape had been stretched in a large, rough rectangle, sealing off the front entrance to the apartment block from a growing crowd. Uniformed officers stood by the tape keeping the rubberneckers at bay. A couple of technicians walked by Callum carrying black valises for the corpses up in the fouled apartment.

Ruiz yelled, '*No me estés divariando, respóndeme la pregunta!*'

She paused like something caught in her throat then held the phone at arm's length. After a second she shoved it back on the hook and joined Callum.

'I kinda asked for that,' she said. 'Arthur hates when I use Dominican slang.'

'Irene used to switch to Cantonese when she was angry,' said Callum. 'I couldn't understand ninety percent but it was her country, you know? And I figured, if I got her that pissed, I must have deserved at least some of whatever I was hearing. It isn't easy being married to a cop.'

'You're so full of shit, Cal.' Ruiz tossed him a smile seemed to warm the cool April air. 'I can tell you're a nightmare to date. One of those soulful Celtic types with your rough hands and your quick temper and your goddamn baggage. No wonder the Irish flooded the Job way back. You don't know how to live a quiet life: never happy unless you're miserable.'

He took a drag on his cigarette and tossed it on the concrete.

'Well, I should be ecstatic right now,' he said. 'You know the paperwork we got coming thanks to the two flycatchers bled out on that carpet upstairs?'

'Hey, not a shot fired. That's something. And you, baby, cracking that guy with the Mossberg.' Ruiz looked him up and down like he'd just fed her a line. Some day, he thought.

'And me,' he said, 'cracking that guy with the Mossberg as I fell on my ass thanks to Alexander shoving me in the back.'

'Could have been worse than a shove. We are talking "Johnson" here.'

Callum rustled up a stage grimace.

Trish "Johnson" Alexander, so called – but never to her face – thanks to a Buy and Bust operation years ago. The story went that Alexander was undercover as a junkie hooker and called in the cavalry from a payphone after her buy went down. Unknown to her, the psychotic Jamaican she was targeting had followed her. The dealer didn't hear the phone call, but he did like Alexander's legs in the denim mini-skirt and stilettos she was wearing. He liked her too-tight t-shirt, her lips you could get lost in for days on end. So he grabbed a fistful of hair, pushed her down and unzipped his fly, looking for a free taste. Alexander's team arrived just as she was ratcheting the cuffs tight on the 250lb perp's cock. The word was the Jamaican's johnson turned blue as an NYPD shirt. Forever after, Alexander was doomed to be known as "Johnson". But thanks to her Christian sensibilities, cops shyed from using the nickname when she was around. Plenty of cops went to church, many to the odd mass. But Alexander never drank, never swore, and was fast to rile at the odd blasphemy thrown around by her colleagues.

Cops were wary of that which they didn't understand.

Callum said, 'She looked bad in there. She got a lot of blood on herself in the bust.'

Ruiz shrugged her shoulders. 'Not exactly washed in the blood of the lamb.'

They saw Martin and Sarge in conversation with a couple of officers over by an ambulance.

'Patrosi won't be playing baseball any time soon,' said Callum.

'Yeah,' said Ruiz. She sounded like her mind was off in an alternate universe for a second. She turned to Callum.

'What do you think normal people would do if they saw what we just saw up there?' she said.

'You mean civilians?'

'No, I mean *normal* people.'

'Come on, Georgie.'

'I got a pissed husband who's got to take our kids to the pool for their lesson, make dinner, get them to bed. He was supposed to have a couple beers with his friends tonight. Now he gets to sit up waiting for me to come home and not talk about the shit that ruined both our days. Because if I don't lock him out, I'm scared of what I'm gonna say, or what he's going to know about the cop version of me. And that ain't fair, on him or me.'

'I go home to an empty apartment and framed photographs of my estranged wife and little girl,' said Callum. 'I leaf through more brochures about Cleveland, and try to imagine walking around with Irene and Tara in those places I see on the pages. And I say to myself I'll book the tickets next week. Again.'

He dropped his spent smoke, fished the packet of Camels from his pocket and slid another cigarette out, jammed it in his lips. He flicked his zippo open, then stopped and grabbed the cigarette again.

'I've been running the same routine for a year, Georgie. I play with the idea of going to see Irene and Tara, then crack open a bottle and think it over some more. Because I'm scared to get on the goddamn bus and take the trip. And that's some twisted shit: scared of your own family. But tomorrow you'll see your kids and make them breakfast, and snipe at Arthur or kiss and make up and you'll *be* there. You might be scared of them knowing the version of you on the Job; but I'm a fucking coward.'

Someone yelled from the crowd of onlookers and a ripple of laughter ran along the line. A couple of uniforms looked up out of reflex, checking for airmail hurled from the rooftop. Then the uniforms remembered there were cops up there surveying the area and turned back to the crowd with a roll of their shoulders.

It was a frozen crime scene but not quite a level one mobilization. They had the tape up. Six-Oh cops were searching for further evidence through garbage, in the building incinerators, around the front and rear entrances of the housing block. There was a half-assed mobile command in a laundromat on West 23rd with stripped back coms. But no choppers, no brass, no ESU pitching in on the evidence search.

A detective had once listed the priorities in Homicide to Callum, ticking them off on mustard stained fingers in order of importance:

1 and 2: Cop killing or child victim.

3: Cases a Boss wants solved because he knows the deceased or for political shit.

4: Some vic. They can wait.

Charles Beresford and Willie Mayhew were *likelies* – characters who would probably end up dead before their time one way or the other, through murder or overdose or whatever. They didn't merit a priority level one. But Patrosi's injury and the threat to life of Callum's team ratcheted up the importance of the case a notch.

One of the homicide detectives walked out of the building, sighed and approached Sarge. He'd be juggling cases, keeping several files in the air at once. This was a slam dunk but it would still eat into his time. He and Sarge went into a huddle and Gerry Martin strolled to the tape to speak with a uniform.

'You know they'll go over this again?' said Ruiz. She resettled a fugitive strand of licorice hair and crossed her arms.

They had related the forced entry to Beresford and Mayhew's apartment to the homicide detectives and would have to do so again at least once back at the 60th Precinct. The detectives had listened and jotted down notes and settled into their default mode of weary scepticism at the facts as relayed by their witnesses. They would have to take this to a District Attorney. The DA would tear them a new one if the case didn't hold water when brought before the Grand Jury. Discrepancies in witness statements, particularly from cops, could sink a case early on, even if the suspects had been found up to their elbows in blood and gore.

In the eyes of the law, thought Callum, who was to say the two psychopaths carving up the bodies had actually murdered the victims? Sure, they were butchering the corpses – but that didn't mean they had pulled the trigger on the Makarov or revolvers that peppered the dealers with bullets.

So the detectives had looked at the narcotics team like teachers who suspected the kid before them was cooking up some story about their lost homework. It made Callum feel …

'Guilty as shit,' said Ruiz. 'I felt guilty as shit. And we do it, too, to regular citizens. No wonder people stay the hell away from cops.'

'Hey, if I weren't a cop, I'd stay as far-a-fucking-way from any of you reprobates as I could.'

'Reprobates? You are so Irish sometimes. What, am I – a rascal, too?'

'You're smiling, huh? You like that one? Arthur can call you that next time you're working on a brother or sister for the kids.'

'Better than mouthing it at the mirror in your sad-ass Village apartment.'

Sarge walked up and said, 'You alright?'

Ruiz said, 'Sure.'

Callum said, 'Yeah.'

'We gotta' go to the Six-Oh and do the paperwork. Patrosi's in Mount Sinai. The leg's shattered.'

'Can we see him?' said Ruiz.

'Maybe tomorrow. McKee ain't too happy this landed on his lap. Stevie was close to a result on the Aquarium shooting. Now he gotta push it back in his case load for this shit.'

Callum could imagine how pissed Stephen McKee would be. Homicide detectives had several meetings each week with their commanding officer in which they reviewed and reprioritzed their ongoing cases. The dealers' bodies upstairs had tossed a grenade in their workload, and other cases would have to wait a couple of days until the grand jury ruled if the butchers who cut up Beresford and Mayhew could stand trial on a murder charge.

Callum said, 'How about Patrosi's CI? Can we bring her in for interview?'

'Nothing's gonna happen there until Patrosi is out of surgery and comfortable.'

Ruiz and Callum nodded.

'Okay, we're almost outta here,' said Sarge. 'We finish up at the Six-Oh, then it's the Anchor for a drink if anyone wants.'

'You got it,' said Ruiz.

Callum caught the tired flicker of her eyelids when Sarge walked away.

'You know, you don't have to go for that drink,' he said.

Ruiz offered a smile didn't make it to her eyes.

'And pass on the chance to spend an extra hour with a *reprobate* like you?'

She cocked her head to the side and the smile made it home. Her eyes lit up for a second. Then she reached out, grabbed Callum's hand and squeezed it. As she let go and walked off, he felt the sun burn through the April chill and watched her disappear behind an RMP.

They were bonded.

She knew the Callum who'd lived undercover with the worst the New York Irish mob could offer. She knew the Callum she'd helped pull out of an industrial hulk, busted to hell, amid Chinese and Irish bodies as the feds rubbed their hands at the RICO case he'd helped build.

He saw her push the hard street cop angle in Brooklyn South Narcotics. He saw her do her best to reconcile with the rawness of those hours on the Job. But she never quite buried the wife and mother in Astoria during the Buy and Busts. She put on a good show for the others, but he'd been close to that woman who held her family back in Queens together for too long to be convinced.

He rubbed the back of his head and rolled his neck. It was as he strolled over to the P-Van that he caught a glimpse of the face among the gawkers. There for a couple of seconds; then gone like an acid flashback. The young, choirboy face that had winked at him as the team made for the housing block a couple of hours ago. The choirboy blinked as he was jostled in the crowd and Callum saw he wasn't wearing eyeshadow. He saw words. Words in a foreign script.

The young man's eyelids had been tattooed.

Three

Clack. Clack. Clack.

He saw the car in his head, climbing the track, straining for the peak. Soon he'd face the heart-plunging, violent downward rush as the car crested the first summit of the roller coaster and dropped.

The climb began after breakfast.

Clack. Clack. Clack.

Tikhon would finish his toast and coffee and look out his window at the municipal parking lot, the boardwalk beyond dusted with sand a shade paler than concrete in the morning light. He lived on the top floor of the building in a corner apartment, on the corner of Brighton 4th Street and Brightwater Ct. The unit next door was empty, the floor quiet. Not so the noise from below. A senile, deaf old woman blared her radio and television early in the morning until eight or nine at night. Tikhon let her be. The clamour downstairs helped keep some of the fear and rage at bay.

As he left his building, he'd imagine the rollercoasters at Astroland, a short walk west at Coney Island. Rollercoasters: they translated as *American mountains* in Russian.

Clack. Clack. Clack.

All day, his anxiety rode that slow climb to the climax of his fear and shame and the fucked-up space in his head. There was no way off the ride. Then, when night fell, the tip over the edge, the plunge into madness, the screaming. Tikhon would try to drink it away sometimes, even though he knew that would end badly, and not for him. Instead, some man would be left on a barroom floor with a broken jaw, or a shattered eye socket. He'd been lucky so far – some joker back in the military had nick-named him Tikhon for his luck – as it was always the right kind of man. The kind who wouldn't go to the police. But one day, if he didn't stop, that luck would run out.

Other nights, Tikhon would lie in a waking dream. He'd hear the *Dukhi* – the *ghosts* – whisper in the dark of his room; feel the *telnyashka* vest cling to his sweating chest; he'd smell the oil of an APC trundling by with marines or airborne men, or the tobacco of a freshly lit Yava cigarette. He'd wait for the flash of AKs, the screams of soldiers shredded, Afghans halved by heavy fire. The bleat of dying sheep or comrades.

Then, when the first shards of cold light slipped through the crack in his drapes, Tikhon would drift into a short, dreamless sleep.

Clack. Clack. Clack.

Now it was dark and the coaster's summit was approaching like a snow-capped peak through the windshield of an Mi-8 chopper: some jagged shard of mountain that had been there even longer than the rangy, bearded Afghan fighters Tikhon had hunted and evaded back in the war. He sat on the B Subway Train to West 4th St station. Upon arrival he'd catch the C or E to Chelsea and his shot at stalling the plunge into the night-mares.

Clack. Clack. Clack.

The subway car bucked as it entered West 4th. Tikhon stepped onto the platform and saw others like him among the crowds. Young men bound for the West Village and Boots and Saddle near Village Cigars, or the Ninth Circle, or other low-lit spaces where men could drink and talk and touch on Christopher St and all points west of 7th Avenue.

He caught his connection to Chelsea fifteen minutes later.

On the street, Tikhon walked by an immaculate east Asian man and pushed through the door of the Hung Jury bar on 8th

Avenue. It was thronged, bodies pressing and coalescing in a dim orange light. Tuesday night. The leather-chaps-and-cowboy-hat shit was a couple of days off on "Longhorn Evening". Instead, a class drag act singing Broadway tunes was draped on a baby grand on the stage at the end of the narrow barroom, a guy in an old-time saloon shirt and sleeve garters playing the ivories.

Tikhon flinched as a spotlight roved the crowd and lit him up for a second.

ClackClackClack.

He felt a panic course through his limbs like a MiG was flying strafing runs around his body. He closed his eyes tight, drove it out and opened them again before he could flash scenes from the war. The spotlight was back on the stage.

Fuck it. He'd have a drink to even himself out. Just one, not even a vodka. Some of the weak piss that passed as beer in this country.

Threading his way through the crowd, he tried not to touch the men. He turned away when two of them locked bodies. Most were casual. Tight t-shirts packing hard-toned stomachs and bruised loneliness. A few were in business suits. A safe, conservative crowd. He made the counter after waiting for a short, loud man to finish a half-hearted flirt with the bartender and ordered a Miller. The bartender popped the cap off a bottle, took the cash and made to throw him a line. Then he caught something in Tikhon's gray, Muscovite eyes and moved on to the next patron.

Tikhon eased his way to the front window, blacked out against the street, and sat on the inner ledge. The crowd seemed to merge into one mass of flesh; breathing, seething under the lighting. There were no stools or tables or chairs, just a mass of undulating bodies filling the space. The smell of sweat and cologne clogged the air.

He looked for Avda.

Avda had told him he would be bar-hopping in Chelsea tonight, that he'd be in the Hung Jury around 9 pm to catch some of the drag act. But the light was so murky and the faces were so numerous: some hungry, some laughing, some sad as those of the young boys Tikhon had seen fight and die in Ghor and Herat and Kandahar.

Clack. Clack. Clac –

'Hey, you're empty.'

Tikhon snapped to – as though a sergeant in the 345th had screamed a command – and saw a man in an unbuttoned shirt over a t-shirt of dark hoop design smiling. The man nodded to the now empty Miller bottle sitting on the window ledge.

Tikhon said, 'I'm fine, thank you.'

'I like your accent. Are you German?'

'No.'

'I dated a German once. Great conversationalist, physical in a ... I guess teutonic kind of way.' The man laughed like a shy kid. 'I don't know what the hell I'm saying.'

'I'm not German,' said Tikhon.

'No,' said the man. His eyes roamed over Tikhon's body for a couple of heartbeats. 'You sure I can't get you another beer?'

'No, thank you.'

'I guess not,' said the man. 'You don't stay in that kind of shape by sucking down calories, huh?'

Tikhon looked around the crowd. He glanced at the door to the street just six feet away. Anywhere but at this man.

The man leaned close to set his own drink on the window ledge. Then he took his shirt off to reveal more of his gym-bought body molding the tight, hooped t-shirt. The bold dark hoops on the white cotton caught Tikhon's eye. They were the wrong thickness – but the design was close to the tight *telnyashka* vest of the Soviet navy, marines and special forces; and the airborne.

The man moved closer. He smiled but seemed, to Tikhon, to mock. This pampered, judgemental American with his ridiculous body sculpted in some Manhattan sweat factory. This simpering, insidious *goluboy*.

This was the "wrong guy". Tikhon knew that to beat him here in a Manhattan bar in front of so many was foolish. If not the wailing faggot he left bleeding on the floor, some of the other homos might tackle him. At least one in the crowd would report him to the police. But Tikhon didn't care. The car was teetering on the climax of the coaster's huge rise.

Clack ...

It was cresting the summit. His stomach began to lurch as he felt the violence rise in his throat like acid, ready to spew over the man before him.

Clack ...

His fists balled. Fists that had punched and cracked and shattered. Fists that had wrapped around rifle stocks, grenades, filthy Afghan necks.

Cla –

Avda stepped between Tikhon and the man. He stared in Tikhon's eyes and something burned through the rage like the sun through cloud.

Tikhon heard him speak – *Sorry about my friend, his English is not so good ... new to this country. He is not a big drinker. Sure, sometime. Have a good night ...*

Then he found himself out on the street. The east Asian man was still there. Tikhon wondered if he was summoning the courage to step through the door.

A taxi appeared and Avda ushered him in. Soon the city was rolling by the windows like a looped movie, block by block, and he was safe with his protector. His strength.

Saint George the Dragonslayer.

*

After, he sat on the edge of the bed and watched Avda walk naked to the ensuite bathroom. The young man's back was smooth, the ridges of his shoulder blades like fins under hairless skin. He had a light sheen of sweat.

Tikhon was soaked. He touched his own chest, peppered by puckered craters of skin, and ran a fingertip along the thin discolored line on his left side.

When they first met, Avda had told him he was nineteen but Tikhon knew he was older. The tattoo that ran from the young man's shoulders to the concave at the base of his spine, spanning the width of his back, was proof of that. It was of a great warrior on a rearing white charger with sword held aloft in preparation for the death blow, a shield gripped in his left hand. At the charger's feet snarled a thrashing, three-headed dragon on its back. Two bloodied heads lay on the ground while the last surviving snout breathed flame. The dragon's belly had been split and innards boiled out.

Saint George slaying the dragon.

Tikhon had no sexual interest in any male besides Avda. He watched him lean over the sink in the ensuite through the door. There was a shower cubicle by the toilet and a cream carpet in the bedroom with a couple of hardened stains in one corner. A functional room in a functional hotel on the fringes of Manhattan's gentrifying Hell's Kitchen.

Avda's tattoo gave Tikhon a stillness, even as they fucked. Saint George was a powerful Russian symbol of valor, courage and the triumph of good. When he watched the saint strain and heave across his lover's skin, Tikhon drifted gently, rising, rising until he finished and was spent. For a time after he was at peace. It helped him channel and center his violence on the right targets. There was only one other who could give him such respite from the endless cycle of fear and rage.

Avda walked back to the bed and sat by his side. He put a

hand on Tikhon's knee and laughed. It was a high pitched sound, almost girlish. Feigning bashfulness, he closed his eyes. Tikhon read the words in Cyrillic, tattooed on the lids in dark blue ink: Never/Wake.

He lay back on the bed.

Avda was good for him. He needed these nights.

It would be a shame when the time came to kill him.

Four

Mahon's Anchor was a dive bar in three acts. Early in the evening some of the locals would come in to fill up on the happy-hour deals before heading to more sanitary, and expensive, nightspots. Act two saw the more hardcore drinkers drift in. Some drew the expletive laden wrath of Paulie Mahon or Davey Cameron as patrons dumped bags of small change, scraped together by collecting the deposit on empty bottles in the trash, on the counter to pay for drinks. Others tried to grab a couple of shots with food stamps. Those with a steady welfare check or working income found their spot and sat rooted to their stools putting in a heavy shift of boozing.

Act three introduced a few shift workers, a hooker or two, and some women in search of the late arrivals.

The cops.

It was close to one and the police who had finished up shifts were working on a soft, or hard, buzz; Callum's team was working off the raid, the abbatoir scene in the apartment. Someone schooled in the art of irony had put Gangsta's Paradise on the jukebox and a couple of cop-babe-groupies were dancing in the open space bordered by tables at the back of the bar, near a swaying Narcotics detective called Billy Hutchinson as he talked with two uniforms who'd finished a four-to-midnight shift. More cops sat at the tables along the walls.

Callum stood with Georgie Ruiz on his left, Gerry Martin on the right at the long counter that began at the door to the street and ended where Hutchinson stood swaying. The team had got word they would relocate to the 60th Precinct for a temporary period, so the homicide detectives could have easy access to them. After two interviews, at the crime scene and in the precinct, they had wondered what the hell couldn't be handled with a phone call but the White Shirts – the senior ranks – had decreed it should be so, and thus, it was.

Gerry Martin was buying a drink for a cop worked the switchboard in the Six-oh, Danny O'Neill. O'Neill sat on a stool next to Martin. He had been topping up his coffee at work with some Jameson's from his hip flask, which had an Irish harp engraved on one side and a phoenix on the other. He was deep in his cups. O'Neill snorted something as thick as his Bronx accent from his nose to his throat and swallowed, then smiled at Callum.

'Hey, Burke, how come you always drink that Canadian shit? American beer not good enough for you?'

Callum peeled a couple of bills from his stash on the counter, handed them to Paulie Mahon and grabbed his bottle of Molson. He said, 'Got used to it a couple years ago.'

'Oh yeah, when you were playing Irish with the Walsh Mob? Thank God almighty for you ridin' in on your white horse and saving us from the shit stains left in the bowl after the Feds flushed the Westies. And the fuckin' chinks on Mott Street too, no less.'

Callum raised his beer in salute but kept his eyes on Paulie's back as the bartender turned and shoved the bills in the register. He took a slow pull and set the bottle on the counter, rolling it between his hands and thought about not popping Gerry Martin with a right for giving this old soak Callum's operational history. Callum could feel O'Neill's small, hard eyes, honed nasty by the alcohol, watching. Waiting to see if he would bite at the insults.

It's been a long day, thought Callum. Drunken logic kicked in: who was gonna blame him if he dropped a loudmouth hairbag like O'Neill off his barstool for coming at him with a smart mouth? Half the drinkers in this place wouldn't remember in the morning anyway.

He felt Georgie Ruiz's foot press on his like some kind of morse code, like she could read his mind – *not tonight, not ever, Callum.*

Georgie looked at O'Neill and said, 'You seem a little cranky tonight, Danny. Tough day on the switchboard?'

O'Neill sniffed and sat taller on his stool.

'You know what, Ruiz?' he said. 'The Job is on a slippery fuckin' slope. I'm workin' that switchboard, and these days I'm putting calls through to Alvarez's, Chen's, Ivanov's, Yin and fuckin' Yangs. Every color of cop under the sun. And now they got the likes of you and fuckin' Alexander executing warrants, so a good man like Angel Patrosi gets his leg busted to hell, because you're too busy thinkin' about what you're gonna make your old man for dinner.'

'My husband better not be waiting for me to cook him anything, this time of night. And Patrosi's leg got busted because Gerry here was too busy thinking about getting out of the line of fire when the door gave on the first swing, and let go the goddamn ram.'

Gerry Martin looked up from the glass of whiskey he'd been studying and said, 'Hey!'

'Typical woman,' said O'Neill with another snort, 'anybody's fault but your own. Just like that fuckin' Jewess, Messinger. God help us if she becomes mayor.'

Martin nodded. 'Go Rudy.'

'PBA might not agree,' said Georgie.

O'Neill slammed his whiskey glass on the counter.

'See, that's a fuckin' broad! Always gotta have the last word. Youse are all the same, like my ex. But any cop in this bar will tell you, honey, he's wrestlin' with some asshole in a fuckin' alley: he'd want his partner to be packin' more than a tampon in his pants. There's a reason you're the weaker fuckin' sex.'

Callum said, 'The only thing you've been wrestlin' with the past decade is the cap on that hip flask, Danny. There's the reason you're a hairbag house-mouse, in the fuckin' bag after twenty years on the Job.'

His voice was even. He kept his eyes on the photograph of rural Tipperary taped to the mirror above the banks of bottles behind the bar. Then he glanced at Danny O'Neill's reflection in the glass. The older cop sat staring at him. O'Neill's bottom lip quivered and his eyes seemed caught between drunken rage and wounded tears. Callum checked Gerry Martin. Martin was blinking at O'Neill. Then he closed his eyes and Callum figured Gerry was making his peace with the fact he'd have to come at him for insulting his friend. Callum turned away from them to Georgie. He raised his eyebrows. She frowned at him like he'd just kicked a walking stick from under a limping man. She peered around him and said, 'Danny, Callum didn't – '

'This job is family, Burke,' said O'Neill. His voice caught for a second and he took a slug of whiskey. 'We say you're never alone as a cop in this city, you got thousands of brothers. But you? You're an outcast, you mongrel fuck.'

Martin put a hand on O'Neill's shoulder but he shrugged it off, pitched forward off his stool and grabbed at the counter. He caught his fall and looked at Callum with bloodhound eyes.

'You ain't an American, Burke. And your Brit mother – you mighta' been born in Belfast, but you're no Irishman in my eyes, or plenty of the other boys. And you sure as hell ain't Narcotics after two years on the Job. Your rabbi can only take you so far – you'd still be a rookie without Bocchini in your corner, whatever you mighta done undercover.'

Callum felt a wild spike of anger and his eyes widened. Gerry Martin moved toward him, hands out like he was talking down a tweaker. Martin's eyes would've shit if they could and his fear stoked Callum's fury.

What the fuck are you scareda me for? thought Callum. *I'm a brother in blue, right?*

He knew Gerry was scared and he knew Martin hated Callum all the more because of it. Callum felt rage, hot as a straight shot of Bushmills, surge from his face to his arm to ready the right hook he would throw at Martin because O'Neill was too old and used up to take it. And because he wanted to beat the resentment out of him. Out of all of them.

But the anger was tempered by a cold rush of fear in his belly that he really was an imposter; and that he really could take another cop apart right here and now in this shithole, maybe do him real damage. He was on the verge of losing control, the red mist gathering.

He dropped his gaze; he dropped his fist.

Then Callum grabbed his jacket and got the hell out of there.

O'Neill put a hand on Gerry Martin's shoulder.

'I knew it. Fuckin' pussy.'

Georgie shrugged on her coat, shot them both a look that could have soured their booze and took off after Callum. Martin opened his mouth to shout something but Danny O'Neill beat him to the punch.

'Speakin' of pussy, looks like Bocchini's brat's gettin' some tonight.'

He grabbed his crotch with one hand, cocked his other thumb after George Ruiz and said to the bar, 'We ain't seein' her fine Latino ass again tonight.'

*

They were lucky and caught a train fast so they got to Callum's apartment on Bleecker Street eighty minutes later. Georgie had fallen asleep in the subway car. They ascended to 7th Avenue and walked onto a Bleecker in the wee small hours, quiet bar a few clutches of NYU students stumbling their way home.

As they passed a café, she wondered how he could live here.

While undercover, Callum had stayed for a while with an Irish mobster, Paddy Duggan, in Duggan's apartment on Bleecker. Just a couple of blocks from his current apartment. Callum said he liked the area and it reminded him of how he'd got started in the city but still ...

'Great location on a cop's salary,' she said.

'You know the story,' said Callum, 'the landlord knows a guy who knows a guy who knows someone at One Police Plaza.'

'And he likes having a cop in the building for security, at reduced rent. Sure.'

They were silent until Callum opened his door on the third floor of his walk-up and stood aside to let her enter.

She had never been in his place before and it felt wrong when she thought of Arthur sleeping in their bed in Queens, little Isabella and Sammy down the hall. It felt downright criminal when she saw the framed photograph of Callum with his estranged wife Irene and little girl Tara in some Asian market, sat on the table in the short hallway.

Fourteen years a cop and she could count the number of nights she slept in a strange bed or crashed on a sofa other than in a precinct basement on one hand. And Callum had looked goddamn scary for a second, when she thought he was about to take Gerry Martin apart earlier. But then he'd looked so goddamn wounded, and maybe a little scared, and she'd just thought he shouldn't be going home alone.

It sounded weak as water in her own head – but it had seemed reason enough to come here and see him back to his place in one piece. That was what cops did, right? They supported and looked after their own.

'I won't stay long,' she said. 'Maybe a couple of hours on your couch, then I'll grab the subway out to Astoria in time for the kids waking up.'

Callum said, 'Sure.' He looked like he was the visitor and this was her space. 'Arthur would worry if you weren't there in the morning.'

'Arthur would worry if I chose Cap'n Crunch instead of Cheerios for breakfast.'

She looked at another photograph on the table, a man and woman in front of a red brick house, hair, clothes and color tones fading with the march of time. Callum's parents back in Ireland, in the Eighties, she guessed.

'Speaking of cereal,' she said with a frown, 'you sound kinda like that leprechaun from the – '

' – Lucky Charms commercial. Yeah, I heard that once or twice.'

They smiled and he walked past her, down the short hallway and into the kitchen at the end. She followed and he opened the refrigerator and grabbed a carton of orange juice, pouring two plastic tumblers. They sat at the table in the center of the small space and she took in the kid's drawings on the wall, the map of Hong Kong, the soccer club crest magnet stuck on the refrigerator door.

She tucked her chin into her chest for a second.

Then she said, 'Arthur is a good man.'

'I know.'

'He's strong. All my time in Intelligence, I was a goddamn chauffeur. You know how many arrogant morons work at the UN, we had to ferry around between restaurants and Tiffany's and The Knickerbocker Club?'

He smiled and nodded. She thought he was pleased she'd said "morons" while with other cops she would have said "assholes". She didn't play the hardboiled gig with Callum because, with him, she had nothing to prove, and because he loved her all the more for it.

'All that time I felt I was some kind of fraud. A cop didn't do any policing. I'd come home and Arthur would listen to me bitch and moan about how I was wasting my time on the Job, how I wanted something investigative out on the street when that was the last place he wanted me. Then the task force came along and I got my shot with Narcotics and now I come home and he endures my goddamn silence; because I don't want to bring what I've seen and done into my home every night.'

Ruiz looked at Callum and she felt something tight in her chest loosen when his dark eyes stared somewhere inside her under those heavy black Irish brows. His lashes were long for a man, she thought. Maybe God gave them to him to shield those eyes that were so open, so expressive and guileless. They drew your gaze from the busted nose and made you wonder what they might have seen. She looked at his daughter's drawings on the wall to stall the warmth blossoming in her neck.

'And now,' she said, 'I haven't gone home at all.'

She wasn't sure what she'd wanted him to say, but couldn't deny a jab of disappointment when he brought his wife into the conversation.

'It was tough for Irene, too.'

'You must be glad she's here in America now, huh? With Hong Kong going back to China in July?'

He smiled and his eyes crinkled like some Rockwell Santa Claus for a second.

'Yeah,' he said.

She'd seen the brochures on the floor of the hallway when she came in. Cleveland. He'd been a couple of times, had told her how it had made him feel he could move mountains when he felt Tara's small arms around him, her warmth against his cheek. How he felt the strongest, best part of himself slowly drain away the farther the Amtrak took him from them at the end of a visit; the closer he got to New York again.

Georgie reminded herself to savor the next goodnight hugs from Isabella and Sammy. And when next she lay beside Arthur and felt his body.

Callum told her how he'd lay in the guest room of Irene's apartment at night and thought of knocking on her door. But it never happened. He had stolen glances at his child and estranged wife in unguarded moments and locked them inside to play back on the reel in his head when things got hard in New York. And he looked at the brochures and thought and planned, and thought and planned. But he hadn't seen his family in eleven months now.

Ruiz finished her orange juice.

'Was it tough, being a Hong Kong cop?'

'I doubt it's easy anywhere.'

His history was concealed, in his apartment as on the job. The only photos that hinted at his life before he joined the NYPD were the shots of his wife and daughter, and his parents. Nothing in uniform: the khaki green of the Royal Hong Kong Police Force, of which he'd been a member when they first met on the joint task force with the DEA; or the bottle green of the Royal Ulster Constabulary before that, in which she knew he'd served before leaving his hometown of Belfast.

Callum said, 'Northern Ireland was a lot harder.'

'To be a cop?'

'To stay alive.'

'I saw they had to cancel some big horse race this month because of a bomb.'

'In England, yeah. That's what you get on the news over here.'

'It's a lot worse if you're there, I guess,' said Ruiz.

'You have no idea.' Callum stood and went to the refrigerator again. 'I think I'll have one more before bed. You want a beer?'

'I'm good.'

He grabbed a bottle of some imported lager she'd never heard of and popped the cap, then took a long pull. Georgie had seen this Callum before. He was off-balance.

She let down her hair and pulled it around one side of her neck.

'Do you still think about Ireland?' she said.

He sat down heavy and slumped. His eyes were glistening and he dropped his gaze. Then he came to some decision as his shoulders straightened and he raised his head. Whatever tears might have been coming had stalled.

'I hadn't thought about those days for a long time,' said Callum. 'Even when I get some of that "secret Brit" shit that O'Neill was throwing around about my mother. But today, when we hit that project, it's like it just flicked a switch.'

Georgie nodded. 'Those bodies. Man, to see those guys digging in their guts like they were Dreyfuss doing the shark autopsy in Jaws.'

'No, Georgie, it wasn't that. I saw worse undercover.' He hit the beer again and reached for his pack of Camels. 'It was that kid winked at me when we were walking to the set.'

It took her a second to remember what he was talking about. Then it popped in her head – Callum had told her about some pure-as-the-driven-looking white kid with a twinkle in his eyes and tattoos on the lids. The kid passed them on their way to the housing block, then watched among the gawkers after.

It hadn't freaked her at the time – she saw so many wierdos on the Job that some cheeky asshole kid barely registered – and it didn't worry her now.

But the look on Callum's face did, the black hardness in his eyes. She wondered if what was lost in that darkness might be clawing its way back to the light of day. And she sometimes wondered if she really knew Callum Burke at all.

Five

Like someone flicked a switch. That's what he'd told Georgie.

What he thought as the cool lunchtime sun burned through the beer-haze in his head was that it was more like someone pulled a trigger. The kid's wink yesterday had felt like a sudden violence – a detonation.

He descended the steps to the street from the elevated train at West 8th Street at a trot, the loose change in his head clattering around his skull with each jolt, punishing him for last night's booze. He knew he'd freaked Georgie in the bar. At least she'd taken the bed while he lay on the couch snoring his ass off. He had a vague memory of her leaving his place before sun-up.

Callum lit up a Camel, swung a sports bag over his shoulder and walked to the 60th Precinct. RMPs and other police vehicles were lined by the curb or on the sidewalk leading to the squat brown building. He crossed the street to stand opposite and finish his smoke. The day was clear, but a breeze skimmed his short thatch of hair and did its occasional best to slap the booze out of his head as he worked on the cigarette.

He thought again of the kid, the wink, the tattoos on his eyelids.

Callum had seen the same look of casual contempt when a cop in Belfast. Always from the young, divided by old loyalties but united in their hatred of police. For a moment he was hurled back to days on patrol in armored landrovers, puffed up with a flak jacket and weighed down with a Ruger Security-six in his holster and a Heckler & Koch MP5 in his arms. The fear of springing a tripwire when hitting an arms stash; of rocket attacks on vehicle patrol. Colleagues like Henry Beattie, shot in bed beside his wife. Steve O'Connor, gunned down on the steps of the chapel as he left Mass at St Malachy's.

And Callum's friend Jimmy Gilliland, shot by a sniper at the gates of their station at the end of a foot patrol.

Sarge, Georgie, and Trish Alexander had all said the kid was probably a customer. Just one of the white students who cruised by the projects like it was a fuck-yourself-up-mall for whatever shit they were smoking or dropping or shooting to get back at mom and pop for having the audacity to raise them in the suburbs.

Too long a cop, he thought, too cynical.

But that choirboy yesterday, that wink told Callum the kid *knew*. He hated cops and he *knew* there was something bigger and badder out there – and the butchers up in that apartment were part of it – that could chew them up if they got too close. Callum finished his smoke and ground it under his boot.

He approached the desk inside the entrance of the precinct house and the sergeant scribbling in the command log. It was fifteen minutes into the four-to-midnight tour and the desk sergeant was making an audit of portable radios, property stored in the evidence locker and cops still on the street from the previous tour. He glanced at Callum and gestured to the stairwell.

Callum said, 'Thanks sarge. You got a snack machine on the second floor?'

The sergeant – Bukowski on his nameplate – went back to the command log and said, 'There could be a sauna and health spa up there, wouldn't matter to you, Irish.'

'Your detectives are upstairs, right? I saw them yesterday before we executed a warrant.'

'The DTs are upstairs, and you're in the basement. There's a Butterfinger I left down there in '82 if you're hungry.'

Callum hefted the sports bag on his shoulder, caught a smile from a cute redhead civilian staff walking out of the 124 Room, and headed down. In the basement he threaded his way through the lockers to the break room where the rest of the team were lounging on busted couches and mismatched chairs around a space with a battered dining table in the corner. A microwave looked like it should have a biohazard sticker on front perched on a rickety bookshelf. He cocked his thumb over his shoulder at the rows of seven-foot-high gray lockers and looked at Sarge.

'Do we get any of those?'

'I'm working on it. Couple of the old timers take two for themselves so I'm trying to free a couple up for us to share.'

Gerry Martin said, 'You can donate yours to a rookie when we finish up here, Cal. Oh wait, you *are* ...' He put his hand to his mouth in mock shock.

Straight in the door and Martin was hitting him with rookie jokes. Callum guessed he deserved something for being an asshole in the bar last night.

'How's Patrosi?' he said.

Sarge said, 'Stable. It's a double fracture so we ain't gonna see him for a while but he'll get there. Billy's gonna schedule a racket to raise some cash to help him out.'

'We're thinkin' somewhere near Borough Command, maybe Lacey's,' said Billy Hutchinson.

The rest was the Job. They had a Buy and Bust op in West Brighton with Trish Alexander as the undercover and Gerry Martin "getting on" as the arresting officer, so Martin and Sarge would go pick up the Buy money and photocopy the serial numbers. While they were gone, the DTs on the second floor wanted to talk to Callum about a detail from yesterday's raid.

He died a little inside. He'd probably contradicted himself in his statement about the shade of mauve of the goddamn carpet in the apartment and would have to justify the discrepancy to some detective looking to make his name on this one.

When Sarge and Martin took off he braved the coffee and made for the stairs and a smoke out front of the precinct house. Georgie followed him up.

Out on the street she said, 'I saw a ghost of a smile when you heard Johnson was undercover today.'

Callum had had a flash of Trish Alexander slapping on the cuffs as a perp screamed in pain and said goodbye to any distant hopes of fathering little baby drug dealers.

'It did conjure certain images, yeah. Not sure if it was a smile or a grimace.'

'Maybe you ask, she'd give you the same treatment.'

'Ach now, she's a fine looking woman,' he said, laying the Belfast accent on thick.

Georgie smiled, as she always did at the cornball Irishness, but he caught something in her look that said she knew he wasn't just bullshitting.

Fact was, Trish Alexander looked great. Not a beauty but statuesque, her legs making her look taller than her five-seven. Skin the color of roasted coffee beans. Dark eyes on the small side, lips the opposite that revealed large white teeth when she – rarely – cracked a smile. The kind of woman entirely comfortable in her own skin, aware of her own worth, never willing to compromise or settle.

Callum said, 'How was Arthur when you got home?'

'Pissed. He hadn't slept until after midnight, then I woke him when I climbed into bed.'

'You guys fight?'

'We didn't have a lot of time for that. Those MTA buses won't drive themselves, and he had to get the kids ready for school.'

Callum lit up and took a drag of his smoke, chasing it with a mouthful of coffee. It tasted like the break room: old and mouldy and used up.

'That kid,' he said, 'I'd like a shot at him.'

Georgie said, 'And if you ever saw him again, ask him what?'

'That kid knew something.'

'Dig it: he was a white kid on a shopping trip for junk in the projects. You know how many dealers hang out in that area? No reason he was buying from Beresford or Mayhew.'

They stood for a few moments, Callum sucking on his Camel and swigging coffee, Georgie gazing at the street. A huge woman with a Pekinese struggled into the precinct house. Callum finished his coffee.

'Okay, here's a question,' he said. 'How did Patrosi's CI walk out of this unscathed? She knocks on the door, right? The dogs are quiet so the killers have already finished them off. By now Beresford and Mayhew are probably already on their way to the hot place downstairs, and the shooters have started carving them up. The CI knocks on the door of a charnel house and – what?'

Georgie shrugged. 'She said there was no answer when she knocked but she heard people moving inside. So she called Patrosi to confirm.'

'She called Patrosi, who said this after the fact to detectives from his hospital bed? A man who was lying with a busted leg, doped up, possibly going into shock. No one wondered if Patrosi's recollection was solid? And no one followed up on the CI?'

'Not yet.'

'Because,' said Callum, 'that's gonna take time. We don't even have a CI name for her yet, like "Blue Eyes" or "Sweet Cheeks" or some shit. If we're lucky, we'll get a code: CI-001-000117 or whatever. Only one of the White Shirts and the CI section know who this woman is if Patrosi registered her, and that isn't a given.'

Georgie crossed her arms and a notch appeared between her brows.

'You want to go ask him at Mount Sinai?'

'Yeah, I do.'

Georgie gave him that look he figured she saved for when her her kids found out there was no Santa Claus. He could handle her anger; pity was something else.

'Oh, Callum,' she said.

'No, no, don't "Oh Callum" me now. You said that in the past when I fucked up. This isn't me fucking up.'

'You've been on this team three months. You hopped in after two years on patrol – *two years*. You might not like being reminded but it's the truth: the other cops on this team clocked up to four times as long before they got their shot in an investigative unit. And now you wanna go and interview a wounded brother-cop in his hospital bed because you think something's rotten in Denmark with his CI? If you think the likes of Gerry Martin resent you now, just try that shit.'

'I might have got Narcotics after two years on patrol, but I been a cop on three continents for eleven years. And I'm tellin' you, somethin' doesn't fit with the CI. It'll come out in the course of the investigation anyway, I'm just speedin' up the process.'

'Not with me. I'm sorry.'

He had no right to expect her to follow his line but it still stung. He had no right, either, to hit up Patrosi for the identity of his CI. They were *confidential* informants for a reason. He didn't even have skin in the game. His only concern should be the Buy and Bust that afternoon, and making sure Trish Alexander, as the undercover, went home in one piece tonight.

But that kid with the tattooed eyelids … he lit a fuse.

That wink bugged him like the bad memories from home kept stabbing at his brain today. Maybe Danny O'Neill set something in motion last night – Callum had far too much shit stashed away in his head from way back that seemed a lot closer to the surface than a day ago. Working the angle on the kid, pushing

Patrosi on the CI, was some kind of action he could take. It might help stem the tide of bad juju crawling toward his dreams tonight.

So he shrugged and gave Georgie the best smile he could rustle up.

'You're probably right,' he said. 'Anyway, the vics were only dealers. Saved the taxpayer three hots and a cot on Riker's.'

It was all he could do, when he saw her look at him all crooked, not to cross his goddamn fingers behind his lying-ass back.

*

Detective Parker sat at a department desk on a department chair in a suit and tie worse matched than Michel Jackson and Lisa Marie. Callum sat opposite. Parker spread four photographs on the desktop with a huge hand and said, 'Yesterday's perps with their shirts off. You seen this kinda thing before?'

'Yeah,' said Callum, 'in Hong Kong. Triads.'

He studied the photographs.

'They were a lot more sophisticated than this work, though. This is more primitive, if that's the word.'

The killers' faces were set like statues – gargoyles popped in his mind – and their bodies knotted with muscle and sinew. Both sported an impressive collection of tattoos. Stars had been needled in ink on their clavicles, epaulettes on the shoulders of one.

The epaulettes wearer had the head of a roaring bear on one pectoral and a cross running from his clavicle to his lower stomach. Flanking the cross at the base of his ribs, a cartoon hare sat drinking something from a bottle, a wolf on the other side smoking a rolled-up cigarette with a leer and a hand of cards in his paw. Another photograph showed his back, dominated by a Russian Orthodox Church with four spires. At the foot of the church lay a syringe, knife, bag with a dollar sign on, and a naked woman with a bottle.

The other man, minus epaulettes, had an inked skull on his right pectoral with a knife through the crown. On his stomach, a woman stood like Marilyn Monroe on the grate – but a devil, rather than a gust of air, lifted her skirt. She was naked underneath. The thug's right arm was raised and the little finger was missing at the first joint. A band was tattoed around his wrist.

Detective Parker smoothed back hair on the retreat after years in the trenches of homicide. He was a heavy-set man a couple of roast dinners from jowly, with used up eyes that had seen well past the limit of what they could process with any hint of emotional capacity. Callum thought he could have been a criminal in different surroundings.

'We come across this every once in a while,' said the detective. 'Russian mafia shit. They usually keep it local in Brighton Beach, though, take each other out; not the dealers around Coney.'

Callum said, 'The two areas are side by side. The Six-oh is right in the middle, covers both.'

'But the Russians keep it in the family. They don't trust anyone with a darker complexion than me with a suntan, but they fuck each other over constantly. Go figure.'

'Any idea what the tattoos mean?'

'Yeah,' said Parker, like he was figuring odds on the Mets game rather than engaging with this narcotics rookie with the funny accent. 'I got a vague idea. The stars mean these guys are the real deal, like they're connected to an organization. The cross and the church on this guy mean the same. He's steeped in their world, and the bear is probably some Russian shit. The perp's name is Alex Turgenev.'

'How about the other guy?'

'He's bad fuckin' news. Ilia Oblonsky. The skull with the knife says he's killed before, and the devil lifting the woman's skirt means he's a rapist.'

Callum smiled. 'Looks like they picked up a couple of bruises between the project and the room these shots were taken in.'

'*Corrective interview*,' said Parker. He returned the grin. 'One of our own is in the hospital because of these assholes.'

One of our own is in the hospital because Gerry Martin couldn't control the ram, thought Callum. Not that it mattered. *Corrective interview* would go on the DD5 report, cop language for a solid beating. He figured the story about Patrosi got twisted and exaggerated somewhere along the line and the uniforms took some time with the perps before they got to the detectives. The DTs wouldn't care: the two killers weren't the type to co-operate, so a tenderizing before interrogation might ease the process some.

Parker took some more photographs from a drawer and handed them to Callum.

Willie Mayhew and Charles Beresford – or what was left of them. He looked at the images of tearing, sawing, slicing.

'The butchery,' said Parker, 'is 'cause they were diggin' the bullets out of the bodies to fuck with our ballistics. It's somethin' the Ivans like doin'. Sometimes they'll leave weapons from a different murder at the scene. They hadn't got around to pullin' the teeth and slicin' off the fingertips yet.'

Callum placed the photographs in a pile.

'The thing of it is,' said Parker, 'if your team hadn't walked into this shitstorm, we'd probably have dodged the bullet on this. The Russians like driving bodies to the Bronx and dumpin' them. They know the DTs up there have to catch the case if the body is found on their turf, and those guys are snowed under. They don't have the time or inclination to put so much effort into a dead dealer from south Brooklyn.'

'Sorry we dropped you in it.'

'Hey, it's what they pay me the big bucks for.'

They both laughed at that one.

Callum checked his watch.

'Look, I gotta go – just wondering to what I owe the honor here.'

Parker sat forward and grabbed a coffee cup on the edge of his desk. He took a gulp.

'You identified the pistol as being a Makarov, right?'

Callum shifted in his chair. 'Well, yeah,' he said, 'but the sarge and Alexander had seen them before, too. I was just the first to say so.'

'I spoke to them yesterday. I'm just gettin' around to you. You had much experience with Russian criminals?'

'Less than you, I'd guess.'

'You worked abroad before, though. How about there?'

'I saw Makarov's when I worked in the RUC, but that was in terrorist weapons stashes.'

'RUC?'

'Royal Ulster Constabulary.'

'How about China with those Triads?'

'Hong Kong,' said Callum. 'No, we got a few Russian merchant ships comin' into port but no military.'

'You speak any of the language?'

'Cantonese?'

'What the fuck is that?'

'It's what they speak in Hong Kong.'

'So just say Chinese.'

Callum said, 'It's a dialec – ' Then he stopped. What was the point?

Parker said, 'You speak any Russian?' slow, like he was talking to a foreigner struggling with English.

'Not a word.'

'Okay,' said Parker.

'Okay?' said Callum. 'That's it?'

Parker spreads his arms wide. He looked big as a bear.

Callum said, 'Mind if I ask you one?'

'Sure.'

'You know our guy ended up in Mount Sinai with a shattered leg. His CI brought us the intel on the original bust of the two vics, Beresford and Mayhew. The CI told us it was a go because the vics' dogs were asleep. Said she was gonna knock on the door and ask the vics for a loan, would see if the dogs barked.'

Parker sighed and tapped the desktop.

'This how you construct a question in Ireland?' he said.

Callum said, 'Have you interviewed the CI yet?'

'You know we can't access a criminal informant until the paperwork's through.'

'She's a potential witness.'

'Who we have to wade through the relevant bureaucracy in order to access.'

Callum knew he'd get nowhere. Still, he figured he'd pitch one anyway.

'You don't think it's strange that Patrosi gets a call says the dogs are asleep and all is as it should be, and when we bust in the door the dogs are dead and two Russians are carving up the vics like they're sides of prime beef?'

Parker looked hard at Callum, tired eyes flickering to life. He grabbed his coffee cup but held off on taking a drink. Callum held his stare.

'You know what else I think is strange?' said Callum. 'I think it's strange a DT is talking to me about two Russian hitters on the pretense I could identify a mass-produced pistol two others on my team knew straight off, too. You think that's strange, detective?'

Detective Parker broke off his stare to look at his watch. He made a show of reading the time, then sipped his coffee and smacked his lips.

'Your time is up, Officer,' he said. 'So take your question and your Canton-fuckin'-ese, and get the fuck out of my office.'

Six

Tikhon watched a well-preserved woman he guessed to be in her sixties, erect and assured in the wealth she wore with practiced indifference, walk west on Brighton Beach Avenue. He thought of Moscow: the lines, the empty shelves of his youth.

He stood by a coffee store holding a copy of Novoye Russkoye Slovo, the New York-based Russian language newspaper, rolled up and unread. A tan Ford pulled up to the curb. It looked like the cars in the old Seventies movies he saw on TV in the midnight hour when he couldn't sleep. An old man struggled out of the driver's door onto the avenue. He panted with the effort and hobbled around the back of the car onto the sidewalk. He fished some candy from his pants pocket and unwrapped it, tossing the wrapper in a wire trashcan by the crosswalk.

The man was halved by shadow and light, the elevated train tracks above the street throwing shade on his left side, the pale spring sun bathing his right. He wore a striped shirt under a brown sports jacket and black slacks, and a silver-gray pork pie hat. A tall man now stooped and gaunt. Tikhon wondered how long the old Jew had lived here. Had he made his way to America after the Great Patriotic War, when the Nazis were driven from the borders and the small nations which hugged the Motherland, like tiny fish swimming next to a shark? The old man, he knew, was Ukrainian.

A police car glided by on the avenue. The man walked past a couple of store fronts before stopping in front of a door with frosted glass above which a sign proclaimed 'Fogelman Apparel'. He fussed with a ring of keys until the door gave with a jolt and he shuffled inside.

Tikhon checked his watch. 1330.

They crossed the avenue five minutes later. Two men in heavy jackets for the season and cropped hair. One had a small, flat forehead and a chin that receded into a bull neck. The other, an aquiline nose and small, mean eyes set deep like bullet-holes in a face cratered by acne. They walked in complete control of their environment. They would fear nothing. They had *Krysha*, a *roof*: a man of power and influence somewhere in the chain above their position as enforcers, who gave them security by association.

They entered Fogelman's store.

A couple of minutes, thought Tikhon. That should be enough. Have them throw their weight around, have the old man plead – *I'm sorry, business has not been so good. Next week I'll have more. Next week, come back then.*

Tikhon waited.

A train crawled into the elevated station overhead with an agonized scream.

Clack. Clack. Clack.

He shoved the folded newspaper in his hip pocket.

The door of Fogelman's Apparel had a "Closed: Please Drop By Later" sign hung inside the glass. Tikhon slipped into the store, reaching up to silence the bell above the inner door. The space was long and narrow, dotted with circular racks holding jackets and pants. The styles were as dated as the old man's car and the wall was covered with shirts sheathed in shiny plastic hung on a metal display grill. A glass and wood counter, ancient and robust, sat at the far end of the store, behind which the old man stood, the hat still on his head, his cheeks flushed. The two enforcers flanked him, standing on the near side of the counter. No one realized Tikhon had joined them.

The mens' Russian was rough and brutal.

'You think we are scum? We come for our *dan* and you tell us

49

– like a Jewish, child-eating troll – you have no tribute.' Bull-Neck spat on the floor.

'Please,' said the old man, 'I swear, business has been slow, the blizzard this month, no one saw coming.' His voice was as robust as his counter despite his age. 'The heating failed, I had to call Gottesman to come out and fix it.'

'Another fucking Jew,' said Bull-Neck.

The man with the mean eyes walked to the corner of the room by a door marked private and grabbed a broom propped against the wall.

'Perhaps,' he said, 'as you want to fuck us so bad, we should fuck you.'

Bull-Neck said, 'Come here old man. I'll take your pants down.'

The old man looked from thug to thug, his eyes wild. These were men of local mobster Maxim Volkov and they would leave him crying on the floor with a broken nose and a bloody ass.

Bull-Neck reached across the counter to grab his lapel.

Mean-Eyes laughed.

'*Yob tvoyu mat,*' said Tikhon. *Fuck your mother.*

The enforcers turned and stared at him, Mean-Eyes gripping the broom with bone white knuckles.

'Don't fuck him,' said Tikhon, his Russian coarse like theirs, 'Go fuck your mother.'

The thugs were simple beasts, he thought, shock written across their faces as bold as the print on his newspaper. No one spoke to them with such insolence. They had courage through their *Krysha*.

Mean-Eyes recovered a trace of his swagger first. He looked Tikhon up and down, liking the odds as he saw the tight but wiry frame ranged against the thick, solid savagery in the powerful bodies of he and Bull-Neck.

'You,' he said, 'are on *seduksen* if you think you can make this

50

your fight and walk out of here. Now fuck off and leave the men to do business.'

A former soldier, thought Tikhon. He had seen many loose themselves in doses of the medical drug, *seduksen*, in Afghanistan.

Bull-Neck was walking in a wide arc on Tikhon's right while Mean-Eyes held the broom and approached him head-on. They were two, Tikhon one, and each had at least ten pounds on him.

He reached behind his back. The thugs checked their advance.

Tikhon withdrew the newspaper. The men smiled and resumed their slow walk toward him.

Bull-Neck said, 'You should move to Rego Park, or Fort Lee. It might be safer there.'

Tikhon took a step to meet Mean-Eyes by a rack of sports coats. He held the newspaper up and smiled.

'You know, it's wonderful,' he said. 'We can buy a Russian language newspaper right here in our own neighborhood.' He nodded at the thug. 'Or, as you say, Rego Park. Anywhere where decent, honest Russians like the owner of this store gather to live.'

Mean-Eyes snorted.

The rolled paper cracked off his jaw with a speed and controlled fury – impossibly hard – that made Bull-Neck take a step back. Mean-Eyes staggered and dropped the broom. Tikhon stepped inside the bigger man's reach and drove the newspaper into his groin. Mean-Eyes doubled over as Bull-Neck moved in. The paper now in a dagger grip, his body fluid and light, Tikhon drove the bottom of the roll hard into the thick throat. Bull-Neck's face flamed scarlet and his eyes bulged. Mean-Eyes was still doubled over. Tikhon turned and drove his boot hard into his skull. The thug dropped to his knees. Tikhon drove his boot in again. And again. Each dull crack slowed the climb of the car on the rollercoaster. It was as though the war and fury and terror was rushing through his limb and into this thug's thick head. Tikhon had a brief image of Saint George last night, swelling, surging on the smooth skin of Avda's back.

He turned to Bull-Neck, still hunched and gasping, and battered him about the head with the rolled paper. It made a sound like a flat detonation mixed with strangled cries. He hammered still, driving the thug down to his knees.

Tikhon shoved both men onto the floor and drove two hard shots into the crown of each. Then he withdrew a dagger from inside the rolled newspaper and pulled the blade from its slim scabbard. He yanked Mean-Eyes's head back and exposed his throat. The knife pressed on skin.

'This *kinjal* was my friend's,' said Tikhon. 'A Georgian in the 345th. He killed six Mujahideen with this dagger. What say we try it on a Russian throat?'

He turned the blade, caressing the neck, and nicked the skin over the larynx.

He turned to Bull-Neck, 'Leave here and tell Maxim Volkov he no longer collects a *dan* from this business. Arkady Kuznetsov protects Mr Fogelman now. Or I'll come looking for you both with that broom, and spear you like skewered *shashlik*. Understand?'

Bull-Neck grunted. Tikhon wrenched his head back and heard something pop.

'OK,' said the thug. 'OK, OK.'

They rose like old men, Mean-Eyes cupping his balls and Bull-Neck gagging, and shuffled from the store. Tikhon went to the door and turned the lock on the inside, keeping the "Closed" sign streetward. Fogelman stood propped against the far side of his store counter. He wiped his brow with a handkerchief and shook his head.

'Such violence,' he said.

'If you think that was violence, old man, you have lived a sheltered life.'

'I saw more in two years than one should experience in a life-time of war,' said Fogelman. He raised the handkerchief to dab at his forehead again and Tikhon saw the tattooed number on his wrist.

'Brutality is everywhere,' said Tikhon. 'Brutality is in Arakady Kuznetsov. Now you will pay your tribute to him. You have traded one tiger for another.' He held the *kinjal* dagger in his right hand and approached the counter. As the old man watched him come, a tired resignation washed across his watery eyes. He took off his pork pie hat and placed it somewhere behind the counter. His hair was damp and matted at the front but a shock of white curls sprang free on his crown. He smoothed back his hair and caught Tikhon looking at the number on his wrist.

'I'm not a victim,' said Fogelman. 'Those thugs try to do what the Reich couldn't – possess me. They mistake control for possession. Because I hand over a few dollars each week to keep my windows unbroken, this is not possession. This is economics. Arkady Kuznetsov will charge less than Maxim Volkov for this, so it is economics also. Your criminal master is cheap.'

'He isn't my master, old man.'

Tikhon trailed the dagger along the counter's edge. The blade scraped small chips from the pitted wood. He walked around and behind Fogelman. The old man's belly rose and fell like a that of a newborn clinging to life.

Tikhon raised the dagger.

'This,' he said, 'is control.'

The room was silent as a body bag.

He leaned close and pressed the tip of the blade to a button on the old man's chest. Fogelman looked down at the dagger.

'I'm not a victim,' he said. His voice sounded frail for the first time.

Tikhon thought of drawing the blade across the withered neck.

Then he sheathed the dagger and slipped it back inside the rolled up newspaper.

'Arkady Kuznetsov's men will be here tomorrow,' he said, 'for their first pound of flesh.'

As he walked away the old man called after him.

'How will I know those two won't come back?'

Tikhon turned.

'If the one with the thick neck shows up, call Kuznetsov. His men will give you a number.'

'And the other,' said Fogelman, 'with the small, evil eyes?'

'I nicked him. The blade was dipped in thallium,' he said. 'You may want to wash your shirt.'

Then he was gone.

Seven

Callum thought of Trish Alexander.

He thought of watching Gerry Martin handing over the buy money and Trish grabbing the roll of bills and shoving it in her cleavage, already assuming the role of junkie before the operation began. Her halter top was low cut, her denim hot pants high. She wore killer heels and blood red lipstick. He wondered what the folk in her church congregation would make of it.

Now she turned the corner back to Sarge's car. Callum was surprised how fucked up she looked, at how good she was in the role.

'She OK?' said Lee, a cop shanghaied from another team to cover Patrosi, sitting in the front passenger seat.

'Great, isn't she?' said Georgie behind the wheel.

Callum sat in back. Gerry Martin, Sarge and Billy Hutchinson were in a Ford a hundred yards up the street and a rented car was a block over with two more men on loan. A last loan cop sat in the P-Van a block further. A detective come over from Manhattan South Narcotics was undercover as Alexander's ghost: back-up for her at the housing complex two blocks away.

Her ghost jogged around the corner after her and leaned on the car roof as he stooped in the window talking to Sarge. Trish sauntered over to their Chrysler rental and opened the rear door on the left. She stumbled and slumped onto the seat next to Callum. The skin under her eye was swollen some.

'What the fuck?' said Callum.

'Guy smacked me,' said Trish. 'Wanted a trick with my treat. I said I was on my period and it was kinda heavy and he took at pop at me.'

Lee said, 'Motherfucker.'

Georgie said, 'You OK, Trish?'

Callum said, 'We got a "move in" yet?'

He wanted to go, take a shot at this bastard and tune him up before processing.

'Your compassion is overwhelming,' said Trish.

'No, no,' said Callum, his face burning up. 'I just care about you is all. I mean not care about you like *care*, you know? I mean ... I ... uh ...'

'He means he can't wait to get in there and defend your honor or some old country bullshit,' said Georgie. She smiled.

Trish matched her grin.

'Geez, Burke,' she said with her long fingers to her chest in mock abashment, 'I didn't know you got feels, baby. I mean, not feels like you *cared* or nothin'.'

'Let me see that,' said Callum, and he reached out and touched her cheek. She flinched like now *he'd* taken a pop at her, eyes wide for a second before they narrowed and looked pissed.

'I'm sorry,' he said. 'I box and I see this shit all the time and I thought – '

'How many dealers?' said Georgie.

Trish looked at Callum like she'd never noticed him before and kept her eyes on his for a couple of heartbeats, before turning to Georgie.

'Three. Could be three hundred in that park though, so people are gonna scatter like roaches from a flashlight when you go in there. Perps are black males – 5'6 in gray sweat pants and a red basketball shirt under a gray puffer jacket, shaved head; 6'1 wearing loose blue jeans and a Lakers sweat shirt, no jacket, dreads; the one who smacked me is 6'3, maybe 4, in blue jeans and a white sweater under a Davoucci brown leather jacket, hair in cornrows. Shaved Head and Dreads are in sneakers but corn-rows is wearing Timberland boots.' She pulled her top up an

56

inch over her cleavage and Callum caught the loan guy, Lee, look away. 'They got a stash behind a loose brick on the corner of the public john, but left by the men's room, not right like in the tac plan. They also got a pistol hidden behind the dumpster at the left side.'

Her eyes slid to Callum again. He held her gaze and felt something pass between them, saw something soften in her features. He had a wild urge to stroke her face and plant a kiss on her damaged eye, and the idea surprised him. A shriek of static made her wince and Sarge's voice cut through on the radio, giving the order to move in.

Trish sat tight while Callum and the others climbed out of the Chrysler and checked vests and guns. They made for Sarge's car at a light jog. Callum felt the old surge in his limbs, the feeling of pure energy careening around his body as his guts went hollow and the adrenaline kicked in. They turned the corner.

Past a hardware store, a pet supply store, a nail salon. People watching the police jog by, identification out, guns holstered on belts. Five cops, Callum, Georgie and the rest. Now seven, now eight as the loan guys jogged over to join them. Cold sun on the concrete, a tree scrawny as a junkie struggling up from the sidewalk, ringed by an ankle-length iron fence like it was doing time.

They split as the housing project appeared around another corner, huge with a tarnished brown-brick facade. Thicker trees now cloaking the entrance and the park by the housing tower. A basketball court. It emptied and Callum heard hissed warnings.

'Po-po! Shit! Po-po!'

Onto the lawn of the park and a concrete rectangle with swings, a Jungle Gym, a couple of slides. Fish in a barrel if they wanted it. Junkies scattered, baggies flying through the air like hats at graduation. Clinking crack vials on the ground. Scrawny shitheads draped in gold dropped off the Jungle Gym and lit off for the housing tower block, the street, anywhere but where the po-po were on the hunt. By the Jungle Gym, a block of public restrooms. Callum saw three men already running, the loan cops sprinting in from the left side where they flanked. Martin made for the restrooms to check for drugs and guns.

Callum moved up through the gears, the vest tight against his body, his badge flying around his neck. He saw Shaved Head dealer go down hard to a body check from a loan guy, saw Georgie run over to help. Dreads was making for the street. He tripped and went into a crazy run, arms spinning as Hutchinson caught him from behind and pulled him horizontal mid-air by his sweatshirt hood. Sarge ran in, took a swing and planted a sneaker in Dreads's gut.

Callum ran on, scanning the park for Cornrows.

He'd lost him.

Come on, he thought, you're in Timberlands with 6'4 inch-guy feet. Like fuckin' clown shoes on this grass.

His heart hammered in step with the pounding of his sneakers and he crunched crack vials underfoot. He was twenty yards from the sidewalk when he saw the leather jacket, Davoucci emblazoned on the back, crossing the street toward a McDonald's. Big, loping gait but those long legs covered ground. A security guard pressed his nose to the McDonald's inner window pane then ducked further back inside. Callum ran across the street and felt a cold shot down his spine: felt someone chasing him. The runner drew alongside and he saw it was Lee. The McDonald's was in the center of the block and Cornrows banked right. Callum followed. Lee split left to round the block and come in from the opposite direction.

Cars honked. People watched. A couple of kids clapped.

Cornrows turned the corner. Callum tried to see if he had a pistol. He cursed as the fucker disappeared out of sight.

His breath came in sharp rasps. His Glock rubbed against his hip. Thoughts raced: Trish's black eye, Georgie in his kitchen, a warm fantasy snapshot of a right hook to Gerry Martin's jaw.

Around the corner he saw Cornrows passing a drugstore and an old lady gawking. The bastard vanished left.

An alley.

Callum reached it and slowed. His throat was raw and scratchy; the run and years of smokes had hit him hard. He stood at the entrance of the alley and drew the Glock. The alley bisected the buildings in the block and ended near the opposite street in a chainlink fence maybe 12 feet tall.

He couldn't have made it, thought Callum. He isn't that fast.

The alley was lined with the rear of various stores. There were a couple of shutters, lots of locked doors. A bank of trash cans. What looked like a couple of hiding holes where buildings were shorter than others. He pulled the Glock.

There was the radio. He could call for help. Lee must finish his lap of the block in a minute, see the alley and follow Callum in.

He took a step, his breath still harsh.

Another step, another breath.

Then he couldn't breathe at all and 6'4 of criminal terror and rage was barreling into him, driving him against a steel door. It felt like his ribs were making to crush his lungs. His head reeled. His limbs lost it for a second. The Glock hit the ground.

Callum grabbed Cornrows' jacket and they went into a crazy dance. The clothes were good but the man smelt like he was rotting away from the inside. Body odour, decaying teeth and spicy fear burned Callum's nose. He felt panic wash in like a tidal wave and the sharp terror that this could be the one – the lucky break for the bad guy and a messy death with a bullet, a hidden knife, even a dirty needle and a slow death from infection. He heard Cornrows grunt, heard his own desperate breath rising in pitch.

He tried to use the dealer's height against him, tried to pivot and unbalance the fucker but they both went down and he landed on something which bit into his shoulder on impact. They rolled and he knew it was the Glock. The dealer's fist cracked his temple and Callum lost purchase on the bastard for a second. Then he saw the gun as Cornrows, fast for a big man, grabbed the pistol. Callum flailed, kicked, cursed. He caught the dealer's wrist and they rolled on the alley floor over yesterday's headlines and broken glass.

Then Callum threw back his head and launched his skull into the shitbag's nose. He heard the crunch above his own breath roaring in his ears and felt the man flinch. He slammed the dealer's hand on the concrete once, twice. Three times the charm; the Glock clattered free and Callum was scrabbling, grabbing the gun and slamming it into the dealer's face.

It wasn't as solid as a revolver but it was tough enough. Cornrows' cheek split and he called out.

Then came a thick, red mist.

Lee pulled Callum off after seconds, minutes: who knew how long? He had been locked in another place like a hidden world, just Callum Burke and an asshole dealer – Callum pummeling, the dealer screaming and rolling, going fetal. Until the screaming stopped and the grip of the Glock slammed wet skin over bone. And then Lee was dragging Callum back to the surface, to the real world.

'Jesus Christ,' said Lee.

Cornrows' face was a ruin.

Callum said, 'Fuck. He isn't movin'. Fuck!'

He dropped the Glock and saw the blood on his hands.

Then Sarge ran up and stood looking at the dealer curled on the ground and Callum kneeling beside the body.

'Oh shit,' he said.

*

'You are one lucky son of a bitch.'

Callum said, 'I'm sorry Sarge.'

'You say that one more time, I'll beat you like you beat that dirtbag asshole, you hear me?'

Callum nodded. They sat on the swings in the concrete rectangle a distance from the rest of the team who drank coffees grabbed from a nearby deli. Shaved Head and Dreads were in the P-Van. Cornrows was on his way to ER. Trish and the other undercover had made for the Six-oh to have her eye looked at.

Before, Callum had looked at Cornrows' body – and it had looked like a body at a crime scene then, rather than a living, breathing person.

'That's it,' Callum had said. 'I'm over. If I'm lucky I'll just lose my job.'

Sarge had called the paramedics. The medic had checked over Cornrows. The dealer was still, like the dummy they used for first aid training.

'I'm done,' Callum had said. 'He could have brain damage.'

The paramedic stood up and leaned in close.

'He's banged up for sure,' he said in a whisper. 'You did a number on this guy. But he's faking.'

'Fakin' my ass, the asshole isn't movin'.'

'He's faking. I'll be back.'

Callum opened his mouth to talk. Sarge put a finger to his lips to silence him.

The medic returned.

'Subject is unresponsive,' he said loudly. 'Bodily functions will be uncontrolled. I'm going to insert a catheter.' He produced a tube and began unbuttoning Cornrows' jeans with his gloved hands. He pulled down a pair of filthy boxer shorts and grabbed the dealer's dick in one hand, gripping the catheter in the other.

'*Get the fuck out of here!*'

Cornrows went bug-eyed and flapped his hands like a swarm of bees were honing in on his cock.

The paramedic had turned to Callum, winked and stood. 'I'll take it from here,' he had said. 'You can do what you gotta do once he's at the hospital.

Sarge had shook his head like a disappointed father, or maybe an exasperated master with an unruly mutt, and gestured for him to join the rest of the team.

Now Callum eased off the swing and lit up a smoke. He saw Georgie look over and hold his gaze for a moment.

'You think I got any comeback from this?' he said.

Sarge sighed. 'You're covered.'

'Listen, I don't want to lean on Bochinni on this,' said Callum. He got enough grief for his rabbi fast tracking him into Narcotics, he didn't need Bochinni covering his ass on an arrest beating too. 'I'll take my medicine.'

'You got help, but it ain't your rabbi,' said Sarge. 'Although he could be behind what's comin'.' He looked at the ground, one hand on his hip, the other resting on his holster.

'The luck of the Irish, huh?' he said. 'You know, I'm Greek, despite what Martin believes. I been watchin' your clans carve up this department for years. There ain't no luck for you guys, not in the Job: just Mick scratchin' Mick's potato-pickin' back. One day the Irish won't run roughshod over Department procedure – but, for now, you got another Paddy pulled you outta this one.'

He whistled and the team looked over. Sarge yelled, 'Georgie!'

Georgie Ruiz walked over.

'You know, this fucks my quota for today. I got two perps in the P-Van, one in hospital, now I gotta lose half my team after just one goddamn B&B.'

'Who you losin', Sarge?' said Georgie.

62

'You and Iron Mike here.'

Georgie looked at Callum, questions writ large on her face, then back at the sarge.

She said, 'I don't get it.'

'I don't either,' said Sarge. 'I get one Paddy stealin' his pal for his team, but why he wants a top-rate cop like you in the mix, I don't know.'

He looked at Callum.

'Gimme one of those cigarettes,' he said.

Callum pulled the Camels from his pocket, passed one over and lit the boss up.

He tried not to hope too hard the olive-pickin', goat-bangin' motherfucker didn't choke on it as he walked away.

Eight

'A top-rate cop? Asshole.'

'Man knows quality when he sees it,' said Georgie. She shot Callum a smile could lift the gray from the overcast sky above. A pissed-looking wasp buzzed above a headstone up ahead. They passed the grave and the insect made a diving sortie between them.

They strolled through Green-Wood Cemetery in west Brooklyn, like a couple taking a walk in the park. The low-pitched hum of the city going about its business lay distant.

Georgie touched Callum on the shoulder.

'Come on,' she said. 'Sarge is just pissed because you battered that perp and he lost bodies when he's chasing his bust-quota. He knows you're a good cop. We all do.'

'Yeah?'

Callum looked at the sky and watched a jet lumber overhead. He thought how easy it would be to grab a flight and go. He'd done it twice in his life: Belfast to Hong Kong, HK to New York. But he'd run from Belfast, then stayed in NYC to be closer to Irene and Tara. He had to stop sometime. He had to go to goddamn Cleveland and see his wife and child.

'Of course we do,' said Georgie. 'Get over yourself, this ain't a job for self-pity, big man.'

That smile again.

'To the rest of the team,' said Callum, 'I'm the rookie got an Inspector on his way to Deputy Chief pulling strings. Without Bochinni, I'd still be pulling on blues every day. You know it, and they know it.'

'You busted two organized crime outfits, Cal, the Irish and the

Chinese. You made Bochinni's career, you got me out of Intel, you got O'Connell his promotion to Lieutenant. A lot of people owe you.'

She stopped him with a hand on his.

'You almost died, Cal.'

He saw her now as he had then. She had kept him sane.

He had been a sergeant in the Royal Hong Kong Police Force, seconded to a DEA/NYPD/RHKPF task force. The heroin came from Asia via Hong Kong Triads to New York, where a Chinatown Tong brokered a distribution deal with a local Irish Mob. Months undercover for Callum with the Irish Crew, living and drinking with the big names. Reporting to NYPD Sergeant Mike O'Connell on the latest rackets, the latest bodies. Occasional meets with Georgie Ruiz as she ghosted him. He'd seen a man murdered, cut up two corpses to preserve his cover. And then, he'd been blown and dodged the final bullet.

Georgie Ruiz had gone to him then. Had cradled his busted up face in her hands.

'You know,' he said, 'when it was real bad, and I was more scared than I ever been ... then ... you ... ' he sucked up air, 'Georgie – '

'So this guy shoves a sausage inside a bun and he gets a pad bigger than my fuckin' house to spend his eternal rest in.'

Georgie's face flushed at the sound of the gruff voice. Callum shook his head and smiled.

Lieutenant Mike O'Connell stood a few feet away in a sweatshirt, overcoat and black jeans. His shield was clipped on his belt by his Colt Official .38 revolver.

Georgie said, 'I heard this one on Jeopardy, Lieu.'

'Hey, Lieu,' said Callum.

Mike O'Connell winced as they both used the usual NYPD form of address for a Lieutenant.

'Christ, don't call me that,' he said. 'Makes me sound like a shitter in England.'

'Or Ireland,' said Callum.

'Not that you'd know, you mongrel limey son of a bitch.'

They walked over to O'Connell and he cocked his thumb at a huge mausoleum on a rise, all Corintheum columns, statues and urns topped by a domed cupola, the archangel Michael perched on top. Two cherubs held a wreath in the center of the pediment emblazoned with the letter "F". Just below was the engraved name Charles Feltman.

Callum read the name aloud.

'He put a frank between a bun and invented the hot dog,' said Georgie. 'We work our asses off to keep the good people of this city safe and we'll be lucky if we get a plot big enough to lie straight in.'

"Twas ever thus,' said Callum.

O'Connell said, 'Walk with me.'

They strolled through the cemetery, all billiard table lawns and well-tended paths. O'Connell talked about the past: the task-force; the names in federal penitentiaries as a result of their investigation. War stories, the foundation of Callum's career in the NYPD, his friendship with both the cops by his side. As they walked, Callum saw Midtown Manhattan looming in the distance across the river through a crack in some brittle-looking trees.

They turned a corner and stopped.

A low stone wall fifty feet around hemmed in an area of raked bone-white gravel. In the center of the gravel lay a slab of marble and on that, a statue of a man in a designer suit and the front end of a Mercedes that disappeared into a massive headstone. Urns sat atop the wall at each corner and an angel, wings spread wide, stood on top of the headstone looking down at the statue of the man and car. A forest, almost photo-realistic, had been engraved on the marble headstone and, barely visible at the treeline, there stood a woman in a fur coat and boots. The name and epitaph were engraved in Cyrillic script.

'The last resting place of Temuri Mikhailov,' said O'Connell. 'I like to think the angel is lookin' down to make sure he's still burnin' in Hell.'

Callum said, 'I'm guessing he didn't invent a fast food.'

'The Feds like to call them Russian Mafia.'

O'Connell had been a sergeant at Manhattan North Narcotics when they worked the task force together. Now he'd transferred within OCCB to the Organized Crime Investigation Division.

'So it falls in my in-tray,' he said, 'except the Organized Crime Investigation Division should be working *organized* crime. The Russians are running around like it's the Wild West down there in Brooklyn.'

Here it comes, thought Callum.

It was O'Connell who had pulled he and Georgie from the sarge's team today. Now he was playing 'through the keyhole', Russian Mafia gravesite edition, in Green-Wood the day after they had stumbled in on two Russian killers inked in mobster art. This was going to be a whole lot worse than busting dealers and junkies in the projects all day.

O'Connell said, 'You hearda Vyacheslav Ivankov? He was a big player in Brighton Beach a coupla years ago before the Feds busted him. Left a vacuum and our boy Temuri here was quick to fill it.' He walked over to the gravesite. 'Trouble is, Temuri didn't have the chops, and lasted four months before someone left his corpse out on Rockaway Beach.'

He stepped over the low wall and motioned for Callum and Georgie to join him.

'So now we got two Ivans trying to assert themselves as leading lights in Brighton Beach. Maxim Volkov, and Arkady Kuztensov. The guys you walked in on carving their brisket were members of the Volkov crew.'

Georgie said, 'And this relates to Brooklyn South Narcotics how?'

'It doesn't,' said Callum. 'Does it, Mike?'

O'Connell smiled and sat on the hood of the stone Mercedes.

'I seen that look before, Callum. Like you maybe wanna tear my fuckin' head off and play a game of your candy-ass soccer with it. It's been a while, but I seen it.'

'Yeah, good times.'

'Light up a smoke. It's good for you.'

Callum and O'Connell watched one another for a minute.

Georgie looked from one to the other, her mouth crooked.

'I was never as close as you guys,' she said, 'but if you got some kinda ESP going on, you need to spell it out for me.'

O'Connell turned to her and said, 'You ghosted him for months while he was undercover, right?' He gestured at Callum.

'I was working with a partner: it wasn't exactly a one-woman show.'

'But you were the drivin' force. And Callum-fuckin'-Burke, the Brooklyn Bomber here.' O'Connell spread his arms like a central-casting wiseguy. 'You went through some dark shit, but you cracked some tough heads, too.'

'I got my ass handed to me.'

'You took some lumps but you dropped Jimmy Mulligan, man. Jimmy-fuckin'-Mulligan! The Irish mob's number one enforcer! And you came through the other side, quit that Royal-Highness-your-Won-Ton-Kung-Pao-Hong-Kong-Constabulary outfit and emerged from your coccoon as a shining blue NYPD butterfly. You *know* clandestine operations.'

'You gotta' lay off that thesaurus you got for Christmas.'

'I never liked Jurassic Park.'

'I ain't goin' undercover with the Russian Mafia.'

'No, you ain't. Clandestine ain't the same as undercover.'

Callum stared at the sky then searched for the sliver of Manhattan again through the trees. It was gone, obscured by a tangle of branches. O'Connell was a hard man. A good man at his core, but a bastard on the Job and him blowing smoke up Callum's ass could only mean bad news. Callum finished his cigarette and moved to drop it on the grass by the path.

O'Connell said, 'Stop.'

He took the smouldering butt from Callum, walked so he stood face-to-face with the dead mobster's statue and ground the cigarette out in the right eye.

'Hear me out,' he said.

Callum hunched and put his hands in his pockets while Georgie crossed her arms and cocked a hip.

'I got a CI,' said O'Connell. 'Russian, lives in Brighton Beach. He's a young guy, a hustler loves goin' to the local bathhouses. One thing the Ivans dig is gettin' naked and workin' up a sweat together. This CI, he tells me Russian men will talk about anything in a bathhouse. So he listens in, talks to the faces in the neighborhood.'

'It's all good,' said Georgie.

'Yeah. He's a kid, you know, at least looks like one. Real pretty if you're a Councilman or Cardinal. Only blemish this kid got is a tattoo on each eyelid.'

Callum leaned forward.

'I heard your interest in the kid from the DTs,' said O'Connell. 'Small world, huh? This CI, he's tougher than he looks. He did time in Russia a couple years before he came over here and he got that ink done while he was inside with a homemade needle. He stuck spoons between his eyes and the lids when he got the tatts.'

Georgie winced.

'His name is Avda Galkin.' O'Connell said. 'The little shit was cheatin' on me with your friend got his leg busted executing the warrant, Patrosi. You won't find him on NYPD records – I already checked. Seems he was makin' double the payoff sellin' the same information to Patrosi and me.'

Callum wasn't surprised there was no record of the kid as a CI. Many refused to be registered due to paranoia, and cops would agree to use the informant off the books to get street information.

He said, 'But Patrosi kept talking about his CI as a "she".'

'I don't know about that. The kid's pretty, kind of feminine. Could be what he meant. Or maybe it was just a smokescreen to protect his source. You gotta ask your friend about that.'

O'Connell sat back on the stone Mercedes hood again and told them how he was pulled in by OCCB when the Russian killers were arrested and taken to the 60th Precinct. He had called the detectives at the Six-oh and found out Callum and Georgie had been on the team who discovered the hoods up to their elbows in blood. He checked the detectives' DD5s and saw Callum's mention of a kid at the scene who had marks on his eyelids. The detectives disregarded the fact as there was always an army of gawkers at a public crime scene like that in the housing projects. But O'Connell figured from the description that it could be his CI. He found out the CI, Avda Galkin, was moonlighting as an informant with Patrosi at Narcotics and asked Detective Parker at Six-oh homicide to have a talk with Callum, then called the sarge to have Callum and Georgie meet him at Green-Wood.

'Why here?' said Georgie. 'Why not at your office?'

'The guys at Organized Crime Investigation love their secret squirrel shit, y'know? We're the elite, all that bull, like they're playin' the Mission Impossible theme in their heads when they go to take a dump. They're protective of their space and paranoid about leaks. It's easier for me to keep you away from the base of operations.'

Georgie said, 'Are the FBI on this? Sounds like their kinda gig.'

'They're too busy with the Columbians right now. The action in Brighton Beach isn't as big as the last couple of years, so the glory boys are giving it a pass and leaving it to us city cops. If they're on Ivans at all, the Feds are too busy spying on the Russkies' Diplomatic Compound up in the Bronx on some dick-swingin' James Bond trip.'

Callum raised his eyebrows.

'And this is off the books, right?'

'There you go with those eyes again, Cal. Now they got "O'Connell's full of it" written across them in letters bigger than the Silvercup sign.' O'Connell looked at the gravel at his feet and smiled. 'Off the books is a little strong. I got you both on a steal but not all day every day, leastways not at first.'

He stood and put a foot on the hood of the Mercedes statuary.

'This little tattoo-eyed shit's been playin' around on me and I wanna know how he's spendin' his days. Georgie, I want you on surveillance. No title IIIs yet, I ain't got enough to push a DA into signing off on a wiretap. But you keep eyes on Avda Galkin. I'll give you his address and you take it from there. Call me on this cell number to keep me updated. I know you can't tail the little prick 24/7 so you work the hours you would on a narcotics shift watchin' him and sign off as usual. You want the overtime, you got it, that's your choice.'

Georgie nodded, but the light faded some from her eyes. When she joined the task force with O'Connell and Callum two years ago, she got surveillance duties. At first it had seemed vital street work. After weeks it became a drudgery.

But she sucked it up and said, 'You got it.'

Callum folded his arms waiting for the sucker punch.

O'Connell said, 'Cal, you go to work with your team as usual. I got a beeper for you. I'll be in touch and your sergeant will know when I need you. You're gonna handle Galkin.'

'But he's your CI: won't he clam up when I turn up at a meet?'

'I'll introduce you. Thing is, this kid, he don't relate to me.'

'He's a hustler with a criminal history – you think he'll relate to me any better?'

'He's an immigrant, like you. European, and he hangs in the Village a lot. You still live in Fagtown, you might know some of the same places. I don't know. I need distance from the kid and you been undercover. Sure, it ain't the same as bein' a CI but you can relate to him some.'

'You know who my handler was when I was undercover, Mike?' said Callum. He stabbed a finger at O'Connell. 'You. The most hard-assed, judgemental, manipulative asshole in the five boroughs.'

'You learned from the best.'

'How did you get the juice to do this?'

'You ain't the only one on Inspector Bochinni's Christmas Card list. He got all the right ears among the White Shirts in the department and he's had dinner with the mayor. When Guiliani beats Messinger in the mayoral race this year – and he will – Bochinni's gonna' make Deputy Chief. That all began with you bustin' the Walsh Crew and the Chinese. I just made the most of a little residual glory.'

Callum sighed and fished another smoke out of his crumpled pack. He lit up, took a deep drag and looked at Georgie. She smiled in sympathy. He turned to Mike O'Connell. It could be worse – and the detail got him out from under the occasional comments and looks in the team. But it would also piss off Gerry Martin and Sarge even more.

'Can I say no?' he said.

'Negative,' said Mike.

Then the lieutenant spat on the Russian mobster's grave and made for the path whistling 'The Girl I left Behind Me' as he went.

Nine

It was Friday.

Tikhon watched a mother and child play on the sand against a wan sky slatted by shredded clouds. There was a beautiful sadness in the scene. It somehow reminded him of a painting he'd seen once in the Tretyakov Gallery, of a lone battleship drifting on the sea, its sails torn and ragged.

Two dreamless nights had passed since he had been with Avda. This morning he had risen, eaten and washed, and made for the beach. The Atlantic spread before him like a massive sheet of tempered steel and he had the crazy idea of walking across the ocean to Europe, then on to Moscow. Pockets of people were on the sand but it was still April and too early for the crowds.

The mother watched the child scoop sand into a yellow plastic bucket.

Tikhon turned and strolled east along the boardwalk then cut back through streets lined by towering brick-fronted apartment buildings to Brighton Beach Avenue. At its eastern extremity, the elevated train tracks had not yet joined the avenue and the space felt light and spacious after the side streets crowded with tenement-style buildings. He walked a block and turned onto Brighton 13th Street, coming to a row of two-floor duplexes with small stoops leading to their front doors. He stopped at one opposite a fire hydrant and walked up the steps, knocking as he stood under a cherry red awning.

The woman opened the door and metal grille and smiled, gesturing with a sweep of her arm for him to enter.

Her dirty fair hair hung straight to her shoulders, framing her face like soft bars of light. Her blue eyes, set wide below a smear of black eyeshadow, had a hint of mischief. She had a sharp nose, high cheekbones and thin lips a fraction from mean. She wore a simple white blouse and tawny skirt to below her knees. A plain woman. The only hint of her profession was the pair of glossy black six-inch heels on her feet.

Tikhon had never asked her to dress like so many Muscovites back then, when he returned from a war no one wanted to mention by name, but he liked it. She had simply read him with her sexual alchemy.

They stood at the foot of the stairs in a simple lounge of hardwood floor, couch, TV and coffee table. He handed her an envelope of money that she didn't open.

She said, 'Would you like a drink?'

The offer was for *chifir*, a caffeine-loaded tea popular among inmates in prisons back home. Another suggestion of how she made a living.

Her name was Marina.

Tikhon said, 'No, thank you.'

Marina nodded and took his hand. She led him upstairs.

*

Afterwards, she wiped herself and ran her fingertips over the puckered skin of his chest. Tikhon knew the bullet wounds excited her. He didn't mind. It was a fair trade: her sex calmed him, like his male lover. His Saint George.

As though reading his mind she said, 'How is Avda?'

Tikhon ran his hand over the sleek rise of her hip as she lay naked beside him. Her smooth softness calmed him. The rollercoaster car would stall for a little more time. The fact she knew he used both she and Avda for sex kept things uncomplicated.

'Fine,' said Tikhon. 'I saw him recently.'

'So which of our teams will you join now?'

'Yours, I think, Marina.'

She chuckled and ran her fingers from his chest down his stomach.

Her question was silly, an allusion to *Boaire*, a folk game played by children where players recruit others for their team. But his answer was earnest. He needed both their bodies; but once he finished with Avda, he closed up. He had what he needed and the rest was formality until they parted. With Marina, he opened up after the sex. It was the one time he allowed himself a scrap of vulnerability.

She curled her fingers in his pubic hair.

'You should get a tattoo of me, like some of the others,' she said.

'My *biksa*.' Tikhon laughed. 'No artist could do justice to your beauty.'

Now she laughed. She knew she was not his biksa and never would be. There were those among the criminals she serviced that might fall in love with a whore, and forge a relationship beyond client and hooker. Some biksa were not professionals but sexually available women who criminals accepted were sluttish but still respected and – in some way – loved above others. There were men with the face of their biksa tattooed on their chest or arm.

Not him. When he wasn't with her, Marina did not exist in Tikhon's world.

'What were the women like over there in the war?' she said.

'They were the enemy, same as the men.'

She put her lips to his shoulder and said, 'Did you kill any women?'

He stretched his arms above his head.

'We were on patrol and a flock of sheep came along a mountain pass. There were nine shepherds with those sheep, and a woman too. They all wore Soviet buttons on their clothes but

75

there were too many men for a small flock, and we never saw a woman with shepherds on the mountains before. She was wrapped up, disguised. We had a KHAD with us, an *Osobist*, too: one of our own KGB.'

He rubbed his temples.

'The KHAD walked over and began shoving his hands in the first sheep's wool. He found a leather girding at its front and back, and sliced through it with his knife. Something heavy hit the ground. There had been a submachine gun tied under the animal. The next sheep had a machine gun and three grenades. They were all laden with weapons.'

He stared at the ceiling as if the scene was projected there.

'The KHAD began beating the shepherds and slapped the woman. Then the KGB officer walked behind her and shot her in the head. He and the KHAD worked their way along the line of shepherds, one bullet each.'

Marina rolled on top of him.

'I'm sorry,' she said – she said it every time – and kissed his chest. 'I shouldn't have asked.'

Again, as every time, he said, 'It's okay. With you it's okay, especially after we fuck.'

Marina reached down and began positioning herself as his eyes met hers.

'And before,' she said.

*

The tea was strong and bitter. It washed the taste of Marina from Tikhon's mouth and he said a silent prayer that her calming sex would see him through the next couple of nights. He turned at a fusilade of raucous laughter and watched a huddle of men in the corner as they stared at James Bond shooting up Saint Petersburg on TV.

The Masha Russian Tea Room sat between two houses on residential Banner Avenue. Arkady Kuznetsov had an apartment out back which he used when spending time with his mistresses. The tea room was named after his wife.

That apartment, like his other residences, was said to have an elaborate model train set. Marina had told Tikhon the Masha apartment had a replica of an old Sakhalin line running on a diorama around the bed. Kuznetsov and his mistresses had to crawl on hands and knees under the hardboard base in order to reach the king size.

Every time Tikhon visited the tea room, the only customers were Kuznetsov's men, a few old folk, and a couple of the other prostitutes he ran along with Marina. The girls were part of a Medicaid scam in which Kuznetsov used a front company to run a home attendance service – good business in Brighton Beach with the number of retirees in the area. But the service was a prostitution ring: the staff attending to the clients' needs were Kuznetsov's hookers. The clients, many of them old men, billed the girls' services as medical expenses.

Arkady Kuznetsov appeared from behind a bead curtain by the counter at the back of the room and walked over to Tikhon's table in the corner farthest from the door. Kuznetsov sat and placed an envelope thick with bills by Tikhon's cup. He looked cadaverous, his aquiline nose like a crooked blade between eyes made huge in the sunken face. His mustache had been trimmed but still obscured his top lip, a cigarette clenched between tombstone teeth. His fat bottom lip hung low, his large ears protruding from a narrow skull. The lobe of the left was missing, a diamond stud in the right.

His voice was thick and deep, belying his scrawny appearance. His Russian was clear, his diction precise.

'That was good work you did at Fogelman's,' said Kuznetsov. 'Should have the *suki* fuck frothing at the mouth all week.'

Arkady Kuznetsov always used the derogatory *suki* – *bitch* – when referring to Maxim Volkov. Kuznetsov was a fully-fledged *Vor*, a proud member of the *Vorovskoi Mir*: the Thieves World. He knew, as did many in their circles, that Volkov had had dealings with the state back in Russia and made a good chunk of his money that way. That qualified him as a "bitch" – a criminal who prostituted himself for the establishment.

Tikhon took the envelope, shoving it into his coat pocket.

'You could call me by that name, too,' he said. 'I served in the Soviet forces in Afghanistan, fought for the state.'

Kuznetsov's eyebrows knit tight. He pointed at Tikhon.

'Not the same thing, brother. Not at all. You fought and sacrificed for Mother Russia. Many Vory fought at Stalingrad and elsewhere against the Nazis, because they fought for the Motherland, not that butcher Stalin. And they were screwed by the state when they came home, denied all they had been promised – just like you and your Afghantsy brothers.'

Tikhon took a sip of tea.

He said, 'Stalin was a Georgian.'

Kuznetsov sat back and folded his arms. His brows relaxed but his eyes narrowed.

It was an open secret that Kuznetsov had Georgian blood. He was ambivalent about his heritage, one of his strengths – there were Chechens in his employ, unthinkable for Maxim Volkov – but, nevertheless, he was a "Bay Leaf", the name given to Georgian gangsters by their Slavic counterparts.

Tikhon said, 'Volkov's men will be back, they will terrorize that old man and Fogelman will pay them as well as you.'

'If so, he'll still make more money than he could dream of in Russia.'

Tikhon drank tea. Kuznetsov traced a circle with his finger around a faded coffee ring on the table top.

'You know,' said Kuznetsov, 'the girls, the protection money, the drugs: these are helpful but they don't pay the rent. In this country, I am a facilitator. The Italians, Jamaicans, whoever – I don't care: I provide vehicles, muscle and storage. But most importantly, I can clean their cash.'

He tapped the table.

'I know a very useful man in Russia. He is a celebrity now and it will be his undoing, but he has much influence: Otari 'Otarik' Kvantrishvili. Do you know how many businesses he runs, how much money he makes? Perfect for laundering the dollars coming from New York. And what is Otarik's blood?'

'Georgian.'

'This is the new world, brother. The Americans call this neighborhood Little Odessa – but we have Russians, Georgians, Ukrainians and more living side-by-side. And I am a Gangster Internationalist of the first order.'

Kuznetsov sat back and regarded him. His eyes lingered on Tikhon's hands, now placed on the table top.

'You know, you are no *byk*. No "bull". I have many, like those men over by the TV. You can crack a head, sure, but you are smarter and a lot more dangerous than any of my foot soldiers.'

Tikhon said, 'And why is that?'

'You're a loner. That makes you unpredictable, beholden to none. More terrifying by far is that I really don't think you give a shit about money.'

Tikhon smiled. It was as dead as the scarred wood of the table.

'I have to live,' he said. 'To live, I need money.'

'But you don't care for it. So why do you work with me?'

'Because I want to hurt – '

'Volkov, yes, yes. But why? Was he in Afghanistan? Did he do something over there?'

For a second, Tikhon's eyes flared like a rocket from a MiG. Clack. Clack. Clack.

Then he thought of Marina less than an hour ago, and of Avda.

He said, 'I have no skills to use save those I learned in the Airborne. Right now there are two big dogs in the fight here in Brooklyn. I see you as the winner.'

Kuznetsov snorted.

'This fight is not about Brooklyn. That bitch and I are butting heads over Brighton Beach and nothing more. This is a village squabble. The real business is fought thousands of miles away in Moscow and elsewhere.'

He shook his head as though saddened by a great waste.

'I said you are no bull, and that is true. But you are a "torpedo".'

Tikhon raised an eyebrow at the Vory slang for professional killer.

'I don't want Volkov removed with a car bomb,' said Kuznetsov, 'or some other mess that brings cops and FBI down on us. Something surgical – that's what I need. I want you to do it. When there is an opportunity, I will let you know. Be ready. I will pay you well.' He smiled and ground out his cigarette in a tin ashtray. 'And so will Marina.'

Tikhon finished his tea.

He said, 'So simple.'

Kuznetsov levered his body up from the table.

'As the proverb says, *Everything that is genius is simple*, my brother.'

Then he walked toward the bead curtain, stopping to laugh at the TV screen before disappearing from sight.

*

Tikhon strolled Brighton Beach Avenue and saw the Fogelman sign from across the street. He thought of the old Jew.

His beeper went off.

He walked to a payphone on Brighton 8ᵗʰ and called a number. The voice was flat, the Russian almost lazy in diction.

'I got him. The bathhouse on Brighton 6ᵗʰ Street.'

'How many others?' said Tikhon.

'I think four, but only two soldiers. Come and take a look.'

It was too much to hope, that he could kill the man now and end it.

Clack.

He didn't have the kinjal dagger.

Clack. Clack.

His apartment was near the bathhouse. He would grab the blade and rip the life from the bastard.

Clack. Clack. Clack.

The voice on the line said, 'Hello?'

Tikhon took a breath and felt the hot flush in his cheeks scuttle up to his scalp. He smoothed back his hair and closed his eyes for a second.

Then he said, 'I'll be there in fifteen minutes.'

Ten

Friday.

Two days Callum had been back on the team after meeting Mike O'Connell. Two days of whispers and asides. He was like the pariah kid in a day-long high school recess and he had found himself waiting for Mike to come calling again.

The one cop on his team who was okay was Trish Alexander. If anything, she'd softened. No big gestures but she chatted when they were in the basement of the 60th Precinct, forcing down the bad coffee. And something in her eyes was different when she looked at him. Like they were bigger and she was affording him a glimpse of new possibilities.

On Wednesday he had left Mike at Green-Wood and gone straight from the cemetery to the Six-oh to help process the day's busts. Thursday he had pushed hard to pull his weight and more with a couple more B&Bs. Then, this morning, he had been pulled by Mike and decided to visit Patrosi at Mount Sinai before hooking up with him.

He'd shown the patrolman on duty at the door of Patrosi's private room his badge and walked into a mess of machines and levers, with the man himself in traction watching a morning soap. They'd shot the shit, Callum gave him a box of cannoli and they each had a pastry. Patrosi bitched about not being able to attend his own racket that night, how Hutchinson chose a goddamn Irish bar for the fund-raising party instead of a good Italian joint.

'You have a couple for me, alright Cal?' Patrosi had said.

Callum had smiled but he worried at the thought of all those cops, all that booze.

Then he had said, 'Your CI, that was some bum information he fed us, huh?'

'I guess,' Patrosi said. 'The assholes were there. Just in body rather than spirit, right?'

'And their bodies were spread out all over the carpet. Your CI, he must not have knocked on that door though. He must have listened from the corridor and heard the dogs were quiet, otherwise the kid would've been riding in a body bag like Beresford and Mayhew.'

'Mighta saved me a couple of months in traction.'

Callum had smiled and looked at the floor for a second.

'Hey, Angel,' he said, 'I just called your CI a "he" three times, but you always said they were a "she".'

'Oh yeah? Must be the drugs they got me on.'

'I called them a "kid" too: you didn't flinch. You never told us they were young or old.'

A shadow passed over Patrosi's face.

'What're you trying to say here?'

'That you're a good cop,' said Callum. 'You're still protecting your CI with a smokescreen after a bum steer. But I know about the kid, the tattoos on his eyelids. Your CI was informing to another cop I know in a different team behind your back. Kid's a Russian, right? A hustler?'

'I never put him on the books.'

'I know. Small world, huh?' Callum thought of Mike sitting on the macabre statuary of a mobster grave. 'I won't tell anyone else.'

Patrosi said, 'Gimme another cannoli.'

He took a bite, worked his jaws, swallowed and sighed.

'This is better than if you'd snuck a bottle of booze in here,' he said. 'This kid, he's okay. I ain't goin' soft, don't worry, I still wouldn't bring him home to meet Annabel or nothin'. They are them; and we are cops. But compared to a lotta others he's human. He told me a couple of his tattoos were like a branding in prison because he was a fag. Some hoods in a Russian shit-hole caught him with another prisoner and forcibly tattooed him with symbols that said he'd become a woman or some shit. That was a reason I called him "she". And it was a good somescreen to protect his identity.'

'The eyelids?' said Callum.

'No, somethin' on his body. Now he works Manhattan for tricks, and not in a bathroom stall in Port Authority. Pretty high-end clients, I think. He always has money, anyway.'

'So why inform?'

'He said he hated the way the worst seemed to rise around Coney and Brighton Beach. It reminded him of the monsters branded him in prison. Also, he took a beating from some rich asshole he serviced one night in Yorkville. The guy was high on some bad shit so the kid used to feed me a line on dealers supplying Manhattanites, too. Good stuff.'

Callum nodded. He hadn't cultivated his own CIs. He hadn't been in his investigative post so long and criminals could be just as choosy as cops. He wasn't a detective yet, so he might not be taken seriously by some.

'So you protected him as a source.'

'Of course. And he seemed kind of scared sometimes. I asked him once why he was so jittery and he told me some of the guys he fucked were rich and powerful. They had wives and families and if it ever became public that they paid for it with him, he could get hurt. You never know, so I didn't push him to go on the books.'

'Does the kid use?' said Callum.

Patrosi shook his head. 'I don't think so. I mean, he might take a pill once in a while when he's workin', or hittin' a club in the City.'

'What happened with the bust on Tuesday? What'd he say?'

'I got word to call him on my beeper. When we spoke, he told me these two assholes – Beresford and Mayhew – in Coney had come across a pretty big stash of junk and they'd be steppin' on it and baggin' it at their apartment. It looked like a good bust so I went to Zhang: hey, you ever need a DA to push for a warrant, use him – he's one of the good guys.'

Callum had said, 'And the rest is history.'

'Yeah,' Patrosi had said, 'like my CI. I won't be usin' him again.'

Then he had taken a bite of cannoli and turned up the volume of the soap on TV.

*

Callum had called Mike from the hospital and waited for him to come pick him up. Thirty minutes later, he jumped in Mike's Ford and they made for Kings Highway, heading south.

'You takin' me back to the Six-oh?' said Callum.

'Nope.'

'Where's your driver?'

'I dunno', ferryin' some asshole around actually thinks a lieutenant needs a chauffeur.' He sniffed. 'When's the last time you washed that shirt?'

'Since you ironed that rag you're wearin' by the looks of it.'

They watched Brooklyn rolling by. Mike picked at something on the dashboard. Callum remembered Mike's wife, how she freaked if the car, or the house, or his clothes got dirty.

'How's Marcie and the kids?' he said.

'The kids are great. Declan's really started getting into his sports. He's playin' a lot more baseball, you know? We got stuff we can do together. Lily, she wants to be a vet. Loves animals. It's good.'

They passed a hulking industrial shell slathered in graffiti.

'Marcie,' he said, 'well, Marcie's OK. She's, ah, she's fine. She misses you. You should come over for dinner soon.'

'She hates me.'

'Yeah, she does.'

They laughed.

'What do you expect?' said Mike. 'I live with the Good Housekeeping Guide and you're a smoker.'

'I smoked in the yard.'

'Shit's still on your clothes, man. She said she could smell it on the plastic cover on the couch for weeks. Hey, if Marcie liked you, I'd be checking the closet when I got home at night.'

Callum held back on a jibe. Despite the cracks, he knew how protective Mike was of his wife, and how he carried his guilt deep inside for her obsessive moods. One night, years ago, Marcie O'Connell had received a phone call to say her husband had been killed on duty. Something broke in Marcie that night. Mike had returned home to find her curled in a corner clutching their wedding album and a butcher knife. The bastard who made the call had been a brother cop, jealous of a big collar Mike made on a prolific dealer.

The view became more low-rise as they turned onto Coney Island Avenue and drove south. Mike grabbed his radio and called in. Georgie Ruiz's voice came through. Mike asked where the CI, Avda Galkin, was and Georgie reported back he was in a building on 6th Street. Mike told her to keep eyes on the building and let him know when Galkin left. He turned to Callum.

'You open up the window, you can smoke. This is a department car.'

They crossed an overpass bridging the Belt Parkway and passed a cluster of stores. Somewhere beyond was the maze of projects in which Callum had stumbled in on the murder scene a couple of days ago. Nearing Brighton Beach Avenue the first Cyrillic signs appeared.

'These Russians,' said Mike, 'they're fuckin' cowboys. The wops got structure, they gotta pay tributes, all that shit. But the Ivans, they're like atoms, all crashing off each other. Like I said, they ain't really organized but the Feds insist they're a mafia and the Feds got the money and the big ugly building in Washington – so a mafia, they are.' He fished a pack of mints out of his pocket as Callum got the window down and took out a cigarette.

Georgie came through on the radio again to report that Avda Galkin had left the building, which had the word *banya* on a sign above the entrance, on 6th Street.

Mike grunted, 'Ten-four.'

'I'm gonna fill Ruiz in on this, too,' he said, 'but what you should understand is *Vory* and *Krysha*. The Vory are like a criminal class. Like a "made" guy, I guess, but without all the family bullshit. They're the criminal elite in the Motherland, got a code, but they don't belong to one gang or organization. They got special tattoos to show their rank and all that Halloween bullshit.'

Callum smoked and said, 'I saw the ink on the two hoods we busted in on, on Tuesday.'

'Yeah. They're both Vory. You saw the stars near their collar-bones? That's a Vory mark. One had epaulettes on his shoulders, means he's got some seniority.'

'Parker at the Six-oh gave me some details. One of them had a bear tattoo – that mean anything?'

'Roaring, right? It's what they call a "grin". It's like a "fuck you" to the system. Sometimes it's a wolf with bared teeth or a lunging snake or whatever. To be a Vory, you got to reject the system totally. You hate the cops, the state, the military. You hate the government.'

'I could be an honorary member.'

'Not a fan of Slick Willie, huh?'

'You know willy means cock in Ireland.'

Mike said, 'You just described half the Presidents of the United States.' He cursed a cab pulled out on his left.

Callum flicked his smoke out the window and said, 'How about Avda Galkin? He's got tattoos.'

'He ain't no Vor. A hustler would never be tolerated by these guys.'

A cab pulled out.

'So what's a *Krysha*?' said Callum.

Mike gave the cab a blast on his horn and the finger through the windshield.

'The translation is "Roof". It's to have one of the Vory guys behind you. You're minor league and you get one of the Vory's blessing – you have muscle, protection, more influence. If you're a business and you pay protection, you're paying to a Vor, or the asshole collectin' from you has a Vor behind him, probably takin' a cut.'

'Same shit the world over,' said Callum.

More Russian storefronts appeared, scattered among fried chicken joints and bodegas. They passed a laundromat with a Cyrillic sign and an old lady, crooked like a character in a child's nursery ryhme, hobbling out the front. A Russian grocery with shining windows, a couple of women in jeans and long coats wrangling kids by the door. Larina's Delicatessan, Mitkaleva's Russian Bookstore. A beautiful woman and brutish-looking man eased out of a BMW by a restaurant with a painting of an Orthodox church above the window.

Callum said, 'So these guys buttin' heads down here – Maxim Volkov and Arkady Kuznetsov – they're both Vory?'

Mike clicked his tongue.

'See, that's why I need you on this, Callum. I been workin' this shit for months, I still gotta wipe the spit off my collar after I butcher the Ivans' fuckin names: you get it right first time.'

The elevated subway tracks above Brighton Beach Avenue cut across the view up ahead.

'Arkady Kuznetsov's a Vor, yeah,' he said. 'Now that don't mean as much here in the land of opportunity as it would back in Russia but he got connections back there that can bring muscle. Volkov, no. You read his file – he served in their military. Pretty distinguished record, too. That kinda disqualifies him as a Vor 'cause, bein' a good soldier, he worked for the establishment. He's just a thug made good since he came to America – but word is he got a shit-hot Krysha behind him.'

'And his Krysha – his Roof – is a Vor? One of this criminal super-class?'

'Don't know what else it could be.'

Mike swung the car right onto Brighton Beach Avenue.

'Look in the glove box,' he said.

Callum found a couple of photographs inside. They were copies of shots Mike had handed him in an envelope before they left Green-Wood cemetery a couple of days ago. The initials M.V. were scrawled on one, A.K. on the other. Volkov and Kuznetsov. Shaven-headed, they sneered at the camera. In the shots, they looked to be in their early forties.

Mike said, 'You had a good look at these?'

'Yeah, I been imagining we write letters to each other and take walks in Washington Square. You told me before, the pictures are about four years old.'

'These were taken in Russian prisons,' said Mike. 'Volkov is forty-eight now, Kuznetsov forty-four.'

Callum looked at the defiance and hatred in the faces.

'How'd they get in to the US?'

'We got a huge number of Russians coming here in the early nineties. Our immigration always say they were overwhelmed, couldn't investigate the background of every person comin' in. They say they had to depend on the Ivans, and the Russians were too lazy or inept to do their job. Some immigration guys say it was a chance for the Kremlin to empty a few gulags, pull a Castro and give us their worst.'

'What do you think?'

'I think there are assholes in every civil service. Look at you and me. But New York was destination number one 'cause the Russians didn't need a grant to settle here – sponsorship and so on – like they did in Philly or Boston.'

They drove west. The tracks overhead seemed to hang low, thick iron struts set in concrete on the sidewalks and central reservation every few yards. The effect was of a huge insect lumbering above. Callum saw the same street life as most other neighborhoods. Families, the elderly, the workers darting here and there, the slouchers, the couples, the shady. Somewhere among the people living the best lives they could manage were the wolves. Same as Belfast, Hong Kong, same as Timbuk-goddamn-tu.

They turned south onto Brighton 6th Street and parked up by the curb about twenty yards from a two-story building with a façade of faded sea-green tiles. The word *banya* was painted on a sign above the entrance, along with Cyrillic. Further down 6th on both sides, tall, flat-fronted Brownstones ran to the beach.

Callum felt something gnaw at his insides. 'So ... what are we doin' here?'

Mike ran his fingers along the steering wheel. He kept his eyes on the Brownstones as he spoke. 'You really do need to wash, you know?'

'It's my religion,' said Callum.

Mike nodded at the tiled building. 'This is a Russian bath-house. You should go for a dip.'

Fuck you Mikey, thought Callum. I'm not gonna make this easy for you.

'I'm good,' he said. 'I'll catch a shower at the Six-oh.'

A pulse worked in Mike's jaw. He turned to face Callum.

'Look, I don't have a speech for this one, OK? I moved to Organized Crime, I'm drowning. I fuckin' hate it but I'm there and they gave me the Russians because the wops are weak beer now, so the long-timers are enjoying the easy ride to their twenty.'

Callum saw a shadow of the man a couple of decades in the future: tired, burned out, drinking a beer and boring his kids with war stories – not the real bad shit, but the parts that made the Job, as a lieutenant in Brooklyn South once said, "like High School with a gun". Callum prayed he wasn't looking at his future reflection.

'I need you,' said Mike, 'just like I needed you to bust the Irish, and the Chinese. No undercover, though. None of that. This hustler-kid, Avda, he goes here a couple of days a week. He told me Maxim Volkov has a conference with some of his heavies every Friday around this time. Just go in there, take a bath and a sauna, tell me who you see and get a feel for the vodka-swillin' assholes. Who knows, you might get lucky and see Maxim himself.'

'One can only dream,' said Callum.

'Do not engage, though. Stay quiet, don't open your thick brogue mouth and talk to anyone other than a "yes" or "no" when you pay. I'll be in Dino's Grill around the corner drinkin' a coffee. I'll see you in an hour, got it?'

'And what if Avda comes back and makes me for a cop? He saw me at the projects.'

'You heard Ruiz, he's gone. Just go in, have a look around, come out and I'll buy you a coffee.'

Callum held out his hand palm up. 'You ain't gonna' pay for the bath?'

'You see a department credit card in my glovebox?'

Sounds drifted in through the open window. The hum of machinery working somewhere and the low street-murmur back on the busy avenue. The el-train screamed into Brighton Beach station. Mike sat back.

Wily bastard's trying not to smile, thought Callum.

'I slip on a bar of soap in there, I'm coming for you where you live,' he said.

Then he opened the passenger door of the Ford and climbed out.

Eleven

Callum felt the hot, heavy air in the sauna clog his throat, felt the booze and smokes from last night leaking from his pores.

He sat in the corner with a towel wrapped around his waist, sweating hard. The wooden bench cooked his ass through the towel as he watched a huge man beat a smaller companion with a bundle of oak twigs and leaves on the floor. An old man was at Callum's side, at a right angle against the wall. Like Callum, he sat on the lower tier of the double-tiered bench. He had an ugly scar, like a shark – or maybe cancer? – had taken a chunk out of his body just below his collarbone. Another scar, like the kind left over from major surgery, was across his ribcage lower down.

Shit, who'd wanna get old? thought Callum. Especially not on a cop's pension.

Two friends with generous middle-aged spread sat on the lower tier by the other wall in animated discussion near the smouldering coals heating the wooden sauna. Occasionally, they shot furtive glances at Callum under heavy brows. At the far diagonal corner sat the clutch of men with an assortment of body tattoos.

Callum would have called the ink primitive: ugly images of violence and fetishized perversion crudely rendered on bodies ranging from steroidal to obese. One man sat on the upper tier of the bench. Gray-white hair like dirty snow cleaved to his large skull. His body was like a heavyweight gone to seed, huge in size; powerful at its core, but sheathed in flab. His legs were spread wide and the calves below the hem of his towel were solid muscle.

The man was Maxim Volkov.

Three men sat below. One spoke to his master, two surveyed the room.

Callum recognised Volkov's face from the photographs he'd studied at home and in Mike's car. The cheeks were more full now, the neck thick with fat. The sweat sheen on the reddened skin gave him the look of a freakish baby doll. He gestured plenty but moved slow. A man who set his own pace and expected others to follow. The acolyte on the lower bench sat with his torso twisted and back to Callum. He had a double-headed eagle tattooed across the breadth of his broad shoulders and down to his tailbone. His hair was close-cropped. He looked sick and frail. Occasionally he laughed and slapped his side or thigh. Callum couldn't hear what they said. He didn't speak a word of Russian anyway.

The two men with the oak twigs in the centre of the room stretched, grunted and shambled out the door.

The scarred old man near Callum studied his knees.

The two middle-aged friends worked hard to avoid looking at the party of thugs in the corner.

Callum stared at the floor and stole glances at Volkov's two bodyguards. One had a flat forehead with a low hairline. His chin was swallowed by a neck as thick as a child's thighs. Give him a loincloth instead of a towel and he could have been mixing it with sabre-toothed tigers. He snorted and ran big hands through cropped hair, sending droplets of water and sweat flying. The other had a scar running from jaw to left ear and dark eyes that looked black in the steam. The eyes darted around the room and to his companion. He scratched his face and adjusted whatever junk lay below his towel from time to time.

They couldn't be packing in here, thought Callum. Could they?

It was the man with the dark eyes who caught Callum's eye first.

He leaned forward a little, resting his thick arms on his knees to peer through the moisture and heat.

Callum saw himself through their eyes. In shape, with no tattoos and a nose like a boxer, sitting here alone around lunch on a Friday afternoon – he just didn't fit. A stranger in a close-knit neighborhood. The other bathers were probably regulars; Brighton Beach, like many other ethnic enclaves in New York, was in some ways a glorified village. The other men would be seen walking the area. They might own stores or restaurants where the local criminals ate or shopped or drank.

The dark-eyed thug elbowed his thick-necked companion. He nodded toward Callum. They made a show of checking him out. The air was like a thick slab of moisture, almost solid, filling the room. The walls seemed to sweat like the bodies on the benches, seemed to warp and contract. Callum was vulnerable, naked, almost off the books as far as the NYPD was concerned. The only other soul who knew he was here was sitting in a coffee shop around the corner reading the fucking Post.

The muscle said something to Volkov's acolyte, leaned toward Volkov, still watching Callum, and spoke.

Shit, thought Callum. Now the boss got a good look at me.

The bodyguards crossed the sauna.

They came and stood over him, hands by their sides. Their tattoos were sharply defined at this distance. An Orthodox church, a devil on a woman's back, a roaring tiger. They had stars inked on their knees.

The neanderthal with the thick, bull neck said something that sounded like *baklany*. Callum sat staring, feeling antsy and dumb and holding down his adrenaline. Some expression crossed the neanderthal's cruel face but it was hard to tell if he was pissed or amused. He growled something else and Callum caught a couple of words: *yob tvoyumat*. The thug with the dark eyes laughed and said something like *opuschiny*.

Callum looked up and dragged a scrap of Cantonese from his heat-fried memory.

'*Aa mauh jing beng.*'

The Bull-Necked thug blanched while Dark Eyes froze. Callum tensed and waited for a move from one of the hoods. He saw the old man on his right look up in his peripheral vision. Bull-Neck shifted his weight.

Shit, thought Callum. I'm fucked.

From this position he had no leverage to spring up and put any power behind an attack. They could come at him from above and pummel him before he landed a punch. If Bull-Neck had a knife in that towel, he could shank Callum five times in a heartbeat. Callum had ceded the high ground by sitting on the lower tier.

Shit.

He caught a movement at the doorway of the sauna, a couple of yards from where Volkov sat. Another man entered the room, slim, no tattoos. The new arrival walked with his hands close to his sides, his towel pulled tight as though something wedged at the back was stretching the material. He had small marks on his chest. He stopped a foot or two inside the room as though someone had hit him point blank with a 9 mm round.

Then the old man sat by Callum stood up.

*

Tikhon saw enough.

Clack. Clack. Clack.

He reached the doorway and slid back the glass partition to find Maxim Volkov just a few feet away. A wall of soaking heat hit him full in the face and his lungs seemed to fill with a searing vapour. Volkov, the vicious bastard, was engrossed in a small drama playing out at the other end of the sauna. Two thugs were standing over a fit-looking man in the corner. A beating was coming, maybe worse.

ClackClack.

It was an aberration in the moment. Enough to abort.

Volkov turned to see who had entered the room, just as the old man sitting by the stranger stood and reached out to the thugs in the far corner. One of the thugs turned to face the old man.

ClackClack.

Tikhon had recognised Bull-Neck from Fogelman's, even from behind. That great slab of meat supporting the cropped head was unmistakable. As the other thug turned, Tikhon saw black shark-eyes in a scarred face he didn't recognise.

The old man began speaking, the words quiet and smooth, lost in the heat and wet and buzz of violence heavy in the air. Volkov was studying the scene. The old man had his hand clasped around the fit-looking man's arm – the potential victim of the thugs – pleading with the dark eyed thug.

The kinjal blade wedged in the small of Tikhon's back by the towel was getting hot against his skin as he stood in the doorway of the sauna. The blade pressed hard into his back as another body pushed against him from behind.

'Avda,' said Volkov, 'what are you doing here?'

Avda shoved past Tikhon into the room. He looked at Volkov, glanced at the scene in the opposite corner, and stopped dead. His eyes flickered with recognition and his mouth worked silently.

Then Bull-Neck turned to look at him and caught sight of Tikhon.

*

Callum willed the old man to stand back and save himself a beating. If Callum was lucky, he'd take some lumps – it wouldn't be the first time – and get tossed on the street. He'd limp to Dino's and report to Mike, who would give him some shit and buy him a beer. But if the old man got involved things could go much worse.

He glanced at the new arrival in the doorway.

Greyhound-lean and erect, he looked like every fibre of his frame was muscle and sinew. His eyes were darting around the room but his body was still. Were those small scars on his chest bullet wounds?

The old man had let go of Callum's arm and was edging closer to the thugs as though approaching a pack of snarling dogs. His voice was slow and deep, his eyes clear and strong. He was not afraid. He spoke constantly without inflection. It was almost hypnotic. The thugs, too, seemed transfixed, like the old man was a wrangler and they the wild animals under his commmand. The room seemed to breathe again, the walls to expand. The thick fug of testosterone and violence thinned. Callum forgot all others in the sauna, even Maxim Volkov himself.

Another movement in the doorway grabbed his attention.

Volkov spoke a name and a trigger pulled in Callum's head. *Avda.*

The hustler kid with the tattooed eyelids pushed into the room. His body was smooth, almost underdeveloped. The kid looked at Volkov. The kid turned to the drama playing out around Callum.

The kid looked at Callum.

The kid knew. His eyes went wide with recognition.

Callum waited for Avda to blurt out that he was a cop; waited for a fist to his face or a hidden blade into his side. He cursed Mike O'-fucking-Connell for all the bastards of the day under his breath.

Then the thug with the bull neck turned to look at Avda, and everything tilted.

*

Tikhon was gone before Bull-Neck spoke a word. He slipped out through the doorway and heard a shout as he ran down the corridor to the changing area. The wooden floorboards were warped and canted and he barrelled into a couple of flabby middle-aged men as he fled. As he hit the lockers in the changing room, he heard the thunder of heavy bodies running in the corridor and knew they were coming. His clothes were in a woven basket and, unlike most, he had no valuables in a locker save a cheap watch and some change. He had left the envelope of cash at home when he fetched the dagger.

He grabbed the clothes and ran for the back exit through which he'd entered the bathhouse. He had needed Avda to get him in with a key. The door was locked only from the alley out back and would open with a shove from within. He ran to the short corridor leading to an office, a storeroom and a kitchen with the exit at the end. He sprinted and shouldered the exit open as he heard the thugs yelling back at the lockers. The air outside felt cool on his skin and the damp towel clung to his legs. The kinjal dagger fell and clattered on the ground and he saw the thugs turn into the corridor as he picked it up, the door still open. The thugs froze. Although they were at the opposite end of the corridor, Tikhon slashed wildly at the air in warning. The door shut. He grabbed a stack of crates and wedged them against the outside. Then he was sprinting down the alley and cursing the idiot stranger in the corner who had been on the verge of a beating from Volkov's thugs. Who had ruined his moment for the kill. A kill he'd been waiting for for an age.

Clack. Clack.

The bastard idiot.

Clack. Clack. Clack.

The bastard idiot with the old man defending him against the thugs like flesh and blood.

ClackClackClack.

That bastard would pay. When the car crested the peak of Tikhon's rollercoaster, that bastard would be there, tied to the fucking tracks to be ripped apart.

ClackClackClackClackClackClackClackClack.

Twelve

Maxim Volkov was an impressive prospect. He had the combination of girth and latent, inner power below the fat that Callum had seen in Sumo wrestlers at an exhibition match in Hong Kong. He wore his position of power well, his head tilted back to gaze down a strong, straight nose at Callum and the old man.

The old man was talking in Russian, salvos of words that sounded pleading or reasoning at turns. His neck was lined but the skin stretched taut – no rolls of fat on the old geezer. He had a thick white mustache that twitched as he spoke and gray eyes that sought grace, from his bowed old head.

Callum took in the catalogue of tattoos on Volkov's body. There was a ring tattoo on the index finger of the left hand, a playing card split diagonally with a club at one end, a spade at the other. When the gangster gesticulated, slow like a large animal, Callum saw a butterfly tattooed on the back of the hand. The Madonna and Child covered his chest and a large bear head roared from below each shoulder. A topless woman smoked and played cards at a table on his right bicep. When he crossed the great slabs of his arms, Callum saw a gun, a pile of cash and a bottle of something on the table at which she sat. On the left arm, the grim reaper sat on horseback with Cyrillic text at the beast's hooves.

After a minute of the old man talking and the occasional grunt from Volkov, the criminal boss nodded and waved them away. The old man pulled at Callum's arm, betraying surprising strength, and led him from the sauna.

Callum wondered where Avda Galkin had gone. Galkin had exchanged a few words with Volkov before the gangster waved him away. No one had messed with Callum, so he had to figure the kid hadn't told Volkov that he was a cop. Maybe Galkin was protecting himself. As a CI, he'd have been in bigger shit than anyone if the truth had come out.

Callum and the old man walked down the corridor with the warped wooden floor that led to the changing area, and the old man watched Callum find the basket with his clothes on one of the shelves around the room. The man grabbed his own basket and set it on the bench by the shelf. He looked around, saw no one within earshot and leaned close.

'What are you doing here?' His English was fluent with a Slavic accent.

Callum began towelling himself without showering the sweat from his body.

The old man said, 'You are not Russian. You don't speak Russian.'

'How do you know?' said Callum.

'I saved your skin. Don't insult me. It was all too obvious, to me and those animals who were ready to carve you into chunks and barbeque you on the coals back there.'

'I'm fourth generation, never learned the language.'

'With an Irish accent. I never knew the glorious Union of Soviet Socialist Republics had stretched all the way to the Atlantic Ocean. We should have improved upon that black swill you call beer, with which you poison half the bars in New York.'

'Now who's insulting?'

The man studied him like he was trying to figure out a magic trick. His hands were on his bony hips, his scrawny arms tensed. He was thin but for a small pot belly, and he had a few wisps of white hair on his frail-looking chest. After a minute he smiled and nodded.

'Okay, Irish,' he said. 'At least take a shower and buy me a cup of tea. I did get you out of there in one piece.'

'And the goons who were making a move on me?'

'They won't be back this way. They work for the man I spoke to just now, Maxim Volkov. Their employer will tell them to leave you be when they return to the sauna and they have a separate changing area away from the other patrons. There is no need for them to come here.'

Callum said, 'How do you know that?'

The old man shrugged and beckoned for him to follow to the washing area.

'I know because I set the arrangement up for them in that way. You see, Irish, I used to own this bathhouse.'

*

They sat in a small cafe down the street, all flower print wallpaper and wooden tables covered with red checked tablecloths, Russian dolls on shelves around the walls. A large woman bossed the counter and a girl who looked of high school age, in a micro-skirt and heels, worked the floor serving customers.

Callum checked his watch – it was fifty-eight minutes since Mike dropped him off. Mike would be expecting him in Dino's any minute.

What the hell, thought Callum, let *him* sweat.

The old man wore a brown leather flying jacket, flat cap and white shirt with rifle green pants. The pants looked a little like the RUC uniform Callum had pulled on each time he went on duty back home.

'What did you say to Volkov's thugs?' said the old man. 'When they were threatening you?'

'It was Cantonese. It means, "Mr Stupid bakes cakes".'

The old man choked on a sip of tea.

Callum laughed. 'That's a literal translation. Basically, it's an idiom means *this is pointless.*'

'You speak Cantonese?'

'No, I just spent some time in Hong Kong and picked up a couple of phrases. I could tell you three different ways to talk about jerking off, too.'

'I take great pride in knowing I saved a man of letters,' said the old man. He looked at the table top, smiled, shook his head and took another sip of tea.

Callum said, 'What did the two brain trusts say to me in there, anyway?'

'One of them called you *baklany*: a punk. Then they told you to have sexual relations with your mother, and one speculated you may have been raped in prison thanks to your feminine demeanor.' The old man wiped his moustache. 'Volkov's men are known for their excellent judge of character.'

And just what kind of character is this old guy across the table? thought Callum.

The old man took a deep breath and explained that he had told Volkov's men that Callum was more trouble than he was worth, some American tourist wandered into the bathhouse to soak up local color. Anything happening to him would bring a lot of attention, a lot of police. Far-fetched. The geezer could have been saying Callum had cop written all over him and it was best to get him the hell out of the bathhouse, but in one piece to avoid the heat the public murder of a police officer would surely bring.

The old man said that Volkov bought his story.

Callum wasn't sure he bought the old man yet.

He said, 'You seemed pretty calm talking to men who look a lot like Russian gangsters. You know nothing about me but your lie came easy in a tough spot. And I still don't know your name.'

The old man sat back and folded his arms. The leather of his jacket creaked like tired joints.

'Or I, yours,' he said. 'You know, the reason I no longer own the bathhouse was sitting in that sauna with his tattooed bulk, like a *bies* demon from a child's story.'

He stroked his mustache and ran a finger down the narrow spear of his nose. His eyes, watery a moment ago, hardened and a furrow slashed the papery skin between his heavy brows. He rolled up his left sleeve. The ragged, discoloured stripe of flesh ran from the crook of his arm to a couple of inches above his wrist. Callum had noticed it in the shower after the sauna. The old man undid a couple of buttons at the top of his shirt and pulled it and the yellowed vest underneath aside. Callum saw the wrinkled skin that had been gouged out below his right clavicle like a trench.

'I have a six-inch scar on my right side below the ribs, also,' he said. 'You probably noticed these in the bathhouse. Those animals you met in the *banya* can be very persuasive if the mood takes them.'

Callum thought of Charles Beresford and Willie Mayhew, cut up on the apartment floor in the Coney Island bust.

He said, 'What'd they use on you?'

'What else? Knives.'

Callum looked from the scars to the old man's face. Both told a story of hardship and pain. The newfound strength in the voice, the hatred in the eyes, told their own tale.

Callum had a card with his name, a number and an NYPD crest in his pocket. It didn't have the word "Officer" printed on, just "Burke, NYPD Narcotics": he worried some might realise he wasn't a detective and not take him so seriously. Bullshit, he knew – to most people, skells or not, a cop was a cop; but he couldn't shake his concern. He considered handing his card to the man.

He looked at the worn face again. He had seen that fury before: a mother whose son had his knees shot out in Belfast by Provisionals; a couple whose child had died in a bombing in the city center; an old man whose house was trashed by junkies in Manhattan. Victims, but fighters. He decided the old man's anger was real.

'I'm Callum,' he said, 'Callum Burke.'

The man's features relaxed. The eyes softened.

He said, 'My name is Kolya Slavin. I am a product of the Soviet Union. I came here via Israel. The Law of Return granted me immigration rights there and, from Tel Aviv, I made my way to New York.'

Kolya Slavin said he had worked hard back in Russia – 'The Soviet system taught us a solid work ethic, at least'. He saved some money for passage to the US and to establish himself in Brighton Beach. He inherited a grocery business from a bachelor relative, sold it on and opened the bathhouse.

'It did well,' said Kolya. 'But like any successful business in this area, it attracted the kind of vermin you met in the sauna. First it was a "tribute" paid every other week to Maxim Volkov for his patronage and protection. Then he "requested" a stake in the business. From that point on, I knew it was over. I sold to him and got half of what the business was worth. At least I get to bathe for free.'

Callum said, 'You're Jewish?'

'What? Of course not.' The old man looked irritated for a moment, a flicker of anger in those hard, gray eyes. Then he smiled.

'Ah, the Law of Return,' he said. He poured more tea and clasped Callum's hand. Then he sat back again and took a sip. 'I paid a bribe to a man of standing within the state machinery to fake my ancestry and get me – as is so popular a phrase in the West – the fuck out of there.'

Callum fished a cigarette out of his pocket and gestured as to whether Kolya would mind if he lit up. The old man spread his arms in agreement.

'If you had the means to pay a bribe,' said Callum, 'I'm guessing you were part of that state machinery.'

Kolya nodded.

'Russia was a hard place. It still is. In the country, there were two words for law. *Prestupleniye* is the technical definition, as the police might see it.' He raised an eyebrow and shot a look at Callum. 'Then, there's *zlodeyanie*. This is more murky, opaque like this tea. I might break the law on a technical level, but *morally* I did nothing wrong. There is an old peasant proverb: "God punishes sins, the state punishes guilt". My morals no longer permitted me to stay in the Motherland, performing the duties which my occuptaion demanded.' He rolled down his sleeve again and buttoned up his shirt. 'Are you going to arrest me?'

'Your status is legal now. Let's just say what happens in Moscow, stays in Moscow.'

Slavin smiled and nodded. 'Back in Russia, in the days of the Soviet Union, I was a member of the Internal Troops of the Ministry for Internal Affairs of the Russian Federation. The MVD.' He sat forward and gave Callum a look so loaded it seemed to hang in the air. 'You might say, Irish, in the lingua franca of the New Yorker, that I was, to all intents and purposes, a cop.'

Then he grabbed his cup and finished his tea with a satisfied sigh.

*

Mike O'Connell rubbed his face with his hands when Callum eased into the booth opposite at Dino's a good forty minutes late.

'Where the fuck you been?' he said. 'I drank so much coffee I'll be pissin' half the night away.'

Callum said, 'I almost got rolled.'

'Jesus. You're worse than the President. You gotta cause drama everywhere you fuckin' go.'

'Volkov and his goons were inside. They saw I didn't fit. Then your CI, Galkin, turned up. Some old guy talked Volkov's goons down, your CI split and I went for a cuppa with the old geezer.'

'While I sat on my fat middle-aged ass reading the sports pages over three times,' said Mike. 'Where's my CI now?'

'Don't know. He said a couple of words to Volkov and lit out. Call in with Georgie.'

Mike said, 'You can tell me what happened in the car.'

'What about my coffee?'

'It tasted like mud anyway. I'll buy you a jar of that freeze dried shit you people from the Old Country like so much.'

They drove for Manhattan. Callum told Mike about the sauna, Maxim Volkov, the thug catching Callum's eye. Then the confrontation, the fit-looking guy with the scars on his chest and the old man, Kolya Slavin. Callum now had his phone number on a scrap of paper. He had taken a shot and given his card to Slavin in exchange.

Mike said, 'You think this old geezer is legit?'

'That laceration on his arm and the chunk out of his body was real enough. And that was some righteous anger when he talked about losing his business.'

They headed for the Brooklyn Bridge on the Belt Parkway.

'You takin' me home?' said Callum.

Mike shook his head and grabbed the radio. Georgie came on and said she'd ditched her car at Brighton Beach and tailed Avda Galkin on the subway, and was sitting on Christopher Street in Greenwich Village having a coffee while Avda grabbed a bite in the Strongarm Restaurant.

'Figured he'd be somewhere around the Village,' said Mike.

They hit downtown and drove north past the twin prongs of

the World Trade Center, mundane concrete and glass at street level, enveloped by the churning madness of Manhattan. Mike was quiet. Callum saw him kneading the wheel, his knuckles white. He drove west past the Stonewall Inn and the sliver of central reservation opposite. They crossed the six-way intersection on 7th Avenue and pulled in by a five-storey walk-up. The Strongarm was a hole-in-the-wall place opposite, the door smothered in handbills, the windows tinted.

'You ever been there?' said O'Connell.

Callum said, 'Not my kind of place.'

'Too faggy?'

'Too expensive.'

After a short time, Avda Galkin left the restaurant. He glanced around and began walking west.

Callum grabbed the door handle when Mike gunned the Ford and they shot into Christopher to the wail of a truck's horn behind. Mike swerved to the sidewalk and Callum jumped out. Avda's eyes went wide.

Mike roared, 'Get the fuck in the car!'

Callum grabbed the kid, opened the back door and shoved him inside. They pulled out again and Mike hit fifty as they took off past St. John's Lutheran and swung south, then west onto Barrow.

The CI was muttering to himself. His voice was whiny and he sniffed thick snot. He was crying. They rode the cobblestones to an empty industrial shell and pulled in at a loading bay. Callum braced on the dashboard for the hard stop. Galkin hit his head on the back of Callum's seat.

Mike twisted and faced the CI.

'You little fuck! You left that bathhouse, then went back a while later and put my man here in the shit! You said somethin' to that fat fuck, Volkov, when you saw my partner here in that sweatbox on 6th – what was it, dickhead? You told that Russian asshole my man's a cop, I'll fuckin' kill you here and now with my bare hands and your fuckin' body'll bob up somewhere around Florida as shark food before they find you!'

Avda Galkin went white as his sneakers. He drew his knees up on the seat and screamed 'No! No!', then babbled in Russian. His eyes kept staring at Callum.

Mike leaned over the seatback and slapped him on the ear.

'I'm talkin' here. And English, you fuck, English.'

Mike's voice dropped a couple of octaves. It was steady.

'Why'd you go back to the bathouse after you left?' he said. 'What'd you say? Breathe. Breathe.'

Avda wiped his nose. A string of snot stretched from his nostril to his knuckle when he took his hand away.

Mike made to slap Avda again. The kid screeched.

Callum tensed up. The scream was piercing.

Mike tossed a Kleenex in the backseat and said, 'You better talk to me, you fuck.'

Avda sniffed. He'd been wearing a trace of black eyeshadow which smudged with his tears. His thin chest heaved. His English was fluent but accented.

'I'm sorry, OK? I forgot I left some cash for him from a client in Chelsea I fucked this week. I left it on a desk in the banya office. For Volkov. I just wanted to make sure he knows it's from me. OK? That's what I told him – there was money from me in his office.'

Avda eyed Callum.

'Not winkin' at my man now, huh, fuckface?' said Mike. 'This is Burke – and, if you think I'm a bastard, get your bony ass over to Woodside or Chinatown and ask about the man who busted the Irish and the Tongs in New York. You ever come close to fuckin' him again like in that bathhouse, he will beat you to death.'

Callum played it straight. He focused on the killers in

Beresford and Mayhew's place back on Tuesday in his mind's eye, the carved up dealers with the dead dogs out back. It made his eyes dull and inexpressive.

'I got it, I got it,' said Avda.

Mike said, 'He's your contact now. Give him your number, he'll give you his card. Now, who was the guy in the sauna with the scars on his chest?'

Avda's eyes flickered.

'Scars?'

Callum summoned up that fear and anger he'd felt when the goons were standing over him in the steam. He leaned in and snarled, 'Who was the guy with the bullet holes in his chest? The little round scars – I know bullet wounds and that's what they were.'

'The guy?' said Avda.

Callum gave him a tap in the gut. Not enough to have him gasping for air but still food for thought.

'Don't fuck with me, Avda. The guy in the doorway when you came in the sauna.'

'I don't know.' The CI gasped, clutching his stomach. He retched for a second, then whispered, 'I swear I don't know. He is not working for Volkov. He is not gangster – no tattoos.'

'You aren't a gangster and you got tattoos.'

'He was just there. In the door. I don't know, I swear. Just a bather.'

Callum pulled a card, same as he gave the old man Kolya Slavin, from his pocket with a contact number on.

'You're gonna know, got it?' he said and threw the card in Avda's lap. 'You're gonna find out who he was and you're gonna call me. Give me a number I can get you on, and God help you if you don't pick up.'

Mike tossed a pen and notepad in the back and Avda scribbled a number, nodding – *OK, OK*.

Callum said, 'It's Friday. We don't talk by next Tuesday, I'll meet you on the central reservation outside the Stonewall Inn at 1200. Got it?'

'Got it, got it.'

'So,' said Mike, 'how come you were playin' around on me, Avda?'

The CI looked at Callum, then O'Connell. His cheeks were flushed scarlet and more liner had smudged around his eyes. The skin below his nostrils shone where his nose had run. He looked like a scared little boy.

'I don't know – '

'Detective Patrosi,' said O'Connell. 'You were two timin' me with a Narcotics detective called Patrosi. If I weren't the thick-skinned type, I could take that shit very personally.'

Avda seemed to sink back into the seat and his face flushed deeper red. He looked at Callum again. Mike sighed.

'Look. At. Me.'

Avda said, 'I'm sorry, Detective O'Connell. You know how it is – lots of people like me have a couple of cops they meet. More money, you know? It's nothing personal, and it was different in-formation. Just drugs stuff.'

Callum said, 'Maxim Volkov doesn't deal drugs?'

'Of course,' said Avda. His voice went small. 'But the informa-tion I gave Detective Patrosi was never about Volkov's drugs. Just other stuff my clients used, yes?'

'So your tip on Charles Beresford and Willie Mayhew had no connection to Maxim Volkov?'

Callum watched the CI's eyes. They were on him, but for a couple of seconds, not looking *at* him. They were somewhere else, he thought, formulating a story in response to the question. Callum hadn't pressed Patrosi this morning – the guy was hooked up in traction and medicated for pain – but he'd press this asshole 'til he bled from his pores if he had to.

'Avda, you lie to me, you'll get more of this.'

He flexed his hand into a fist. Avda stared at Callum and now he was *really* looking at him.

Callum said, 'Was the tip for Patrosi connected to Volkov?'

'Yes.'

'Don't make me hit you again ...'

'Beresford and Mayhew were small time. Mayhew is – was – gay. He used to see me at a couple of clubs around the Meatpacking District. One night, he saw me with this rich client I meet. The man is very powerful, lives off Water Street downtown.'

Callum remembered Patrosi telling him that Avda feared for his safety should some of his upmarket clients be exposed as gay men who paid hustlers for sex.

'Mayhew started talking to this rich client. Volkov had been dealing to this man and Mayhew struck a deal and cut in on Volkov. Mayhew knew the two Russian killers, who you found in the apartment, through a middleman around Coney Island. The Russians had an arrangement to rip-off Volkov's supply and deliver it to Beresford and Mayhew. Volkov found out but didn't tell the killers. He ordered the killers to deal with Beresford and Mayhew; then he told me to set them up by telling Detective Patrosi there would be a drug stash in the apartment.'

Mike's eyes bugged. 'Volkov knows you're a CI?'

'Only to Patrosi,' said Avda. His words came in a torrent. 'He would kill me if he knew I informed to you. You are Organized Crime. You are targeting him. Patrosi was Narcotics. Volkov could use me to set up rivals. He knew the police would find his men with Beresford and Mayhew's bodies. The men betrayed him – so he betrayed them and got rid of the dealers at the same time. Like you say, killing two birds at once.'

'With one stone,' said Mike.

'You mean,' said Callum, 'you've been playing us all this time?

Playin' Patrosi and having us do Volkov's work for him? My partner got his leg crushed clearing rivals off the board for your fat Russian-fuck-boss?'

He felt something hot and relentless rise inside. It almost frightened him. Mike saw it coming and grabbed him, pulling him back, holding him.

Mike glared at Avda.

'Get the fuck out,' he said. 'You call my partner's number every morning and afternoon with something from today until Tuesday. You miss a call, I'll go to Volkov myself and tell him we been hearing war stories on his operations from you for months.'

Avda froze. Callum didn't notice or care. He strained to get at the CI and hurt him, tear at him, beat him bloody.

'Get out!' yelled Mike. 'Now!'

The CI opened the door and slid out. Then he ran for the Hudson river like he was going to leap in and swim to the Jersey shore.

Thirteen

'It's *foot*ball.'

'It's soccer and it's a fag sport,' said Billy Hutchinson.

'It's a working class symphony,' said Callum.

'How much have you drunk?' said Trish Alexander.

Hutchinson slurred, 'Football is the Giants and the Jets. Cheerleaders. Fireworks. Superbowl.'

'No,' said Callum, his face earnest like he was debating the meaning of life. 'That's *entertainment*. Football is West Ham, Bayern, Falmenco. It's Europe, the Americas, Africa, Asia playin' in the World Cup.'

'It's a girl's game in junior high.'

'No shame in that,' said Trish. 'I was a girl in junior high, once.'

Hutchinson wavered, his brain – soaked in cheap booze – calculating his response. He decided on a compliment.

'Well, you're all woman now, baby.'

Trish shook her head.

'And you're one hundred percent asshole, Billy.' She walked off.

Callum and Hutchinson stared after her.

'Did Trish just say asshole?' said Callum.

'I never heard her swear before,' said Hutchinson. He turned to Callum and gave him a sloppy wink. 'I'm honored.'

Callum watched him wander into the throng of cops putting in serious drinking time at the racket for Angel Patrosi. Lacey's Lounge was a barn of a place with an Irish flag behind the bar and a threadbare string of green lights strung over the bottles of spirits. A plastic sign above the door to the bathrooms said

Tipperary 3,000 miles. At the far end of the main lounge, ten creaking wooden steps led to a raised area on which stood Gerry Martin and Danny O'Neill. The whole place was rammed.

Callum leaned over the counter and ordered a bottle of beer. He almost spilled it when a cop from Queens Borough Command bumped into his shoulder. He shot the guy a look. The cop gave him a drunken grin.

He and Mike had left Avda Galkin in the Village and driven to a pizza joint. There they talked over the CI playing Patrosi and Narcotics for Maxim Volkov. Was he doing the same to Mike? Of course, Mike wanted to let it play out, see where it led. His theory was they could feed bullshit to Volkov, maybe push him in the right direction for a collar. And now Callum handed over his card, he was in the firing line. Goddamn Mike O'Connell!

'Hey.'

Someone grabbed Callum's ass and he spun.

Georgie giggled and withdrew her hand.

'You got to hit the StairMaster, Cal, that tush is getting flabby.'

He saw the glaze in her eyes. She wasn't a big drinker.

'Hey,' he said, 'not babysitting Avda Galkin tonight?'

'A girl's gotta have some fun or I'll be old before my time. You don't think I look old, do you?'

'You look younger than the first day we met. Least the crack of your ass does.'

She laughed. His first sight of Georgie had been her ass-crack above the waist of her jeans as she crouched at a low window, watching a drug location with a telephoto lens.

'I've been bathing it in Oil of Olay.'

'More like formaldehyde.'

She gave him a punch on the shoulder that was harder than she meant and said, 'Oh God, sorry!'

'You punch Arthur like that, I'll book you,' said Callum.

Her face went sad-drunk.

Callum said, 'Everything OK?'

'Let's not talk about that right now.'

He took her in. Her licorice hair, fine nose, strong-boned features. He loved the lines of her face, loved the sloppy arch of her eyebrow now she was drunk. He decided, as he did every time he saw her, that she was beautiful.

In another time, he thought, in another life ...

An image seemed to swim through the booze and smoke in the bar of Irene and Tara in a small park in Hong Kong. Before cop life and the bad shit crept in. He'd had stand-up fights with Irene but, on the whole, it had been a slow rot in the marriage. Like a tub on the ocean battered by a few too many storms that finally rusts away.

'You know what,' he said, 'there's a jukebox over in the corner and a sliver of space beside it. What do you say I throw on a song and we have a dance?'

Georgie smiled.

'I'm Domincan, Cal,' she said. 'I was born to dance.'

*

Tikhon cradled a beer and picked at a sliver of wood on the counter. The bar was on the western fringe of Brighton Beach, bordering Coney Island.

Clack. Clack. Clack.

He had been climbing the slope since the escape from the bathhouse. He had fled toward the beach, the towel flapping high around his ass, his clothes clutched in his arms. He'd scrambled under the boardwalk to dress – and it was there, in the gloom, that the car had begun its climb up the coaster.

Clack. Clack. Clack.

It had been a shot at the target. Avda had told him the routine was always the same. The civilians in the room were always the same at that time. The hour kept the number of patrons low. The younger men of Brighton Beach were working. But someone new was there. The stranger in the corner who had a look of violence about him. The stranger had sparked the interest of Volkov's muscle who, by that time, would otherwise have gone for a short break in the cold pool, leaving the target exposed for a brief time.

And worst luck: that one of the bodyguards that day would be the same idiot Tikhon had chased off at the old Jew's store on the avenue. It had been a confluence of ill fortune. Were he a more superstitious man, he would have considered the bird pecking at his windowsill earlier a bad omen.

Avda had called him when he finally got back to his apartment and told him the stranger in the sauna was a cop. Avda had seen him with a group of police entering a project in Coney Island a few days ago.

What was a policeman doing in that bathhouse with Maxim Volkov?

Tikhon had told Avda to meet him tomorrow night and begun drinking to dull the rising insanity that began as a cold fire in his belly and spread like a virus through his body as the day passed into night. The drink did little to tamper the fever. The walls of his apartment closed in; he walked. The bar seemed as good an option as any. Russian name, Russian bartender. Shitty beer.

An overheard name brought him back to the here and now: the small, L-shaped counter, the knife-slashed booths around the walls, the blacked-out windows. Tikhon sat at the end of the counter farthest from the door by the men's room, and a Soviet-era poster of Lenin. He could smell piss. Two men sat at the counter talking.

The taller man had said *Seduksen*. It was a medical drug used during the war in Afghanistan. It had become a high of choice for many soldiers during those long, hard years.

Tikhon listened to the man talk. His Russian was slurred with drink but he used military jargon and slang: "yoghurt", diesel fuel; *dukhi* or "ghosts", the Mujahideen. "Black Tulips", the planes used to transport bodies back to Russia.

Another veteran, thought Tikhon, still fighting that damn war here in the United States.

Then he caught the place names. Gardez and Khost.

'The fucking 345th,' said the man, 'all they talk about is that stretch of road from Gardez to Khost. It's like the British with Waterloo.'

'Like the Airborne can forget the rest of us were out there, because of one fucking battle!' said his companion, sinking a shot of vodka.

'Six paratroopers killed in a day? We lost eight just before Magistral. What makes them think their shit doesn't stink?'

Clack, clack, clack, clack.

The car climbs.

Tikhon is no longer on the rollercoaster.

He is on a mountain.

Evening tempers the peaks around them a dull gray. The ground shakes. A column of APCs passes on this lower slope. The drivers' faces glow in the lights from their dashboard instruments. Tikhon and his patrol watch them from under their panamas, the hats offering some protection from the exhaust fumes, the dust, the sand.

As darkness falls, the stars crowd the sky like thousands of bullet holes in the fabric of night. Bad for the paratroopers of the 345th Independent Guards Airborne. A clear sky means too much light for the ghosts to hunt them. They begin to trek south, climbing the slope from the road to Peshawar. An Afghan guide leads, a man of around forty with a coarse beard and murderous eyes. At the rear of their patrol is an Osobist – a KGB officer. He appears of a similar age to the scout, maybe even older, but is in peak condition. He carries as much kit as the paratroopers and steps lightly on the rocky terrain.

The cold begins to bite their faces as they climb. Their sweat-soaked collars freeze and scrape their necks like sandpaper. They are lucky, whispers Dolidze the Georgian, they are on an old mountain – the slopes are more gentle than the younger peaks.

'You are an old fart,' Tikhon whispers back, 'but your tongue is as sharp as any.'

Then they see the lights far off streaking across the dark. A battle in the distance – too far to hear. They pause for a moment to rest and watch the tracer fire criss-cross the black hulk of a distant mountain.

*

'Callum, I love you,' said Georgie, 'but I gotta go.'

Three strippers had arrived and were putting on a show downstairs, thinning the herd of male cops boozing on the main floor of Lacey's. Georgie had sunk another couple of beers, a real bender by her standards, and called a cab. Callum walked with her to the door.

Her goofy smile and strong features seemed slack and softer. Callum loved her a little more.

As the cab pulled up, Gerry Martin appeared at the door.

'Jesus H. Christ, I could see what that chick downstairs had for dinner,' he said.

Georgie grabbed Callum and held him tight. She burrowed into his shoulder for a second and he felt her skin on his neck.

'Night, Cal,' she said, 'I love you.'

It was only when she broke the clinch that he saw she was

crying. His brain, dumb with booze, took a minute to process it, and by then she was in the cab with the door closed.

'I heard you did some boxin',' said Martin, 'but you are seriously punchin' above your weight there.'

Callum watched the cab as it pulled away and said, 'No, it isn't like that.'

'A woman like Ruiz all over you? You got a dick, she got a pussy. What else would it be?'

'Goddamn!' said Callum, a flicker of heat under his eyes. 'You really are a grade A asshole, Gerry.'

Martin stared at him, wheels turning through a drunken fog. Callum had seen it before: the idiot was weighing up his options to back down, square up, or cozy up. Callum saw the slack shoulders and figured Martin had settled for door number three.

Then Danny O'Neill popped up and said, 'You know, Burke, you think your farts smell of roses thanks to the English in you from that Limey mother.'

Callum went rigid.

O'Neill saw the spark of murder in his eyes.

'Yeah,' said O'Neill, 'must be that Brit bitch bred that shit in you.'

Martin grimaced and shut his eyes tight.

Callum ignored O'Neill and said, 'Best not let your girlfriend talk you into a fight you can't win, Gerry. That hairbag asshole is too old and lazy for me to beat on.' He felt something hot and savage stretch close to snapping in his head.

O'Neill's face went tight. He muttered, 'Brit half-breed dickhead.' He made a gun barrel with his index finger, his thumb as the hammer, and pointed it at Callum. 'We know where you live, right Gerry?'

He fired.

Callum heard the shot in his head, felt liquid cold drop in his gut. He was back in Belfast: the shot rang out across the city.

It was eight years ago.

The shot had come from a Barrett M82 sniper rifle which sent a .50MG round through Callum's friend, Jimmy Gilliland, as he had walked toward the gates of the Royal Ulster Constabulary station in west Belfast. It took a big chunk of Jimmy with it.

Callum could smell the cool dead musk of the leaves in October. Felt the comforting heft of the Heckler & Koch MP5 in his hands. He heard the clatter of the army helicopter overhead as he stood at a road block near the Grosvenor Road – out of their usual patrol area, but still B Division – and there were rumors of a planned bombing somewhere near the Royal Victoria Hospital where it fronted the lower Falls Road. He stood with other uniformed police and two British soldiers. Three armoured Land Rovers were parked nearby, two side-by-side. Traffic cones were on the road and a couple of RUC were crouched by the wall of the hospital holding Sterling submachine guns.

A nurse gave him a wink and he chatted her up for a while. Then one of the other officers called out to him that there'd been a shooting outside their station and it might be Jimmy Gilliland.

Callum felt ice cubes in his chest and made for his vehicle to pick up the radio. As he ran the ground seemed to give way and his ears split with a huge roar. He caromed off the armour plating of one Land Rover into the door of another, the metal grille across the windows slashing his face. Then he was on the ground and his cap was on the concrete by his head. His scalp felt wet and hot and there was a burning above his left ear. Everything was happening through a bubble of dull sound and the narrow view as he lay on his back looking upward, wedged between the Land Rovers.

As the smoke had billowed from the bomb detonation by the gates of the hospital a few yards away, the sky turned black and he knew his friend was dead.

*

They make makeshift pillboxes with rocks on the slope and hunker down. They are set to ambush a Mujahideen group dragging weapons to a kishlak at the foot of the mountain in the morning. Dolidze the Georgian tells Tikhon he will take a watch, that Tikhon should get some sleep. He lies on a couple of ponchos in a silence that roars with threat. The ground is bone-chilling. He pulls his pakistanka coat over his body.

Tikhon doesn't realise he's been sleeping until the soft beeping wakens him.

Dolidze hisses, 'Shit!' His digital watch is beeping. He kills it. Then he says, 'Dukhi.'

With that, the silence is pierced by automatic fire. Flashes strobe the dark and thunder erupts from Tikhon's side as Dolidze opens up with his AKM assault rifle. Tikhon struggles to his knees, hears the crack of bullets passing close by, the rounds moving faster than sound so he catches the bang of the enemy fire seconds later.

He wills himself to fight. He has bested the dukhi before: has killed and even captured them. But tonight he is frozen with a terrible fear. He can't force the primal man inside to rationalise all the sound and fury surrounding him.

Tracers stripe the dark.

A shadow leaps for their position. Tikhon sees it, sees the silhouette of the bastard's RPD in a flash of fire and waits to be cut apart by the light machine gun. Dolidze yells and fires a burst point blank. The Afghan screams and his clothes spark with fire.

Tikhon opens his mouth to yell his thanks over the crackle and roar of gunfire when a face appears before the Georgian, strobe-lit in the blackness.

Dolidze freezes.

123

This doesn't make sense: Russian features, hard and sharp as the rocks in which they fight, wrapped in a lunghee *turban atop a* shemagh *shawl. His eyes are huge.*

This Russian raises a Stechkin APS pistol and fires four shots into Dolidze's face, the muzzle flash illuminating a fine spray of blood-mist in black.

The man doesn't see Tikhon cowering in the rocks among the ponchos and scuttles away into the cruel wastes of these freezing mountains in a land two and half thousand miles from Moscow.

The man is the Osobist with their patrol.

The KGB.

*

Callum remembered there had been a riot that night. He had picked himself up after the explosion, strapped on the gear and clambered into the back of the Tangi Land Rover to hold the line. The locals had kicked off in Andytown after Jimmy was shot, and the sky over Black Mountain looked like it was burning with the blaze of buses across the Glen Road. A couple of choppers were hovering above, another across the Lagan Valley somewhere near east Belfast. He wondered if A Division were taking a hammering, too.

They prepared to do what they mostly did – stand there sweating in helmets and protective gear, batons out, gripping their shields and just fucking taking it. But tonight, some stray managed to thread his way through the alleys, hit the side of their Tangi with a petrol bomb and lit it up. At least they weren't in one of the Hotspurs. But the steel armour plating cooked and the men inside began to sweat like bastards while they waited for the word to pile out the back.

Callum sat in silence. His mate was dead.

Alfie and Susan Gilliland would be crying now, maybe touching Jimmy's cap, the neighbours over and a female PC sitting drinking tea and feeling helpless. In a few days there'd be the honour guard, the flag-draped coffin, the usual ghoulish footage on BBC local TV of the family struggling to hold it together. Jimmy's funeral probably wouldn't make the BBC in England, not without a British soldier going down too: even at that he'd be second string for the news ghouls in London. The wake would be traybakes and tears and other police staring into their glasses and thinking it could have been them.

The heat fried the steel of the Tangi. Callum's brain burned but he felt something pure and cold and relentless bloom in his gut – and when the doors swung open he was a greyhound off the blocks and bolted for the line.

The lads had had to hack their way into a crowd of rioters to get him. They had pulled him back behind RUC lines with blood splattered across his face.

It hadn't been his.

Fourteen

Callum woke with the vague memory of the racket for Angel Patrosi the night before and a worm gnawing in his belly that he'd fucked up somehow. He'd had a drunken black-out. An angry drunken black-out – never good. He grabbed at a shred of memory: a flashback to Jimmy's murder with the sniper years ago; the explosion at the Royal Victoria Hospital in Belfast; the riot that night.

Now, he was in his own bed in his apartment in Greenwich Village, New York City. He was naked. He had no idea how he'd got back to the Village from Lacey's across the East River. Then he heard someone in the kitchen.

'I got coffee, you want to get out of bed.'

He was on the tail end of his drunk but sober enough to wonder if he heard right.

The voice came from the kitchen again.

'You get some clothes on, you can have a cup of the real thing. I brewed a pot instead of spooning that freeze-dried slop in a mug.'

He threw on sweat pants and an AC/DC tour shirt from their gig at the Garden last year. When he shuffled into the kichen he saw his ears hadn't deceived him. Trish Alexander shot him a smile and held out a mug of coffee. As he took the drink she looked at his expression and laughed.

'Anything you think might have happened in this apartment last night,' she said, 'didn't. I slept on your couch. You weren't exactly in shape to do much more than pass out soon as I got you in the door. Why'd you have to live in a walk-up? And what do you weigh, anyway?'

'Whatever it is, isn't between my ears,' said Callum. 'Jesus, I feel like shit.' Then he flinched at his own language and said, 'Sorry.'

'I'm a Baptist, not a nun,' said Alexander. 'I been out in the real world before. You might remember I'm a cop?' She shot him another smile and the hangover cloud forming above his head lightened a little. Trish still wore her clothes from last night, a white wraparound top and tight blue jeans with biker boots. She looked as fantastic as Callum felt shit.

She said, 'You think you can shock "Johnson" Alexander with a little coarse language?'

Now Callum grinned.

'That story is true,' said Trish. 'And the reputation comes with it can be a bonus. You know Gerry Martin hit on me the first couple of days he was on the team? Then Sarge told him the "Johnson" story and he backed right off.'

Gerry Martin hit on Trish? thought Callum. The man had better taste than he thought.

Then he remembered Billy Hutchinson's sloppy compliment at Lacey's and laughed.

'Billy backed off last night when you called him an asshole.'

'Like I said, I live in the real world. I'm a Christian cop. That's a hard thing to be sometimes, and I think The Lord will cut me some slack if I forget myself once in a while and drive the truth home a little harder than usual.'

'Preach, sister.'

Callum took a sip of coffee. It was good.

He said, 'I guess you're sayin' all sorts when you're making a buy undercover.'

'When that's going down, I'm not Trish Alexander. That may not make sense to you or a few in the congregation of Blessed Calvary Baptist Tabernacle, but it makes sense to me. For the greater good, you know.'

'I gotcha. Don't make it public, but I go to church sometimes when I have a Sunday off.'

Trish looked him up and down.

'Callum Burke got some churchin',' she said. 'So which chapel you go to?'

'First Saint John's Faith Baptist Church, West 120th and Malcolm X Blvd.'

'You go to church in Harlem? For how long? I thought you'd be a Catholic, being Irish.'

'Over a year. And Irish come in all kinds of flavors. I'm a Presbyterian but the Baptist thing – the, uh, the joy of the whole thing – just kinda hooked me.'

Alexander shook her head and took a sip of coffee.

'The Good Lord must be watchin' over you, your lily white behind been walkin' that area for over a year without a scratch.'

'I made it known I'm a cop,' said Callum.

Trish sat in a kitchen chair. She draped one long leg over the other and held her coffee cup in her slim, delicate fingers. She raised an eyebrow.

'You kinda forgot your Romans last night, Callum: "Repay no one evil for evil"? You repaid Danny O'Neill pretty good when you knocked him on his rear end out front of Lacey's.'

There it was, thought Callum, the black-out fuck-up. He remembered a scrap of spoken words – *We know where you live, right Gerry?* Then he'd laid out an old hairbag in front of half the Borough at a boozing party. He hoped that was the worst of it. His cheeks burned but he sat down and said, 'Ephesians 6:13, right back at you: "Take up the armor of God".'

Trish leaned back in the chair. She ran a finger through long, straight hair and pursed lips already primed for lying down and falling asleep in.

'See, that's what got you in trouble last night, this macho crap all the guys on the Job push day in day out. Some moron mouths off on the street and a cop has to pop him with a nightstick. You chase a guy down an alley and don't call back-up, then end up almost killing him. Some old House Mouse from the Six-oh, hasn't been on the street since Carter was in office, mouths off and you can't just brush it off or talk him out. You gotta swing for the guy.'

'The drink probably had something to do with it.'

'And that's just more macho garbage. Contrary to what some might think, I'm a woman, and guys getting so drunk they can't take their pants off when they soil themselves is not attractive, trust me on that. It doesn't inspire much faith in the guy's judgement as a cop either.'

Her face split in a smile.

'No, you didn't soil your pants, don't worry. But you get what I'm sayin'? Every hour of every day doesn't have to be a contest, Callum.' Trish looked at her hands. 'You care for Georgie Ruiz, right? How do you think she'd have felt, she saw you like that last night? After you dropped O'Neill, you had a pack of drunk cops baying for your blood. Lucky for you, I was around to grab you and haul you into a cab to get you home.'

'You got my address from my wallet?'

Trish nodded and studied her hands.

'You know,' said Callum, 'Georgie saw me like this before, when I was undercover. I got in a mess and she helped pull me out. We're like partners, you know? I wouldn't want her to see what happened, but she'd understand. Not her husband and kids, though. They're good people.'

Trish looked up.

'You met them?'

'Sure, I've been to the house lots of times. Been to watch a couple of Mets games with Arthur.'

She cocked her head and shrugged like – *oh, so that's how it is*. She almost looked relieved. Callum felt something spark in his chest and pushed it down.

Trish said, 'And the woman in the photographs, in this apartment?'

'My wife,' he said.

Her eyes wavered and the spark lit again. She looked honest-to-God disappointed.

'We're separated,' he said. 'Been that way for a few years now. Her name is Irene. We met in Hong Kong when I was a cop over there, had the best thing ever happened to me in Tara. They left and went to live in Cleveland. I haven't seen them in a year.'

He saw a look on Trish's face he couldn't have imagined on the Job. There was a tenderness that softened everything about her.

'Why?' she said.

'I love my daughter more than anything,' said Callum. 'When we're together it feels so great – so acutely, incredibly great – that when I leave it's like the end of the world. I'm a shell for weeks after. Things between me and Irene are pretty much dead now, too, which doesn't help.'

'So you stay away.'

'I'm a coward,' he said. Then he looked to the ceiling and blinked. He felt tears coming and cursed himself. 'And last night, I just got a flash on some bad memories – real bad memories – from back home. Everything swelled up and I couldn't hold it back anymore; and Danny O'Neill talking bad shit about my ma, he was like a lightning rod or something. He just caught what was coming anyway.'

He had his face down now and wiped away the hot, salty tears with fingers wouldn't stop trembling. When he looked up, Trish was standing right in front of him. She put a hand under his chin and raised it up. Then she bent down and her long, slim fingers went to the sides of his face and she leaned in and kissed him slow and deep.

After, she stepped back and said, 'Now go take a shower. You smell like a brewery after an army of bums had a party and wrecked the place.'

*

He wished he was on a swing day when he walked into the 60th Precinct later that morning. Callum's heart sank when the desk sergeant greeted him with a hearty shout of, 'Hey, it's Slugger O'Toole!' as he made for the stairs. He was back on Narcotics for the day, Georgie too. Trish had told him she had the day off to attend a family event so the team was short-handed. Avda Galkin was free to go about his business without an NYPD tail, not that he knew he had one.

At least Trish had a day off, so Callum could deal with the fallout from smacking Danny O'Neill without his face burning up every time she came within ten feet of him.

Her face had burned this morning, he remembered. He'd taken his shower and come out wrapped in a towel to find her sitting on his bed in her wraparound top and panties, the jeans folded in the corner. She had stood and they'd kissed a while.

Then she said, 'Not all the way.'

So he had taken her as far to the edge as he could and her face had burned on his cheek and he'd felt her hot breath on his neck. Then they'd lay together and talked shit and laughed some. She gave him her number, he his, and she'd slipped out the door leaving a good memory and her scent on the sheets.

He took the stairs down to the lockers and found himself craving some of the mud passed for coffee in the precinct.

'Hey, Lennox, you need to get some sun, man. Lookin' a little pale there.'

Sarge slapped Callum on the shoulder sending a wave of nausea through his gut.

'What kinda patriot are you?' said Callum. 'Evander got the WBA belt, and he's a 'Murican.'

'Too clean, man. Too busy pluggin' Coke and Sega games. I like Lennox Lewis's upright style, you know. That straight right. Like the punch you hit O'Neill with last night.'

'Shit,' said Callum. He looked around. Only he and Sarge were in the room. 'Is he okay?'

Sarge laughed. 'He ain't ready for an Inspector's funeral just yet, man. You knocked him on his ass but you were both so drunk it was like you smacked him with a balloon of booze. He cracked his elbow on the concrete when he fell but that's about it. Took the day off, though.'

Callum said, 'I thought about it, too.'

'The best part? He'll pick up a CD 'cause he called late.'

Callum's misery turned up a notch. Danny O'Neill would be issued a Command Discipline. It was minor, probably issued by the desk sergeant who had goaded Callum on the way in the precinct door. It could be a verbal warning; it could be up to five days docked vacation.

He said, 'I'll talk to the Integrity Control Officer, get it cancelled.'

'Don't even blink,' said Sarge. 'You think the Boss here hasn't been lookin' for an excuse these past years? Danny O'Neill is a bitter hairbag oiler needs a kick up his ass. It's a precinct matter, not even Inspections Division shit. It'll stay on his record for a year and then get wiped.'

Callum rubbed his temple to soothe the swarm of bumblebees partying in his head.

Sarge said, 'You're pretty banged up, huh?'

'Yeah. No idea how much I drank, don't remember getting home.'

'You were "Johnsoned", baby. Trish took charge, threw you in a cab and took off.'

'No shit?'

Sarge watched him, like cops do, for a couple of beats. Callum waited him out. Then he shrugged and said, 'You want some of that instant swill they got down here? It's still caffeine.'

'Yeah, sure.'

Gerry Martin came in after five minutes. He tossed out a greeting but kept his head down and spent too long in the john. Billy Hutchinson walked in next, armed with a takeout coffee. Last came Georgie. She looked worse than Callum. Red rimmed eyes, pale, hair pulled back to reveal a haggard face. She wasn't a drinker, thought Callum, but she looked like it was more than a couple of glasses messing with her head. She said 'Hi' to everyone and shot Callum a wink when no one was looking.

Sarge laid out the bust.

'We got a Controlled Delivery on Ocean Parkway. A Postal Service Inspector picked up something suspicious about an international package from London at the local depot and called it in. The dogs smelled drugs. After testing, we got heroin.'

Georgie said, 'How about a warrant?'

'I got it. DA Mazurek went with me. Judge Pennington signed off on the papers after we listened to him arrange a drink at the Plaza tonight on his phone. Mazurek told me that the woman on the other end of the line wasn't Mrs Pennington, either.'

'Maybe the DA is going to the party, too?' said Martin.

Hutchinson said, 'With that rod up his ass he couldn't climb the Plaza steps, never mind jump in a three-way.'

'OK, OK,' said Sarge. 'The package is resealed and Gerry is playin' dress-up as the mailman. Once he delivers to the address, he radios in and we bust them.'

Georgie said, 'Which floor?'

'Fourth of a walk-up.'

A communal groan ticked the sarge off.

Georgie said, 'Who lives at the address?'

'A Nikolai Popov.'

'Ah Christ,' said Martin, 'sounds Russian. I hope Niki ain't gonna be carvin' up any locals when I knock on the door.'

Sarge ignored him. 'Popov is twenty-eight years old. Five-four. Scrawny, brown hair and eyes.'

There was another moan when they heard a couple of uniformed officers from the Six-oh would be along for the ride. Sarge figured the Precinct Commander thought his COMSTAT figures might look better with some local cops invoved in the bust.

'I don't give a fuck what the Patrol Guide says,' he said, 'they're takin' their caps off soon as they walk out of the door of this station house.'

All cops groused about the cap badges on their uniforms. It was a sunny day and the glint on the metal badge could give away a cop's approach from more than a block away if the perps had spotters. Sarge said the uniforms would ride in the P-Van as it had tinted windows, and wouldn't appear until the Narcotics detectives had executed the warrant. The Precinct commander wanted them to use ESU for the entry but, as with the Beresford and Mayhew warrant, Sarge had argued the Emergency Services Unit would slow down entry and search. Narcotics cops knew where to look for the drugs off the bat. They'd have a guy on loan to bolster the numbers because Trish Alexander was on her day off, too.

'Speakin' of Trish,' said Martin, his eyes darting to Callum, 'how come she didn't change her day? She tuckered out after last night's partyin' or what?'

Callum felt his face ignite. He looked around the room. Martin watched him for a beat and turned to Sarge. Hutchinson was oblivious but Georgie caught Callum's eye.

Sarge said, 'She got family business to take care of.'

'I heard her nephew's getting baptised,' said Hutchinson.

'Shit,' said Martin. 'I'm a good Catholic so I never got the snip.'

'That's circumcised, dickhead.'

Sarge said, 'You're here in body, Marty, but you sure as shit don't do much work.'

He laid out the tac-plan then they started grabbing vests and guns, cuffs and car keys. Gerry Martin had a postal worker's uniform and strapped a S&W .38 snubnosed special to his right ankle and slipped a Glock in his mailbag. Then they all hit the street.

*

Same as it ever was, thought Callum.

He sat next to Georgie in a Buick rental a hundred yards from the *set*, a seven-story brick walk-up next to Ocean Parkway. Georgie had a Mossberg shotgun between her knees. The Prisoner Van was parked up around the corner with the uniforms and Lee, the cop on loan: the same cop who'd pulled Callum off the perp in the alley a few days ago. Sarge sat in a rented Toyota a block away by a mosque with Billy Hutchinson, who had a second Mossberg. They were short on bodies on this one. Gerry Martin was making his way along the mail route toward the target, Nikolai Popov.

The radio hissed on channel SP-TAC H, tuned so only their team would be on the frequency. Callum watched an old couple totter across the street, hand in hand.

He said, 'You OK?' He kept his eyes on the road.

Georgie said, 'No.'

'You wanna talk about it?'

'Not right now.'

He thought of her last night. She was a messy, beautiful drunk. He couldn't imagine Trish Alexander that way. Trish wasn't exactly buttoned-up if this morning was anything to go by, despite the façade she presented at work. He just couldn't imagine her out of control on booze.

Callum caught sight of Martin walking up toward the target building in his mailman uniform.

He said, 'Did Arthur take care of you when you got home last night?'

'Not right now means not now, Cal. OK?'

'Ten-four.'

They sat and watched Martin enter the building. After a couple of minutes, he walked back down the path from the walk-up and continued on the mail route. The radio crackled to life.

Martin had made the delivery.

Sarge's voice came over garbled by static. 'Move in.'

They left the car and jogged at a crouch across small patches of lawn out front of the buildings on the tidy street. Not too close to the walls – this wasn't the projects, but nothing in the rule book said the perp couldn't have a spotter on a roof somewhere ready to drop some airmail on their heads. They saw Sarge and Lee coming from the opposite direction with the ram, Billy Hutchinson behind. Callum had his hand on his Glock and drew it as they reached the walk-up. A couple walking a beagle saw them and went back to picking up dogshit. Cars slid by on the Parkway. Some asshole sounded his horn.

Into the building and up the stairs, and Callum and Hutchinson took the ram. They were breathing hard by the fourth floor. Hutchinson switched with Lee and grabbed the shotgun. He leaned against the wall of the corridor, his chest heaving. Callum had a sudden craving for a smoke. His hands were slick with sweat on the ram.

Cinderblock walls, shining waxed floor, faint, musty smell of disinfectant. Same as a thousand apartment buildings across the city. How many of them had a team of cops crouching to catch their breath before they busted a door down and threw a perp around?

They edged up the corridor and fanned out either side of the apartment door. Sarge tried the handle – no one wanted a repeat of the Coney fuck up. Locked. He nodded. Lee and Callum hefted the ram and started swinging as the others yelled, 'NYPD, open up! NYPD! Open the door!'

This time there was no easy entry. This fucker had his door locked up good. After four attempts, Callum and Lee passed the ram to Sarge and Hutchinson, Callum grabbing Billy's Mossberg. They took up the shout.

'NYPD! Open this fuckin' door you motherfucker!'

There was a sound like bones snapping and the door splintered. They started kicking at the edge. Callum waited to hear the sound of a toilet flushing as Nikolai Popov tried to get rid of the heroin but all he caught was a whimper and the sound of something tearing.

The door gave at the edge like lightning cracking a tree and they piled in.

'Get your ass down!'

'Getthefuckdownyoumotherfucker!'

'Policedroponyourbellyasshole!'

Callum felt his heart battering his ribs harder than the ram on the door. He had a bad booze sweat on and felt all dried out and weak inside. He could taste stale beer and reeked like a bum on 9th Avenue.

But however he looked and felt, it must have been better than Nikolai Popov.

The man lay on the floor and looked up at the cops as Georgie sat on his back and snapped the cuffs tight. His forehead had a swelling like a baseball, his face the colour of bruised fruit.

Lee laughed and held up a package well wrapped in brown paper and masking tape. Too well wrapped for Popov, who hadn't flushed the heroin because he couldn't get the package open to get at the drugs, and hadn't had the presence of mind to throw it out the window. Instead, the paper was shredded and torn like a kid had been clawing at a Christmas present. The guys who resealed the package had bought the team time on the entry by throwing a couple of extra layers of paper and strips of tape over the product.

Popov craned his neck and looked up at the package.

'I broke a nail on that,' he said.

Sarge radioed to the uniforms to come in.

Hutchinson took a look at Popov's face and said, 'Shit, he looks like he ran into Cal last night with his bad drunk on.'

Georgie said, 'What?'

And Callum looked at the tip of a tattooed epaulette showing from Popov's shoulder at the neck of his stretched t-shirt, and knew the man was a ranking Vor in Maxim Volkov or Arkady Kuznetsov's crew.

And someone had handed him a thorough beating.

Fifteen

Tikhon crossed his legs and watched Avda squirm like a sand racer snake he'd once speared on a combat knife near Kandahar.

When he spoke, his Russian was clear and precise.

'No, I do not want to fuck now. Tell me more about the policeman.'

He saw the fear in Avda's eyes. His lover's pupils flitted left and right, as though two competing sides of his brain were pulling at the truth of the matter. Tikhon thought he was weighing which entity he feared most: him, or the police.

Avda pushed his delicate frame up from the dresser on which he'd been leaning and crossed the small bedroom to stand before Tikhon, sat in a wicker chair next to the bed. Tikhon had surprised him by buzzing Avda's apartment rather than waiting for their rendezvous that night. Avda had glanced at Tikhon's knuckles when he opened the apartment door. They were bruised and split from pounding the two drunkards in the Russian bar last night. The bartender had yelled and hauled at Tikhon to drag him from one after the other fled.

'Don't you know who you are beating?' he had said.

What did it matter? A broken jaw was a broken jaw, no matter to whom it belonged.

To others, though, it would have mattered a great deal. It would have mattered when one of the idiots Tikhon had pulverized had fallen and a semi-automatic pistol had dropped from his coat pocket and clattered on the floor of the bar. Now Tikhon reached behind his back and produced the gun. A Tokarev. He'd used them in the war.

Avda's face went ivory-white. He stared in silence.

Then he sank to his knees in front of Tikhon and placed his hands on his legs.

'I could make you feel good,' he said. 'You can ride my dragon and then we can talk. It's so much easier to talk – '

Tikhon kicked him hard in the chest with his crossed leg. Avda yelped and shrank back.

Tikhon felt nothing. Why would he? Avda was a receptacle and nothing more. He absorbed the fear and hate and violence when they fucked, and his Saint and Dragon offered hypnotic calm. But there was no emotional connection. He uncrossed his legs and leaned forward on the chair. The little shit knew that cop from the sauna better than he'd said. He could see it in his weak eyes, eyes that glorified in victimhood.

'You met the policeman from the banya and spoke with him. I am right, am I not? And don't lie to me or you will get much worse than a kick.'

Avda began crying and nodded.

'Where and when?'

'He was with the other one. They came for me yesterday in the Village. I don't know how they knew I was there.'

'The other one: the Italian, Patrosi?'

'No, the angry one. O'Connell.'

'Go on.'

'They took me somewhere in a car and beat me. They wanted to know why I was in the banya. They saw me talk with Volkov and wanted to know if I said anything to endanger the cop who was in the sauna. I told them ... I told them I went there to give Volkov some money. It was a coincidence the cop was there. That's all.'

Tikhon shoved the gun in his waistband and watched Avda in silence for seconds that stretched to a minute. He had watched tribesmen like that in Afghanistan but it had been like staring into a dark well. Their eyes gave him nothing but cold hatred.

'Please, say something?' said Avda, his voice a tremolo whine.

'You say his name is Burke? The pig in the sauna?'

'Yes.'

'And he knows nothing about me?'

'Nothing.'

'Did he ask about me?'

'No.'

Tikhon stood and kicked Avda like he was punting a soccer-ball. Avda screeched and Tikhon knelt and clamped his hand over his mouth.

'Be quiet,' he said. 'Be quiet.'

Avda looked up at him skull-eyed, his face red and blotched with tears. He quietened.

'The policeman, Burke, asked about me, didn't he?'

Avda nodded.

It was obvious, thought Tikhon. The man had appraised him from behind Volkov's thugs in the moments when they shared the sauna.

'Tell me.'

Avda closed his eyes as though a noose were being fitted over his head. Then he spoke.

'He asked who you were. He said he knew the scars on your body were bullet wounds. I told him I didn't know anything, that you were no one. You had no tattoos, had no criminal connections. I said you were just a random bather. I swear.'

'But he didn't believe you, did he?'

Avda lowered his gaze.

'No,' he said. 'He told me to ask around and find out who you are. He gave me a card with a number and said if I didn't have anything useful by Tuesday, we should meet near the Stonewall Inn. That's it, I swear.'

His eyes went back to Tikhon with a wild hope and he became eager and animated.

'He knows I work for Volkov – but he has no idea you were there to kill. He has no idea we are lovers.'

'He never will,' said Tikhon.

Avda began crying again. His face seized up like crumpled paper.

He said, 'Please.'

Tikhon said, 'Hush.'

*

He left the apartment.

Tikhon decided it was a good thing he had let Avda live. To have a contact plugged into Maxim Volkov and the NYPD was an asset. The fact he disregarded the hustler when they weren't fucking was another matter. Avda was a dog with several masters: but he hated Volkov, hated what the animal made him do, and was eager to help Tikhon destroy the gangster. He could live a little longer.

Avda had, again, tried to seduce Tikhon before he left the apartment. Tikhon refused. For one, he hadn't wanted the little rat to think he had ingratiated himself any; for another, he wanted to hold onto the edge he now walked.

Beating the two idiots in the bar last night had already fed the beast some, slowed the rollercoaster. He'd heard the talk before. Drunk men bitching about the war, the Soviet government of the time: and the inter-regimental rivalries. And the men last night had been, like so many before them, in the wrong place at the wrong time.

But the new cop, Callum Burke, worried him. Until he understood more about him, he would keep the tight, sharp needle of doubt pricking at his spine. It helped him focus and kept him alert.

Could he trust Avda? Would the little bastard stick to the

script and call the cop to arrange a meet that Tikhon would observe from a distance? Or would he call the policeman and tell him the truth about everything?

No. He had looked in Avda's eyes and seen a tug of war born of fear: fear of the cop versus fear of Tikhon. Tikhon had won.

He watched a mother and child as they crossed the street, the child eating candy in American sneakers. These people, he thought, have no idea how easy their lives are. They consume and consume, and have no concept of what it's like to be truly hungry. To have nothing. And that was why Tikhon would win out over the cop. Why Avda would obey him despite any threats the police might make.

Tikhon was a man with nothing. No family, friends, or life.

He had nothing to lose, and that made him a very dangerous prospect.

And one day, when he appeased the ghosts, he'd be a man with no fear.

*

'No fear,' said Callum.

He and Georgie were searching Nikolai Popov and Georgie had made a crack about the Russian's ass, a pair of gloves and a Camel cigarette. He laughed but she didn't usually go for the dirty jokes and banter. Something was bugging her.

The paper package they took from the controlled delivery was on a metal table in the room. Callum and Georgie had the usual field team duties – searching, vouchering evidence, taking mugshots and fingerprints. Upstairs in the 60th Precinct, Sarge, Martin, Hutchinson and Lee were working through the mountain of paperwork required for each arrest. They had asked Popov if he was okay with a female detective in on the body search, and the macho asshole had said he didn't mind giving some lady cop sweet dreams tonight if she was game. He hadn't even winced when he gave her a smile with his busted-up face.

Popov eased his shirt off.

This asshole's been giving some unlucky lady a lot more than sweet dreams, thought Callum. A crude tattoo of a woman in a dress and a prancing devil lifting the back with a fishing line had been etched on the right side of his stomach.

Callum glanced at the video camera in the corner of the room. Georgie caught the look and raised an eyebrow.

Callum said, 'How many women you raped, Niki?'

Popov looked at him as though he'd discovered a new species. The Russian unbuckled his belt and began unbuttoning his Levis.

'You think I need to rape anyone?' he said and shot Georgie a leer. 'I'll show you why lady cop here's going to be dreaming about me tonight.'

'How many, asshole?'

He remembered detective Parker's short lecture on the Russian tattoos on the killers who carved up Beresford and Mayhew in the projects.

'See, these guys wear the story of their lives on their bodies like a comic book,' he said to Georgie. 'Like the assholes we busted on Tuesday cuttin' Beresford and Mayhew. What were their names?'

'Andro-something and something-ovich. I dunno',' she said, 'all these guys blend into one for me.'

Callum snapped his fingers.

'Turgenev. Alex Turgenev. That was one. The other was Ilia Oblonsky. Those names mean anything to you, Niki?'

Popov shrugged. 'Nothing means anything to me until I have a lawyer, policeman.'

'They had a Tokarev. You ever seen one of them?'

Popov's eyes shifted like a guilty schoolboy. His back pushed back against the wall and his hands dropped to his sides, went to his waist. He scratched his chest. Something had struck a nerve.

'No, Makarov,' said Callum, 'that was it. Ever seen a Makarov?'

Popov shrugged, almost sweating with the effort at indifference.

Callum cocked a thumb at the video camera mounted on the wall and said to Georgie. 'That thing work?'

She shot him a fast look said *don't go there*.

He lit a Camel.

Georgie stared at him – *we can't smoke in here*.

Callum walked over to the camera and pulled a wire out of the back.

He pointed with the lit cigarette and walked over to Popov. 'This here masterwork, the devil and the woman, looks similar to a tattoo Oblonsky has on his body. You know Oblonsky?'

Popov rocked on the balls of his feet and tilted his head back. Angry fear and resentment had kicked in now and he looked at Callum as though deciding which part of him to slice off first. Callum turned away to face Georgie.

'This gradeschool artwork here, with the devil and what, I guess, is supposed to be a woman: means this piece of shit has raped someone.'

Something inside had crawled out of Callum's darker nature and taken hold of him when he got his drunk on last night. The thing that had tipped him over into smacking Danny O'Neill. And now it was whispering in his ear.

Georgie, hands on hips, stared at him hard with eyes somewhere between furious and concerned. Her face made him want to pull back but he couldn't stop. He gave her a wink and turned to Popov. Then Callum brought the tip of the cigarette close enough for Popov to flinch.

The Russian said, 'Hey!'

'One more shot, Niki. Do you know Oblonsky?'

The thug snorted. His neck was scrawny. The tendons worked under the skin as Callum closed his fist around his throat and pinned him to the wall. Popov's bruised face went a purple-red with the choke. With his other hand, Callum brought the lit Camel up to the Russian's clavicle.

'See, these stars here,' he said over his shoulder to Georgie, 'mean Niki is a Grade A asshole – a Vor.'

Georgie said, 'Callum – '

'Who gave you the hamburger face, Niki?'

Popov strained against the choke but kept his hands down. He knew he'd take a far worse beating if he socked a cop.

'C'mon, man,' said Callum, 'someone fucked you up and it was pretty recent. Who would pound on a Vor like you in this neighborhood?'

'Callum, stop,' said Ruiz.

'Who?'

He saw another tattoo on Popov's shoulder. A candle aflame.

'Now,' he said. 'What's this mean, Niki?'

Popov looked at him with red eyes made small by the choke. He smiled and his swollen purple cheek puffed up more. Callum brought the glowing tip of his cigarette less than an inch from the candle.

'What say we light this for real, huh?' he said.

Popov spluttered, 'Ffffuck you!'

'Alright, man, have it your way. But I ain't gonna' waste a smoke on you.'

Callum wedged the Camel in his teeth and pulled a Zippo from his pocket. He snapped it open. It sparked first time.

Tears welled in Popov's eyes. Blood vessels were close to popping. He clawed at Callum's hand as the lighter moved to half an inch from his skin.

Georgie was beside them.

'Callum, no!'

Callum looked at Popov and saw terror. It felt great.

Popov whispered, 'OK!'

Callum let go. The Russian folded and began coughing, gasping, wheezing. His nose was pumping snot, his eyes streaming. Georgie was next to Callum wearing a *what the fuck?* glare. He blocked it – couldn't lose his edge now.

'Niki,' he said, 'do you know Oblonsky?'

Popov shook his head. 'No, no. But I know Turgenev.'

'How?'

'He does some of the same shit as me. Collections around Brighton Beach. Some courier work.'

'For who?'

'Uncle.'

'Do I have to grab you again to get a full sentence?'

'Maxim Volkov. You'd have known soon enough – he will send my lawyer.'

Callum said, 'Maxim Volkov is your uncle?'

Popov nodded.

Callum grabbed a pad and pencil from the table.

Georgie mouthed to him, *We can't use this.*

He gave her a hand sign like he knew, she should bear with him.

He said, 'Why were Turgenev and Oblonsky carving up two dealers in the Coney Island projects? Don't shit me now.'

Popov said, 'You're crazy, none of this is admissable.'

'Good word. You let me worry about that.'

'I don't know – really! – I am related to Maxim Volkov but I don't have much responsibility. Just donkey-work like receiving this package. But I heard the two niggers were dealing to some important people, and some homo whore works for my uncle was fucking those people. That's it, that's all I know.'

Callum scribbled in the pad. The story didn't contradict Avda Galkin's, which was a start. He pointed to the ripped package on the table.

'Tell me about this,' he said.

'I swear, I didn't know what was inside. Donkey work, you know? I just heard a package was coming to me and I should wait for someone to come and collect it from my place.'

Callum snapped the lid of the Zippo open and shut a couple of times and said, 'You shittin' me, Niki?'

'I swear.'

'Alright,' said Callum, 'I believe you, brother.' He gave the thug a pat on the shoulder hard enough to keep him alert. 'Who gave you the face?'

'That, I don't know either. Some guy was in a bar last night. I was drinking with a friend and we were just talking shit. This guy was in the corner by himself. About your height, similar build but maybe a little more skinny. He just came over and started beating on us.'

'You sure you didn't know the guy? Maybe you said something to piss him off?'

'I didn't pay attention until he punched my friend in the neck.'

Callum said, 'What were you and your friend talking about?'

'Afghanistan. We were over there. We're Afghantsy. Before I got involved in this shit.'

'What were you saying about Afghanistan?'

'We were...' Popov looked at the floor. He looked at Georgie. She had moved to the door to slow down anyone coming inside the room. 'We were complaining about the Airborne troops over there.'

'Which troops?' said Callum.

'The 345th Airborne Regiment. They were in Operation Storm-333. They fought on Hill 3234. They did a lot, but they sacrificed no more than many other men and yet some looked at them like the rockstars of the war.'

'From what I've seen,' said Callum, 'wars don't make rockstars of anyone. So he punched your friend.'

'He was very strong, very vicious. I hit him a few times but he didn't feel it. He fought like a Vor – dirty, smashing us with anything he could find. He cut my friend with a bottle, had no worries about really hurting or killing us. But he had no tattoos. Not on his body, anyway.'

'How do you know?'

'I pulled at his shirt and split it open. His skin was clean – but he had scars.'

Part of Callum knew the answer before he asked the question. The universe had turned its volatile gaze on him this week. 'What kind of scars?' he asked. 'Where?'

'On his chest. Little holes here, here, here. I've seen them before. Trust me when I say, they were bullet wounds.'

Callum dropped his smoke on the floor and ground it out with his heel. He hadn't taken a single drag. Then he patted Nikolai Popov on the cheek like a brother-in-arms.

'I do trust you, Niki,' he said. 'I really do.'

Sixteen

Later, when they had searched Nikolai Popov, taken the mugshots, vouchered the evidence and the rest, Georgie and Callum stood outside the 60th.

'Let's call Mike,' said Callum. 'He can pull us off Narcotics for the rest of the day.' Sarge and Martin were taking Popov for processing so the team was now too small for any other street operations anyway. 'We need to get our heads together. This Russian hit on Beresford and Mayhew still doesn't make sense to me.'

Georgie said, 'Yeah, sure.'

'Where has Avda Galkin been leading you recently?'

Georgie dug her hands deep in her pockets and said, 'His place. A club near Long Island City. And a swank address on East 35th Street and Lexington Avenue.'

'Low friends in high places.'

'You got that right. The townhouse looked like someone lifted a chunk of Vienna and dropped it in midtown Manhattan. Like something out of "Emma".'

'You can bet Gwyneth Paltrow doesn't live inside, though. Whoever's paying for Avda's services there has some serious money. Our boy Popov said Beresford and Mayhew were supplying important people with drugs. Could be a connection to their murders. I'll get in touch with Mike.'

'Try his cell or beeper. He's been on Galkin today with me back on the team.'

Callum said, 'Sure.'

He sucked in tobacco smoke and thought about how Georgie was different – had been last night, too. He wanted to tell her about Trish but now might not be the time.

Georgie looked in the direction of the Atlantic, hidden behind the buildings on the boardwalk.

'In there,' she said, gesturing to the precinct building, 'what Popov said is useless in a prosecution.'

Callum said, 'I know that. He knows that. He'll lawyer up and what will be, will be. But it isn't useless to us. Something's going on with the Russian gangs around here and we need all the information we can get.'

'What if your bad cop act endangers the narcotics case?'

'They got that whole macho mafia culture shit goin' on. He won't hide behind what I did. Maybe he won't have to. So someone sent a package of drugs to him. How do we prove he was expectin' it? He tore at the paper while we were swingin' the ram. He panicked. The cops are battering the door down and he gets scared someone's framing him by sending him some nasty shit in the mail.'

Georgie pursed her lips then said, 'Why were you so interested in whoever beat Popov and his friend last night?'

'Anyone works over a Russian gangster is pretty interesting.'

'I saw your face when he mentioned the bullet wounds.'

Callum looked her in the eyes and said, 'I went to a Russian bathhouse yesterday. Mike asked me to go in, take a look around, see if there were any bad guys in there. Familiarise myself with this area and their world. A man who fit the description of the bullet-scarred guy beat Popov walked into the sauna where me and Volkov were sweating. The Russians don't know who I am but Volkov knew my face didn't fit. A local old guy took me under his wing and got me out.'

'Jesus.'

Georgie's face went pale then flushed red.

'And you didn't think to tell me this today?'

'We were with the team or Popov until now.'

'How about in the car?'

'You didn't want to talk.'

'Last night then?'

'I was drinking to let off some steam. It wasn't the right time.'

'Jesus,' she said. Then she grabbed him and held him tight, her fist scrunching up his jacket at the back. 'I don't want to lose you, OK? I can't lose you.'

Callum looked around, his face on fire, to see if any cops were wandering in or out of the precinct watching. Just a large lady with a shopping bag and a scrawny guy in a pork pie hat passing by. He had to admit, it felt good with Georgie's arms around him sober. Not like Trish, but good. But he gently eased her away.

'Georgie,' he said, 'nothing's gonna happen to me. You know this city. The cream don't rise to the top, the scum and the shit nobody wants – like me – does.'

He smiled. Georgie looked at him with eyes that said plenty about pain.

She dropped her head and kept her face down as she said, 'Would you have burned Popov if he hadn't given you something?'

Callum took a long drag on his cigarette. He blew the smoke out in a thin stream.

'Would you have tried to stop me?'

Georgie said, 'Yeah, I would.'

'Then I wouldn't have burned him,' he said and killed the spent smoke under his heel.

*

Callum got two calls on his beeper just before he and Georgie walked into the small coffee shop on Bleecker Street, a few blocks from his apartment. The place was next to a supermarket and across from the towering NYU buildings between LaGuardia Place and Mercer Street. Two blocks north sat Washington Square Park where students, locals and dime-bag dealers would be strolling in the afternoon sun. Mike was waiting in a booth in jeans and a sweater.

The coffee shop was going the way of much of the neighborhood, straining so hard for an affected chic the walls were practically sweating with effort. A loud group of money sat in the corner sharing their nasal whine with the other patrons, and the distressed wooden booth was hard under Callum's ass. He saw Mike look around with despair.

They compared notes on what Nikolai Popov and Avda Galkin had said about the reasons for the murders of Beresford and Mayhew in Coney. None of them trusted Volkov's nephew or the hustler kid. Georgie gave a run down on where Avda Galkin had been over the last few days, most of it mundane. There were a few assignations around West Village, a couple of hours spent in bars or clubs. She gave Mike the high-class address in midtown east and he said it sounded interesting, a scrawny hustler hitting an address in the Manhattan mid-thirties. He'd check it out. They spit-balled the connections: Volkov and Avda; Volkov and the Russian killers in the project; Popov being Volkov's relation. Heroin, hustling, murder. The constant in all of it was Maxim Volkov.

Mike said, 'Everyone on your team OK with what you guys are doin' for me?'

'Nobody *knows* what we're doing,' said Georgie.

'You ain't got any grief from your boss, Cal?'

'Nothin'.'

'Heard you thought you were back in the ring last night.'

'Jesus!'

The rumor mill of the NYPD, thought Callum. Incredible. Then again, he probably shouldn't have popped Danny O'Neill at a big-time racket for an injured cop.

He said, 'You know what? Droppin' that old hairbag has given me an easier ride with a couple of the team. Every cloud, huh?'

'Who knew?' said Georgie. The temperature seemed to drop a couple of degrees with the disapproving tone of each word.

Mike took a mouthful of coffee, put a fist to his chest and belched.

'Alright,' he said. 'So where do we go from here?'

Callum said, 'I got Avda Galkin on my beeper on my way in here. And next minute, that old guy from the bathhouse, Kolya Slavin. I'll call them back and set up a meet with each.'

'In Brighton Beach?' said Georgie.

'I wouldn't advise it,' said Callum. 'Some of these neighborhoods are like back in Belfast. They're small, close-knit. Most people know someone knows someone. It's almost like they're under seige.'

Mike slurped caffiene and said, 'In the case of some of the older folks, they think they are. Lot of the locals don't trust the blacks from Coney Island. They blame them for a lot of the crime in the neighborhood.'

'Surprise, surprise,' said Georgie.

'Not that they think their local Russian skells walk on water. Organized Crime interviewed one guy who came here as a political refugee in the eighties. He was in his fifties, comes from the Soviet Union where the government practically wipes your ass, right? He mighta been broke but there wasn't shit to spend money *on* over there and everyone's in the same boat. The state runs everything. Then he comes here, he don't have a job to start with. He can't believe the welfare system, can't understand why the welfare officers are so hostile and talk to him like a cockroach. He sees a lotta the brothers livin' on welfare and resents it, because he hates the handouts, wants to work. So, he don't trust a lot of the folk in Coney.'

Georgie looked like she swallowed a fly with her coffee.

'Did he realise plenty of "the brothers" want to work too?'

Mike sniffed. 'Wood for the trees shit. But I can tell you he fuckin' hated the Russian gangs. Most all the people in Brighton Beach do. 'Cruel' is the word I keep hearin' to describe them from citizens in the neighborhood.'

'But?'

'But what else, Georgie?' said O'Connell. He was heating up, his face screwing a little tighter. He said, 'The people are fuckin' terrified. Same as East New York, or Bed-Stuy, or Washington Heights, or South Bronx. And while your sergeant was chasin' quotas, the old guy I interviewed got dragged to a warehouse off Neptune Avenue a week later. The Vory-Russian-fuckin'-mob, whatever, they tied the guy so he's lyin' flat on his back under some shelves. Then they climbed on the shelving and jumped off on top of him. On top of him – you imagine that? They snapped his ribs and drove them through his fuckin' lungs like they were spears.'

Georgie was silent. Callum knew the drill. Mike O'Connell was an asshole, a brute, a loyal and indefatigable friend, and a fantastic cop. Probably, Callum thought, the asshole who put Marcie O'Connell on a psych ward with the crank call saying Mike was dead all those years ago, had a part to play in O'Connell's make-up. And the cop part of him mostly came from Mike's passion for crushing the assholes who provided stories like the one he'd just told. At volume.

The table of money sat and stared.

'Hey,' said Mike, 'excuse my language, folks. Still, the Mayor's puttin' your tax dollars to work cleanin' up the city. Other people's dollars, of course. Yours are tied up in the fuckin' Caymans, am I right?'

He winked and leaned toward their table.

Callum said, 'Mikey ...'

Mike continued, 'What I heard, Rudi Giulliani's gonna' have Manhattan so fuckin' sterile the subways won't even smell of piss anymore.'

One of the men at the table grimaced and said, 'Really! Outrageous!'

Callum flashed his badge and said, 'He's undercover. You take this further and I'll have to bust you for interfering with police business.'

A woman in Versace stood and corralled the others to leave. As they walked off she said, 'This is why no one likes cops.'

*

Mike agreed Callum should set up meets with Avda Galkin and Kolya Slavin. Callum was still wary of Avda's motives, but the meet would be public and he knew they needed to stay in touch with the hustler to see how things panned out.

Georgie would go back to shadowing Avda after her two consecutive swing days, tomorrow and Monday. Callum thought she looked like she needed the days off. She left to check in on the Six-oh before heading home to her family. Come Tuesday, Callum should have met with Galkin and they'd have a better handle on what kind of game the kid was playing.

It was four in the afternoon. Rain kicked in, blanketing the city in a fine drizzle. The Old Peculiar Pub was a block away on Bleecker. Mike wanted a beer.

They sat in a booth next to an embossed mirror with a logo of a defunct beer which probably hadn't been on tap since the Native American on the NYPD badge was supping a brew by the Hudson. The taps were micro-brews that ranged from horse-piss to a pretty good pint. There were tiles on the floor and a decorative ceiling desperately wanted to emulate a London pub but came off like it was molded out of plastic. But the bartenders were good and it was cheaper than many drinking holes around the Village. It was quiet too, hours before the weekend crowd got their booze on.

Mike stuck with a bottle of Budweiser. Callum grabbed a pint of something West Coast.

He said, 'You know, a guy at Borough Command was in San Francisco last year. He said he went to a micro-brewery had cigarette girls walkin' around like it was the forties.'

'You can forget that happenin' in New York, Cal. Pretty soon you won't be able to light up your cancer sticks indoors.'

'Marcie runnin' for City hall?'

'She'd have a better shot at mayor than Messinger. How're Irene and Tara?'

'OK, you know. Tara's doing really well in school.'

'You ain't seen them for a while, huh?'

Callum smiled but it came across like a grimace of pain.

Mike's face dropped its ever-present semi-scowl. His features seemed to open out and Callum saw his friend as Mike was with his family.

'I'm not one to tell a man how to run his private life,' said Mike, 'but don't let them go, Cal. Just a phone call, so your little girl hears her pop's voice. You'll find your way to them again – but if you don't keep in touch, they may not wait around until you do.'

Callum said, 'Yeah.' He thought Irene was done with him, though. He remembered Trish last night, her hot face against his.

Mike clinked Callum's glass with his bottle and took a long pull. 'Do I need to worry about you?'

'I know you care,' said Callum. 'It's why we connect on a spiritual level, kinda like we were together in a former life. Maybe Laurel and fuckin' Hardy.'

'You ain't so fat,' said Mike, running a hand around his waistband. 'I mean you ain't gonna end up at Lefrak Plaza on me, right?'

'Psych Services? I took the MMI exam same as everyone.

Drew the bullshit pictures of houses and trees. Only mental problems I got is I'd want to be a cop in the first place.'

'You used to drink in here with Paddy Duggan.'

Callum had a flash of his time undercover boozing in the Old Peculiar with Duggan from the Irish Crew. They'd got into brawls outside a couple times.

He said, 'Different time, different me.'

'You were drinkin' a lot then, getting into fights. Then you clock Danny O'Neill at a fuckin' 10-13 party last night.'

'He was talkin' shit about my family. My mother.'

'And you got your Irish on.'

'That's kind of what he was talkin' shit about.'

Mike rolled his eyes to the ceiling.

'Jesus Christ. You're gonna let some bitter hairbag asshole push you into throwin' a haymaker, how am I supposed to trust you on this job? I set you up with my CI. What happens if you kick the shit out of him on a bad hair day? In the bathhouse, if you'd lost your shit I coulda been firing shots over your coffin.'

'I got this Mike.'

'You got my balls in a vice, you fuck up.'

Callum clinked glass and bottle again. He looked at his friend, sat hunched like a Silverback across the booth table. Mike was strong medicine for some but he moved heaven and earth for his cops. He went to the counter for another beer.

When Mike had a fresh Bud and Callum a pale lager from some Wisconsin backwater he'd never heard of, he cleared his throat.

'I keep sayin' it, but small world: the guy who worked over Popov in the bar soundin' like the guy in the sauna. The bullet wounds in his chest.'

Mike downed half his bottle in one.

'You think that's why Galkin's in touch? He found out about the guy?'

'I think Galkin's full of shit,' said Callum. 'He's been playin' some kinda game with Patrosi and you, and I figure none of us understand the rules yet. And I guess he's been deliverin' product for Volkov. The heroin comes in – like this afternoon's bust via London – and some of it gets to the rich and powerful through Galkin. His clients are payin' for more than sex when he comes around.'

Mike rolled up his sweater sleeve and scratched an arm carpeted in black hair. He watched Callum stare at him doing it and said, 'This guy with the scars got you worried.'

'Yeah,' said Callum. 'He doesn't fit. No tattoos, it didn't look like Volkov knew him when he walked in the sauna. Then he takes off after a second. He just keeps poppin' up in places where these Vory assholes hang out. I saw plenty of guys like him when I boxed – compact, quiet, but there's some real violence bouncin' around inside and it just kinda ...vibrates around them.'

'Only thing vibrates around you is that 12 inches of molded plastic you got in your bedside drawer for the cold, lonely nights,' said Mike. His face was deapan but his timing told Callum he was worried like him, had to throw in a gag to keep things on an even keel while they chewed the fat.

Callum said, 'Popov was in the Aghan War. He was bad-mouthin' the Russian Airborne guys over there and then our mystery man rearranges his face. What if this guy's ex-Soviet special forces or somethin'? I bumped into a few SAS in my days in Belfast. Similar look, similar aura.'

'Aura? You'll be buyin' crystals and meditatin' to whales givin' birth next.' Mike looked at the table and picked a little at a wood chip. 'What if Maxim Volkov was in Afghanistan too? We know from his file he was in the Russian military. Imagine if we had some revenge shit, or a vigilante happenin' here.'

'Or Volkov got a private army of ex-Russian military.'

They both drank. A guy behind Mike started diggin' for gold with his tongue in his girlfriend's throat. He was pushing into her so hard, Callum thought they could go through the wall. The place was filling up with students, Bleecker store attendants, business people passing through on their way uptown. Saturday night. What was happening in the Brighton Beach bars and restaurants? Callum guessed much of the same – the good people of the neighborhood letting off some weekend steam. Only cops and criminals were lurking in the background, shovelling society's shit.

Mike said, 'Talk to Arkady Kuznetsov.'

Callum took a second to tune in to his friend. Then he laughed. It had to be a joke, meeting with the *other* Brighton Beach Russian godfather.

'For real,' said Mike. 'I'll broker the meet. Talk to him, ask him about the mystery man. Do it before you meet Avda so you got a wider picture before the kid starts layin' any fairytales on you. Watch Kuznetsov while he's talkin' to you, see if he's hidin' somethin' when you talk about the bulletscars guy. Be a cop, you know?'

'He's under investigation with Organized Crime.'

'When you were investigatin' terrorists back in Ireland, did you harass them?'

Callum nodded.

'Yeah,' he said. 'But we didn't invite them for tea and biscuits.'

Mike shook his head. 'They were terrorists. Their purpose in life was to blow you away.'

Callum saw Jimmy Gilliland in his head, half his face gone from the sniper's bullet back in Belfast.

'But,' said Mike, 'Arkady Kuznetsov is a criminal. He just wants to make money so he ain't gonna waste a cop – that's bad business. I'll set it up so you ain't steppin' on OCI toes. I promised you, you wouldn't go undercover: you meet Kuznetsov and he'll know you're a badge. I'll ghost you myself.'

Callum thought it over.

Mike said, 'If this is about Volkov, his main rival in Brighton Beach will sleep better thinkin' we're all over him. You'll make a friend in Arkady Kuznetsov, I'll be there somewhere watchin' your ass; and you know what they say about keeping your enemies close.'

Callum shrugged. Why the hell not? He was in pretty deep already. And Mike was a lieutenant, his boss on this caper, so it was following orders. It was all investigative work building to a detective shield.

'Alright,' he said. 'You can really set it up?'

'Is the Pope a Don? Sure I can. I'll reach out through a few channels.'

'OK,' said Callum. 'I got a swing day tomorrow but it's fine if you can set it up then, I could use the overtime. Not the mornin', though.'

'You gonna' tie one on tonight?'

'I got church.'

Mike laughed.

'Oh yeah, you like a little "Praise Jesus!" and dancin' in the aisles up in Harlem.'

He drained his bottle and pointed to it to show he wanted another.

Callum said, 'When are you gonna pay for one on your lieutenant's salary?'

'When you got a wife and kids to support on a cop's pay,' said Mike. 'The only people get rich in our job are the dirty cops and the flirty cops. You go to One Police Plaza, you'll find plenty of both.'

Seventeen

When he got home, Callum found a message on his machine from Trish Alexander. He was surprised she got in touch so soon and called back. She came over. The rain stopped and they went to Café Figaro for a drink at a sidewalk table and watched Bleecker Street light up. The crowds of weekend revellers swirled around the corner of Bleecker and McDougal. Callum savored the time, knew you didn't get many moments when two people sat in the middle of millions, wrapped in their own magic for a night. They talked about themselves, New York, Trump's split from Marla Maples and the Eddie Murphy scandal.

The Angelika had a late night show of Grosse Point Blank and when they came out Callum asked Trish to stay. She smiled and took his hand and began walking back toward Bleecker through another rain shower. When they got to Callum's place she looped her slender arms around his neck and it began. They explored one another, talked, explored some more.

After, she ran her fingers through his hair and frowned at something felt off on his head.

'You felt that, huh?' said Callum. 'It's a skin graft on my scalp, just above my left ear. Feels like a small dip, right?'

Trish nodded. 'What happened?'

'Shrapnel. When I was a cop in Belfast, a bomb went off nearby and a piece of metal winged me above the ear. I was lucky. There was some blood. Thing was, I didn't even realise how deep the wound was until next day – a few hours after the bomb I was cracking heads in a riot.'

'My Lord.'

'Funny thing was, the bomb was right next to a hospital, the

Royal Victoria. The Royal had some of the best people for burns and gunshot trauma in the world. They performed a skin graft so's you can't really notice. It's so shallow.'

'But the hair grew back.'

'It's a little wiry but I keep it short so you wouldn't notice. You're the only person in the team knows about this. They took the skin from my groin. It even grew back a little down there, and the pubic hair pretty much covers the patch anyhow.'

Trish laughed.

'Just to verify,' she said, 'let me take another look down there.'

An hour later, they fell asleep to the lullaby of helicopter blades somewhere high overhead and the wail of a siren in the street below.

In the morning, Callum felt a stab of fear.

This was great. He was happy with a great woman. They were good together, good in bed as far as Trish would let things go. He felt like he was a better person when he was with her.

But they worked in the Job. Together. And the Job didn't make him better, in lots of ways.

He slipped out of bed. Trish lay with the sheet snarled around her waist.

Jesus, he thought, she has great legs. He ran his hand up her thigh. She moaned, opened one eye and smiled. The dance began again.

*

She didn't go to church with him up in Harlem. He'd asked if it was a guilt thing, singing psalms after what they'd been doing. She'd laughed and said no, but it would have felt like she was cheating on Blessed Calvary Tabernacle if she went to First Saint John's Faith with him.

Later, he had another shot of fear laced with doubt. He

worried she hadn't wanted to be seen in Harlem with a pasty white boy, churchin' or not.

*

At lunchtime he grabbed a coffee and sandwich and wandered through Central Park to the Alice In Wonderland statue. Alice sat on a giant mushroom, eleven feet tall in bronze. He'd always thought it was one ugly-ass effort, that statue. The Mad Hatter's face looked like he was melting. Then again, his favorite New York statue was the knotted gun at the United Nations.

Kids wandered around and he thought of Tara. He'd had to stop her clambering on the Buddhas when they went to a temple grounds for some quiet, back when they lived in Hong Kong. Back when they lived together.

His brother had married a woman from two streets away in Belfast. His cousin, a girl from their church congregation. Callum had met and married a woman six thousand miles from his homeland. He had a daughter with Irish and Chinese heritage. Now he was falling for an African American woman he feared might be ashamed to be seen with him in a black neighborhood.

Still, he thought, God loves a trier.

His beeper went off. When he found a phone and called the number, Mike O'Connell's voice came over the line shouting at his kid because the dog was chewing something it shouldn't in the kitchen.

'Sorry,' said Mike. 'Listen, you wanna come over for dinner?'

'Marcie OK with that?'

'Hey, I'm the man of this house,' he whispered.

Callum smiled. 'I'm good, Mike. I like wandering around, it's a beautiful day.'

'Wait a second.'

Callum heard the sound on the line change. A plane flew overhead on O'Connell's end and he knew Mike had gone outside.

'You're on for Arkady Kuznetsov but not today,' said O'Connell. 'Long Island City, tomorrow, 1300. I got an address at Hunters Point for you. I already cleared the time with your boss.'

'Why Queens?'

'Neutral. Busy. They're buildin' the park out there so plenty of hard-hats around. You know what he looks like from the photographs, he don't have a clue about you, so you got an advantage.'

'He'll have someone watching.'

'Of course. So do you: I'll ghost you.'

Callum thought of the statue. That mean "I-got-ya" grin on the Hatter, the weird fox thing lurking on Alice's right.

'OK, Mike. I'll leave my gun with you. Just in case.'

The sound of Mike ushering one of his kids away came over the line. Then he cleared his throat.

'I'll be there,' he said.

*

The beach had a healthy smattering of bodies under the afternoon Brooklyn sky. A few people dipped toes in the chilly waters. Callum sat on a bench on the boardwalk at Coney Island, looking out at the sand. At his back sat a few shacks selling franks, heros, ice-cream. Behind those were the amusement parks. He watched Kolya Slavin approach, far enough from Brighton Beach that the old man felt safe meeting a cop.

Slavin wore brown slacks and a jacket that looked too warm for the mild day. He took his flat cap off to scratch his healthy head of white hair. As he sat, his mustache twitched.

He said, 'You look tired, Irishman. You don't sleep since the bathhouse?'

'It's just the light,' said Callum. 'You look good. Maybe you could trim that caterpillar on your lip, but besides that...' He sat back on the bench like he was taking in the cut of the man, then said, 'You put on some weight?' Slavin looked as scrawny as he had naked in the bathhouse but Callum leaned over, unzipped the old man's coat and put his hand on the small pot belly, jiggling it playfully. He ran his hands over Slavin's torso.

Slavin waited until Callum was finished and said, 'Satisfied?'

'You'll do.'

Callum had frisked the man well enough.

A woman cooing into a baby carriage nearby began fussing with a blanket. A man stood at a snack shack behind their bench, sipping something from a paper cup. A gull screamed overhead. Callum shook a cigarette from his pack and lit up with the Zippo.

'You still don't trust me?' said Slavin.

'You were a cop: those bastards are some of the most untrustworthy assholes I know.'

Slavin chuckled. 'Why is your nose like a shovel?'

Callum exhaled smoke. 'You mean it looks like someone hit it with a shovel.'

'No, I mean it is flattened like a shovel.'

'It was broken a couple of times.'

'Ah,' said Slavin, like he remembered some indisputable fact. He nodded in self-confirmation. 'Fighting Irish.'

'You wanna be careful believing stereotypes.'

'But you fight.'

'I do some boxing.'

'That would require *you* hit your *opponent,* no?'

'You should see the other fella,' said Callum. 'Look, it's great to catch up and all, but there's stuff I could be doing right now.'

'Do you like being a policeman?'

'It's probably been a while for you but the way it works, the cop usually asks the questions. Like, "why did you want to meet"?'

Something hard and dark slid behind the old man's gaze, like a shark's black eyes with blood in the water. For a second Callum felt a sea breeze ripple across his shoulders. His smoker's cough made him shudder.

Slavin said, 'It has been a while since *I* was a policeman. It has been a while since I sat in a Moscow police car holding an AKR submachine gun in one hand and my balls in the other, screeching through the Golyanovo district with lights blazing, stopping for nothing and no one. That was what we called a patrol, back then.' His jaw worked as though he were chewing the memories. 'Undermanned and underequipped. The *Mineralny Sekretar* hadn't helped before, but it got worse under Yeltsin.'

Callum looked at the lady still fussing at the pram as he said, '*Mineralny Sekretar*?'

'Gorbachev. Under his direction, the Party's Central Committee issued a resolution on "Measures to Overcome Alcoholism". It was like American Prohibition. As alcohol became more scarce and expensive, the gangsters stepped in to meet demand for those who couldn't afford to buy their drink at the stores.' Slavin looked at his hands. 'You have a gun,' he said, 'but much of the time – from the late years of Gorbachev into Yeltsin's *bespredel* – in the MVD, our best weapons were our heads. They had to be. We used old revolvers; the criminals had state-of-the-art weaponry. We didn't have enough bullets. The radios didn't work in our cars. Some of our men were reduced to tailing suspects by bus. By bus! Can you imagine?' He laughed, hard and bitter. 'A few years ago, there was a shoot-out in Moscow between Vory and MVD. A policeman was killed. Two rounds pierced his "bullet-proof" vest. And for this, we were paid $30 a month.'

Callum finished his smoke. He crossed his arms and looked at the slow churn of the water in the distance.

'But you came here,' he said. 'You paid a bribe for false documents to get in here. On $30-a-month.'

The old man smiled and there was real warmth in his grin.

'What do some Americans say? Homo Sovieticus? The sly Russians; the untrustworthy Russians; the corrupt Russians.'

'I'm not American.'

'No, you are not,' said Slavin. 'Are you paid well for the job you do?'

'More than $30-a-month – but I ain't booking a foreign trip anytime soon ...'

'The MVD once had social perks, like special housing for policemen's families. Then we all realised the state was broke and many police families had to live hand-to-mouth. I knew men with two, three or more children existing in a filthy communal hostel, waiting years on an apartment. So there was corruption, yes.'

Callum said, 'What did you do?'

'Took a few bribes from speeding drivers. But the main source of cash was the media. They wanted to ride in our cars with us for their newspaper stories. Many foreign journalists were desperate to report on the sorry state of once-mighty Russian society. We charged them thousands of dollars for the privelege. Some of the money went into buying better equipment to keep us alive on patrol. Some went into our pockets.'

'Don't know if I can blame you.'

'I think not, when one considers your own, NYPD "Dirty Thirty". How many cops were arrested in Harlem?'

'A lot more than were convicted.'

'Don't worry, I don't pass judgement. I have read up on the NYPD. The rank, the equipment. This city – it must be impossible to police.'

Callum noticed the lady with the baby carriage was gone. He glanced to his right and saw the man at the snack shack was still standing with his drink. He turned and looked at Kolya Slavin. The sad eyes, the wrinkled face, the scrawny body. Slavin was in decent shape for an old man. His hands looked young, he had a spry glint in his eyes.

Callum said, 'How old are you?'

'Fifty-nine.'

'Jesus.'

'A hard life. But at least my nose is not squashed like a flattened *kolbasa*.'

Callum watched as the guy at the snack shack walked off.

'Yeah,' he said, 'it gives me character. So, why am I here?'

Slavin said, 'I am old before my time. Not just my looks but my scars – they hurt in the cold winters. I want to help you, give you information so you can lock up the poison in Brighton Beach that gave them to me. Give the people who live here the neighborhood they deserve.'

'You want to be a CI?'

'An informant. Yes.'

'But you aren't a criminal. You don't move in their world.'

'I am in Brighton Beach, I am in their world. I can get close to Maxim Volkov through the bathhouse. I am an old man wandering the streets. People don't notice me. I was a policeman so I know what to look for.'

'You want paid?'

Slavin sat back a little on the bench and appraised Callum.

'Has anyone ever said no to that question?'

Callum shrugged. Slavin was right for CI in many ways. He could be discreet; he could fit most places. If nothing else, he might be another pair of eyes on Avda Galkin.

But Callum still wasn't convinced.

Don't get paranoid, he thought. Had enough of that undercover a couple of years ago. Ladies with baby carriages are just mothers strolling the boardwalk; guys grabbing a coffee are just citizens at a loose end. An old geezer wants to stop bad men doing bad things in his neighborhood could be just that.

He said, 'Call me when you have something interesting and I'll see. In the meantime, I'll look into putting you on the payroll.'

'But off the register,' said Slavin, his face hard. 'I don't want to be on a record or some such. Even if we have some codename for me, only you and I know it. Nothing on paper. If Maxim Volkov had an inkling I was informing to the police, he would take me apart.'

'I'll see what I can do,' said Callum. 'You got a safe number I can reach you at?'

Slavin handed him a crumpled piece of paper.

Callum stood. He was tired and now he had to drag his ass across the city to meet Avda Galkin.

'Call me,' he said. Then he walked off toward Brighton Beach and lit another cigarette, cupping the Zippo against the chill ocean breeze.

Eighteen

Arkady Kuznetsov opened the door and said, 'Tikhon, welcome.'

Tikhon didn't return the Vor's predatory smile. He took a deep breath.

Clack.

The lament of a rough male voice drifted through the doorway of Marina's house. Kuznetsov was playing *blatnye pesny* – Russian criminal songs – on a videotape on the VHS player in the lounge. He wore jeans and a black t-shirt. His belt was undone, his shoes by the stairs.

Tikhon thought he would kill Kuznetsov with his bare hands if Marina was dead – not for any sense of revenge for a lover, but because the bastard would have deprived him of an outlet to assuage his rage and fear.

Clack.

He stood on Marina's stoop and debated whether to enter her house or not. Why was Kuznetsov standing in her doorway? Tikhon had made this appointment with her yesterday. She should have been expecting him.

The answer came with the sound of her voice behind Kuznetsov.

'Come in, Tikhon. I've been waiting for you.'

Kuznetsov stood aside. Marina wore a man's shirt, her hair loose, face flushed. She was barefoot and, when she walked over to offer him a drink and take his arm, a breeze caught the shirt and he saw she was naked underneath.

'Marina, dear,' said Kuznetsov, 'why don't you go upstairs and prepare yourself? I need to talk with this man before he has you earn your dollars.'

She gave Tikhon a loaded glance, then looked at Kuznetsov and nodded before padding upstairs. The sound on the tape faded out. The singer was Villi Tokarev, an émigré to Brighton Beach whose music had become popular in the Motherland. Another song, a dark, romantic ballad, began.

Kuznetsov said, 'Marina is excellent, isn't she? I hadn't visited her for more than a year and forgot just how skilled she can be.'

'Very,' said Tikhon.

'I hope you don't mind: just before you arrive. Some men would find that insulting. To have a man open the door of the woman they are ready to fuck – it would kill the ardor of many.'

'It means nothing.'

Kuznetsov smiled again and looked at Tikhon through hooded eyes.

'No,' he said, 'I don't suppose it does.'

He walked to the couch and sat, picking up a copy of Novoye Russkoye Slove and flicking through the newspaper.

'Nothing worth reading,' he said. 'A few years ago, Yaponchik was tearing south Brooklyn apart. The cops were shitting themselves, money was flowing like piss in a gutter. Now? We have been neutered. The FBI convinced themselves – or the money men – that there was a Russian mafia in New York. The NYPD are getting a handle on the area. People in the neighborhood are beginning to suspect the police can make a difference – on a good day. The younger generation at least. Before, they wouldn't go to a cop out of fear, of them as well as us.' He shook his head.

Tikhon said nothing. He had nothing to say. This was irrelevant to him. All that mattered was killing his target in Brighton Beach – sooner or later. His personal mission. Then he would be done.

Clack. Clack.

He had a stabbing memory of the the mountains, the tracer

fire, the screaming Afghan as Dolidze the Georgian fired into the man point blank. And the KGB officer in Afghan clothes, rucksack over his back. The pistol. Four shots into Dolidze's face.

Clack. Clack. Clack.

He washed the memories out with the thought of Marina upstairs, like swilling mouthwash to kill a sour taste.

'If you're finished,' he said and made for the stairs.

Kuznetsov chuckled and stood again. 'Not one of my men would dare walk away from me. You are truly unique.' He still held the newspaper and pointed with it at Tikhon. 'I have some work for you. Tomorrow, I will meet a policeman. The cops contacted me and this man wants to ask me some questions. Not about me, about Volkov.'

Something kindled in Tikhon's eyes. Kuznetsov saw it, his own eyes narrowing in interest.

'I want someone to be there, unseen. Watch for other cops, even federals. Be sure the area is clean before I sit with this pig, keep an eye on us while we talk. From a distance. That's it. I will pay you well.'

'Why would you trust me over your own men?'

'Put most of my men on a city street and the majority of people will cross the road to avoid them. You could blend in to the surroundings a little more. At least with your clothes on – those scars on your chest are another matter. And,' Kuznetsov folded his arms, 'you are professional, I think. I don't need loyalty tomorrow, I need competence.'

'And you will deal with the police? A Vor? Might this be another reason you don't want your men around?'

Kuznetsov rubbed at his left ear where the lobe should be and bared his large teeth like the wolf in a children's fable.

He said, 'This is not Russia, the rules here are different. You will be there: yes or no?'

Tikhon looked back with eyes as dead as the wood of the table in the center of the room.

'Tell me how much you will pay. Give me the details. I will be there.'

*

Tikhon and Marina finished.

He lay back and looked at the ceiling.

'Was I good?' said Marina.

'Yes.'

'I am sorry. I didn't know he would be here. He knocked on my door an hour before you arrived. I couldn't say no.'

'It's fine.'

And it was, for the most part. The physical act was like taking a dose of medicine. But he found he couldn't open up to her today, after they fucked. It was not jealousy – she was a whore, he was a customer; Arkady Kuznetsov was her employer. But something in the balance of their moments together had altered with the presence of Kuznetsov, even if he had left before Tikhon joined Marina upstairs.

Balance.

Clack.

Tipping over.

Clack. Clack.

He was losing his equilibrium: Avda and Marina both tainted now. He thought of the gun he'd taken from the drunk in the Russian bar, locked in a closet in his apartment. A Tokarev. He would keep it there until the right moment.

Clack. Clack. Clack.

He had to complete his objective and kill the man he'd been hunting since that night in the mountains back in the war no one talked of, before he lost total control.

It had to be soon.

But first he had to deal with the policeman. He got out of bed and dressed. He had to be in Manhattan in an hour.

Nineteen

The rain started, coating the cobbles of the street with an oily gloss. Callum stood under metal sheet awning in front of an old loading bay and looked around. A couple of trucks backed up to meat wharehouses with cracked and peeling walls. Men smoked and hauled rough cuts of beef and pork. Someone walked toward the river in a sharp suit with an umbrella. A lost-looking couple tried not to be too obvious as they checked a crumpled map. Little West 12th Street in the Meatpacking District.

Avda Galkin had asked for a meet here.

Galkin appeared around the corner and approached with shoulders hunched and hands deep in jeans pockets, coat open over a pale blue and white lumberjack shirt. He could have been a student on campus. Then he closed his eyes for a second and Callum saw the tattooed lids.

Galkin joined him under the awning and looked at the slick cobbles by the curb.

'Thanks for coming,' he said.

'You call, I come,' said Callum. 'Hey, you could use that as a motto for your hustlin' business.'

Galkin looked at him with a smile weaker than a handshake from a White Shirt cop.

'Do you have a motto?' he said.

'Fortuna Audaces Juvat.'

'What does it mean?'

Callum said, 'Means I'm a big football fan. So, how's business?'

'OK. You didn't mark me when you hit me, so that's good.'

Callum said, 'You smoke?'

'Sometimes.'

'Here.'

Callum fished a pack of cigarettes from his pocket and Galkin took one. He leaned in to light up from Callum's cupped Zippo. When the tip was in the flame, Callum flashed the lighter in front of the hustler's eyes and caught his head with a side swipe of his elbow. The young man yelped and Callum put an arm around his head, covering his mouth and pulling him back until they were sitting on the lip of the disused loading bay in shadow. Avda Galkin froze like the weak kid at school playing dead with the bully. Callum closed the Zippo and leaned in close.

'You think I give a fuck about how many closet fags you been fuckin'?' he spat. 'You think I care I mighta hurt your feelin's with a slap last time we met? Here's how it works, shithead. I own you. Own you all the way. You stand here like a sullen kid brother, that don't work for me. Either I call Maxim Volkov and tell him you been takin' tea with a cop, or I drag you round back of this buildin' and beat the ever-lovin' fuck out of you. Got it?'

Galkin moaned and nodded.

'Alright, Avda, you called me. It's rainin' and I don't like this neighborhood, so what you got?'

*

Georgie Ruiz sat in the kitchen sipping a coffee while Arthur played with the kids outside. She felt detached, couldn't settle into her swing day. With each sip she felt a pressure build behind her eyes. This Goddamn job, she thought. No wonder Callum was on edge recently. O'Connell was an asshole at times, but Mike could compartmentalise, keep the best of himself for home.

Cal was like her – he couldn't switch it off.

Being a cop changed people and she couldn't imagine doing this job in three different countries – hell, three different continents – like him and not have that mess with your head some. But he was angry now. Some memory from Ireland, maybe. She couldn't relate. Whatever was there in her face when he brought up his home country told him so and he hadn't talked about it much for a long time.

She saw it in Arthur, too.

In the past, those nights she was home and Isabella and Sam settled in bed, and she and her husband lazed on the sofa or lay in bed after making love, she let him in a little about the Job. She'd moan and he'd be a goddamn man and try to fix her life singlehanded when all she wanted was for him to listen.

But she realised now she had loved him for it. And those problems had been an asshole boss or a bitching partner or a crappy detail. Then she joined Narcotics and the Job got real. She'd tell him about the violence and devastation out there. Arthur would try, his eyes searching hers, to find a way in. To get what she was saying. His forehead would crease with the damn effort. Then his eyes would glaze over a little and she'd know he was somewhere else: balancing the books for the housekeeping, thinking of what to cook for dinner for the kids tomorrow evening, when her folks would next visit.

And the less she talked about the Job, the less she talked.

And now she might lose him.

*

'The guy in the bathhouse,' said Avda Galkin. 'The one with the marks on his chest.'

Callum said, 'Bullet wounds.'

Galkin nodded. 'Right. Bullet wounds. I know who he is.'

'I'm waitin'.'

'Another hustler, like me. On Volkov's books. Never seen him before, but now I hope I do again: we could compare notes.'

Callum read false bravado in the young man's stage leer, the raised eyebrow. The hustler might be good at faking it for his paying customers, but he couldn't bluff a cop for shit.

'Oh yeah?' he said. 'So you work some of the bars and clubs, right? Like the Hellfire down here? This guy work them too?'

'Maybe. Like I said, I hadn't seen him before. Those places can get pretty busy.'

'How about the high-end clients? You service some pretty rich and powerful zipcodes: him too?'

The leer faded. 'I don't know.'

Callum folded his arms and watched a couple of guys down the street haul a rack of meat from the back of a truck. The shouts of workers echoed around the street over the ever-present hum of New York, dulled by the rain.

'You know so little about this guy, how'd you find out he was a hustler?'

Galkin glanced toward 9th Avenue to the east.

'I asked,' he said.

'Asked who?'

'I asked – ' his voice slowed, the last word trailing, ' – Volkov.'

He almost flinched when he saw Callum's face. It was obvious his lie was failing.

Callum said, 'Seems to me this guy, with his chest scars an' all, got outta that bathhouse like his arse was on fire. Like he saw someone or something he didn't like and ran. He sure as shit didn't look like he was cosy with Volkov.' Callum watched Galkin's face crumple. 'So cut the bullshit and tell me what you know.'

Galkin stared at the ground. He shifted from foot to foot.

'Alright,' Callum said. 'Don't try to bullshit me again.'

Then he faked a punch at the CI, saw him flinch, and wandered off toward the west side and the Hudson beyond peppered with rain.

Twenty

Avda left the room and wiped his lips with a crumpled tissue. The man still lying on the bed, basking in their sex, disgusted him. A fifty-six year-old father of three young children, with a huge loft apartment in SoHo and a trophy wife twenty-two years his junior. The man had refused the rented accomodation offered by the German Mission to the United Nations. Instead, he funnelled that country's taxpayers' money into paying for the shiny hardwood floors, generous views through large windows, and roof garden of an apartment on Mercer Street.

Tonight, though, he lazed in a four-poster in a discreet boutique hotel on Rector Street overlooking Trinity Episcopal Church.

Avda remembered a joke from the old days in the USSR: the worker pretends to work and the government pretends to pay him; and another, post-Soviet: The people pretend to vote and the government pretends to govern.

He slung his small pack over his shoulder and closed the room door with a soft click. His heart rate quickened and his stomach went cold. Disgusted as he was by the 'client', he felt safe in the room. Now, he was out in the wild again, left to fend for himself in the streets of this vast city so far from the place of his birth. He hadn't felt this anxiety before but, with Tikhon's ruthless violence, and the cop Burke's bullying, his nerves were shot.

Did the UN delegate have a security detail watching over him? If so, were they sworn to secrecy about his gay trysts with the scrawny Russian prostitute with the delicate face? Avda had no idea. The German was always in whatever hotel room they met beforehand.

It was Sunday night.

He had run that afternoon from Little West 12th Street, when the cop rejected the story Tikhon had concocted to stop Burke looking into his identity. A weak cover, Avda knew Burke would see through it because he knew he couldn't convince: ask him to suck the cop's cock and he could fake it like a movie star. but tell that lie and he was as transparent as the window in the hotel room. He knew Tikhon had been watching from a distance and had seen the failure. He knew Tikhon would punish him. Tikhon scared him; the cop scared him.

So Avda had run.

He hadn't stopped all day. He went to a friend's place in Chelsea and hid out until seven, when he showered and borrowed an outfit for his appointment on Rector Street with the German delegate. Now he would go to his friend in Chelsea again.

He was more alone than at any time since prison back in Russia. Even then there were rules, and a food chain within the camp. He could dream in his head and service the strong for protection. It was easier for him than some of the straight men they raped. Eas*ier*. He had almost learned to live with being brutalised. He never learned to accept it.

Today he had run because he feared both his lover and the cop. And he feared Volkov.

He wished Tikhon had already killed his prey, and satisfied his vendetta or whatever dark presence drove him. Avda wished he were someone else entirely.

Rector Street was narrow. The hotel had a European look – Baroque, perhaps. The railings of the church perched on a low brick wall opposite, a short lawn sloping up to the building. Tall stone offices and soaring skyscrapers reared high over the street at either end. It was dark, the lighting in the buildings low in the dying hours of the weekend. They scattered hulking shadows on the streets below, still greasy from the earlier rainfall.

He walked to the corner of Rector and Trinity Place, and the entrance to the Wall Street subway station. The street was empty. Downtown was quiet on a Sunday night: better to be in the subway with its ticket booths and the possibility of a random cop patrolling the platform for residual protection.

Avda was almost on the top step of the subway steps when something seized the pack slung over his shoulder and yanked him backwards. A hand clamped over his mouth and he was dragged backwards across Trinity Place. He was hauled into a recess in the side of a huge, decorative building and shoved against the wall. It had happened so fast, so efficiently, he was unsure of where he was. Only, he knew someone with great, controlled power had snatched him.

He was spun around and looked into the eyes of Tikhon. They were black sockets in the shadows.

Something sharp pressed on Avda's kidneys. It felt like the tip of a knife.

Tikhon whispered, 'Where have you been?' The Russian was cold, smooth with no malice in the intonation. The pressure of the blade increased.

'With a client for two hours over there.' He nodded in the direction of the hotel.

'Avda Galkin, do not treat me like a fool. Where did you go this afternoon?'

'For a walk.'

'You met the policeman. I was watching. He left. You looked around the street and ran. Where?'

Avda swallowed hard, fighting down a yell of panic that might push Tikhon to drive the knife home.

'To a friend,' he said. 'I wanted company.'

Tikhon stared hard with his black eyes. Avda saw his future in the gaze, the empty vacuum of death. His tears came hot and salty, his breath in ragged gasps. He wanted to slide down the wall and curl up, but the strong arms held him straight.

Tikhon said, 'Where are you going now?'

'Home.'

'No. You come with me. You can stay at my apartment. We can spend the night together. I need Saint George.' The voice was flat like a chalk outline at a murder scene.

Avda raised a hand slow as though daring to pet a fighting dog and touched Tikhon's cheek.

'I'd like that,' he said through gulps of air, 'but I'm so tired. I'll give you my key. You can come by in the morning. I'll do anything you want.'

Tikhon bent with the knife still at Avda's side and picked up the small backpack from his feet where Avda dropped it.

'You will come to my apartment. You will sleep there. I will even sing you a lullaby,' said Tikhon. 'One of the old death lullabies my mother used to sing when I was a child. Before I died again and again in the mountains of Afghanistan.'

*

They got to the apartment around one. Brighton Beach was a ghost town at that hour, on the turn from the weekend to the nine-to-five. As they entered Tikhon's building, Avda heard the shushing of the ocean.

He had gone like a lamb.

He was terrified. He knew now of what Tikhon was capable. They had rarely spoken of the war but it was there in his lover's eyes. Something had soldered Tikhon's emotions closed to those around him. Avda had walked down the steps to the subway with a knife at his back; had sat in the car of the Q, then R trains with the blade at his side. Now he lay naked on the bed while his sometime lover made coffee.

Tikhon wore a t-shirt and boxer shorts. They had not had sex. Instead, Tikhon had insisted Avda strip, then went to the kitchenette to make coffee. The apartment was one large room with a bed at the end, a kitchen area along one wall and an open space with a couch, a chair and a table. There was no TV.

It was now almost two in the morning.

When the brew was finished, Avda sat on the bed and covered himself with the sheet. He looked at his backpack, lying in the corner by the kitchenette.

Tikhon spoke with slow, deliberate Russian. 'Tell me about the man you were with tonight.'

Avda sipped the bitter coffee. It bolstered him.

'He is a German delegate to the United Nations.'

'How often do you meet him?'

'Once, sometimes twice a month.'

'Does he know you are Russian?'

'He thinks I'm Polish. He books me through an agency Volkov staffs with Ukrainians, Polish, some Czechs.'

'Does he frighten you?'

Avda snorted. 'He disgusts me. But the situation scares me sometimes, yes. He is a rich and powerful man. He has a family. If it were made public that he pays men for sex, it could be very difficult for me.'

Tikhon nodded. They had discussed some of these clients before during the few scraps of chat before or after sex.

'And in which area does he work within the United Nations?'

'The Security Council. The Germans want a permanent seat.'

'Does he have any security detail – bodyguards?'

'Perhaps, but I have never seen anyone and he doesn't talk about it.'

'Does he talk?'

'He tells me I'm beautiful, makes jokes, says dirty things. He never mentions his work or family.'

Again Tikhon nodded.

'You fuck other UN staff?'

'Yes, an Italian and a Britisher.'

'Are they involved with security?'

'The Englishman is an aide. He works in economics and trade. He has a lot of money and comes from a powerful family but I think he is lazy. His position is not so important.'

'Does he talk about his job?'

'Just bitchiness about colleagues,' said Avda, 'and citicising America. He is single.'

Tikhon sipped his coffee and said, 'Tell me about the Italian.'

Avda raised his eyebrows. 'He is gorgeous. Younger. He is not one of the more important staff, more like an office worker. He has a fiancee back in Turin. We met at a club and I told him I was professional. He didn't mind. I think he is lonely.'

'In what area does he work?'

'Agriculture.'

They sat and drank in silence for a while.

After they finished and Tikhon rinsed the cups in the sink, he sat next to Avda on the bed. He put a hand on Avda's leg. They had discussed the cop, Burke, how he had rejected the cover story concocted by Tikhon that afternoon.

Tikhon said, 'The policeman, Burke, still knows nothing about me?'

'Nothing,' said Avda with eagerness.

'The other cop, O'Connell, who met you before – he knew your hangouts, your routine, so they could be watching you. They have my description now from Burke.'

'So what shall we do?'

'You will stay here for a while.'

Avda felt a cold plunge down his spine like falling mercury in a thermometer. He ran his tongue around his mouth gone dry and said, 'I need to work. My things are in my apartment. I had a date for lunch with a friend.'

'Meaningless now. I am so close to the end. You have helped

me all the way – I know you want to see this through to its conclusion.' Tikhon pulled his t-shirt up and over his head. 'Besides, were Maxim Volkov to hear of how you have been helping me work to destroy him, your life here would be finished.'

Avda hung his head. He had no one to blame but himself. He had let his emotions run riot with this beautiful, damaged man and his tragic scars, his hard body and his huge inner darkness. Now that darkness would consume Avda. He was trapped.

A great weight of hopeless exhaustion fell upon him. Tikhon ran his hands over Avda's body.

Avda said, 'I'm sorry, I'm so tired. May I sleep?'

Tikhon nodded.

He began to sing an old Russian death lullaby. His voice was soft but clear and sweet.

'Bye-bye, bye-bye,
Quickly die.
In the morning will be frost
And you'll go to the graveyard.
Grandfather will come
And will bring the coffin.
Grandmother will come
And will bring the shroud.
Mother will come
And will sing the prayer song.
Father will come
And will take you to the cold, dark earth.'

Twenty-One

Callum, Georgie and Mike sat in a booth in an all-night coffee shop two blocks from Georgie's house in Astoria. Her kids were in bed. Her husband, Arthur, sat fretting and fuming at her absence. The street outside lay quiet save for the occasional rumble of a train on the N and W el-tracks nearby.

Georgie had called Mike and Callum and asked that they meet up for a Sunday night coffee at the bakery café by the station on 31st and Broadway. It was 2300. In a few hours, the smell of fresh baked bread would fill the shop. But now it was just the three cops and a guy reading Newsweek behind the counter, ignoring the TV playing quietly on a shelf in the corner.

Georgie was studying her tea like the leaves held the secrets of the universe.

'You OK?' said Callum.

'Sure,' she said. Her voice was sharp.

Callum figured Arthur heard that voice a lot these days.

She looked at him, saw she'd cut with her tone, and said, 'Sorry, it's just Arthur. He's pissed I'm here this time of night on a swing day.'

'Believe me, I understand,' said Mike.

Ruiz didn't know much about Mike's wife. She didn't know about the delicate balance of their marriage, the destruction wrought by the job on their family.

She said, her voice hard, 'So I gotta hold my husband's hand because he's an emotional cripple, instead of doing my job?' She turned her cup around in her hands. They were shaking a little. 'Anyway, Mike, if you say it's OK, I'll put this down as hours worked. I need the overtime. Regular pay won't cut it right now.'

Mike said, 'I can live with that.'

Georgie's eyes glazed wet with a red tinge. Her lips scrunched, then twisted and trembled. She lost it, a sob took her. She cried hard but quiet. Mike gave Callum a look. For him, this was agony. He couldn't offer her a shred of TLC – it wasn't in his DNA. Callum sat feeling like shit and running through options in his head of what the hell was going on with his friend.

After a minute, Georgie wiped her face with her sleeve. When she looked up, she seemed all broken but, Callum thought, more beautiful than ever.

She said, 'Arthur is sick.'

Callum said, 'How sick?'

'I don't know. First off, he got arthritis. Not just a couple of aches and pains, this is going to be crippling in a while. How you gonna drive a bus when it's agony to move your arms?'

Mike said, 'Ah shit.'

'Yeah. There's this doctor, thinks they can ease the pain for him – ease it, not cure it, with gold injections. Gold. You know how expensive that is?'

Callum said, 'I can imagine.'

Ruiz took a sip of tea and sniffed. Her voice was hoarse and thick when she spoke.

'I can't take time off. I need to work and I need overtime. I got a few years to my 20 and, even then, I'm gonna have to keep workin'. I figure my street time is limited – I can't work shifts when things get worse, and they will. So I don't want vacation, I don't want anything in a report that some boss might find and force me to take a 28. I got to work.' She looked at the table. 'He might have cancer.'

Callum was so enrapt in Georgie he almost asked who she was talking about.

'Christ,' said Mike.

'Arthur gets forgetful. He blacks out sometimes. He gets these headaches, short but real painful. He's tired all the time. They said it could be a brain tumor.'

'Could be,' said Callum. 'They aren't sure.'

'No.'

She looked at him and part of him cracked and splintered inside. He never wanted to help anyone more than at that moment, and he never felt less useful.

Georgie said, 'Sorry, Cal.'

Callum gaped. 'What? No, you don't – '

'I stayed over in your place. I just needed a night away. I dunno, I couldn't handle going home. I got drunk at Patrosi's racket. I was all over you. All that sloppy *I love you* crap.'

'Hey, you're only human,' he said.

She smiled and it was bleak and fragile. Her voice broke again.

'I don't know what we're gonna do.'

'I tell you what I'm gonna do,' said Mike. He sat back in the booth and drew circles on the table with his finger. 'I'm gonna order you to stay home tomorrow and Tuesday.' He raised his hand to stop her protesting. 'Shut the fuck up. You're off the books and you stay that way. You do a little creative writin' when the kids go to bed and put some surveillance reports together – general shit can't be followed up. I'll type your DARs each day. Callum's due to meet Avda 1200 on Tuesday – I'll be there watchin'. You, Detective Ruiz, sit on your ass at home and I'll call you Tuesday night. Then we'll see if you can come back Wednesday.'

Georgie wiped her face again and concentrated hard on her cup. She frowned. Callum knew she liked doing things right – the idea of fudging reports and cutting class didn't sit easy with her.

But after ten seconds she said, 'Thank you, Mike.'

Mike grunted, 'Alright, now get the fuck out of here and get some sleep with that man of yours.'

Georgie stood. She eased out of the booth and said goodnight. She took three steps when Callum called her name.

She said, 'Yeah?'

Callum smiled and gave her a wink.

Then he said, 'I love you, Georgie.'

She nodded and walked away.

*

'I love you,' said Mike as they stood under the el-train station. 'You fuckin' sap.'

Callum shrugged. 'I been readin' Men Are From Mars.'

It was close to midnight. Mike offered Callum a ride to the Village on his way home.

'I'll take the train,' said Callum. 'I ain't tired and the the ride will help me think.'

'Yeah, that's some tragic shit Ruiz got goin' on.'

Callum thought of the shitstorm Mike would catch if anyone found out he gave Georgie paid-up overtime for a couple of days at home, and faked her daily activity reports.

'You're a good man, Mike.'

'I'm a dead man, I don't get home before one. And you look like shit. Go sleep. You got your meet with Arkady Kuznetsov tomorrow in Long Island City.'

'Alright.' Callum slapped Mike on the arm. 'I'll see you.'

'And no stoppin' for a nightcap, shithead. You ain't gettin' any younger.'

*

But Callum did stop for a drink.

He wanted to calm the dull ache had started in his head, drilling into his skull just above his ear. To dampen the fury clawing its way up from his belly. He wanted to wash away Jimmy Gilliland, lying with half his head missing from a terrorist's sniper round on a Belfast street. Over ten years ago but the memory was as sharp and strong as the Bushmills he drank with a brace of beers. Each shot seemed to stoke the angry fire some more, like oil on flames.

And now Arthur Ruiz was sick, and Georgie couldn't work, and the world stank worse than the toilet in the corner of this dive bar on East 5th and Avenue A.

He left before he started tearing the place up and staggered back to Bleecker.

Next thing he knew, it was morning and he was lying on the couch and the TV was still on.

He got up, stretched out some kinks and went to bed for another couple of hours before he had to shower and go meet a Russian mobster across the river.

Twenty-Two

Something huge and powerful was churning the earth nearby. The area by the waterfront in Long Island City was being torn up and re-laid as Gantry State Park. Midtown Manhattan, across the East River, watched on as the docks were flattened and re-planed. The great steel frames of the transfer bridges and gantries on the piers would stand as a nod to the industrial heritage of the neighborhood, but the clutter and detritus of the working men's tools, buildings and workshops would be cleared for gleaming towers of commerce and riverfront apartments. In a couple of years, investment brokers and media types would be sipping lattes, rather than dockers munching on sandwiches.

Callum sat on a stone bollard across from a fence screening the construction.

He checked the street again.

Twenty yards to the south, a gate in the fence led into the construction area. A couple of workers stood around talking and smoking. The same distance away, on Callum's side of the street, Mike O'Connell sat in a Buick LeSabre. An empty industrial building lay behind Callum. To the north, a bum was propped against the fence cradling a bottle in a brown paper bag. Occasionally he stirred and took a swig. Further on was the Pepsi bottling plant with its giant neon sign.

Callum lit a smoke. A silver Mercedes swung onto the street forty yards to the north and pulled up by the curb. Three men got out of the car. Two wore leather jackets, one a Nike top and sweatpants.

Mike had suggested Callum use a cell phone the NYPD had developed that acted as a listening device. He'd seen them on a couple of Buy & Busts. But he knew in himself he'd be too on edge. His eyes were his tell and he was already tired and cranky after last night's drinking. He was off the books – so was this conversation.

Unless Mike had wired the location somehow. You never knew with Mike.

The men from the Mercedes walked down the street. Two of them would be the bodyguards, thought Callum, but the man in sweatpants wasn't like his companions. He didn't have the bulky, steroidal frame or fuck-you attitude in his step.

One of the construction guys was still at the gate. The bum twitched across the street. Mike sat tight in the LeSabre. The men reached Callum and the man in sweatpants matched his clothes to O'Connell's briefing, leaned forward and offered a hand.

He said, 'I am Arkady Kuznetsov.'

Callum held his cigarette in his right hand, kept his left in his pocket.

The leather-jacketed goons glared. Kuznetsov smiled, unleashing large, domino-sized teeth below a trimmed mustache. He gestured for Callum to walk to the Mercedes.

Callum said, 'I don't feel like going for a ride.'

Kuznetsov shrugged. 'Fine, have a good day.' His accent was light with a tang of American in the rhotic 'r's' and strained vowels.

Callum glanced at the contruction worker, at the bum.

He said, 'A walk would be good, though.'

He shoved his smoke between his lips, and his right hand in his pocket, then stood.

Kuznetsov gave him an approving look.

'OK,' he said.

*

They stood looking over a pier south of the gantries. The leather jackets had frisked Callum and pronounced him clean. All they found was the outline of his badge, hung on a chain around his neck below his t-shirt, and a switched off radio. He flashed the tin and they were satisfied. A helicopter flew over UN Plaza across the river.

'I have never been here,' said Kuznetsov. 'The view is like a movie. Like The Devil's Own – did you see that? It was in the theaters last month.'

Callum spat. 'Jesus Christ,' he said, 'that piece of shit's like a fuckin' comic book. Brad Pitt sounds like he's retarded.'

Kuznetsov looked him over. 'Your accent. You are Irish?'

'Born and bred in Belfast.' Callum cocked a thumb at the panorama across the river. 'Got a favourite building?'

Kuznetsov smiled. 'I like the Chrysler. It could almost be European, you know? And some of the old skyscrapers down-town. You?'

'I don't know why, but I dig the Citicorp building. Maybe it's because we drank a lot of Chock full o'Nuts in my old precinct.'

Kuznetsov was relaxed, more approachable than most White Shirts in the NYPD.

Trish Alexander came to Callum's mind: she'd probably quote Corinthians – *the Devil disguises himself as an angel of light.* Callum lit up another cigarette. He didn't offer one to Kuznetsov.

He said, 'You know why I'm here?'

'You think we can talk business.'

'I got no business with you. But there could be people you know, I need to get in touch with.'

'I'm listening.'

Callum thought about a light starter before the main course. He'd called Avda Galkin before taking the train to Queens but no one picked up. It was probably nothing, the kid sleeping off a late night. But still, things were moving – Beresford and Mayhew murdered; Volkov's connection with Nikolai Popov; the mystery man from the sauna ...

He said, 'You know a young man called Avda Galkin? He's a male prostitute, lives in Brighton Beach.'

'No.'

'You sure? He works for Maxim Volkov. Could be, I could use him to bust Volkov's prostitution business. You won't cry any tears over that.'

'You work Public Morals?'

'Narcotics, but I got a lot of friends.'

'And why is a Narcotics policeman interested in a hustler?'

'When you need to know that, I'll send the answer on a post-card. You want to hurt Volkov or not?'

Kuznetsov looked across the river and ran a finger down the narrow ridge of his nose.

'This city,' he said, 'is incredible. Compared to St Petersburg it looks like a child's Lego set, but never mind.'

He turned to Callum and flashed those piano-key teeth.

'It is a shit-hole. We know this – you and me. We are not American, we just suck at the tit. Much as he is an asshole, Maxim Volkov is the same.'

Callum watched a barge heading toward Randall's Island and Hell Gate.

'You're a Vor, huh? Can't be seen to cooperate with the authorities, even against your rival.'

'Yes, I cannot work with the police.'

'No,' said Callum. 'You can't be *seen* to work with me. You're standing here now breathin' my smoke, you hypocritical piece of shit.'

Kuznetsov laughed. His men glanced over.

'Tell me more about this Avda Galkin.'

'He looks young, like early twenties, but could be older.

Delicate. Dark brown eyes and hair, tattoos on his eyelids. I heard he services some of the great and good over there.' He nodded at Manhattan. 'Upper East Side, Midtown, you get the picture. Men wouldn't be too thrilled if word got out they were bangin' some street kid for cash.'

'Just ask Jimmy Swaggart,' said Kuznetsov.

'We're more in Barney Frank territory here.'

Kuznetsov looked at Callum for a couple of seconds. There was something in those eyes seemed to be trying to get out.

'Who knows,' said Kuznetsov, 'even the assholes want to run the world over there could be paying young men for it.' He cocked his thumb across the East River toward UN Plaza. After a couple of seconds, he said, 'But I don't know this Avda Galkin. Sorry.'

Another helicopter flew overhead, this one an NYPD chopper. The insidious, husky whisper of the city churned on. Callum looked at the UN Building and the pall of tobacco-stained air hanging over Manhattan Island.

He said, 'Volkov was in the military, right? How about you?'

'No, I am a Vo – '

'Yeah, a Vor, I got it. You know anything about Volkov's time in the army? Military record, anything unusual?'

'No. Many immigrants come to the United States. Most leave their old lives back in the land of their birth. Volkov has left some things behind, too, I'm sure. It's why immigrants are always drinking and remembering.'

'You got that right.'

Callum finished his smoke and flicked the butt toward the river. It landed on the pier and smouldered on the damp stone. He turned and looked straight at Arkady Kuznetsov.

'I'm lookin' for another man. About my height, slim but solid-looking, like he can take care of himself. Gray eyes, dirty-fair hair cut kinda' military. Like a crew-cut. He got high cheekbones, like this.' Callum gestured with his fingers at his own face. 'Straight nose, thin, not all busted like mine. Lips are on the thick side.'

He watched Kuznetsov. The man's face was as cold and hard as the cobbles at their feet.

'No tattoos. This guy may not be a criminal at all, least not in the sense of what the Feds believe constitutes a Russian gangster.'

Kuznetsov's lip, shaded by the mustache, was pulled tight over his teeth. No smile. No message in the eyes. His face was a death mask.

'And,' said Callum, 'he got a bunch of scars on his chest, like little puckered holes. Bullet wounds. You know who I'm talkin' about?'

'No.'

'This guy, he looks kinda military, like he's old enough to have served in Afghanistan. Volkov was military, and could have served in Afghanistan too. See, this mystery guy turned up in a Russian bathhouse in Brighton Beach when Volkov was holdin' a pow-wow with some heavies. Our mystery man appeared outta nowhere, took a look around, then disappeared with a couple of Volkov's goons on his tail.'

Kuznetsov's stare was so hard he could have been stuck on a plinth and covered in pigeon shit.

'I was figurin' he didn't look like he was on Volkov's books. Maybe he was there for a hit and he found the place too crowded? I was there – maybe he knew I was a cop and hesitated. But, see, the only reasons I got so far why he would even be interested in Maxim Volkov is revenge; or he works for you, and you're tryin' to cut down the competition.'

Kuznetsov said, 'This conversation is over.'

He turned to leave. Callum grabbed his sleeve. Kuznetsov turned and glared, his teeth bared below his mustache. He barked a command in Russian and a fleck of spit hit Callum's cheek as the two goons snapped to and moved in. Callum felt his heart follow suit and make a break for it against his chest. He put his hand to his chest and pulled his badge from under his t-shirt on the chain around his neck. He ripped the razor blade taped behind the leather and tin clean off. The goons froze. In a second the razor hovered at Kuznetsov's jugular.

'Stay the fuck back!' spat Callum. 'I got the cavalry up the street and a blade at your boss's neck. Go on! Fuck off!'

Kuznetsov gestured for his men to step back. Callum hooked his arm around Kuznetsov's throat with the blade next to the skin. He fished his radio out of his pocket with his free hand. He fumbled, cursed, got it turned on. He buzzed Mike to come pick him up. The goons hung back with hunched shoulders and arms by their sides like jackhammers waiting to begin pounding. When the LeSabre drove into view, Callum shoved Kuznetsov forward. He looked at the goons.

'That's my boss in the car,' he said, 'with his .38 Service-Six, and my Glock. You ladies might want to crawl back to whatever south Brooklyn hole you came out of now.'

He turned to Arkady Kuznetsov as Mike pulled up.

'This is for you,' said Callum, offering a card with his name and an NYPD contact number. He felt a stab of shame when he saw how much his hand shook. 'You remember anything about Mystery Man, you give me a call.'

Kuznetsov looked at him as though he were checking his morning bowel movement in the the bowl.

He snorted.

He spat.

But before he turned and walked north towards his Mercedes, he took the card.

Twenty-Three

Callum jumped in the LeSabre and turned on Mike.

'You goddamn son of a bitch, you set me up, you fuck!'

Mike said, 'Take it easy, Officer Burke, before you say something you might regret.'

'Regret? You wanna know what I regret?'

Mike gunned the car and flapped his hand at Callum like he was nagging.

Callum said, 'I regret – '

Mike punched him on the shoulder. Not hard, just a jab, but it was like 20,000 volts through his system to Callum.

Mike gunned the car east through Hunters Point. Low-level buildings, parking garages, auto body shops sped by. Across Vernon Boulevard, both men stewing in their thoughts. On Jackson Avenue they swung left. Callum grabbed his Glock in its hip holster from the door pocket where Mike had wedged it. He taped the razor blade back on the back of his badge.

They came to the el-train, its pillars on either side of the Avenue like massive gateposts. O'Connell swung the LeSabre off the street into a complex of empty industrial shells. It looked like a strategic explosion at a paint factory. Every inch of the walls was covered in lettering, paintings, stencils in multi-colors. There were Keith Haring knock-offs, cartoon characters, shit looked like gang tags. Someone had slapped up a cartoon John McClane in a Knicks shirt.

The Fun Factory, at 45-46 Davis Street.

They climbed out of the Buick.

Neither spoke for a beat. The ride had calmed the initial storm.

Then Mike said, 'Look at that.' He smiled. 'That's why you gotta love New York. Every inch put to use. The whole fuckin' city is a work of performance art, y'know. But we lose the people give it life, it might as well be a suburb in goddamn Jersey. That's the way it's goin'.'

'City Hall would call it progress.'

'If it don't add a few zeros on a spreadsheet, City Hall ain't interested.'

Callum said, 'You should have told me the Feds were watchin' us. Kuznetsov probably made them. If I hadn't moved the meet, he'd have thought I was settin' him up.'

Mike looked tired. He folded his arms on the roof of the car and laid his chin on top.

'How'd you make them?'

'The morons at the meet site. You got a construction worker with spotless jeans and a bum with Oxford-fuckin'-shoes. Had to be Feds: cops woulda dirtied-up for the job.'

Mike nodded.

'Same as the idiots used to watch Gigante's place. The "Chin" made one of 'em was dressed up as a hobo 'cause the asshole had polished his boots.'

Callum yawned. Jesus, he was beat.

'They got the dough, they run the show, Cal. They called me yesterday to find out what my next play was. I lie to them, I could lose my job, so ...'

Callum said, 'If they're all over this, don't they got taps on Volkov? They gotta be up on his phones.'

'The asshole don't do business on the phone. Instead, he calls meets in places like that bathhouse you were sweatin' in.'

Callum thought of the bullet-scarred man in the sauna.

'We tried our Mystery Man in the department databases, right?'

They had fed descriptions of the bullet-scarred man through

the NYPD system. Nothing. Ditto for NYSPIN, the Staties' database.

'Way ahead of you,' said Mike. 'I had the Feds try. NCIC, everythin'. No hits. They ain't takin' him seriously, figure he's some loser owed Volkov money or some shit.'

They leaned on the roof of the car. Someone was in a third-floor window in the building ahead with their back to them. Probably with a mask and a box of spray paints, thought Callum. In years to come, this spot could be listed in the National Register of Historic Places.

He thought of Avda Galkin, the Russian criminals and their crude body art. Avda visiting high-end addresses in midtown to service clients. Kuznetsov gesturing across the East River a short time ago.

He said, 'The Feds are working an angle on the United Nations, right?'

Mike smiled. 'You can be a sharp motherfucker when you feel like it, Cal. Riff on it, let's see what you got.'

'Maxim Volkov runs hookers, hustlers – same as any name with a game. But you got the Feds giving him special attention over Arkady Kuznetsov because his hustler – Avda Galkin – is screwin' some people work at UN Plaza. Galkin probably acts as a courier deliverin' Volkov's heroin to them, too.'

Callum stared at the building opposite.

'I figure Avda screws these diplomats, envoys, whatever they are and, somehow, he gets compromising material on their gay sex and drugs kick. Volkov uses the material to, what, blackmail them?'

'Maybe,' said Mike. 'Or maybe he don't give a shit. But the Feds wanna be sure so they're diggin'.'

Callum snorted. 'I saw Volkov in the bathhouse. Give him an Italian, or Irish, or Albanian name and he's the same as any asshole been running rackets and breakin' legs in this city for decades. Tell me the Feds don't think he's a spy.'

'Fact is,' said Mike, 'they know he's just a hood on a good thing who won't burn his bridges by compromising his customer base. But they're bored watchin' the Russkie's diplomatic compound up in the Bronx; and someone's gotta burn up those taxpayer dollars. Besides, it's just possible Volkov could be using the hustler and heroin angle to wring some money outta these UN idiots.'

'And the drugs,' said Callum, 'come from Afghanistan?'

Mike gave him a *who knows?* look. 'That bust on Nikolai Popov? We're gonna test a sample of the product. London's in the right direction. Could be the heroin comes from Afghanistan through a European route.'

'And if Volkov was in the Afghan War, he uses some old contact from those days to secure product for his New York operation.'

They stood for a while looking at the technicolor buildings.

Then Callum said, 'So the Feds know me and Georgie are working this.'

Mike slapped the Buick's roof.

'You're insulated. This is on your record as an Organized Crime detail, on loan from Narcotics. I have control, I can cover Ruiz for a few days like I said. You moved location with Kuznetsov today, no problem. I write it up you were compromised and took the meet elsewhere. They had the spot you met him miked. Fuck 'em. You tell me what went down. Like the old days.' Mike shrugged. 'Look, I ain't on their team, so to speak. This ain't a task force like before where we're on equal terms, on paper anyway. More I'm kinda like their office boy. They give me shit to do, I report back. You and Ruiz help me do it. I'm peripheral. They fuckin' use me.' He faltered. 'I saw you tape that razor blade to your badge in the car – that what you had at Kuznetsov's throat when I drove up?'

'His dogs were gettin' restless.'

'Hey, no problem. Whatever gets the job done. Just a little...'
'What?'
'Dramatic. But it's all good.'

Callum said, 'How about I come take a piss on your lawn next BBQ, right in front of Marcie? Give you some real drama, you bogtrottin' prick?'

'Takes one to know one,' said Mike. 'Come on, let's grab some lunch and you can tell me what went down with Kuznetsov before I came chargin' in and saved your skinny white ass.'

*

Callum went to the Six-oh around 1500.

He and Mike had chewed the fat of the Kuznetsov meet over a couple of falafels could have fed the five thousand. They had both figured Kuznetsov at least suspected Volkov's UN angle. Most criminals knew of a rival's business concerns in neighborhoods defined by an ethnicity, nationality or cultural identity. It was a small world within a small world. The nod to the United Nations building across the river had been a tip-off. Callum thought Kuznetsov knew who Mystery Man was, too. He clammed up too fast, got way too defensive too early.

The two cops split after the meal, Callum to check in on the Narcotics team at the 60th Precinct, Mike to write reports and figure out how to appease the Feds after Callum ditched their surveillance.

Callum walked down the stairs in the Six-oh past a bored-looking duty sergeant and found Trish in the locker room alone. She had her head bent in front of a mirror on the wall, her face cupped in her hands.

He said, 'Trish, are you OK?'

She looked around, wide-eyed for a second.

'Just tired is all,' she hissed, 'and lay off, Callum. Someone walks in here and you're giving me TLC, the whole precinct's gonna suspect we got a thing going. I don't need that right now.'

'What, I can't express concern for a fellow cop?'

'Put your hand down – you aren't touching me, any more than you would Gerry Martin if he took a shot.'

Callum looked at her and saw eyes hard and cold. Then something in his look stung her. Her eyes softened and she checked the doorway was empty.

Trish said, 'You free tonight?'

'Sure.'

'You wanna rent a movie?'

'My place?'

'I'll call you after.'

She smiled and suddenly she was a different person, like she slipped off a uniform.

'I still got this ugly bruise under my eye,' she said. 'Guess it makes me look more skanky for the Buy and Busts.'

'Hey, I don't care if you got a high-top fade or a Hanson cut, you're still the most beautiful woman out there.'

She shot him a stern look and raised a finger. Then she shook her head, cocked her hip and said, 'The team're doing paperwork upstairs, a couple are at central booking. So get outta here and do whatever secret squirrel nonsense you're in the middle of. I'll tell Sarge you called in.'

'I'll see you tonight.'

She nodded, turned her face to the mirror and probed at her bruise with a long, slim finger.

*

He hit the Village. It was too early for a drink and he wanted to stay sober for tonight, so he trawled a couple of cafes west of Hudson Street. Crazy idea, but he hoped he might sight Avda

Galkin in a bar or restaurant window. He glimpsed the twin towers of the World Trade Center down the straight shot avenues when he crossed, the skyscrapers of Midtown to the north.

He bought a Village Voice in a tobacconist's and sat at a sidewalk table with a Vietnamese coffee and a fresh pack of cigarettes. He'd quit next time he got a chunk of leave – maybe when he booked a Greyhound to Cleveland and visited with Irene and Tara. It was time. He'd been working and drinking in the city like a backpacker just discovered the wider world out there for long enough. Now he had a shot at something real with Trish. What? He didn't have a clue, but something. So he had to get out there and talk it over with Irene. And he missed Tara. He missed the joy of being her daddy.

He saw in Mike the pressure valve – call it an escape route – of family. When cop-life began to burn away the world above, where the citizens lived, Mike could remember the wife and kids waiting back home. It kept Georgie grounded, too, and he felt a cold spike of fear for her. If Arthur passed, how would she cope? She had always resisted the callouses that formed as a street cop: the fact that, when you spent so much of your life in a dance with the worst people, you lost some of what made you good. It was a weird dichotomy: so many cops lost faith in humanity because they existed amongst its worst. But show a cop a person in trouble, and most he knew would run into a collapsing building without a lot of thought.

He looked at the pages of the Voice without reading much. His head switched thoughts like a finger on a remote. Irene and Tara, Mike, Georgie, Trish, the Russians' tattoos, the Fun Factory buildings smothered in art out in Queens.

His beeper went off.

He jumped and dropped his smoke, peppering his coffee with ash, and said, 'Shit!'

*

The number was that printed on his NYPD card as a contact. When he called it from a payphone, he heard Avda Galkin's voice, small and haunted on an answering machine recording.

'I can meet tomorrow, 12 o'clock, like we planned. But not the Stonewall – too open. There's a small gate between buildings on Grove, where the street bends. Through the gate is Grove Court. It's private for residents but a friend has a key. I called him and he will unlock it for us. I'll see you there, noon. I think I have something for you.'

Callum called Mike to tell him about the meet.

Twenty-Four

Avda rubbed his wrists as he sat on the toilet. His skin was red raw where Tikhon had tied him to the bedframe with twine, then later, nylon zip ties. The bathroom door lay open and Tikhon stood there, leaning against the frame, watching him piss. They were both naked.

Tikhon spoke with calm efficiency. He rarely employed *mat*, obscene or profane language, in his Russian; he never used the criminal dialect, *fenya*. He said, 'Have you finished?'

'Almost. It's difficult when you are watching, and to piss sitting down.'

He tensed, frightened. It slowed his stream to a trickle. Then he stopped urinating.

Tikhon uncrossed his arms but said nothing.

He had told Avda to pass water sitting down after he had missed the bowl and trickled urine on Tikhon's bathroom floor. If he couldn't piss like a man, he'd sit like a woman, Tikhon had said.

Avda willed himself to relax. How many men had he found repulsive, yet dug deep and discovered a space far within that enabled him to endure their touch, and for him to touch them? Now all he had to do was pass water. A natural bodily function. He thought of Dostoyevsky – "whoever conquers fear and pain will himself become God."

But could he do so with the devil looking on from the door?

*

The fucking policeman was haunting Tikhon.

The Irish cop, Burke, that Arkady Kuznetsov had met in Queens.

Tikhon had observed the meet from a rooftop.

He had secured Avda in his apartment, locked the door tight and made his way to Long Island City then lain up on a flat warehouse roof to observe. He had felt like he was on a mountain post back in the war. He had seen the surveillance team: from above it was easy to see the tramp and construction worker were keeping an eye on proceedings. But Kuznetsov and the cop had moved location and Tikhon had crossed several rooftops, climbed down to a cross-street and scaled a fire escape to observe them again at the pier. He had been impressed when the cop produced a weapon and held off Kuznetsov's goons until his back-up arrived.

Later, he reported to Kuznetosv about the surveillance team, of which Kuznetsov already knew, and that the cop seemed dangerous but legitimate. That was all.

Clack. Clack.

Avda sniffed and ran his skinny forearm across his nose. This morning's whine was that, as a man, he couldn't piss comfortably sitting down. As if the little *goluboy* had a shred of masculine strength in his pathetic frame in the first place. Tikhon had used Avda twice this morning and the anger still buzzed in his head. The spell was weakening.

Avda finished. He washed his hands. He wiped his hands on a towel and his eyes with his red-raw wrists.

Tikhon gestured for him to go back to the bed and sit. He watched the saint on the smooth back as Avda walked across the small apartment. He was pleased to see that, despite the occasional beating, he had not marked the young man.

Tikhon said, 'Would you like a drink?'

'Yes, please.'

'Let's have some tea.'

As the water boiled, Avda said, 'Did I do well with the call?'

'You did as you were asked.'

The call to the policeman had been short and gone to a recorded message, all the better as Avda could deliver the message with no interrogation from the cop. The meet was set: midday tomorrow in a small garden behind a street in Greenwich Village. Avda had a client lived in the square who would unlock the gate for an hour – for a promise of a future fuck.

Avda said, 'I am your lover.'

The kettle whistled.

He said, 'When will this end? When will you kill the man and find your peace?'

'When I have dealt with the policeman, Burke,' said Tikhon.

'Will you kill Burke, too? Tomorrow?'

Clack. Clack. Clack.

'I don't know,' said Tikhon.

'Do you have a plan?'

Tikhon carried the tea to the bed and handed him the cup. Then he walked to the couch. On the couch sat Avda's Nike backpack. Tikhon opened it, reached inside and produced the small Camcorder hidden in a padded false bottom. He walked back over to Avda.

'You record your clients with this?'

They had never really talked about this aspect of his work. He nodded.

'You hide the camera somewhere in the room to record them with you?'

'Yes.'

'When?'

'I ask them to shower before.'

'Then you take it out when you finish.'

'Yes. They usually piss or some such when we are done. Then

I grab it. Once or twice I couldn't find an opportunity, so I called Volkov and he sent a man to retrieve it shortly after.'

Tikhon weighed the recorder in his hand.

He said, 'You give the tapes to Volkov and he uses them for... what?'

Avda said, 'I don't know.' He heard the whine in his own voice and seized control of the tight fear in his stomach. 'I imagine it's blackmail of some sort. I only tape certain clients – mostly married – who have money and positions which could be endangered by – '

'By you.' Tikhon set the recorder on the bed. 'You recorded last night's client?'

'Yes.'

Tikhon nodded.

Avda searched his mind for the reasons he had helped Tikhon at first. There was the initial attraction. Then the tale of the traitor, the KGB officer who had turned on his own men, murdered Tikhon's comrade, the Georgian, Dolidze – the quest for revenge. The stories of Tikhon's nightmares and how the traitor was now walking the streets of Brighton Beach. Avda had been excited. He had been flattered and gratified when he lay with this beautiful, quiet, damaged man. He had already been frightened of Maxim Volkov, and the powerful and connected clients he fucked. Of the constant stress, of how terrible might be the repercussions were his nights with these men to be publicised; or Volkov to no longer have use of him.

So he had helped Tikhon. He had loved him with his body and fed him information and compromised Volkov through his dealings with the policemen, Patrosi and O'Connell. Boxing the gangster boss into a position where he might be vulnerable. Forcing Volkov into more and more conferences with his lackeys until the moment seemed right to strike. They had thought that moment came in the bathhouse.

He looked at Tikhon and thought, now I see. I was being groomed by this dispassionate monster to be discarded, or worse, once he had his revenge.

He started when Tikhon spoke.

'You are a valuable young man, my sweet. Eventually you will be missed, and this tape with you. That bastard will want you back. I will use you to lure him out. And that will be the end of him.'

Then Tikhon walked away.

Avda sipped his tea and spilt some scalding liquid on his hands.

*

Callum and Trish rented The Birdcage and watched it, lying on his floor leaning against the couch. They made it through a half hour before they began to fool around. It went further again this time. They were both naked. Callum reined himself in a couple of times, scared he'd push her too far but Trish pulled him close and breathed hard, whispering he shouldn't stop. Then, when he was down between her legs with his mouth, and her back was arched and her thighs began to shudder, she pushed him back with her hands on the top of his head.

'I want to feel you inside,' she said. 'But I can't. I'm sorry.'

He lay with his head by her stomach tracing circles on the skin with his finger. She stroked his head wound from the old days and te skin graft hiding it.

'It's fine,' he said. 'I understand.'

And he did. She had her faith. No sweat. It was when her stomach twitched and he heard a small sound that he realised she was crying. Panic set in and for a second he hit a disconnect. This was "Johnson" Alexander, tough-as-nails street cop; this was Trish, the beautiful woman who trusted him and lay naked with him in his apartment. He moved up to her face and held her.

'This isn't fair,' she said, 'I'm sorry.'

'You got nothing to be sorry for. I knew from the start you wanted to save that part of yourself. You've been honest with me from the get go.'

'Maybe,' said Trish. 'Maybe not. At least, maybe not with myself.'

She put her head close to his chest but kept her body curled a little away from his.

'Look at us, Callum. We're both cops. You know many couples in the Job go the distance?'

'Jonathan and Jennifer Hart.'

'I don't know who that is.'

'Doesn't matter, they weren't cops. More kinda amateur detectives.'

Trish pushed him away.

'I'm serious,' she said. The street-cop edge flared in her voice.

'Alright,' said Callum, 'but it *can* work out. And you aren't the typical cop. Hitting a dive bar and drinking 'til dawn isn't exactly your profile.'

'And you?'

'A man can change.' He reached out and touched her cheek. 'I'm a long way from Popeye Doyle. I go to church on Sunday, for a start.'

'I don't know who that is either,' she said. 'And the church thing – I get it. But...' She took Callum's hand and brought it to her mouth. She kissed his fingers.

Goddamn, those lips, he thought.

'But ... you're white.'

Callum said, 'Jesus.'

'It matters.'

'It shouldn't.'

Trish sat up with her back against the couch and drew her knees up to her chin.

'How many black people you got in Ireland?'

'Ah shit, I left the census in my locker.'

'OK, how many black people did you know in Ireland?'

Callum sat up and joined her. He leaned the back of his head on the cushion of the couch.

'I get it,' he said. 'Listen, I asked you to go to church with me Sunday and you said no. Said you felt you had to be loyal to your own congregation. At the time, I thought maybe you didn't want to be seen with me because I'm pasty. Was I right?'

'Kinda.'

He seemed to deflate.

Trish said, 'Callum, I see the worst of all creeds and colors in our job. I know people are people and all that, and there are good out there as well as the bad. But people are also assholes. And you don't have roots here like I do; you don't have a whole team of white people to get all secretly shocked about you being with a black woman.' She ran her fingers down his cheek. 'If I go to your church in Harlem, some folks are gonna look at like me like I'm betraying my race, or I hate black men, or some other nonsense. If you come to my church, same story – and I got to stomach those same people every time I go to worship.'

She turned to him and rested her head on his arm.

'I feel something for you. I care about you, and it scares me. It scares me with what we both do for a living and it scares me because of who we are. You know what my pops would say if he knew I was lyin' naked with any damn man, never mind an Irish white boy? Not to mention, you're still married.'

He made to speak and she stayed him with a finger on his lips.

'I got some peace with that right now,' said Trish, 'and I'm not giving up on us. What I'm saying is, this could go further but until it does, until this gets deeper, I can't do everything I want with you, like go to church or introduce you to my folks.'

He smiled. 'I gotta be worth it, right?'

She bit her lip and smiled back.

'That's right,' she said.

Callum leaned forward, cupped her breast and moved in for a kiss.

'So let me work on that,' he said.

Twenty-Five

Over a breakfast of Cheerios and Pop-Tarts (Trish said, 'What are you, nine?') Callum took a leap of faith and gave Trish a key for his place. He saw the look she gave him and raised his hands in surrender.

'I trust you,' he said, 'but you break in here and steal my stuff, I'll call the cops on your ass.'

'Callum – '

'Look, just keep it. It isn't a huge commitment. Think of it like a next of kin listing on my 10-Card. Something happens, you got a key to get in here.'

She laughed. It was kind of deep and kind of sexy and all good, hearty food for a growing boy's soul.

'Next of kin? Nothing says *I care for you* like the threat of imminent death.'

But she took the key and held onto his hand at the table. It was quiet but for the wail of a fire truck somewhere outside. She jumped when Callum's beeper went off and dropped the key. It clattered on the kitchen floor and she crouched and picked it up as he checked the message.

'Listen, I gotta go,' he said. 'Leave the dishes in the sink and call me later, OK? I think I'll be back with Narcotics for a day or two later this week, but it'd be great to see you before then.'

Trish stood, holding the key, and smoothed down her denim skirt. She stepped close and kissed him long and slow. His hand slid around back of her t-shirt.

When she broke off, she said, 'Yeah, it'd be great.'

*

Callum called Kolya Slavin from a phone by a Korean grocery a block from his apartment.

'You paged me,' he said. 'What's up?'

Slavin's voice sounded younger on the phone.

'If you are free I would like to meet – I am in Manhattan right now.'

Callum checked his watch: 0920.

'I got time,' he said. 'When and where?'

*

Slavin sat on a metal chair at a glass-topped table and raised a coffee cup as Callum approached.

Worldwide Plaza at West 50th and 8th Avenue: trees crammed in circles of brutal concrete; cold, hard surfaces and angles everywhere; the Four Seasons fountain holding court in the center. The development was an early shot fired in the city's gentrification of Hell's Kitchen, and the local hoods bitched and moaned about the loss of the old neighborhood to the money from downtown. Callum figured they really hated the fact the Italians made good on the construction and cut the Irish out.

He sat opposite the old man amid serious-minded people in serious-looking suits scattered across the plaza. Slavin pushed a cup across the table to him.

'I took the liberty,' he said. 'Black coffee.'

'You know I can't accept gratuities,' said Callum, raising an eyebrow before taking a grateful sip.

Slavin turned to take in his surroundings and Callum saw an ugly purple and red bruise on his left cheek, a fat maggot of swollen skin below the eye. A small red trench was cut into his upper lip.

He said, 'Jesus Christ.'

'It is kind of you to evoke the name of our Lord and Savior, but I fear I am left to heal these wounds alone.'

'What happened?'

'You happened,' said Slavin. 'I returned to the bathhouse yesterday. Maxim Volkov was there; I hadn't seen him since your encounter with his goons. He spoke with his lackeys – with more muscle now than ever – in the sauna while I sat sweating in the corner, as he often does, paying me little mind. There was no one else in the room. I heard snatches of talk, which is why I called you.'

'And then he gave you a beating?'

'Then his men gave me a beating while he watched. I interfered when his apes confronted you. I had to be chastised.' Slavin folded his arms and shivered. There was no breeze. 'And I was *musor* – as you are now – in the past, so they put in a little extra effort.'

'*Musor*?'

'Literally, it translates as garbage. For a Russian criminal, it means police.'

Callum felt his face flush.

An old man beaten because of me, he thought. Christ, this job can suck.

He said, 'Why does Volkov talk so frankly in front of you when he knows you were a cop?'

'In America, I am just a civilian. In the culture of the gangsters, they consider me nothing – they have nothing to fear from me. Do you see many people in Brighton Beach going to the police when they have to pay protection money, or they take a beating from a loan shark, or a dead body is dumped in front of their house?'

'That's changing.'

'Not fast enough. There is a langauge barrier, cultural issues. The bottom line is that they are more frightened of the criminals than they trusting of the NYPD. It would not occur to Maxim Volkov that I would run to you with information.'

Slavin put a hand on Callum's arm. 'Another reason Maxim Volkov does not fear me, is he believes the beating I took will cow me. This is enough, in his world, to secure my silence.'

'So why talk to me?'

'Because I am the one in a million who doesn't care. I have no family here. My brother in Russia died two years ago. And, while in Moscow I was the underdog – I told you of how ill-equipped the MVD were – in New York I believe you, as a policeman, have a chance of breaking these people.'

He spread his hands like a priest ready for benediction.

'And, you are Irish. The American police sometimes see us as a nuisance, backward "Ivans" coming to their country with our superstitions and our black stares and vicious criminals. But you are an immigrant, like me. You understand. I can trust you.'

Slavin looked around. 'This area is famous for Irish, is it not? Hell's Kitchen – how wonderfully histrionic.'

'Once, maybe,' said Callum. 'The old Paddies are a thing of the past.'

'Surely not. The Fighting Irish?'

'Yeah, yeah,' said Callum. He looked up at the towering façade of One WWP. 'Fightin' Irish. Like that's all we're good at. You know what Americans call a hangover? An Irish flu. And some lush at the bar starts mouthing off about someone, so drunk he doesn't realize the guy is right there listening? That's an Irish whisper. You lose your temper and you "get your Irish up". Fucking stereotypes. Christ.'

'Stereotypes.' Slavin nodded. 'All Russians are spies who live on vodka and Borscht.' The old man's face crinkled like a bird just shit in his coffee.

Callum took out a cigarette and lit up. 'So what're you doing in Midtown?'

'TKTS. I wanted tickets for a show: A Doll's House.'

'You get them?'

'Yes.'

'And what have you got for me?'

'Maxim Volkov is unhappy. One of his young men has gone missing. This young man was valuable, and he very much wants him back.'

'And you overheard this in the sauna?'

'Even Russian gangsters will talk more openly in a bathhouse, more so when they are with associates and I am the only civilian in the room. You remember we have history, he and I.' Slavin chuckled. 'You still don't trust me. I don't blame you – I wouldn't have believed everything some old man told me when I was a policeman.'

In fact, Callum had asked Mike to run Slavin's name through the system. Slavin came up clean. But he shrugged and threw out a joke.

'Like you said, every Russian is a spy.'

The old man laughed with gusto. Then he winced with the pain of his battered face.

They drank and chatted some more.

No, Slavin didn't know why this young man was so valuable to Volkov. He had heard Volkov say his men had paid a visit to this man's apartment. It was empty. Slavin had guessed the young man was a prostitute from a phrase he overheard.

Avda Galkin popped in Callum's mind.

'How about our mystery man in the bathhouse? The guy with the bullet wounds on his chest? Any word on him?'

'I heard only bits and pieces,' said Slavin. 'I am not sure, but I think this man works for another criminal, Arkady Kuznetsov.'

'I heard of him.'

'Volkov was talking about a *byk* who works for Kuznetsov. A *byk* is a bull: a footsoldier or thug. Volkov said something about this bull having a *pika* – a knife – when his men chased the thug from the bathhouse. You realise, these words are criminal slang.'

'So this thug drew the knife on the men chasing him?'

'Yes. He had also confronted Volkov's men – one of those who threatened you in the bathhouse – in a local store in Brighton Beach. A clothing or shoe store, owned by a Jew. The *byk* had the knife then and represented Arkady Kuznetsov.'

Callum finished his cigarette. 'How'd they know it was the same knife?'

'Volkov mentioned a *kinjal*. A Georgian knife. Some Cossacks used it too. Quite distinctive.' Slavin produced a small piece of paper with a rough pen sketch on it. 'They look something like this.'

Callum turned his Zippo over in his fingers. They drank coffee. The suits around them came and went. Callum checked his watch. He thought of Avda again, the meeting today.

'I have to go,' he said. 'One thing, how'd you work out this young man Volkov's been looking for was a prostitute again?'

Slavin said, '*Voronoy.*' A darkness washed across his eyes for a moment. 'It means goat. Prison slang for a homosexual slave.'

'And on that note,' said Callum, 'I'll leave you. Next time, coffee's on me.'

The darkness passed from his gaze and Kolya Slavin stood to bid farewell.

'In the words of our American friends and neighbors,' he said, 'have a nice day, Officer Burke.'

Twenty-Six

Avda lay naked on the bed in Tikhon's apartment. His wrists and ankles were sore and raw with the fastenings tying him to the bedposts. He wanted to piss and was terrified to soil the bed, lest Tikhon punish him when he returned.

After feeding him and offering a sip of water, Tikhon had secured him to the bed and told him to sleep. The bag with the Camcorder was gone. The drapes were pulled.

Just before Tikhon had left, before he had dressed, there had been a knock on the door. Tikhon had opened the door a crack and had a hushed conversation with someone on the other side. It had been a short exchange. Then he had closed the door and walked to his clothes folded neatly on a chair, the kinjal dagger on top, to dress. He had finished, secured the dagger in a shoulder scabbard under his left armpit, and gone from the apartment.

Avda lay and thought of Russia; then of nights out in New York, living as a young man should in this vast city. Nights when he had danced until dawn and enjoyed the illusion that he was like the other people in the club or bar. Untainted by the parasites who lived off the neighborhoods and communities, and who exploited fears and grudges and avarice for their own gain.

And he wondered why, when he had returned from his brief discussion with the hidden caller at the door, still naked, Tikhon had carried the scent of a feminine perfume with him.

*

Georgie Ruiz lay close with Arthur on the bed. The kids were at school. The neighborhood was quiet.

For a couple of hours, a least, life was good. Her man was with her. They had made love. It was like she rediscovered him. An older husband and father, a little frail, but still the man who had chased her with persistance, who put a ring on her finger and gave her years of happiness and support – some headaches and sleepless nights – but above all, love. They were partners. Whatever was eating him away from inside, they'd face it together.

And her other partner, Callum? What was he doing right now? What was he fretting about, or raging on? She'd never seen anyone more tempestuous in their moods. He was a good man who could be real bad: but at his center, a good man. She hoped he found his happiness.

Arthur ran his fingers through her hair. Her head rested on his chest.

He lifted her chin with his finger and smiled.

'You want to order takeout for lunch?' he said.

*

Arkady Kuznetsov sat in the Masha Tea Room and brooded.

He couldn't say he liked Tikhon: admired him to a degree, yes, but liked? No.

No more than he could have liked any other wild animal, indifferent to all around it but the prey it lived to hunt. However, Kuznetsov found a new sentiment had crept into his appraisal of the man. Jealousy.

It was Marina. When Kuznetsov had fucked her a couple of days ago, before Tikhon arrived for his appointment at her place, she had been good. She had always been one of his best girls, a true actress: so good he sometimes wondered if she used some form of self-hypnosis to will herself into a momentary connection with whoever had taken her body for a time. But, that last time, she had been good only like a bottle of American beer, or a burger from White Castle. It had been enough to satisfy an immediate need but no more. It had been mechanical. This *baklany*, Tikhon, had got into her head and her mind had been on him while Kuznetsov heaved on top of her.

For a man like Kuznetsov, a Vor, it was unthinkable. To be cuckolded by another, with a fucking whore. And now the *musor* policeman, Burke, was asking questions, the time had come to settle Tikhon's account. A friend, when Kuznetsov was enduring a rough patch in his marriage, had once said the equation was simple: if his wife gave him more happiness than grief, it was worth perservering with the relationship. The balance with Tikhon, as efficient a weapon as he could be against Maxim Volkov, had tipped into the negative.

But first, Arkady Kuznetsov needed to work off some of his aggression and think more clearly. He needed to reclaim Marina. He could summon her to the apartment behind the tea room, but he didn't have the inclination to bend under the model train tracks before he worked her over. The replica Sakhalin line, with its little steam trains running on electric, seemed childish and facetious today.

Marina would be at her place. He would go there, invade her space and then invade her. Restake his claim and reconfirm his dominance

He picked up the phone.

*

Trish Alexander sat on Callum's couch and stared at the tube without watching the daytime show. She would work later. Now, she couldn't find the will to leave the apartment. The place felt ... safe. She could smell Callum on the sheets in the bedroom, see his touch in the soccer team mugs in the kitchen or the photograph of the shipyard in his hometown in the hall. This was the first, enchanted stage of a love affair, she knew. They couldn't get enough of each other, lay awake for hours through the night yet felt fresh next day. The world outside evaporated when they were in bed together; they no longer heard the honking and the sirens and the occasional yells, and the endless low groan of the city churning around them. The universe contracted to their four walls.

But the cruelty of the world was always there, even if they were temporarily blind to it. It was there in his pale skin, made whiter by the jet black hairs on his limbs and the coal-smudge of his morning stubble. It was there in the dark of her leg draped over his, the gray of her nipples; her – what did Callum call it? – coffee bean skin.

Galatians 3:28 swam into her head. "There is neither Jew nor Gentile, neither slave nor free, nor is there male and female, for you are all one in Jesus Christ."

Try telling my pops that, she thought, God-fearing man that he is. Especially the slave part.

She thought about going to Le Figaro Café for a coffee, but it wouldn't be the same without Callum. Somehow, this felt like his neighborhood and she would trespass if she stepped out without him. Dumb, she knew.

Neighborhoods, territories, divisions. It was the way of the world.

No, she thought. I'll just sit here awhile, and enjoy the peace.

*

Tikhon held the straps of the backpack as he walked through Greenwich Village. He looked like a student at NYU, or one of the priveleged kids who moved into the neighborhood and lived out their bohemian fantasies with chain-café lattes, Oakley shades and spotless Spitfire sneakers.

He remembered the thrill of visiting the neighborhood when he first arrived in New York. Tikhon had always been ambivalent about sexual pleasure – he found he could be attracted to men or women, although Avda had been his only male lover. With women, he could talk to them, share a little: not much, but enough to function in society. Women helped him fool the world that he could feel and think like everyone else.

Women like Marina.

Now, as he looked around, he thought Greenwich Village was acquiring the feel of a suburb. Clean, ordered, quieter than before.

Tikhon thought of the cop, Burke.

Clack.

He had been ready to kill him, with all the blood and thunder that would surely bring down from the NYPD. But it was too messy. Burke's connection with Avda Galkin was a factor. Killing a policeman was not the answer.

He had watched Burke at the meet with Avda, and then Kuznetsov. The policeman was smart, dangerous. Perhaps driven. Better to intimidate the cop. Show him his vulerabilities.

And toss him a crumb.

One of the tapes of Avda, with the German on Sunday night. A compromised UN staffer would be enough to push the investigation on Maxim Volkov. Enough to force Volkov's hand and make it that much more imperative for the man to recover Avda.

It would be a death sentence for Avda.

Tikhon swiped at something buzzing around his ear.

Then the target would be drawn out (he saw the mountains in his head). Then Tikhon would use the kinjal dagger and vengeance would be served (he saw the KGB bastard fire into Dolidze's face). It would be over. Perhaps the nightmares and the fear and faces in his head in the small hours of the night would be over, too. And then?

He rolled his shoulders under the straps of the backpack, and crossed Hudson Street.

*

Callum said, 'Jesus, bad memories.'

Mike yanked at the Kell device strapped to Callum's chest under a loose baseball shirt to make it sure it was secured fast. Callum thought of a close call when he'd had a wire when undercover.

'You're still here and breathin', ain't you?' said Mike.

'You ever thought about being one of those life coaches, Mike? You got too much empathy for this job.'

'What, like Ms Cleo? I see a child down a well – he's holding a teddy bear and saying "Red Rum" over and over.'

'Forget it. We good to go?'

'We're good.'

They sat in the back of a rented Ford van on Commerce Street, a couple of blocks from Grove. It was 1150. The street was quiet, the buildings straight out of a period drama. Tidy, Colonial, ordered. The Founding Fathers could have walked around the corner and not looked out of place. There was even a clapboard house.

Callum said, 'Your Fed friends tested that heroin from the Popov bust yet?'

'There's a backlog, you know?'

'Yeah, poor FBI. So underfunded, so unloved by the federal government in comparison to a PD.'

Callum stood as straight as he could from the bench seat in the back of the van and bent down to test the give in the strap on his chest. Mike spotted a small bulge in his jeans hip pocket.

'What's that?' he said.

Callum touched the bulge for a second. 'A pocket dictionary

of Russian. After I met Slavin earlier, I picked one up from the bookstore on West 48ᵗʰ and Broadway. Wanted to check a few words he said at the meet.'

The plan was simple.

No Feds on this one. They wanted to avoid clutter – Avda Galkin wasn't exactly a candidate for the Violent Felony Squad. Callum would jump out of the van and walk to Grove Street. He would make his way to the small courtyard behind the buildings, Grove Court, to meet Avda. Mike would drive the two blocks to Grove and park down the street. He would have the antenna needed to receive the audio from the Kell wire and listen in on the conversation. Mike had batted aside Callum's complaints and insisted on a wire since Avda was no threat.

'It's almost the Twenty-First Century and we gotta work with this?' said Callum, pointing at the antenna.

'You know the Job,' said Mike. 'No expense spared. The FBI aren't in on this caper so the money ain't there.' He slapped Callum's shoulder. 'Hey, what do you care? This kid's light in the loafers, right?'

'See, Mike,' said Callum, 'empathy.'

Then he threw on his jacket, opened the doors at the back of the van and jumped out.

Twenty-Seven

Callum walked north on Bedford Street along the sun-dappled sidewalk. More New England-style townhouses, a stone crest on a wall above stable doors proclaiming "J. Goebel & Co. Est. 1865". He checked his watch. It was 2 minutes to noon.

He hit Grove Street and turned left. Callum could see where the street curved to the right and the townhouses shrunk to two-story walk-ups. Right on the south side of the bend was a small entrance to the courtyard, Grove Court, hidden from the street behind the townhouses. He looked up at a pale spring sky clawed by the branches of sidewalk-trees. Somewhere nearby, Mike sat behind the tainted windows of the Ford rental with the Kell antenna.

The gate to the courtyard was open. The entrance, set between two red-brick pillars, was maybe wide enough for two slim adults to squeeze through. He walked into a courtyard of flat cobblestones with what looked like a small fountain and fixture in the center, overgrown with ivy. Victorian-style lamps were on some of the brick walls and a red-brick bank of rowhouses stood opposite with white window trim and the heady smell of money.

There was no sign of Avda Galkin.

Callum checked his watch again. 1202.

He had a flash of unease at the quiet. The place creeped him out, it was like a scene from some Gothic horror, or a haunt of Jack the Ripper. He turned and looked behind, half expecting the gate to creak shut of its own accord. His hand went to the Glock on his hip under the loose baseball shirt. He felt the weight of his badge hanging on the chain under his shirt with the razor taped on the back.

Nothing and nobody.

He whispered, 'He ain't here. The place is empty.'

Mike would be listening, maybe getting an uneasy breeze across his shoulders just like Callum. Maybe not giving a shit.

Then he saw her. She was sitting on the low wall around the fountain in the center of the court on the ivy, her dress green and hair straw-colored, hanging around her shoulders like a shampoo commercial. Elegant, long-limbed. Sharp, European features. She looked as though she belonged here among the money, a permanent fixture just like the fountain. A well-kept secret mistress of some Episcopalian old-name-trust-fund-geriatric, hidden from view behind the iron gate.

Looking at her, for a second he forgot Avda Galkin and the mystery bullet-wound man and the Motherland gangster shit of Brighton Beach. As she stood like she was light as air, he thought how Georgie would have laughed at him: *men, such simple animals*.

He hoped Trish might have been just a little jealous.

Then he was back in the game. She walked toward him, a small bag on a gold chain slung over her shoulder, smiling. He smiled back.

*

Tikhon crossed the tiled entrance and started up the stairs of the apartment building. He had been lucky, the occupant of 203 buzzing him in after he'd tried three other apartments. It had been the flaw in the plan – that he could be stuck here on the street, waiting for someone gullible enough to open the building door, and he breathed a sigh of relief.

He had faith in Marina. He knew she could hold the cop, Burke, up for a couple of minutes. Grove Street was several city blocks and ten minutes on foot from Bleecker; Tikhon would need only seconds. Leave a card with a number, a written message to show Tikhon had been there, in the cop's apartment. To show Burke how vulnerable he was in his own home. And to leave the tape: Avda Galkin with the German diplomat.

That would set the cat among the pigeons, and push Tikhon's target into action. Expose the bastard and force him to deal for Avda's return. Then Tikhon would have his moment. His friend, Dolidze the Georgian, would have his revenge. All the men who had fought on that freezing mountain, betrayed by the KGB scum who turned to the Mujahideen, who valued a heroin pipeline above his country. His comrades.

Clack. Clack.

He breathed deep and thought of Marina's willowy sex in the long, green dress. Her wheat-field hair. She would be in Grove Court now with Burke. Tikhon reached the door. He checked the apartment number. Yes, this was it.

Clack.

He took a moment for the rollercoaster to slow. His watch read 1203. Then he dialled the number of Marina's cell phone, a gift to her from Arkady Kuznetsov. Tikhon had bought his own. It felt like a toy – but he supposed they were the future. Her phone, in her bag, would vibrate. She would know Tikhon was at the apartment and would leave Grove Court, and the cop, behind with a simple clue as to what was really happening here.

He placed a hand on the *kinjal* dagger, snug in its shoulder scabbard slung under his armpit. He felt a security in its weight. Tikhon unslung the backpack and took out the tape, ready to leave it in a conspicuous spot for Burke to find.

He took the tool from his pocket. One of the skills he'd learned as a freelancer for Kuznetsov was how to pick a lock. He worked for seconds that seemed to stretch into hours. He had a trick for any security chain that might be on the other side, too – most any apartment in New York seemed to have one. At worst, he could break the door open and be gone in less than a minute.

But the lock clicked and gave and there was no chain slung across the inside. There was no secondary lock to deal with. No bolt.

Just a woman standing barefoot in the hallway with a phone in her hand and something unreadable in her eyes.

*

Callum saw the woman was holding a cell phone in her right hand. Her left clutched a map.

Clutched, he thought, like her life depended on keeping hold of the folded paper.

Up close she looked older – still attractive, but her body was less willowy, more a shade toward scrawny. The skin of her arms was clear and smooth – she had young hands – but she seemed like she had seen a few more miles than at first glance. Not travelled, but seen. The hollows around the eyes. The tight creases at the sides of the mouth. He'd seen the look before in brothels back in Hong Kong, or among some of the junkie chicken heads he'd met on Narcotics busts.

In fact, she looked wrong for a quiet, affluent courtyard in the West Village.

And where the fuck was Avda?

As she got close, she put the phone in her bag and opened the map.

'*Izvinite, ya poteryalsya. Ne mogli by vy pomoch' mne?*'

The words came out in a rush as though rehearsed and she was scared of forgetting her lines.

'I'm sorry,' said Callum, 'you speak English?'

Her smile had lost any trace of legitimacy.

'*YA ishchu adres.*'

'Wait, I – '

'*Bliker-strit, dom dvesti desyat, vy eto znayete?*'

'Wait a second, what did you say?'

'*YA polagayu, net. V lyubom sluchaye, spasibo.*'

Callum glanced at the map. A street map of Manhattan.

'*Blicker*: is that Bleecker Street? You're speaking Russian?'

She hadn't stopped moving and was now between Callum and the gate.

She said, '*Proshchay*,' and turned away.

Callum said, 'Wait.'

A man with a small child walked into the court. She hurried past them onto Grove Street.

Callum said, 'You catch that Mike? I think she spoke Russian.'

He gave a brief description of the girl.

'She's on Grove, grab her.'

He pulled the dictionary out of his pocket and stared at it.

Would Mike see the girl? Should he go after her? She was out in the city now. Why'd he let her go? Because he goddamn froze, that's why.

Shit!

Bleecker, she said Bleecker. She had a map.

Something cold blew through his bones. He got flashes of the bad shit in his life that seemed to be racing around his head these days. Jimmy Gilliland blown away by the sniper in Belfast. The explosion at the checkpoint and Callum on his back, black smoke clouding the sky. The dead dealers at Coney Island with their insides out. Georgie with her sick husband, Arthur. Irene and Tara living life without Callum, so far away.

She said *Bleecker*.

He dredged up a scrap of what he thought he heard; of what he thought was Russian. His fingers searched the dictionary for the numbers section, following his brain on the hunch.

He was right.

She'd said the number 210.

His building on Bleecker.

He set off at a run, startling the father and child. They gave a yell of fear.

*

It took a couple of seconds for Trish to realise someone was at the door of Callum's place. She checked her watch and had a stab of shock at the fact she'd been here all morning, drinking his coffee, looking out his window.

The fussing at the door continued.

Her shoes were right there at the entrance. She stood barefoot, suddenly wired.

She grabbed the phone in the hall.

It could be Callum. It might not. A friend of hers who had studied at NYU had her place on Bleecker rifled a couple of years ago. Some junkie, most likely, one of the Washington Square Park crowd.

Trish moved further away from the kitchen along the corridor leading to the door, stretching the phone cord tight. She pulled at a strand of hair which had fallen in front of her eyes and realised she didn't know who to call.

The door opened.

She remembered her Glock was in her bag, in the kitchen. Sudden fear scrunched her chest tight.

The man in the doorway stood with a small backpack in his left hand and a lockpick tool in his right. He was Aryan youth with a few more years on the clock: fair-haired and fine-featured. The look of his body and how he held it told her he was in shape. His eyes went wide when he saw her. Her legs were lead, her mouth parched. She had maybe ten feet on him in a dash to her bag in the kitchen at the end of the corridor.

She said, 'NYPD.'

Her voice was high and whined in her head above the surge and thump of her pulse.

Come on blondie, she thought, whoever you are – turn around and run back out that door.

But the man stood staring like he had walked in on the wrong scene.

Tin him, thought Trish, show him your shield. It was clipped to the waist of her denim skirt in plain view but his eyes hadn't left hers.

She moved her left hand to grab it.

The spell broke.

He came at her. She swivelled and got four steps toward the kitchen before he had a handful of her t-shirt. Her right foot went from under her and she dropped the phone, yanking the cord from the wall socket. She fell hard on her ass and yelped.

He got a fistful of her hair and pulled her head up and back, yanking her skull like she thought her neck would snap. She cried out, grabbed for his wrist and took a shot on the side of her head. It didn't hurt so much as terrify her with its violence. A skell on the street was one thing. Then it was hysterics and screaming. This was blunt, economical, brutal.

And here, in Callum's place.

The man began dragging her by the hair. Her scalp was a mass of electric shocks, her cheek numb from his punch.

My God, she thought, help me! This is real – I could die!

They reached the door to the bedroom. He threw her inside and she hit the side of the bed. Her body made good with the mattress but her hip cracked off the frame. Trish lay on the floor, her legs splayed and her back half propped against the bed. The man eased through the doorway and she saw the backpack in the hall where he'd dropped it. He came toward her.

No God, no not that, don't let him do that God, not that in this bedroom where I lay with Callum! No!

He slapped her hard and her head whipped sideways and bounced off the mattress. He dropped to his knees in front of her and grabbed at her skirt. She babbled and clawed. He smacked her full in the face. Her vision went as she teared up. Her nose tingled. She felt something wet above her lip. Then he reached in close to his body and pulled out a long, slim dagger like it was a magic trick. He brought it close to her.

She yelled a litany of names, invoking the great and good in her life to help her, give her strength: her mom and pops, her sisters Jessie and Perry. God. Jesus. Even Callum.

The man grabbed her hair again and forced her head back, exposing her throat. She couldn't blink the tears away.

Trish screamed.

She didn't see his head snap to the right but felt the solid hit when she smashed her detective shield into his cheek. He made no sound, didn't ease up his grip on her hair. But the dagger wavered. She hit him again and this time the metal shield bit into something soft, ground against something hard. He let her go and she saw blood in his mouth where she'd cracked him. His head was to the side and she pummelled him, trying to find the leverage to get up off the damn floor and run. He flailed and the dagger slashed her wrist. She cried out.

He swung and she rolled. The dagger hilt glanced off her shoulder. He'd put too much behind the blow and lost balance. Trish scrabbled past him. He grunted behind her and she pulled herself upright by the doorframe.

She tasted blood, felt her top lip fat and firm as a frank. Her scalp burned, her nose felt thick with mucus. Her wrist stung with blood and sweat.

She stumbled into the hall and slipped on the hardwood. She landed hard on top of something. He was behind her, barely breathing hard. Something gnawed at her shoulder and she knew he'd cut her.

She heard someone crying – whimpering, really. It sounded like a woman who knows it's over. All of it. Everything she was and everything she ever would be. Trish realised it was her. She rolled a little on the floor.

The man bent over her and his hand grabbed her wounded shoulder. His grip was iron. He bent further. His face was cool against her head and she was surprised. She felt like she was burning up. His breath was hot, though. It washed over her face like a lover's touch, then blasted her when he yelled out.

She crawled from under him as he stayed bent double for a couple of beats. Trish still held the body of the phone she had landed on. The phone she had driven with everything she had left into the man's crotch.

She crawled a few feet then struggled upright. The man was unbending to his full height, slow and controlled like the relentless killer in a slasher flick. The dagger was stained with her blood. She made six paces from the kitchen. Four. She heard him coming. Something feral burst from her belly up through her chest and split, coursing along her arms. She swung the phone blindly behind her and bellowed. Above her animal roar she heard a crack and saw him stagger.

Fire in her gut, she ran to the kitchen. She dumped the contents of her bag out. The Glock hit the floor. Someone next door banged on the wall. She heard a shout in the corridor outside. Her hand was slick. She almost dropped the gun. She fell to her knees and brought the barrel to bear in what seemed like a lifetime. She was grunting, growling.

She snarled, 'NYPD.'

But the hallway was empty. The man had gone.

Twenty-Eight

Callum got to the apartment ahead of Mike and an RMP car despatched from the 6th Precinct after a concerned neighbor had called 911. He took the stairs two at a time and found a couple of people standing at his doorway. Inside, Mrs Calloway from down the hall was kneeling next to Trish. She had mopped up some of the blood on the floor with paper towels. Trish lay propped against the wall like a marionette with clipped strings. She turned to look at Callum and he flinched.

Her nose was swollen. Her top lip on the right side, too. She had a welt under her right eye and caked blood under her nose. A towel was tied around her shoulder and blood had seeped into the fabric. Her wrist was bound in a homemade bandage. Callum felt torn in two, like the universe had turned on him like a mad dog and reminded him: all that shit you see on the street can make it back home, too.

He muttered, 'Jesus Christ.'

Mrs Calloway said something he didn't catch and he nodded and thanked her for her help. He crouched by Trish. She had been watching him since he walked in the door and now she crumpled and cried hard. Callum wanted to grab her and hold her tight but she looked so damaged, so fragile that he was scared of hurting her more.

Then he did hold her and she pulled him to her. They were still like that when the cops arrived.

*

So that was it. The incident was written up as an assault, probably a burglary gone wrong. The victim was an off-duty NYPD detective in the apartment of an NYPD officer. As Callum wasn't present, he wouldn't be part of the investigation other than confirming it was his place and nothing was taken. Trish could fill out a complaint report if she so wished. With no broken bones, a superficial slash on her wrist, and a shallow shoulder injury from the sharp lockpick rather than the dagger, she'd been patched up and given a couple of shots. She could return to duty tomorrow if she wanted.

All nice and neat for Mike. The Russian investigation remained clear of any interference from detectives at the 6th Precinct who might want to look deeper into the assault. Trish need never know she was collateral damage in a job Callum was working against the Vory gangsters down in Brighton Beach.

Callum felt like shit.

He felt mad. Fucking livid.

So he played it Mike's way because he was going to put the pedal down on this one and he didn't need the 6th in the way. Callum had to know how whoever fucked with Trish knew his address. He was going to find the bastard did it and take it as far toward street court as Mike would allow. Maybe thirty minutes with the asshole before he was carried into his cage for processing.

Like the people said, he was getting his goddamn Irish up.

*

He went to the hospital. He wished he hadn't when Trish's parents showed up.

They huddled around her like a human shield, sneaking glances over their shoulders at him sat in a chair with a coffee. She looked a lot worse than she was. She was a cop, and tough

– but she was their little girl and she seemed plenty banged up right now. And the lily-white Irish boy in the corner – whose apartment she had unaccountably been in – was guilty by association.

It looked like it was going to get worse when Gerry Martin walked in with a bolt of lightning up his ass, hopped up on righteous fury. He stood over Callum and said, 'Can I talk to you?'

His voice was like a tripwire just tweaked, all trembling tension before the big bang.

Callum looked over at the Alexander family huddle once more, sighed and said, 'Sure.'

He hauled his bones out of the chair like he was a hundred and walked into the corridor. He was ready. He knew from Trish that Gerry had hit on her when she first joined the Narcotics team and figured that, in Gerry's fever dreams, she was the one that got away. His train of thought probably ran something like: she'd been having sleep-overs at Callum's and he'd left her undefended in his place, ready for some psycho to come in and kick the shit out of her.

They made it to a Coke machine on the corner. Gerry leaned against the wall. Callum stood in the corridor where it bent to the right.

Gerry put his hands on his hips. Callum hadn't seen him like this, coiled, with brawler's eyes. But Callum was ready. Ready for the shit. Maybe a punch. Ready for Martin to work it off.

He wasn't ready for what came next.

Gerry said, 'You OK, Cal?' and put a hand on his shoulder.

'Better than Trish,' said Callum.

'Yeah, yeah. I was gonna go over but I thought I should wait until her mom and pop left, you know?'

'Right.'

Rather than throw a right hook, Callum thought maybe Gerry Martin was about to cry.

'You OK, Gerry?' he said.

'I got sent home. We were at the Six-oh – me, Sarge, Billy Hutchinson. Jesus, it feels like we're droppin' one-by-one: first Patrosi with his busted leg, then you gone on loan, Ruiz. Now Trish.'

'She's still breathin' Gerry. So, you were at the Six-oh ... '

'Yeah, and word came through Trish took a beating. We heard it was your place, so everyone gets that you were together. But Danny O'Neill was around and, when he heard the news, he made a crack. We got news on her injuries and Danny said some bullshit about her lookin' better than ever, spat some racial poison out. So I smacked him.'

Callum saw O'Neill in his mind at Lacey's Bar – *We know where you live ...*

He looked at Gerry Martin with a new degree of respect and said, 'Hey, welcome to the club.'

'Yeah, I broke his jaw, though.'

'Shit, you been eatin' your spinach.'

'So Sarge sent me home. He's forcin' some vacation time on me. Get me outta the way.'

Callum got some change out of his pocket to buy the man a Coke. 'You gonna face a firing squad on this?'

'The old hairbag bastard wants an assault charge.'

'Danny?'

'Yeah. Sarge laughed at that one. Says he got a couple of witnesses in himself and Billy, and a cop at the lockers, to Danny makin' a racial slur against a fellow cop. Says he'll issue me a Command Discipline with a verbal warning and leave it at that.'

'For breakin' a fellow cop's jaw on the job?' said Callum. 'Nice work.'

A CD was tin-pot stuff, like being late for work or having a button missing from your dress uniform.

Gerry leaned in close. 'Look, I'm gonna roll with the sarge's idea and take a few days vacation off the back of this. But, you got a plan to rectify this situation – ' his eyes darted to Trish's room ' – then I want in.'

Callum bought the Coke. Gerry took it with a nod and a muttered thanks.

'Listen, Gerry, what happened, it was just bad luck. Coulda been any one of us on the wrong day.'

That was when Mike O'Connell strode up the corridor at a right angle to where Gerry stood, unseen, behind the wall and said, 'We know if this asshole beat on your girlfriend is connected to our caper yet?'

Mike stared when he rounded the corner and saw Gerry Martin.

Gerry stared back and said, 'Your caper?'

*

Callum had been listening to Mike do his best to close down Gerry's pleas to help out on the Russian investigation when a man with eyes like wedding-day rain and a mouth torn with pain walked up.

Trish's father looked at Callum from below brows weighted with worry and fear. He had hair shaved close with flashes of gray searing the scalp above each ear.

'She wants to see you,' he said. Then he walked away. Callum wondered if it was the first and last thing the man would ever say to him.

He left Mike and Gerry and went to Trish's room. She was already sitting on the side of the bed. She looked up when he appeared at the door and dug inside for a smile, found one – a little crumpled – and offered it up.

She said, 'Hey.' Her voice was soft.

'Hey. I won't ask how you're feeling.'

'Not too bad, honestly,' said Trish. 'I took a couple of good shots but I'm in one piece. Nothing broken, including my nose: sorry, I won't end up ugly as you.'

'No, that would take some doing,' said Callum, his eyes on the floor.

'Hey, wait a second.' Trish's voice went hard. 'I'm the one supposed to get sympathy here. You feel sorry for yourself, Callum, you're crying over the wrong person.'

He looked up. She looked like she wanted him to hold her – but he saw her beautiful face all hammered wrong by someone he knew, in his gut, was there in that apartment because of him. And, worse, he felt that the coward-bastard who did this to her had thrown some kind of barrier up between them.

'Your dad looks like a good man,' he said.

The disappointment was writ large on her face.

'We going there,' she said, 'when I need you here?' She put her hands on her chest.

And goddamn if she didn't tear down that invisible barrier with eight words. Callum walked over and held her. She cried some again. Callum's eyes went red and raw.

Then Trish looked up at him and said, 'Are we going to be OK?'

'I don't know,' he said. 'I look at you and I feel we got it. But your parents ... the cops thing ...'

'The black/white thing?'

For some weird reason he was relieved she didn't say "race".

'I don't know,' he said. 'I understand what you said before. I got no roots here. I'd die for my daughter but she's in Ohio. And I'm her dad and I know that fear of being a parent, that fear of your child being hurt. I see that in your dad and ... shit ... I dunno'.'

'I wanted you there,' said Trish. 'When that man was tearing into me, I wanted you to come and be there, to help me. Don't feel bad about that, Callum. I wanted *you*. That's got to mean something.'

She brushed his cheek with her lips. Callum held her again.

'Hey, we're cops,' he said. 'We love a lost cause.'

*

They sat in a backroom of a bar on Avenue C in Alphabet City. Callum, Mike, Gerry and now Georgie.

Callum had gone to talk to a doctor after he left Trish. He'd told Mike and Gerry it would take a little time and asked them to meet him later. They'd agreed on this dive at Mike's suggestion. Callum had taken so long in the hospital that Mike gave him a world of shit for leaving him with Gerry Martin when he finally arrived.

'What the fuck were you doin' in there?'

'I was showing the doctor this lump I got,' said Callum. 'It's on my balls, just here.'

Georgie had heard about Trish on a phone call from Sarge and called Mike on his department issue cellphone. She turned up when they were still on their first drink and joined them in the private booth.

'First thing,' she said, 'I think it's great: you and Trish.'

Mike said, 'Yeah, you sure know how to show a girl a good time.'

'Lieu?' said Gerry. He hadn't become acclimatized to the rare air that surrounded Mike.

Mike looked at Gerry and said, 'I'm tryin' to work out why you're still here. This is my investigation and Burke and Ruiz are invited. You get this beer on me and then you're on vacation.'

'Lieu,' said Gerry, 'I know I'm here on my own time. I won't endanger any convictions, I'll do the leg work to speed things up, that's it. But I got skin in the game. Trish Alexander is good people and God knows I ain't always been a decent human being to her – maybe to Ruiz and Callum, too. So let me help out, tip the scales a little in my favor when I hook up with St. Peter, huh?'

'Gerry,' said Georgie, 'I knew there was a soft Irish cream center in that hard exterior.'

'Blow me.'

Callum took a swig of Molson and looked at Mike. 'Hey, we could use the help. I know we wanna push on here and change gears.'

Mike said, 'You know we got a federal element to this investigation. Ghandi here can't be privvy to details.'

'So we call him when needed. He doesn't have to know why he's at an address but he can cover a back door.'

Mike took a swig of beer. He looked at Callum, then Georgie. He ignored Gerry.

'Alright,' he said. 'While Ruiz is out of the game, the Good Samaritan here can do any leg work we got coming.'

'Out of the game?' said Georgie.

'Time to go, Gerry,' said Callum. 'I got your number.'

'Out of the game?' said Georgie again.

Gerry Martin nodded and stood. He said, 'Thanks, Lieu,' to Mike and left.

'*Out* of the *game*?' said Georgie, once more with feeling.

Mike said, 'You stick to your plan, Ruiz. You need to be home for a while.'

'What, to do you boys laundry when you get blood on your shirts?'

'Remember Arthur,' said Callum. 'Come on, Georgie.'

'No, you come on. I'll take the vacation time in a week or two. I work with Trish: I want to catch the bastard beat her up. So you tell me the next move and we figure how to make it happen. Which is what?'

Mike said, 'Avda Galkin. He sure as shit didn't bang up Alexander, but he called to set up the meet. What say we go over to his place and see what turns up?'

'It coulda been tossed already by whoever fought Trish,' said Callum, 'and I got a good idea who that was.'

Mike said, 'The suspense is killin' me.'

Callum took a small sheet of paper out of his pocket. It was of the type doctors made notes on at the end of a hospital bed.

'Trish told me the guy had a knife. It'll be in the reports. When I was alone with her at the hospital, she drew it for me.'

He stabbed the paper with his index finger. The drawing was of a long dagger. The guard was a fraction thicker than the blade, the grip the same size. There was a small pommel on the end. Callum thought it looked like a smaller version of a Centurion's sword in a movie.

'Kolya Slavin told me that Mystery Man, our bullet-scarred guy, had a Georgian dagger.'

'Some Civil War shit?' said Mike.

'Georgian like the country, you idiot,' said Callum. 'Whatever's goin' on here, I'll bet the house on this mystery asshole bein' up to his neck in this shit. And Slavin also told me Volkov is sweatin' because a young man in his employ – a hustler – has gone off the grid. A young man who sounds a lot like Avda.'

Mike nodded. 'OK, so we get over to Avda's, see what you can dig up.'

'We got a warrant?' said Georgie. 'I don't feel like filling out an Aided Card for kicking down a door we don't have a warrant for.'

'He's Callum's CI now. If anyone asks, Avda called for a meet, Cal got the notification on beeper. It'll show on phone records. Avda didn't turn up, hasn't been seen in the neighborhood for a while. Callum goes to his place for a Welfare Check.'

'No answer at the door, but I hear the sound of a struggle

inside,' said Callum. 'I bust open the door. Maybe there's a broken window.'

Mike rolled his eyes. 'Or maybe you pick the fuckin' lock and use gloves.' He raised his glass. 'The Welfare Check story is just in case a resident sees you in the corridor and asks what's up. Then you wait for them to go back to the Late Show and pick the goddamn lock anyway.'

Georgie whistled through her teeth. She looked askew at Callum and Mike, then shook her head. 'You guys are unbelievable.'

They made to answer but she shut them up with a raised hand.

'Seems to me, you shouldn't be there, Lieu. You got Fed attention, and we need someone to stay legit in all this. But I'm not working tonight and I got a perfect alibi back home: Arthur's there and won't work tomorrow.'

Callum said, 'Listen – '

Georgie said, 'I'm your back up. No arguments.'

They sat with their drinks, all three chewing over the fact that Trish could have died; that Avda could very well already be dead; that they were drifting pretty far off-reservation on this one.

'Alright,' said Mike. 'I got paperwork I gotta catch up on.'

Georgie looked at Callum and said, 'How'd whoever did this know your address?'

'No idea. Avda didn't have it, for damn sure. Maybe we'll find something in his place can point the way.'

The sounds of the main bar drifted in through the door to the private backroom. A bartender was yelling at a patron that he wouldn't take food stamps as payment for a drink.

Callum finished his beer.

'Alright Georgie, let's go.' He made to stand, then stopped and said, 'And you better bring the popcorn.' He pulled a video tape from behind his back. 'I picked this up from the floor of my apartment when I first got there and saw Trish. She said it fell from a bag the guy attacked her had with him. I figure if Avda's got a VCR, we watch a late night movie while we're in his place.'

*

They stood in the corridor outside Avda Galkin's apartment, Georgie's car parked on a street nearby. It was 1900. The video-tape was in a bag slung over Georgie's shoulder. They whispered as Callum picked the lock.

Georgie said, 'You wanna stay at mine tonight?'

Callum said, 'Why?'

'I know your place isn't a closed crime scene but I thought maybe you'd want some company.'

'No, you and Arthur need your time.'

'Me and Arthur are gonna' have plenty of time.' A smile heavy with shadows melted on her face. 'And the kids would love to see you in the morning.'

Callum hunched his shoulders and smiled back. It was a worse effort than Georgie's.

'Thanks, but I'll stay in my place tonight. I need to keep this edge I got – remember what went down there with Trish.' And if he was real lucky, he thought, the Russian asshole slapped her around might come back.

He'd been popping images of Trish since he found her; Jimmy Gilliland, too, half his head missing back in Belfast. The two memories had been climbing one over the other in his mind, ratcheting up this rage he felt boiling inside like storm clouds before the chaos and destruction of a big one. And he'd been having flashbacks – the cool sky above the city of his birth, turning black like dye billowing through pale blue water, after the bomb had driven him onto his back all those years ago.

Black. That was his world right now but for a chink of light in Trish and Georgie.

The lock gave. There was a second bolt inside. He used the pick to lever the bolt up a fraction, then slid it across until the door opened. Avda's place was musty but there was no corpse smell. The door opened directly onto the living room, where the drapes were open. Off the living room were two doors that he guessed led to a bedroom and bathroom. A kitchen unit stood against the wall on the left of the front door. It was a decent sized place compared to some, on the third floor of a modern 5-story apartment building on Ocean Avenue.

Their gloves squeaked as they went to work by flashlight. There was a pile of CDs next to a portable player in the living area by the couch. TV, VCR, a couple of Robert Mapplethorpe prints on the wall – was that Schwarzenegger?

Callum looked around the kitchen; Georgie went through to the bedroom. Twenty-five minutes later, they had nothing but a couple of gay lifestyle magazines and a Captain America comicbook.

Georgie said, 'When do you think he was here last?'

'I dunno,' said Callum. 'It isn't too dusty but the air was heavy when we came in. He seems a pretty neat guy. The place is tidy.'

He sat on the couch like he'd aged forty years and slapped his gloved hands on his knees. Georgie sat next to him. The bag was on her lap.

'Want to watch a movie?' she said.

She handed him the tape and he got up and knelt by the VCR. He fiddled with the controls, found a remote on top of the TV, and rejoined her on the sofa. The screen flickered to life. The scene looked like a hotel room. A middle-aged man came out of an ensuite bathroom. He walked to the bed and sat. The camera was hidden, bed-height. A liqor bottle framed the right side of the screen. Then Avda appeared from stage left and the show began.

They watched around five minutes, zipped through the tape, watched the last minute before Avda grabbed the video camera from its hiding place and cut the power. Callum felt hollow with a sudden and terrible sadness for the man, thousands of miles from home, alone, living this life.

Then again, he thought, who am I to judge? Maybe Avda digs this shit.

Georgie said, 'You know the client?'

'Not yet. But when I get this to Mike, I figure we'll get him through hotel records. The bath towel has a hotel name and address on it. The video has a timestamp.'

Callum craved a cigarette but didn't want to leave the smell in Avda's place. He let his head lie back on the couch and sighed hard.

Georgie said, 'You should get some rest. We aren't going to find this kid tonight.'

'Yeah. You remember that grave where we met Mike when all this started?'

'Up at Green-Wood, yeah.'

'The mobster dickhead was called Temuri-something. Avda won't have a grave like that.'

'Hey.' Georgie shoved him in the ribs. 'We don't know the kid's dead. And he isn't exactly a kid, anyway.'

Callum's head lolled on the couch.

'So many people hurt,' he said. He thought of the photographs he'd seen of Beresford and Mayhew. 'Let's go.'

He got up and bent to the VCR again, looked for the eject button and knocked over a cardboard videotape slipcase. It was empty of tapes but a small notebook fell on the carpet. He picked it up, showed it to Georgie. She raised her eyebrows. He sat next to her again and she held her flashlight on the book while Callum flicked through the pages. It was part ledger, part contact book. There were phone numbers, addresses. Not necessarily clients, thought Callum: Maxim Volkov would have that information and much of Avda's business – the business that mattered – would be conducted in hotel rooms like on the videotape.

There were a couple of entries with hearts next to them: one with the name Bobby had a phone number, an address in Chelsea and the word *SAFE* written next to it in English. Another entry, a cell number, had what looked like a code written in brackets: "(D-3185-P!!!)" and a word scrawled in Cyrillic, unreadable.

'We got something,' said Georgie.

Callum said, 'I'll pass this to Mike tomorrow. Let's call it a night.'

Georgie offered him a ride but he refused. His apartment was across the river and out of her way. Besides, he could do with the time to think on the subway. And he thought he might just stop for a drink somewhere around Chelsea on the way home.

Twenty-Nine

The bar was down two flights of stairs from street level. Callum had walked through a metal door cut into a larger, garage-style steel roller entrance. He made his way down a corridor lit in hellish red with shots of cut-bodied men in various states of undress. Then down steps to a landing with a closed door, with a small booth built into the wall on the right. Music pounded. He glimpsed a body-builder physique in baby oil dancing on a pedestal through the other side of the booth window.

SAFE was a gay bar in Chelsea, and the name next to that of 'Bobby' in Avda Galkin's ledger/contact book. Callum knew it from his time in uniform when he picked up a pick-pocket rolling patrons when he took them for a blowjob in an alley around the corner.

He paid the entrance fee and walked through. The room was long, with what looked like a warren of smaller rooms beyond. They were dark, some barely partitions. The place was three-quarters full of men. A long bar ran along the wall of the main room. He went over and ordered a beer. Some men drank, some watched the dancer. Some started fooling around then headed for the darker areas at the back.

Callum gestured to the bartender. Model-handsome, Latino features, immaculately scruffy quiff.

'Hey,' he said.

'Hey,' said the bartender. He had a thousand watt smile with movie star teeth.

Callum said, 'I'm from out of town.'

'I gathered.'

'A friend told me to check this place out. Knows a guy lives around here said I could maybe hook up with. Bobby – you know him?'

'Yeah, sure, I know Bobby.' The bartender gave him a check-out-the-slow-kid look. 'No offence, but you know how many Bobbys there are in New York?'

'He lives in Chelsea. I got his address written down somewhere.'

'What's he look like?' said the bartender.

Callum took a stab. 'About my height, short hair well-cut. Good body.'

As soon as he said it, he knew he'd just described the straight-guy image of a young gay man, right out of central casting. For all he knew, the mysterious Bobby had a limp, bad skin and a two-ton belly.

Now the bartender gave him a knowing smile.

'You a cop?'

Honesty was the best policy, Callum's mother had always said.

'Yeah,' he said. 'But I wanna help another guy – someone this Bobby hangs out with. This friend of Bobby's is missing and I want to make sure he's okay. I got Bobby's address in Chelsea but he ain't home and I thought he might be here.' Callum took a chance. 'The missing guy looks young, Russian, lives in Brighton Beach.'

'Avda,' said the bartender, half to himself. Then he looked Callum in the eye and said, 'I'm Bobby.'

Callum smiled. Thank you Ma, he thought.

*

He dozed in a storeroom on a beat-up couch until Bobby, second name Fernandez, finished his shift. Fernandez shook him awake and they walked three blocks to his apartment in a building

252

Callum figured the guy would soon be priced out of. The apartment was industrial, a metal pole in the center of the room and a hole in the wall where some kind of machine fixture had been torn out. This was the real deal, not the interior designer post-industrial bullshit of a SoHo loft apartment. Fernandez offered coffee. Callum took a glass of water instead. He'd want to catch some more sleep when he got through here. They sat opposite one another on breakfast bar chairs.

'Avda was here a couple of nights ago,' said Fernandez. 'He was scared, asked if he could stay for a few days. I told him sure – but he went out Sunday night for a job and never came back.'

Callum said, 'You didn't report him missing?'

'I was working Sunday night. I got home around six Monday morning. This place was quiet, his door was closed. I guessed he was asleep or still out. It's no big thing for either of us to go clubbing all night and not come home for a few days. Or maybe he had another job and was with a client.'

'You knew he's a prostitute?'

'Sure. Whatever. He told me about some of the people he's fucked, you know? Most of it's pretty mundane, just lonely guys looking to relieve a little pressure. Some is pretty kinky. This one guy had him use a tire hose, for putting air in your Dunlops – crazy shit. And this other guy – real fucking creepy – liked him to wear dresses and shit. Petticoats and knee socks, like a Little House On The Prairie trip. He'd only call Avda *she* or *her* when they fucked but – get this – he was a bona fide *bottom*.'

Callum gave him a blank look.

'On the Hershey Highway: he was the receiver every time. Just lay there and took it.'

'Gotcha.'

'Anyway, after some time I finally knocked on the door, went into Avda's room, and his stuff was exactly as I'd last seen it. It looked like he hadn't been back to my place.'

'This was Monday afternoon? You were concerned then, why not call 911? It's the wee small hours of Wednesday now.'

Bobby Fernandez sipped his coffee and gave Callum an apologetic shrug.

'Don't take this the wrong way,' he said, 'but neither of us have had great experiences with cops. He told me he got mixed up with this bastard cop slapped him around some. And something happened down in the Meatpacking District that freaked him out – that's why he wanted to stay with me. Plus, as I said, he could go on party binges for a few days – it happened before. Hey, am I in trouble?'

'Not at all,' said Callum

Bastard cop, he thought. Is that what I am?

Suddenly it seemed like the most important thing in the world to keep Avda Galkin alive.

He said, 'Avda was scared of some of his clients, too, wasn't he?'

'Shit, yeah,' said Fernandez. 'The guy he met on Sunday night was one of them. A German diplomat, if you can believe it.'

'He told you that?'

'This time, yeah. He was real upset on Sunday. Real scared. He talked a little more than usual.'

Callum leaned forward.

'Tell me more about this diplomat.'

Fernandez shrugged. 'He didn't say much more than the guy was German and he worked at the United Nations. I'm not sure he knew more than that but it scared him – this guy being rich, in politics. The German had a family and a reputation, so Avda would be a liability if anyone found out about their business.'

Bobby Fernandez had been staring into his cup. He looked up and said, 'He told me more about the bad cop.'

Callum flushed. He took a gulp of water to wash down the guilt-bile rushing up his throat.

'Yeah,' he said, 'I treated him pretty bad.'

Fernandez eyes went wide and he drew back a little.

'My God!' he said. Then his eyes narrowed. 'You don't look Italian. I mean, not that there's a *look* or anything. You sure don't sound Italian. This guy wasn't Italian from Italy but he had an Italian name. And I'm so sorry. I mean, if that whole Laura Ingles scene is your thing, who am I to judge?'

'Laura Ingles?'

'Little House On The Prairie? It was the bastard cop liked Avda in little girl bonnets and petticoats.'

'But you said this guy just lay there and took it; and the cop slapped Avda around.'

'Yeah, the cop beat on him when they weren't in bed. Pretty fucked up dynamic, huh? I mean … it isn't you, right?'

Something heavy plunged through Callum and seemed to leave him hollow. Fernandez read the confusion in his eyes and reflected it back.

'No, it ain't me,' said Callum, 'but this cop, he was Italian?'

'I'm sorry, I can't remember the name now. It was real obvious he was a guinea, though. Luigi, Lombardi, Bianchi. Something like that.'

Callum fought back a spike of rage, saw Fernandez flinch. He gave him a hands up gesture.

'Don't sweat it, Bobby, you got nothing to worry about from me,' he said. 'And this Italian motherfucker's name? I think I got it.'

*

Callum called Mike. It was 0630 on Wednesday morning.

Mike was chugging coffee. 'You been to bed yet?' he said.

'I got something for you. I'm gonna leave it with the desk sergeant at the Sixth. He'll bitch but he knows me from my time there. Can you come into the City and pick it up?'

255

'Sure. It ain't like I got a job to do or nothin'.'

'Thanks, I'll leave a note with the package explaining what it's about. And I need you to run something for me,' said Callum. 'Very quiet, use your Feds on this. It's a Detective Shield number. 3185. That's 3 – 1 – 8 – 5.'

'Anyone I know?' said Mike.

'I hope to God not,' said Callum, and hung up.

Thirty

Callum knocked on the door. On one hand, he didn't want anyone to answer; on the other, he'd kick it the fuck down if someone didn't. He was alone. There was no place for Mike, Georgie or even Gerry Martin on this one. He heard footsteps and his heart lurched when a little girl answered. She looked around nine years old in a Space Jam t-shirt and jeans.

'Hey,' said Callum, 'you must be Bria. My name's Callum, I work with your dad. I was just passing and wanted to call in and see him.'

He stood on the porch of the house in Annadale on Staten Island surrounded by trees, sculpted lawns and wide, quiet side-walks. It seemed like a great area to raise kids. The house at which he stood was a good-sized clapboard affair.

Callum read the indecision in the little girl's face.

'Why don't you close the door and go ask your daddy? My name is Callum Burke. OK?'

'OK.'

The girl disappeared. After a minute she was back, her chin tucked into her chest, long hair tied back in a ponytail held by an MTV hairclip.

'Daddy says to go on through,' she said. 'He's out back. Just walk straight to the end.'

Callum said, 'Thanks, Bria.'

Inside, the house was open plan, the living room divided from the kitchen by a partition. A wall on the right was peppered with family photographs, a door set in the center. At the far end of the house was a sunken room with big glass windows looking out on a spacious area of grass, two apple trees in the far corners and a wooden fence encircling the whole deal. Callum was surpised it wasn't white picket.

Angel Patrosi sat on a chair with his busted leg in traction, watching a TV playing Married With Children re-runs. He had a glass of lemonade on a tray on his lap and a remote in his hand.

'Callum,' he said, 'how you doin'?'

'I had better days, Angel.'

A shadow crossed Patrosi's face. Callum glanced at the windows. He took out a pack of Lucky Strike and made to grab a cigarette.

'Sorry,' said Patrosi, 'no smoking in the house, man.'

Callum, somewhere else in his head, said, 'Hmm? Oh, sure.' He set the pack on a table next to Angel's chair with the jug of lemonade on it.

Angel said, 'Sorry to hear you ain't so good, Cal. You wanna drink or somethin'?'

'No, I'm good. Hey, I saw this one – it's the one where the bathroom gets redecorated and Al's all freaked out, right? This is some old shit now.'

'Yeah, daytime TV. No wonder so many housewives get high. At least this is from this decade.'

'You know,' said Callum, 'we used to get a lot of old American TV in Hong Kong. Kojak, The Waltons. My wife used to love Little House On The Prairie. All those pigtails and petticoats and shit.'

He watched Angel. Not a blink of an eye.

'Nice rig,' said Callum. Patrosi had some top-class equipment at home to help him cope with his leg while it healed.

'Yeah, the PBA really weighed in, and the 10-13 party was a big help. Tell all the guys thanks, huh?'

They were silent for a few seconds. Callum looked at some framed photographs arrayed around the room. Angel Patrosi in uniform, with members of the team. One of Patrosi and Sarge bowling at a department tournament. Patrosi and Gerry Martin fishing somewhere upstate. Angel saw him looking and said, 'So, to what do I owe the pleasure?'

Callum took a breath and went for it.

'There's no easy way to say this, Angel, and I'm sorry I gotta lay this down in your house with your little girl at home: but I know you're a sometime client of Avda Galkin – ' he took a shot, ' – and I know you're on Maxim Volkov's books.'

Patrosi blanched for a second.

Al Bundy bitched and moaned on the TV.

Then Patrosi nodded to the door.

'Close that, will you?'

Callum did.

Patrosi hissed, 'Fuck you!'

'But only if I dress up real pretty like a little girl, right Angel? Lucky you're in traction or you might wanna slap me around some between the fucking.'

Callum produced Avda's notebook. He flicked to a page and read out the cell number, the entry in brackets, *D-3185-P!!!*, and showed the scrawl to Patrosi.

He said, 'That's your badge number: D for Detective. The 'P' is obvious. The exclamation marks say you're important. You want I should have a Russian cop translate that Cyrillic?'

Angel Patrosi lay his head back on his chair and took a deep breath like he was tasting free air for the last time. His eyes filled up. He wiped them and cleared his throat several times. Callum pulled open his jacket and shirt, and showed he wasn't wearing a wire.

He played it out – took a chance Patrosi didn't know Avda was missing. 'I turned up unexpected at Avda's place and found this book. I figured he'd been giving me bum information. And that cop he was acting as CI to, same time as you? That guy is OC

Investigation Division. So I was just there at Avda's apartment to scare the kid straight, and he gave you up. I guess he thought it would cut him slack.'

Patrosi blew a long stream of air out of puckered lips. He said, 'I knew I was screwed when you told me that little Russian motherfucker was CI for another cop. Jesus, this'll kill Annabel. I'll lose Bria.'

'You'll go to jail,' said Callum, playing a hunch. He figured maybe, just maybe, Patrosi could be connected with Maxim Volkov. If the Russian hood might be using Avda to get compromising videos on the great and not-so-good, he'd sure as shit jump at the chance of snaring himself a tame cop.

'You know how this works,' he said, 'I call 1-800 PRIDEPD, or tell a CO about your extra-curriculars. You're a C-Case, highest designation the Rat Squad got: A-1 classification for dead-cert prison time. Kangaroo court in One Police Plaza. Prosecution only gotta prove a 51% chance of misconduct for you to get some kinda punishment. At the very least, you're outta the Job for sleeping with a prostitute, and your CI at that.'

'And you're willing to play rat?' Patrosi's voice was strained ready to snap. He kept snorting snot back up his nose and his eyes were hangover-scarlet.

And right there was the rub. Was Callum willing to turn him in?

He knew many cops would say no, but then many cops were never confronted with more than a partner wiping the odd parking ticket and letting a girlfriend walk on a bullshit summons. This was the big leagues. Callum figured cops despised IAB, and refused to rat on fellow cops, because of the old adage – *there but for the grace of God go I*. They were surrounded by the worst humanity had to offer, beaten and abused, often by 'honest' citizens. They saw the scum of the earth make it big on easy money while they sacrificed their kids' upbringing for the overtime slog – collars for dollars – to supplement a paltry salary. They got hooked on booze, the wrong women or men, drugs. Gambling. Christ, Callum knew all about that one from his time in Asia.

He said, 'I ain't always followed the Patrol Guide. Especially in Hong Kong. When I moved here, I got a clean slate and I'm doin' my best to keep it that way. Now you throw this shit in my face, what am I supposed to do, Angel? If this was RICO, my ass could go down too through association, Christ's sake.'

Patrosi looked at the remote in his lap.

Time to take a breath and dive in. Callum threw it out there.

'How long you been on Volkov's books?'

Patrosi looked at the door. Callum figured he saw a couple of futures there, none of them happy endings with his wife and daughter. His eyes drifted to his busted leg then, lazily, up to Callum. They were old bird dog eyes. Tears striped his cheeks.

'A couple years,' he said. His voice was thin. He cleared his throat. 'We all got secrets, huh? Now you know mine. Better you than Annabel or Bria. Me and Avda, we had some times. I knew he was a hustler, met him in a place south of Chelsea. It kept it simple, uncomplicated.' He snorted. 'Who knew? Eventually, Avda works out I'm a cop. Found one of my cards one time stickin' out of my pocket. "Detective Patrosi". So he hides a Camcorder and makes a videotape and, next thing I know, I'm serving warrants on Maxim Volkov's competition in the heroin trade.'

'And that's it? You busted people on Volkov's say-so; you never clipped someone?'

'Fuck no!' Patrosi went red. 'I'm a fuck up but there's a line.'

Sure, thought Callum, there's a line. Trouble is, it creeps on and on.

'So you busted dealers – only heroin?'

'Yeah. Volkov doesn't deal in other product. He got a pipeline leads all the way to Afghanistan.'

'Via London?'

'Sometimes, maybe. Why not?'

'You heard of Nikolai Popov?'

Patrosi said, 'Volkov's nephew, yeah. Not the brightest spark in the fusebox.'

'We busted him last week on a Controlled Delivery,' said Callum. 'He had a stash of product sent from London. Volkov sends product by airmail?'

'If he's having issues with the supply chain, maybe. He's like any other perp: 2% brains to 98% balls. But he's smart enough to keep a distance from the rackets. I'll bet he was insulated from that bust.'

'He used his nephew?'

Patrosi said, 'Kid's an asshole. Nothin's gonna lead back to Uncle V. Volkov probably wanted him out of the way, so he lost some product but put some distance between him and his idiot nephew.'

'Popov knew the hitters we stumbled in on at Coney Island.'

'Some of us stumbled more than others.' Patrosi nodded at his leg.

Callum said, 'Avda told me Volkov was getting rid of Beresford and Mayhew, and the hitters. You know about that?'

'Sure,' said Patrosi. 'The black guys were cuttin' in on his business with some high-rolling customers; the hitters were doin' a deal behind his back. We were supposed to go in there and bust the hitters, clean up what was left of Beresford and Mayhew.'

'And Volkov wasn't concerned the hitters might lead back to him?'

'They couldn't. Contract was taken out in Russia by a third party.'

Callum mulled it over. A lot of faces in Brighton Beach must have contacts by association in the Motherland, but Maxim Volkov would have serious Krysha – the "roof" – Mike had told him about, a name to add some weight and protection to his operation. This was a good indication of why Volkov was one of the top guys in the neighborhood: he had active muscle in Russia to broker hits and, probably, product.

Patrosi was staring at the TV screen. He started to cry a little again.

'Million dollar question time,' said Callum. 'Did you give that Russian motherfucker my address?'

Patrosi stared. His eyes glistened with tears and his mouth worked like a landed fish for a couple of seconds. Then his face went red and he said, 'Jesus, no! You're a cop, on the team! What do you think I am?'

'Why not? He paid you enough, you'd tell him. You ain't got history with me like you do with Sarge or Gerry.'

Patrsoi shook his head. He was on the verge of anger now.

'No fucking way! There's a line, Cal. Even if I had some beef with you – which I don't – that's somewhere I'd never go.'

Callum swallowed down something bitter and made a decision. He felt like he had an angel on one shoulder, a devil on the other. He told the angel to take a hike. The asshole threw a verse at him, Titus 1:15, "To the pure, all things are pure, but to the defiled and unbelieving, nothing is pure; but both their minds and their consciences are defiled". The devil on his other shoulder told the angel to shove his scripture up his ass. The angel threw images of Tara, Trish, Georgie at Callum. Even Reverend Dickson at First Saint John's Faith Baptist. *You'll never sit in that church with an easy conscience again*, said the angel.

Callum said a prayer, asked for forgiveness and kicked him to the curb. The devil laughed. Callum told him to go to Hell.

'Alright,' he said. 'So far three people know about your shenanigans, Angel. Maxim Volkov, me and Avda Galkin. I can keep Avda quiet. You tell me some more of what you know about Volkov and maybe I stay quiet, too.'

The bird-dog in the chair with the busted leg looked up like someone offered him a steak.

'Yeah?' said Patrosi.

'Maybe. Starter for ten – was Volkov ever in Afghanistan, I mean during the war?'

'What war?'

'The fucking Afghan War. The eighties, the Soviets and Mujahideen.'

'The Muja-ma-what?'

Callum thought he should bust Patrosi on the grounds of being so goddamn dumb.

'You ever seen The Living Daylights?'

'The Bond movie?'

'Yeah. He helps the good guys – that's the Mujahideen – fight the bad guys – that's the Soviet military everyone in America was so fuckin' scared of. Ring a bell?'

'Hey, we wasn't scared of nobody.'

'Sure.'

'Listen, if you think Maxim Volkov was in any man's army, you're severely fuckin' mistaken. I saw his record once, some shit he got from Russia when he came over here. The real shit, not the bullshit identity he paid for to clear our Immigration. He was drunk and showin' off, and the only uniform he ever wore was prison stripes.'

The theory of Callum's bullet-scarred Mystery Man hunting Volkov for revenge went spiralling to the floor and crept under the door.

'You sure?' he said.

'Can you be sure of anything with a fucking gangster?'

'OK. You ever seen a fit-looking guy around Volkov or Avda? Not pumped but lean, gray eyes, dirty-fair hair, cut kinda' short?'

'I seen a lotta guys.'

'If he had an open-necked shirt or some shit, you'd see he got these little scars on his chest, puckered skin.' Callum pointed to his own chest. 'I think they're bullet wounds healed up.'

Patrosi's eyes drifted off somewhere – maybe a bathhouse, or a gay hangout, or some drinking hole owned by Volkov. They came back to Callum empty.

'I got nothin'.'

'Did Avda ever mention someone like that?'

'There was a guy,' said Patrosi. 'Some guy he used to see non-business. He never gave me a name or anythin' but he called him his wounded soul or broken man or some shit. Romantic, you know.'

'You never looked into it?'

'I don't want to get caught up in fag business, shit creeps me out.'

The skepticism on Callum's face was easier to read than a large-print paperback.

'Look, I ain't gay,' said Patrosi, 'it's just – '

'You're happier than most, I got it,' said Callum. 'He ever mention where he was going to meet this guy?'

'No … wait a second! I remember, it was a kinda fucked up dynamic because this guy was fuckin' a woman, too, and Avda knew about it. And the weird thing was, he didn't pay with Avda but the woman was a whore. Around 30, I think, Russian. Maybe illegal, I dunno.'

'You got a name?'

'Sounded like a place for boats and shit – Regata? Ma … Marina! Yeah, Marina, that's it!'

Callum grabbed a pen from his pocket and wrote the name down in Avda's notebook. He thought of the scrawny woman with the sharp features who sat in Grove Court among the ivy. How she had looked beautiful from a distance until she got up close and he saw the wear of too many tricks, maybe too many drugs, on her face. How she had spoken Russian with a bone-chilling message: his address – his vulnerability. She knew where he lived and she probably knew Mystery Man. It had to be the woman: it had to be the bullet-scarred asshole who had invaded his home and beat on Trish.

'That's good, Angel,' he said. 'That's good.'

Callum asked more about Volkov. After ten minutes he was ready to leave.

'We're done for now,' he said. 'So here's what happens. You heal. Then you quit the Job.'

'What?'

'You go be a security guard or a train driver or start a drag act, I don't give a shit. But you never work another day for the NYPD. Don't take this wrong, Patrosi, but you're dogshit. If I had bigger balls, I'd take this up the chain. But we got enough dirty cops dragging this department through the papers. We don't need another. And the people of New York sure as shit don't need you on the street workin' their tax dollars and keepin' them safe. You quit, you forfeit the pension, everything.'

'I got nothin' else.'

'A minute ago you were sobbin' about your family. You keep them provided you can live with yourself and not tell them what a low-life piece of shit you really are. You stay out of prison where they won't wear pretty dresses when they use you like a bitch. Now shut the fuck up, you got a Ricki Lake re-run on the TV.'

He picked up the pack of Lucky Strikes from the table and opened it to reveal a small tape recorder hidden inside.

Patrosi rolled his eyes.

'You cocksucker!' he said. 'You don't sound so good on that tape, either, you know?'

'I got the original, I can edit. And I got a shit-hot rabbi in Inspector Bocchini in my corner. How you like them apples?'

Callum went to the door.

As he walked he said, 'Don't get up, I'll see myself out.'

The devil on his shoulder snickered hard.

Thirty-One

Callum went back to his apartment. The place looked pretty much the same as always. Nothing had been broken in the struggle between Trish and Mystery Man: the phone was back on the table near the door. He didn't have a flashback of Trish bleeding and shaken, although there was still a small blood stain on the floor. Her body would heal fast enough; her spirit was stronger than shipyard steel. Callum went and picked up the phone.

He got a kick out of the fact Trish had crushed the bullet-scarred bastard's balls with it as he called Mike.

When he got hold of his friend, they talked for ten minutes before Callum asked him to clear him of Narcotics duty for the next couple of days and keep him on loan. Then he asked if Maxim Volkov was currently under surveillance. Mike said the Feds kept an eye on him, but there was a big operation going down with the Colombians and agents were being directed there where possible. The Feds were stretched but they still checked the phones, and had a tracker on Volkov's cars too. Callum told Mike his plan and asked he try to keep the Feds off him that afternoon; that he would pop up around Volkov today. Then he asked Mike to run the name Marina for a Russian national, around 30 years of age. Callum knew it was probably a lost cause but wanted to try – put the name in an old U49 and hit up the Feds, touch base with Immigration through them if possible. He guessed the girl was illegal but it was worth a shot.

Once he got through holding the receiver away from his ear through Mike's rant, he thanked him and hung up. Then he called the number for the doctor he'd talked with at the hospital, when Trish was brought in. They spoke for twenty minutes.

Next, he searched for the crumpled paper given him by Kolya Slavin and called the old man – he couldn't think of the 59 year-old as anything but old, he looked so haggard. Slavin was at home and picked up on the fourth ring.

Callum said, 'You want to earn some money?'

'I live to serve,' said Slavin.

'I'll call you back in four hours. At that time, you tell me where Maxim Volkov is hanging out.'

'I'll have to check my tracking satellite is in range.'

'I know, I'm reaching. But if you don't ask … '

'And ignorance is bliss.'

Callum said, 'Four hours.' He hung up.

Gerry wasn't home. Callum left a message on his machine.

Next, he called Georgie. He felt kind of bad when her husband picked up and wasn't sure why. Arthur sounded the same as always: better, even. Georgie came on the line and Callum asked if she could be around Brighton Beach in four hours. She could. They agreed a time and place to meet. He hung up.

Then he went to bed.

*

He was glimpsing Prospect Park through lines of brick tenements from the Q Train window when he remembered he hadn't scrubbed the last spots of blood from the floor in his place. He had slept, showered, changed and tried Gerry again. This time he got him and they spoke for around ten minutes. Then Callum had gone out with his gun in his holster and his badge in his jacket pocket.

The train rocked past the backs of houses, garages, tenement blocks.

He laid his head back on the window and thought of Irene and Tara. He remembered how, during shifts with the Royal Hong

Kong Police, he'd ache for Irene. After Tara, how they'd lie together, the three of them inseparable. Now, years later, he'd had a couple of half-assed relationships since coming to New York but Irene had always been there in his head, getting more distant and more perfect with time. All the fights and rough edges had been filed down by distance and years until he was scared – no other word for it – goddamn scared, to pick up the phone and call because of how shit it made him feel about his own life. And yet Tara: what would he give to hold Tara again, hear her laugh?

Then Trish Alexander came along.

He got off the train at Brighton Beach elevated station and walked along the avenue and down Brighton 4th Street to the boardwalk. He pulled his long t-shirt down to make sure his gun was covered.

Georgie was waiting next to a municipal parking lot on the boardwalk. It was a warm afternoon and she took in Callum's leather jacket, not a million miles away from the average Russian gangster's idea of chic.

'When in Rome?' she said.

'It's lightweight. Let's find a payphone.'

When he dialled Kolya Slavin, the old man picked up straight off.

'So,' said Callum, 'you got his whereabouts?'

'I am taking a risk for you here. I had to contact one of his associates with some fiction about needing a loan. Maxim Volkov knows me, he knows this is not how I do things.'

'He's under investigation. When we talk, I can tell him he's under surveillance and I found him that way. You'll be clear.'

Callum heard Slavin breathe on the other end of the line.

Then the old man said, 'He's at the State Restaurant, planning some kind of function there.'

'Got it, thanks.'

The State was a couple of blocks away on Brightwater Ct. The door was open but a "CLOSED" sign hung on the glass. There was a canopy over the entrance and thick pleated drapes would have suited a Funeral Parlor were hung in the windows. A poster in a perspex covered frame advertised a night of cabaret with twin sisters who looked as if they'd spent half their adult life under the cosmetic surgeon's knife. Their lips were so inflated they could have floated the Titanic.

Georgie took her detective shield out and let it hang on the chain around her neck. They tried the door. It was open so they walked in the entrance to a corridor straight out of a Tzarist-Russia acid-dream. Heavy velvet drapes hung at intervals, richly patterned wallpaper held ornate gold leaf light fixtures. The carpet was a tapestry of garish paisley and Russian motifs. Statuary of naked women and cherubs and Bogatyr knights stood against the walls.

A man in a tuxedo came rushing down the corridor, saw Callum and Ruiz, and said, 'I'm sorry, we are closed.'

Georgie tinned him with her shield and said, 'And we're open for business. NYPD. Is Maxim Volkov here?'

The man almost genuflected.

'I'm sorry, we – '

'We need to speak to Mr Volkov in private.'

'You understand, Detective, once a patron is on our premises, they become our responsibility. May I ask with what this is in connection?'

'No, you may not. Police business, unless you and your establishment want to get involved. Are you the owner here?'

The man's face melted a little like wax under a flame.

'No, no, I am simply – '

A deep, rich voice called out from the shadows, 'It's fine, Sacha, I am always happy to provide whatever assistance I can to our esteemed police department.'

Sacha flinched and led them down the corridor into the darkness. He showed them through a door in time for them to watch Maxim Volkov settle his bulk in an ornate chair backed in red velvet with a carved frame painted gold.

A king's throne fit for a Russian mobster's grave, thought Callum.

They were at the end of a long dining hall. Mirrors covered one of the walls; chandeliers hung from the ceiling. The carpet was lush and woven with some design like family crests with a large wooden rectangle for dancing by a stage at the far end of the room. Tables were stacked along the walls, but one was out and laid with a white cloth and small tea cups by Volkov's chair.

The Russian mobster took a sip from his cup, his black shirt-sleeve riding up his thick forearm to reveal the inked woman smoking at a table laden with cash and a gun. When he raised the petite cup to his lips, it made his huge skull look monstrous. A man stood behind him. Callum recognized the small forehead, flat as a board, and the thick, bull neck that seemed to be swallowing his chin. One of the thugs from the bathhouse. Bull-Neck looked Georgie over then turned to Callum. His reptilian brain did the calculations and his eyes widened.

'*Ty,*' he said, '*Ty musor!*'

Callum said, 'Surprise.'

Volkov rubbed his chin and spoke to Georgie.

'Do you have identification?'

Georgie gestured to her shield hung at her chest. 'Detectives Georgina Ruiz and Callum Burke, Brooklyn South Narcotics,' she said.

'No prizes for guessing who is who. Might I see your identification, Detective Burke?'

Callum pulled his badge from his pocket.

'Forgive me, *Officer*,' said Volkov, 'for not giving you your proper title.'

Georgie said, 'You're aware you are under investigation and surveillance by the NYPD and Federal law enforcement. It's how we found you. But I want to assure you that is not why we are talking to you right now, Mr Volkov.'

Volkov's thick frame shook for a moment with a deep chuckle.

'That comes as a great relief, Detective Ruiz. So what the fuck do you want with me, that you have to disturb my afternoon tea?'

'A missing persons case, a Russian woman named Marina. Around 30 years of age, fair hair, slim, sharp features and blue eyes.'

'You have just described a large part of the female population of this neighborhood.'

Callum said, 'We believe she could be a prostitute.'

Volkov kept his eyes on Georgie. 'I don't believe I know any women in that profession. You know, I am a married man.'

'Nina, right?' said Callum. He pulled the name from Volkov's file out of his memory. 'You married her for a $15,000 fee 'cause she had a Green Card. Good work. She used to do some singin' right here, correct?'

Volkov's Bull-Necked bodyguard shifted his weight a little.

Callum thought back to the bathhouse. Through the steam, the face of Jimmy Gilliland emerged, half of it gone. The steam turned black like the bomb-scarred sky. Then he heard Trish Alexander call out in his head as Mystery Man beat her. The steam built with the pressure in his skull; it felt like someone shoved a dagger behind his eyes. Bull-Neck watched him hard and Callum stared back to avoid flinching with the pain in his head.

He felt something snap inside.

'Hey, Igor,' he said, looking at Bull-Neck and gesturing to the rectangle of wood flooring set near the stage, 'you wanna dance?'

He took off his jacket and shoved the badge in the pocket while Bull-Neck smiled like Christmas came early.

Georgie said, 'Officer Burke … '

Callum unclipped his gun and offered it to Georgie with the jacket.

He said, 'This asshole ain't got much of a chin to start with, but I figure it's glass, just the same.'

Bull-Neck watched Volkov, waiting for the word. Volkov watched Callum with a spark of light dancing in eyes dimmed by shadow.

Georgie said, 'Officer Burke, I need you to step back.'

'What,' said Callum, staring at Bull-Neck, 'you think this'll go hard after because I'm a cop?' He pulled up his t-shirt. 'I ain't wired. We can go out back if you like. Detective Ruiz won't report nothin'.'

Georgie spat, 'Officer Burke!'

'Detective Ruiz.' Volkov's voice seemed to fill the space. He ran brutal fingers through his gray-white hair. 'Officer Burke has shown us he is not wired. If you could oblige, I believe we could talk more freely.'

Georgie wore a black jacket and blue shirt. She shrugged off the jacket as Callum, eyes locked with Bull-Neck, shrugged his back on and clipped his Glock on his belt. Georgie unbuttoned her shirt to reveal a simple white camisole. She pulled it up to her chest and turned once.

'Very good,' said Volkov.

Bull-Neck said something in Russian. The sleaze dripping off his words could have pooled at his feet.

Georgie nodded and buttoned her shirt. But not as high as before.

Callum felt the rage seep out of his pores. It left a hollow sense of defeat he couldn't understand.

'This woman, Marina,' said Volkov, 'I never heard of her and that's the truth. You trust me or you don't, it's nothing to me. However, you might want to ask a known gangster in Brighton Beach, Arkady Kuznetsov. He runs girls across the neighborhood.'

Georgie said, 'Hit your competition? That's original.'

'That's close to slander, Detective.'

'Here's another for you,' said Callum, 'you know a man about my height, wiry build? Gray eyes, dirty-fair hair cut short. High cheekbones, kinda thick lips. Got three puckered craters on his chest about here, here and here – bullet wounds.'

He caught the spark in Bull-Neck's eyes. Volkov's poker face never budged.

'I can't help you,' he said.

'Funny, he was in the bathhouse same day as me. Igor over there seemed to lose interest in my face as soon as the guy walked in. In fact, he took off after the guy like his ass was on fire.'

Bull-Neck glanced at Volkov. Volkov poured himself a cup of tea.

He said, 'You must be mistaken, Officer.'

Callum looked at Bull-Neck and said, 'How about you? You got a name for the guy?'

Bull-Neck's eyes flickered. His face bloomed red. Then he shrugged his shoulders.

'No,' said Callum, 'takes more than three brain cells to re-member anything past when you last jerked off. Or maybe you jerk your boss off, instead.'

'Officer Burke,' said Georgie, her voice tight with anger, 'get the fuck out.'

The words hit Callum like a slap in the face. His cheeks felt hot, his stomach cold. Georgie never spoke to him like that. And in front of these animals? He opened his mouth to reply, then saw Bull-Neck's face split in a broken-toothed grin. Volkov had the ghost of a smile on his face. Georgie's face was granite.

He turned and walked out of the room, down the corrridor and into the street.

*

'Asshole,' said Georgie. 'Gentlemen, I apologise for my subordinate's attitude.'

Maxim Volkov said, 'You can't be held responsible.'

Bull-Neck nodded. His grin had taken on a predatory aspect.

'Irish,' said Georgie. 'Born over there. Typical, thinks he's better than some street Spic like me.'

She shook her head and stood straighter. Her chest pushed out an inch or so and she put her hands on her hips, placing her weight on her left leg and straightening the right. Her pants pulled tighter across her crotch and ass. Volkov appraised her like a judge on Miss America. Bull-Neck almost licked his lips.

'Listen,' said Georgie, 'I'm under pressure. Being a woman in the NYPD ain't easy and I gotta deal with assholes like that ignorant mick all day long. You guys are the opposition, but sometimes I wish I worked your side of the fence.'

Volkov said, 'I'm not sure I understand your meaning, but there's always employment with me, if you're interested.'

Georgie rolled her head around her shoulders a little, felt her shirt buttons strain as she arched her back, knew the lace of the camisole would be tracing an outline on her shirt. She brought her gaze to bear on Volkov, then Bull-Neck and laughed. It was throaty and kind of dirty.

'Hell, there's always something sexy about a bad boy, huh? I bet you get so much goddamn pussy.' She pursed her lips. 'But listen, I'm in the shit. I'm working reduced hours. I'm drowning in bills. I gotta find this bullet-scarred guy my asshole partner was talkin' about and get a bump up the pecking order in my squad. Then I got more responsibility; more information. And who knows … you scratch my back …'

She pulled the shirt and camisole up like she was rearranging her clothes and getting comfortable, giving the Russians a flash of her flat stomach. Then she turned on her best thousand watt smile and strolled over to the table. She took a chair, turned it back to front and sat with her legs splayed either side like a Vogue covergirl.

Maxim Volkov studied her for a moment like a taxonomist classifying a newly discovered species. Then he asked her for a business card, accepted hers with a nod and stood. He leant close to Bull-Neck and spoke in whispered Russian.

After a minute he said, 'My friend here will try to help you, Detective Ruiz. Do inquire with Arkady Kuznetsov after the girl: she is probably one of his. Give me a call here anytime, I'll get your message. Perhaps I can help a little with those bills you are struggling with. And tell Officer Burke he may want to step carefully in Brighton Beach.'

Then he was gone.

Bull-Neck sat in Volkov's chair, his knees at 08.20. Ruiz could swear he had the beginnings of a hard-on swelling his jeans.

He said, 'This *opuschiny lavrushnik* that Irish shit was asking about: does he have a knife about this long, this shape?' and described a dagger in the air with his hands.

'Yeah, I think I remember somethin' about that in a report.'

'He was in the *banya* – the bathhouse – like your shithead friend said. He had the scars on his chest, the blue eyes. I chased him out and he waved that dagger around before he got away. It's called a kinjal. Georgian.'

Georgie said, 'The Irishman isn't my friend.'

'That's good,' said Bull-Neck. He ran his hands up and down his thighs for a moment, then said, 'I met the knife man once before then. He was in a store on Brighton Beach Avenue,

Fogelman's. He confronted me and another of Mr Volkov's employees. There was a fight.'

'Who won?'

'Not my colleague. It was a stalemate and the bastard got away, but he cut my friend on the neck. There must have been poison on the blade. My friend is alive but brain dead. Mr Volkov told us to avoid Fogelman's from then on. He has more important business than helping out a small-time store owner.'

'That's very kind of him – and you: "helping out" this Fogelman like that.'

'We help anyone who is deserving.'

'That's an attractive quality in a man.' Georgie stood slow. 'You've helped me out a lot. Here's my card. If you see this dagger guy again, don't confront him – give me a call, huh?'

Bull-Neck took the card with an official department number on, and looked up at her from his seat like a horny schoolboy.

'And if I don't see him,' he said, 'should I give you a call?'

Georgie shot him a wink. 'Goes without saying,' she said.

Then she walked out of the room with a wave and a sashay of hips.

Thirty-Two

'Are men really that simple?' said Georgie.

She stood with Callum by the boardwalk and the municipal parking lot on Brighton 4th Street, off Brightwater Ct. Callum hadn't said words of more than one syllable since she'd met him back outside the State Restaurant. Images and memories were piercing his mind like swords in a magician's magic box: Jimmy Gilliland, Tara, Irene, Trish, Avda Galkin; Belfast, Hong Kong, Greenwich Village. Even the old Irish crew he'd run with under-cover. He had a splitting headache, fuel for the low-fi rage pacing back and forth deep inside. That slap from Georgie – her telling him to get the fuck out – felt like a betrayal. He knew the truth, hoped to God he did, that she was pulling a good cop-bad cop with some method acting thrown in. But everything in his life felt fragile right now, and he couldn't shake that sense of treachery.

Georgie said, 'Cal, you were out of control back there.'

'Yeah.'

'You were calling out Volkov's guy in a public restaurant. The employee opened the door for us was a witness. You could have screwed me with that, too.'

'Sorry.'

'Jesus, what are you, six years old? Stop with the sulk, Officer.'

He looked up at that and she recoiled a little from his eyes.

Fragile, he thought, everything so fucking fragile. Himself most of all.

'How'd you know he'd talk to you with me out of the room?' he said.

Georgie shrugged. 'I didn't, for sure, but they were both staring at my tits the moment we walked in. In their eyes, I humiliated

279

you: they hate you and and they liked my body, so it gave them a reason to talk. Now they're hoping for more – but Hell will freeze over before they come within thirty feet of me without cuffs on.'

He picked up the receiver from the payphone and said, 'You did good.'

And he meant it. Sounded lame as shit, though – like she needed *his* approval.

He called Kolya Slavin. Again, the old MVD man answered after a couple of rings.

Callum said, 'Don't you ever leave your place?'

'I forgot to mention,' said Slavin, 'I'm a vampire. I look so pale because of the sun block I wear during the day. But at night, I wander the streets drinking the blood of nubile young women and thick-headed Irish policemen.'

'I wanna meet.'

'When?'

'Around ninety minutes – no, make it two hours: 1615.'

'You would expose me to the deadly rays of the sun again, after risking my neck to help you visit Maxim Volkov?'

'It's cool,' said Callum. 'He thinks I knew his location because he's under surveillance.'

'Did he remember you from the bathhouse?'

'Volkov didn't say but he knew. One of the goons confronted me in there had been with him. He squared up a little. It was a fun reunion.'

There was a silence on the line. Then, 'Where do you want to meet?'

'In front of Astroland, on the boardwalk.'

'Very well.'

Callum killed the call.

Georgie gave him an *all-set?* look and he nodded. Then he called Mike's cell number.

Mike said, 'Yeah?'

'We're through with Volkov. I think you should come down here.'

'Anything I need to know?'

'We can talk in person. How about Dino's?'

'What time you got?'

'Let's say an hour – think you can make it?'

Mike paused for a second, spoke to someone nearby on his end, then came back on the line.

'Yeah, I'll be there. What're you doin' in the meantime?'

'Mystery Man had a dust-up with Volkov's goons last week in a store on Brighton Beach Avenue,' said Callum. 'Sounds like a territorial thing, probably collectin' dues. Me and Georgie will talk to the store owner, see if we can get somethin' more on Mystery Man. I figure the bastard's definitely workin' for Arkady Kuznetsov.'

'Time for another visit to our other favourite Russian mob boss, huh?'

'Probably. See you in an hour.'

He put the phone down.

Georgie said, 'We good?'

Something in her face stilled the carousel of memories in Callum's head and the deep rage in his gut a little.

'You know I love you, right Georgie?' he said. 'And it doesn't come easy, me saying that to anyone right now.'

She smiled. 'I know.'

'All right.' Callum shoved his hands in his pockets and shot a smile back. 'We're good.'

*

A sign hung on the door of Fogelman's declaring, "Closed: Please Drop By Later".

Callum and Georgie exchanged a glance. Closed mid-afternoon looked wrong.

Georgie tried the door. It opened: the lock was on the inside, unfastened. They entered and took in the store. It was long, more expansive than the façade would suggest. Lots of dependable clothing that would never be in fashion, the kind of wear people picked up for a funeral when they didn't own a suit and didn't want to spend too much. There was a big, solid-looking counter at the far end. No one in sight.

They walked toward the counter.

'NYPD,' called Georgie. 'We'd like to talk to the owner. Hello?'

Callum joined her. 'Is Mr Fogelman here? NYPD. We need to talk.'

They saw the register was open when they got to the counter. A few bills were strewn on the floor. Their eyes met; their hands went to their guns. A door was set in the wall in the corner next to a mop splayed on the floor. Callum nodded to the door and they crept over, Glocks drawn and held in a two-handed grip. Ruiz pulled her shield out, Callum clipped his badge to his belt. They stood either side of the door. Something the color of rust was smeared on the handle.

Georgie mouthed the word, *Kleenex*? But Callum shook his head. She pulled her shirt sleeve down over her hand and turned the handle real slow. Then they heard a click as loud as a hammer-cock on a revolver in the quiet of the store.

They both caught the smell.

'Police,' said Callum.

He shouldered the door like a linebacker on a quarterback. It hit the inner wall with a bang like a gunshot. Then they were in, yelling and aiming at monsters in the gloom, freaking themselves out with noise and fury. They edged around a space full of boxes and racks. A couple of boxes had been knocked over and clothes spilled on the floor. A sink and counter were along the far wall with a kettle and a couple of cans. Callum heard Georgie breathe hard under the rushing sound in his ears. His head cleared some, his heart slowed.

They both saw the figure on the floor.

Georgie said, 'I got a switch.'

The room lit up thanks to a striplight on the ceiling.

'Jesus Christ,' she said. She walked out of the room.

The face had been beaten to a pulp. Shards of glass were embedded in the nose and scalp and water spilled nearby. The base of a smashed bottle was a couple of inches from the corpse's head. The body was dressed in slacks and a poloshirt. There was a dark stain over the crotch. The smashed head was almost severed from the torso; the neck had been sawn through to the spinal cord.

Callum knelt by the body for a second. He saw a number tattooed on the wrist.

'Ah, shit,' he said. 'Ah, Jesus.'

Georgie stood near the counter in the store. Her eyes were red.

Callum walked up to her and said, 'I think we got Mr Fogelman back there. The body has a Nazi concentration camp tattoo on the wrist.'

Georgie crossed herself. She took a deep breath to retake some control. 'You think the bastard had fun in there?'

'I think he couldn't help himself. Maybe he wanted to warn the old guy and got carried away. Maybe he wanted a quick, clean kill and found he couldn't stop. Whatever, that doesn't look premeditated – at least the level of violence.'

Georgie said, 'You OK?' She looked at him a little wrong. 'I mean, you seen anything like that before?'

'Yeah,' said Callum. 'When I was undercover, there were bodies. And you know what a bomb can do to someone? I was police in Belfast, don't forget.'

Georgie shook her head. She swallowed a few times.

'I don't want to work Homicide,' she said. 'I don't want to get used to this.'

They stood for a second, Georgie with her eyes closed, Callum looking at his boots.

Then he said, 'We should call Mike.'

'We should call this in!'

'Let Mike make the call, he's a lieutenant.'

'Make the call? Make the fucking call? We got Jack the Ripper's handiwork in here! That psycho is out there, maybe honing his dagger for the next victim and you want to wait for O'Connell to rule on when we call this in? That's why you're calling him from payphones, you want to keep this off the books – you're fucking crazy!'

Callum held her shoulders and she shrugged him free. He sighed and stood back, hands on hips.

'Listen,' he said, 'you know well as I do our Mystery Man probably did this. Why would Volkov's goon tell you about Fogelman if they were involved in his murder? No, Mystery Man is shutting down any trail leads to him. That means he could be moving to his end game, if he got one. I still figure the revenge angle looks good, we just gotta find the target. We bring Homicide in on this, it blows our investigation wide open – too many cooks in the kitchen, Georgie. It slows us down and we find this guy when it's too late for Avda Galkin. Maybe this woman, Marina, too.'

Georgie's eyes went wide. 'Investigation? We don't have a goddamn investigation, Callum! We got supposition, a mad dog running around Brighton Beach we're no closer to finding than a week ago. Maybe Homicide on this will bring us closer to a result.'

Callum felt something ugly rising in his chest he didn't want Georgie on the end of. He shoved it back down.

'I got an angle,' he said. 'Just give it another day to pan out. Mike reports the homicide. They can process the scene, all that shit, but we don't have to get involved. Give me the chance, Georgie. I meet Kolya Slavin. Then we hit Kuznetsov and look for this missing woman, Marina. Get our ducks in a row, then see.' Before she could speak he said, 'I wanna get the sick fuck did for that old man and while that's a horror scene back there, it tells me our guy is unravelling. He's close to the end and he's losing control. Someone's gonna call this murder in, and now, but not us. No leads to our work – not yet.'

He hated himself for the look she gave him; like he was moving to the other side – the bitter, rock-hard cop who forgot what life in this city was like for regular people who didn't wade through shit for a living. He hated himself because he knew she might be right.

'Homicide still come in. They do their thing and, when we're done with my angle, we give them what we got. OK?'

She said nothing but walked by him and down through the store-racks to the street.

He followed her to find a payphone.

*

'Well, this drops a turd in the stew,' said Mike. 'Poor old bastard. Wait a second, I got terrible reception here.'

He was on his cell, driving toward south Brooklyn. After twenty seconds he came back on the line. 'Alright, I pulled over.'

Callum said, 'How should we call this in?'

'Let's have Martin do it.'

'Gerry?'

'Sure. He can call it anonymously from a payphone, keep the parasites at bay for a while.'

By parasites, Mike meant the press. Not that the media would

285

give much of a shit about some senior citizen killed in an apparent stick up on Brighton Beach Avenue. Mystery Man had made a half-assed effort to stage a robbery by grabbing a few bills from the register, enough to start the investigation off as a stick-up gone wrong.

The store had been clean of blood bar the smudge on the doorhandle and on the floor around the body so Mike figured the killer washed as best he could in the small sink out back. Then he must have grabbed some clothes from Fogelman's stockroom and shoved his own, bloodstained duds in a bag.

'So we should be on the lookout for a fit guy in his late twenties, early thirties with pants hiked up to his chest,' said Mike. 'I'll have Martin call 911 now. He can stick a rag over his mouth or some shit like the movies. You out of there?'

'Yeah. Gerry with you?'

Georgie looked up from scowling at the sidewalk.

Mike said, 'Yeah. See you in twenty.'

Callum killed the call.

They stood a block away from Dino's. Callum said to Georgie, 'You want to go get a coffee while we're waiting for them?'

'Sure.' Her voice was harder than the brick wall by the phone.

When they got settled in a booth by the window, each with a coffee and Danish, Callum said, 'Glad you still got your appetite after that horror show.'

'Speaking of horror shows, you mind telling me why Gerry Martin is sitting in a car with Mike O'Connell driving through Brooklyn to meet us?'

Callum took a slug of coffee and looked out the window. The sun was out and slatted bars of gold lay along Brighton Beach Avenue under the elevated train line. People went about their business. People of all ages, some laughing, some scowling, some walking with purpose and some wandering. Good people. Tired people. Pissed people. Same as any neighborhood.

He said, 'I got a hunch.'

'Cops actually say that anymore?'

She stared at him. The skin under her eyes seemed to have grown darker.

Callum said, 'Gerry's been doing a little work for us – he doesn't know why he's doing it yet.'

'So tell me before my Danish turns blue and furry.'

'Checking on a phone number. That's it. Meanwhile, Mike has the tape we watched. I left it at the 6th Precinct for him to pick up. He's gonna ID the guy in the hotel room with Avda.'

Georgie nodded. 'The towel in the video gives him the hotel, the timestamp tells him the time to check the register on Sunday night.'

She took a bite of Danish. Callum watched her mouth as she chewed. He felt tired and the motion was hypnotic.

Then she said, 'So which number is Gerry checking?'

Callum smiled at the thought of Gerry Martin on the donkey work of luds and tolls: checking calls going from and coming to a phone number. The search for patterns or inconsistencies. Bread and butter investigative slog.

Then he explained what was happening to Georgie.

Thirty-Three

Tikhon stared out the window and held his breath as the car climbed the coaster again.

Clack. Clack.

The cop, Burke, had been standing with a woman at the boardwalk and municipal parking lot over which his apartment looked. They had been standing at the end of his fucking street. Tikhon had been gazing out at the water as Avda lay on the bed and Marina sat in a chair combing her hair. He noticed the man and woman walking along and recognised something familiar in the man's haircut, his body shape.

He grabbed a pair of binoculars from under his bed. The couple had stopped by a payphone. When he observed them through the lenses, he confirmed it was the bastard interfering Irish cop, Burke. He had watched Burke make some calls, then the two had walked off.

He had been watching the boardwalk, the street, the beach, the parking lot through the window since. It was when he turned back to the room that he realised Marina was now standing at his shoulder.

The surprise jarred him.

He jumped: the car tipped. He felt it go – crashing downwards through rings of memory and hated faces: Afghanistan, a Russian bar, Volkov, Burke. He knew what came next and yet couldn't stop it – and then he was rushing headlong into hell. ClackClackClackClackClackClackClackClackClackClack ...

He forced his lips on Marina's. The kiss was too hard. He heard her muffled cry and pulled her against him, ripping her blouse open. Buttons popped and she cried out again when he scratched her skin tugging at her brassiere.

She said, '*Net, net, net!*' Quiet at first but then more insistent. He paused and she cupped his face in her hands. Her Russian was almost sung.

'Not like this, please. It's rape. Not like this.'

He was vaguely aware of tears in her eyes. He had a snapshot memory of Fogelman crying as he cut the life from the old man.

The rollercoaster would not be denied.

He hurt Marina. Hurt her until she could barely breathe for screaming. Then she didn't breathe at all.

When he stopped, Avda was making sounds like a child with night terrors.

Tikhon cared less.

'Stop your crying,' he said. He walked to the bed and kicked him. He began to untie Avda's wrists and ankles and said again, 'Stop crying.' He gestured to Marina's corpse near the kitchen. 'Filthy *dukhi* bitch.'

Avda stared, struck dumb with the terror of confusion at the word *ghost* for the dead Marina.

Tikhon flinched for a second. She *was* a Mujahideen, yes? An insurgent. Another fucking Afghan with their weapons tied under their scrawny sheep, and their booby-trapped cigarette lighters and thermos flasks. She had to die. They all did. Then he looked at the slight young man with eyes wild with fear staring up at him, and it was as though someone had hit the skip button on a remote. He jumped forward into a new reality. America.

For a moment he considered the screaming. Would it bring the neighbors? The old woman downstairs was quite deaf – she woke Tikhon some mornings blasting her radio. His was a corner apartment on the top floor of the building. The next unit was currently empty.

No, it should be fine. But he'd need to move the body.

He looked at Avda, horror-struck and brittle on the bed.

Tikhon breathed, settled and said, 'I'll make some tea. You need your strength to clean that up off the floor and help me get it out of here.'

Thirty-Four

Callum stood on the boardwalk outside Astroland in the late afternoon sun. A smattering of people were scattered across the beach, the great gray sheet of the Atlantic beyond. Georgie was two blocks away on West 15th Street in her car, Gerry on West 12th in a rented Ford, next to the housing project where everything began with the bust on Charles Beresford and Willie Mayhew's apartment. Mike sat in his car on Neptune Avenue. They were all on their radios. Callum's was wedged in the deep inner pocket of his jacket. He was cooking in the leather now the temperature was up.

He'd run through his hunch with the guys in Dino's, and where he figured they would go from here. No mention of Patrosi being dirty, though: that was information he didn't want Gerry and Georgie to know right now. After this meet with Kolya Slavin, Callum would sit down with Mike, just the two of them, and he'd lay Patrosi's work for Volkov out to his friend.

He glanced back at Astroland, at the great, matchstick ridges of the Cyclone coaster and the top of the Wonder Wheel. When he turned again Kolya Slavin was walking from the east on the boardwalk. He came up to Callum and doffed the Knicks cap wedged on his white-haired head. The bruise on his cheek was still vivid, the skin around his eye swollen.

'How's the face?' said Callum.

'I am older,' sighed Slavin. 'It takes longer to heal than before.'

'I like the hat,' said Callum, nodding at the Knicks cap. 'Be careful, I heard they make you go bald.'

'I have managed to cling to a decent amount of my hair as I

approach sixty. Not that you aren't wrestling it away from me with your demands about Maxim Volkov's whereabouts.'

'You're lucky if that's all you have to worry about,' said Callum. 'There was a guy in my old precinct got cancer. He had these thick, blond locks. By the time he passed, his head looked like a used up pin-cushion. You could count the strands of hair on the fingers of one hand.'

'A cheerful topic for a fine spring day.'

'Another girl I knew, she got it on her arm. Now she's got this chunk about the size of a golf ball missing below her elbow. You ever been sick like that? Something real bad like cancer?'

The old man gave a dead-eyed stare. 'Until I met you, no,' he said. 'Now ... only God knows.'

Callum lit a cigarette. 'Let's go in to the park,' he said, 'my treat.'

They strolled through Astroland. Slavin rambled on about an amusement park in Gorky Park in Moscow. They stopped near Dante's Inferno ghost house.

'Shit,' said Callum, 'there was a ghost train I went on as a kid in Barry's, in Portrush. It's a place with rides and stuff: Portrush is this seaside town up on the Atlantic coast back home.'

'Like Coney Island?'

'Not exactly. I bugged my dad to go on that ghost train every time we went there until, one day, he finally caved and took me on the ride. So we rode through and came out and he asked me how it was. "No problem," I says. Fact was, I kept my eyes shut the whole time.'

'A wise decision,' said Slavin.

Callum said, 'There was a story about a ghost house pitched up in Corona Park, up in Queens, with a travelling carnival. Some guy working the attraction got a real bad chemical burn, actually took a chunk out of his body. Some shit they were using on the ride. Can you imagine? Something burning through your skin like that, leaving an actual trench in your body?'

Slavin's eyes were steady as a rock. He said, 'You are rather bleak today, Officer Burke. Your brooding Irish temperament coming through? Would you like a drink to settle yourself?'

'See, there go those stereotypes again.'

'I do enjoy our conversations. However, I wondered why you asked me here?'

'I need your help,' said Callum. He walked toward a snack stand. 'You want something?'

'I'm fine.'

Callum ordered a cup of coffee and they stood by a stand-up table top.

'The young man you told me about last time,' he said, 'this hustler Maxim Volkov was so keen to find: I got a lead.'

He produced the notebook-cum-ledger.

Slavin raised an eyebrow.

Callum said, 'This belonged to a kid name of Avda Galkin. I think it's the missing guy. It's some kind of diary or somethin'. It lists clients, maybe even some information on our mystery man I been hunting – the guy with the kinjal dagger.'

The old man smiled. He gestured to Callum's coffee.

'Perhaps I'll have one of those, to celebrate your discovery of Kashchey's egg.'

'I don't follow.'

'There is a Russian fairy tale about an evil wizard named Kashchey. He seems immortal but there is a way to kill him and one hero does so. He travels to an island where a magical tree grows; under the tree is a chest and in the chest, a rabbit; inside the rabbit is a duck; inside the duck is an egg. Kashchey's death lies inside that egg. Volkov and your kinjal man are Kashchey. This book is the egg.'

'Hey, nobody's trying to kill anyone here, but I'll get your coffee.'

'Metaphorical, my literal-minded Irish friend.'

Callum ordered the coffee, the notebook in his hand. He came back, stood beside Slavin and said, 'I wanted you to help translate a few parts of the book.'

'Don't you have Russian-speaking police in the NYPD?'

'You'd be surprised how few. There's red tape, I gotta have them sign non-disclosure papers. I'll get around to it – but I trust you and you're here. I figured you'd enjoy helping with a little payback for what Volkov's men did to your face. And your body.'

Slavin's eyes glittered in a flash of late afternoon sun.

'Of course.'

'Just one thing,' said Callum. He leaned close to the old man and threw out a story off-the-cuff. 'This missing kid, Avda, he had a client with a scar here.' He pointed to his chest just below the clavicle. 'It's a crazy thought but cops are all about crazy. Can I take a quick look at your scar again, just to make sure it doesn't match?'

Slavin stopped mid-slurp of his coffee.

'If you need me to translate the book,' he said, 'how do you know about this client?'

Callum spun his bullshit. 'See, I got the book from another male prostitute came forward when Avda went missing. This guy told me about the client with the scarred chest and it got me thinking.'

Slavin raised his eyebrows and looked into his coffee. The steam made cotton candy of his mustache.

'Couldn't this client be your kinjal man? He had marks on his chest.'

'Sure he could. But the description doesn't sound like bullet wounds. More like a gouge outta the flesh. Hey,' he raised a hand palm up, 'you were a cop – you know how it is. You get a crazy idea and it just burrows in there, so deep in your skull it hurts, and you have to check it out.' Callum saw Slavin's hands were clenched with knuckles white as a sea-polished rock on the shore. He laughed and said, 'This fuckin' job, huh?'

'This job,' said Kolya Slavin. He smiled but it was heavy and so melancholy that Callum felt a pang of some indistinct regret for the old man and had no idea why. Slavin reached up to the neck of his sweater under his coat and pulled at the material to reveal the chunk out of his chest. Patches of gray hair surrounded it but the skin was smooth. The hollow looked a little discolored. In the center were small creases, like the skin had been split, then pulled into the middle and sewn together. Callum thought it almost looked like a tiny asshole.

He said, 'Jesus, and they did that to you with a knife?'

'Russians are creative people. Look at the writings of Tolstoy, the paintings of Kuindzhi – the mass murder of Stalin.'

Callum shot Slavin a grin. 'Your scar is nothing like the guy this hustler mentioned. The john's wound was more like a slash. We're good.'

'I have a slash in my skin around my ribs, you remember?'

'No, this was definitely on the chest. I knew it couldn't be you; but I just had to *know*, you know? See it with my own eyes.'

He opened the notebook and they worked through a few entries. Callum had a small pad and pencil with him. Sometimes he jotted down notes from what Slavin said, others he gave the pencil to the old man to illustrate some point. There were addresses, a couple of nicknames for clients: "The Hose", "Leshy", "The Mailman".

He flicked to a page with a business card stuck in as a bookmark and pointed to a couple of lines. A sentence in Cyrillic was underlined in red. Slavin peered at the words and craned his neck to get closer to the paper. He took a sip of coffee. His face creased. Either the coffee was real bitter, or something was stuck in his craw.

'Very sad,' he said. 'You see this underlined word here – Afghanistan – you obviously know what this means from my pronunciation. This one is "veteran". This one – *ugolovnoye* – is an adjective, "criminal". The other one, underlined – ' he swallowed and a look of heavy resignation settled on his face, ' – I do not understand. I think it is Polish, not Russian. Perhaps this young man had a Polak client?'

'How do you say it?'

Slavin stared at Callum.

'Osobist,' he said.

Callum scribbled the word in English as it sounded.

'Great. I got one more.'

He turned to a single word written in Cyrillic on the inside back cover of the book.

Ворон.

'This is kinda weird,' Callum said, 'just sittin' here all alone on the page.'

Slavin looked up at the clear blue sky. Summer was on the horizon – which, in New York, meant crushing humidity, sweating sidewalks, thousands crammed on the beach. The rich would emigrate to Long Island and Conneticut at weekends. There would be Shakespeare in Central Park. Summerstage. The Brighton Jubilee.

He smiled and looked at Callum again.

'It reads *voronoy*. Perhaps some introspection from our young friend. It translates as "Goat".'

Callum scribbled the English translation down.

He said, 'Introspection? I don't follow.'

'I told you back at our meeting in Manhattan. The word is slang for a homosexual slave. Perhaps this Avda Galkin looked in the mirror and wrote this down in acceptance of what he had become?'

Slavin finished his coffee and dropped the cup in a trash can by his side.

'You tell me,' he said. 'You're the policeman.'

Thirty-Five

Kolya Slavin had gone. Callum stood under the trees in Astroland and spoke into his radio on channel SP-TAC-L.

Callum:	'Mobile Two, you got Ivan One?'
Georgie:	'Roger Mobile One, on Surf Avenue and West 8th, heading east for Brighton Beach.'
Callum:	'Mobile Three, Ivan Two is yours, K.'
Gerry M.:	'Will shadow, K.'
Callum:	'Mobile Three, stay in contact with Mobile Two.'
Gerry M.:	'Ten-Four.'
Callum:	'Mobile Four, you ready?'
Mike:	'Gimme five minutes. See you on West 10th by the Aquarium, K.'
Callum:	'Ten-Four.'

*

Five minutes later, Mike said, 'A fucking lieutenant and I'm Mobile Four? You're still a goddamn Officer and you're Mobile One. See, that's why the Job is goin' to shit: no respect for chain of command.'

Callum said, 'You drive, I'll talk.'

He gave Mike more details on Fogelman's body, told him Georgie was pissed they hadn't called it in themselves. He related how angry she felt being out of the loop when he told her Gerry Martin had been doing some work on phone records. Then he dropped the bomb: Angel Patrosi was a dirty cop worked for Maxim Volkov, and a kinky client of Avda Galkin's.

Mike was the first person Callum had told – but it didn't help any getting it off his chest.

'Don't go to Georgie with this,' said Mike. 'Leastways not yet. We wanna play this out and she'll go all conscientious and throw a spanner in there.'

'I don't see her as an IAB rat, though.'

'She's under a lot of pressure with her old man bein' sick and all. Best to leave it for now. And Volkov hears anything about us knowing, Patrosi's family could be a target.'

Callum watched streets roll by from the car.

'So, the tape?' he said.

'Gotta love the Feds,' said Mike. 'We got him. Dieter Schmidt, fifty-six, German Delegate to the UN. Lives in SoHo. Three young children, wife of thirty-four years of age.'

'Jesus Christ.'

'You gotta wonder who else has been caught on camera.'

'OK,' said Callum, 'I figure we're upping percentages on my hunch.'

'The result came back on the heroin from the Popov bust, too. Feds figure it originates from Afghanistan.'

'They sure?'

'As far as you can be. The Chinese could fuck with the composition of their product, hide the origin.'

'Yeah,' said Callum, 'but Afghanistan fits.'

'You want it to fit.'

Mike pulled up thirty yards from the Masha Tea Room and said, 'Arkady Kuznetsov got some Arab chick in there he bangs every week. Same time, same place.'

'No Feds watchin' the premises?'

'They don't tell me everythin' but I know they're up on the phones here because they can't cover all Kuznetsov's places of business right now. Even if they're outside somewhere, they won't know what happens when you walk through the door.'

'It ain't wired?'

'Just a Title III on the phone.' He nodded toward the building. 'I'm comin' with you, but I'll stay out front with the customers. It covers you if the Feds are around – I can tell them you were investigatin' some local shit and I came along to keep an eye on you.'

'You got it.'

When they walked in the tea room a couple of old ladies were jawing in a corner over some kind of cakes. A young woman stood behind the counter. A bead curtain hung behind her.

Mike walked up to her and said, 'NYPD. Where's Arkady Kuznetsov?'

'You have warrant?'

'We ain't here for a search. We wanna talk.'

'I just started my shift. I haven't seen him.'

'Is he out back?'

'I think you need warrant.'

Two men eased through the curtain. Both had mustaches and shaved heads. They looked like clones of neanderthal man in Levis and t-shirts so tight they could have been painted on. They only seemed to differ in their arm tattoos.

Mike said, 'How you doin'?' He flashed his detective shield.

Callum said to clone number one, 'What's that word tattooed on your wrist?'

'*SLON*. Death to cops.'

'Gotta love the First Amendemnt.'

'My partner here,' said Mike, 'gotta piss fit to burst. Can he use your john?'

'I don't think – '

'You got a customer bathroom back there, right? Thanks.'

Callum made his move. Mike put his hand on his gun.

The men blocked the way.

Callum tinned them with his badge and pulled his coat back

to show the Glock. He'd yet to meet paid muscle who'd risk the beef that came with smacking a cop but there was a first time for everything.

Mike said, 'I'm Lieutenant O'Connell, Organized Crime Investigation Division. My colleague and I are workin' a case and he needs a piss like you wouldn't believe. If you don't let the man go out back and syphon the python, I'm gonna charge your vodka-swillin', bear-fuckin' asses with interferin' with a federal-linked investigation.'

The thugs shrugged, parted either side of Callum and let the bead curtain fall back so it almost hit him in the face. Callum walked through into a narrow corridor. He passed the customer bathrooms and came to a door at the end with a chair on either side. There were cigarette butts mushed in a tin ashtray, empty tea cups and a couple of pornographic magazines on the floor.

He put his ear up to the door. A woman was yelping on the other side. When he tried the handle slow, it gave enough that he knew it was unlocked.

Callum shoved it open and saw Arkady Kuznetsov's skinny, milk-white ass pumping like a Pekinese on a chair leg, while a woman the color of golden sand, her legs wrapped around his back, squealed underneath on a huge bed. Circling the bed was a miniature railway track mounted on tables with an electric lo-comotive looping Kuznetsov and the woman as they fucked. The woman saw Callum and screamed like a train whistle. She pulled away from Kuznetsov and grabbed sheets around her body.

Kuznetsov glanced over his shoulder and rose to stand next to the bed. He turned, buck naked with hands on hips. His body was a tapestry of stars, epaulettes and symbols. A cross covered his chest, with a dollar bill and the Statue of Liberty stood at its base.

Callum recognised the Cyrillic on Kuznetsov's ribcage and smiled.

'Hey, I know that one,' he said. ' "Death to cops", right?'

The Vor mobster watched him, encircled by the track like a lion in a cage.

Callum nodded at the woman.

'Cleopatra, you can leave.'

'I'm Iraqi, asshole,' she said. She gathered up her clothes and her pink leopard-print panties, ducked under the track, skipped past him and out the door.

Callum took out a pack of Camels. He offered one to Kuznetsov. The Vor refused with a shake of hs head. Callum lit up with an orange plastic lighter and took a deep drag.

Kuznetsov stood like a statue at his own gravesite, so thin he could be made of twisted wire. His face was hard as granite, the thick mustache frozen above the fat lower lip.

'I get it, you're old school Vory,' said Callum. 'Don't get in bed with us cops. You'll fuck an Arab chick, though: I thought you Russian mob guys were racist cocksuckers.'

'I have Georgian blood.'

'Yeah, I read that in a file. Georgian – like a kinjal dagger.'

Kuznetsov bent, pulled some jogging pants up over his dick and said, 'Maybe I will take a cigarette.'

Callum tapped one out of the pack and leaned over the minia-ture train track. He lit the man up.

Kuznetsov took a drag and said, 'I still don't co-operate with police.'

'Ain't nobody here but us chickens, Arkady.'

'I like you, Irishman. But the answer is still no.'

Callum shook his head and whistled. He put his hand on his Glock, ducked under the train track and stood a foot from Kuznetsov. He opened his jacket, pulled up his t-shirt, turned around to show he was wire-free.

'I box,' he said. 'There are some good Russian fighters. Georgian too, I'll bet. But I see it in your stance: you pay other men like those apes outside to do your fightin' these days. So don't force this – you won't like the taste of what comes next.'

'Fuck,' said Kuznetsov, 'you.'

It was a pretty good jab, thought Callum later, when he whipped the Glock out of his holster and smashed Kuznetsov across the face with the gun. The Vor fell back on the bed. He spat and his mustache was wet with blood and a little snot. He began cursing.

Callum heard the roar of blood in his ears, felt his skin itch with violence, his body hollow out with a white-hot fire. He willed Kuznetsov to play hard-ass so he could throw a couple more shots at him.

But he knew deep down this was a poor substitute for laying hands on the bastard who'd smacked Trish around.

So he said, 'I'll lay off your face for a while because I need you to talk, but I'll work your body until I could serve you up with a béarnaise sauce, you hear me?'

Kuznetsov eased himself to a sitting position on the bed.

He said, 'You are no cop.'

'Blue all the way. But you made your bed, Arkady. You're old school. You don't co-operate with police, so you sure as shit won't go bleating about some cop handing you a beating in your personal fuck-pad. I could work you like the bag for hours with no comeback, long as I make it known we had a chat.'

'I'll kill you.'

'No you won't, because I'm with Organized Crime Investigation Division, and they're with the FBI, and the last thing you need is choppers up your ass 24/7 and the shitstorm comes from a cop-killing. Besides' – Callum took a drag of his cigarette – 'I'm gonna help you out.'

Kuznetsov's smoke was smouldering on the bedsheets and he tamped it out with his palm. He sat with his elbows on his knees and asked for another.

Then he said, 'I'm listening.'

'I'm still looking for our fair-haired, well-cut, bullet-scarred mystery man I mentioned back at Long Island City,' said Callum. 'This guy, he fights off two of Maxim Volkov's bulls in a store on Brighton Beach Avenue, Fogelman's. You might remember the protection money the old man paid you. Past tense verb. Mr Fogelman got carved into cold cuts out back of his store and I'll bet the wounds on his neck are consistent with those caused by a kinjal dagger.'

Kuznetsov peered through cigarette smoke.

'I didn't know,' he said.

'I figured. It's bad for business, right? Also, there's a woman's gone missing. We got the name Marina. A little scrawny but she has some class. A little birdie told me she's one of your girls.'

'Volkov,' said Kuznetsov with a snort. 'And you believe him?'

'Let's say it's true. So I got Mystery Man: no name, no leads. But I guess he did a little strong-armin' for you to kick Volkov's guys out of Fogelman's. And I figure he murdered Fogelman – one of your "clients" – and ran off with Marina, one of your girls.'

Callum ground his cigarette out on a plastic pond feature next to the model train tracks. He whistled through his teeth.

'That's some major disrespect, right there. I mean a real insult, Arkady. Imagine what people would think if word got out? Never mind that the homicide and missing girl could both lead lines of investigation to you.'

'And you could make sure they don't?'

'I don't want you – I want Mystery Man. He's losing control, on some kinda mission. That could mean more grief comin' your way.'

Kuznetsov smiled, baring his tombstone teeth. He hated cops, thought Callum, but if he could convince himself he was using them for his own ends, he'd bite. The mobster dropped his cigarette on the floor and ground it out with his bare foot. He stood and stretched to his full height.

Callum pushed a little more. 'Long as this guy's out there, he's a liability to your business. You already lost Marina.'

He caught a flicker in the Georgian's eyes. The girl, he thought, that was the clincher.

Georgie's words came to him: *Are men really that simple?*

'The girl was a big earner,' said Kuznetsov. 'I have been looking for her. Now, I think, there is no point.' He shrugged, making a big show of his indifference. 'The man you are looking for is called Tikhon,' he continued. 'It is some kind of nickname. I have never known him by any other. He did some work for me. He was eager to hurt Volkov. I felt he had some kind of personal hatred for him. Tikhon is an Afghantsy – an Afghan War veteran. Maybe Volkov was there, too, and they have some sort of personal grudge. You know the saying: small world.'

And great minds think alike, thought Callum. Patrosi had said Volkov never served in Afghanistan – but could the word of a dirty cop be trusted?

He said, 'Go on.'

Kuznetsov spat on the floor. It was tinged red. 'Tikhon was helping me eliminate my competition, but he never really worked for me. He was freelance. He could have betrayed me – it is the nature of our business – but I doubted it. He seemed to hate Volkov too much for that.'

'And Marina?'

The Vor stroked his mustache, blood caked on the tips of the bristles.

'Tikhon was fucking her,' he said. 'Just a client, nothing personal. One time, I went to her place. I used her. Tikhon arrived. His face was like a mask – he doesn't seem to care about anything: money, women, power. A man like that is very dangerous.'

'I said I want to help you,' said Callum. 'I figure Volkov is the key. Tell me about him.'

'Your files on him must be bulging with information.'

'But it's never the full picture. How about his heroin? It comes from Afghanistan, right?'

Kuznetsov shrugged.

Callum caught a glimpse of the clock on the wall. He should get moving. 'Volkov brokers hits through Russia. We collared two Russian killers with the bodies of a couple of smalltime rival dealers of Volkov's over in Coney Island. A source told us the hitters were contracted in the Motherland, not New York.' Nikolai Popov, thought Callum, some source. He said, 'Is there a broker for the heroin, too? It comes via London sometimes – maybe there? Or in Russia again?'

Kuznetsov frowned for a second. Callum caught the pop of something looked a little like fear in the Vor's eyes. Then the face set hard again, decision made.

'You will arrest Volkov and leave this conversation out of the case?'

'It ain't exactly admissible.'

'I think you could say the deals are brokered in Russia, in a manner of speaking.'

Kuznetsov folded his arms across his chest, covering the inked cross. Then he said, 'But when is Russian soil, not in Russia? You answer that, you will know where the deals are brokered.'

Thirty-Six

Georgie: 'Mobile One, sitting on Ivan One, on West End Avenue and Shore Blvd,
  K.'
  Gerry M.: 'Mobile Two, on Ivan Two. Still in Matryoshka Social Club, K.'
  Callum: 'Mobile One, Mobile Two, Ten-Four.'

*

Callum and Mike drove in a convoy of two to the parking lot at Manhattan Beach on the southeastern tip of Brooklyn, Callum behind the wheel of a rented Ford. There they parked and walked down to the deserted sand while Mike called home on his cell. The sky was darkening, casting the ocean the color of shark skin. Housing projects loomed in the distance beyond the far end of the beach.

Mike finished his call.

Callum said, 'Marcie OK?'

'Nope. All these years, she still doesn't like me bein' out all night.'

'Can you blame her? A regular lothario like you, no woman over the age of sixty in south Brooklyn is safe.'

Mike's face was a mask in the gloom.

'You know,' said Callum, 'when I saw you in Green-Wood Cemetery, standing by that big-ass Russian mobster's grave, I knew life was about to get more interesting.'

'You missed workin' with me, huh? Needed someone could understand what the fuck you're sayin' with that accent.'

Callum gave him the finger. Mike took a candy bar out of his pocket and unwrapped it. 'Helps me think,' he said then took a bite. 'So, lay it out for me.'

'Alright,' said Callum. 'Let's start with Ivan Two: Volkov, and his heroin supply. He gets his heroin from Afghanistan, according to his nephew Popov, and the Feds. Kuznetsov didn't comment. Then we had a theory that Mystery Man – this Tikhon guy – had some kinda personal issue with Volkov. We figure Mystery Man fought in the Soviet military in the Afghan War: we thought Volkov served in the military in some capacity and could have been in Afghanistan, too. Then Patrosi cast doubt on that.'

Mike said, 'OK. We know Tikhon was working for Kuznetsov, so he could have been targeting Volkov for a cash reward.'

'Except Kuznetsov said this guy has no real interest in money, and I believe it. He's gone rogue: killing Fogelman and taking one of Kuznetsov's girls.'

Callum looked at the dark slab of the water and let things roll in his head.

'Let's spitball that whatever Tikhon wants, it's personal, connected with his time in Afghanistan. But Patrosi says Volkov never served in that war, maybe was never even in the military ...'

'So?' said Mike.

'So, ladies and gentlemen, I give you Ivan One: Kolya Slavin.'

It fit. When Callum spread the pieces out in his head and put them together, they said that Tikhon's beef was with the old guy. Not the Russian mob boss Volkov but, Callum figured, the man *behind* the mob boss.

He lit up a cigarette and listened to the soft lap of water on the shore for a second.

'I had a feelin' from the start,' he said. 'Old guy calm as you like talkin' down some Russian mobster muscle? Volkov didn't bat an eyelid at Slavin when he got in the middle of things at the bathhouse. But Slavin was convincing with me. He was open about having owned the bathhouse. He seemed genuinely pissed about Volkov bein' around.'

'Maybe he is,' said Mike. 'Maybe he's trapped in all this.'

'Could be. Slavin showed me his scars, said Volkov's men gave them to him with knives. But I noticed the one near his collarbone, like the flesh was scooped out, in the bathhouse and my first thought was some kind of skin cancer. I brought up the cancer angle at Astroland today; then a chemical burn for good measure. Just floatin' it to see if he flinched. Nothing.'

'You're reachin' here,' said Mike.

'But he showed the wound to me again today. It confirmed what I remembered. It's got little ridges in the centre, like an asterisk, kinda. And it's discolored. No knife's gonna leave a wound like that. The ridges are where the skin's been blown open then sealed again. The discoloration could be a skin graft.' Callum looked at the two-tone dark of sea and sky. 'My bet is it's a shrapnel wound. I seen enough bomb victims in Belfast. The doctor at the hospital E.R. where they took Trish agreed. I drew a sketch of Slavin's wound for him from memory. That old man's been close to an explosion.'

'In Afghanistan? He's an old guy.'

'Fifty-nine. Put him there ten years ago and he's in his late forties.'

'You believe the Russkies sent men that age to the frontline?'

'I'll come back to you on that one,' said Callum. 'Now, me and Slavin are in World Wide Plaza. The old guy's relaxed, slips up and calls Avda Galkin a *voronoy*. I remember the sound of the word, and I remember Slavin's expression – nervous for a heartbeat, like he knew he fucked up and let his guard down. He tells me the word is Russian for goat, and goat is slang for a homosexual in prison.'

Callum reached in his coat pocket and pulled out his Russian pocket dictionary.

'I went straight to a bookstore and bought this. "Goat", in Russian, is *kozel*. And *voronoy* means "raven".' Callum snapped his fingers. 'A slip of the tongue. Kolya Slavin is an FSB operative.'

Mike said, 'The new KGB? The old guy is a spy now?'

'I know a guy in the Intelligence Division. I called him and he told me 'raven' was KGB slang for a male seducer in a honeytrap operation. You think because the KGB changed names to the FSB they don't use the same terms?'

'It's a stretch.'

'Look at the accumulation of evidence. He wanted to be an informant but he didn't wanna be on the books. That ain't unusual in itself, but it fits my theory. Jesus, after Patrosi and Avda, you gotta wonder who'd be running who.'

Mike scrunched his candybar wrapper. Callum knew he still thought the theory was pretty weak.

'Then there's the "Officer"/"Detective" thing,' said Callum. 'I gave him a card – neither title on there. I'm in Narcotics: no uniform, an investigative division. I *should* be a detective if I'm in that team.'

'All hail Rabbi Bochinni,' said Mike.

Callum made an imaginary toast. 'Slavin referred to me as "Officer" a couple of times.'

'Your average citizen could make the same mistake.'

'Your average citizen wouldn't know, but a man with FSB resources would. And he told me he researched the NYPD, like rank and structure.'

Mike threw his hands toward the dark heavens. 'It's thin, man. He's probably some geezer came off the boat here, built a fuckin' business, had it stolen away from him by some Russian mobsters and harbors a fuckin' grudge. He saw you and wanted to do some good. He took a beating from Volkov's guys after the bathhouse. You told me yourself his face was all busted up.'

Callum flicked his cigarette away, the glowing ember like a tracer round in the dim light. The lights of Brighton Beach and Coney beyond winked in the distance to the west.

He said, 'The marks on Slavin after the bathhouse could have been staged. They looked bad, he took some lumps, but it could be for authenticity.' He counted off points on his fingers. 'We got the shrapnel wound – Slavin lied about it, I know it; we got the *voronoy*/goat/raven thing; we got Officer/Detective Burke. And Volkov did the exact same thing at the State Restaurant today. He never even got my card and called me *Officer* Burke. Someone at that Russian Diplomatic Mission in the Bronx the Feds are so fond of could have checked my rank for Volkov after the bathhouse thing.' He grinned. 'And ... '

'What?'

Callum was riffing. It felt good. 'Maxim Volkov got a broker. Someone who commisions hits. Someone who keeps him insulated, maybe from his Afghan supply. Nikolai Popov said the guys whacked Charles Beresford and Willie Mayhew were contracted by a broker. Patrosi said Popov's arrest wouldn't touch Volkov, even though Popov is his nephew, because of the broker. I asked Arkady Kuznetsov about it and he gave me a riddle: *When is Russian soil not in Russia? We know* the answer.'

Mike's eyes were black wells now in the dying light.

Callum said, 'Tell me what Gerry found out about Slavin's phone records again.'

'He said Slavin called numbers around Brighton Beach, Coney, Manhattan Beach, Gravesend. Same for incoming. Plumbers, food places, shit like that.' He sighed in time with the tide rushing the sand on the beach. 'And a couple of calls incoming from a payphone on Riverdale Avenue.'

'North Bronx. Two blocks from the Russian Diplomatic Compound for their mission to the UN. Russian soil, not in Russia. Back to the honeytrap with Avda. Kuznetsov hinted at it when he pointed out the UN Building at our meeting in Long Island City. Avda was scared – he knew.'

Callum drew another cigarette from his pack.

'We figured Volkov was blackmailin' Avda's VIP clients but it's been a honeytrap all along, to compromise UN delegates.'

'KGB?'

'KGB, FSB: same shit different name. Volkov's hustlers fuck some high class clients, including the German prick on the videotape. The hustlers tape the sex and Slavin gets it to the FSB at the compound in the Bronx to use as leverage against other nations' diplomats. In return for runnin' the racket, the FSB help out Volkov by brokering some of his business.'

'Including contract murder and heroin smuggling?'

'You know the spooks in this country ain't above a de facto hit. And the heroin? What if Kolya Slavin was KGB back in Afghanistan? He establishes some kinda heroin connection through cloak and dagger shit. He's late forties then, so mostly he's behind the scenes – but one time he joins a patrol and gets blown to shit. He's sent home with his injuries. After the war he flows from the KGB to FSB, same shit, different acronyms. Or maybe he quit and really was a cop in Moscow for a while. Either way, he ends up in New York. He's told to connect with Volkov and get this honeytrap sting in motion. Then he uses his heroin connection with Volkov, too.'

'So,' said Mike, 'he's a professional, or a reluctant spy now?'

'He could have been rerecruited over here as an honest to God immigrant, or he could have been stationed here. He told me Osobist was a Polish word, he didn't understand it. I read up, and that's bullshit. It's Polish, sure, means personal or individual maybe. But in Russia, it's a word too: used to refer to intelligence service officers. Like the KGB.'

'He's a real superspy, huh? Or maybe he's givin' you bad translations because deep down he wants to get caught?'

'Who knows, maybe. I know you're diggin' this, don't shit me. Fact is, he's involved. And if he was in Afghanistan, I'll give you odds of ten to one he's the guy this Tikhon asshole's got a beef with.'

Thirty-Seven

Avda shivered on the bed.

Marina's body lay rolled in a carpet in the corner of the apartment.

Tikhon sat a little back from the window, gazing out at the Atlantic Ocean past the boardwalk and beach. He had been quiet since he killed Marina. He had seen the scowls of many Afghan women in Marina's face. Then reality had seeped back in. To beat the breath from someone with whom he shared a bed, a woman who quietened the nightmares: did he feel sorrow? No. That would require him to feel anything other than anger and fear.

Clack.

She had been noisy. Tikhon had waited for a knock on the door. He had watched at the window for a police car. None came. His neighbors, like good New Yorkers, had hugged themselves ever tighter in their homes and turned up the TV.

Clack.

Now Tikhon was gentle with Avda. Marina's death had exhausted a measure of his fury and he wanted to preserve the rest, cultivate the rage, for the old KGB fuck when the moment came. And he needed Avda, so he kept him happy. It was easy: the pathetic *opuschiny* was so grateful not to be slapped or given a harsh word. He would be pliant until the end.

Clack.

Tikhon glanced at the rolled carpet in the corner. He checked his watch. It was dark outside.

Soon he would make the call. He would put Avda on the phone so Maxim Volkov would know his prize asset was still alive. Tikhon would give a time and place tonight. He had decided where. A mountain of sorts – fitting for the end of the traitorous bastard, killer of his friend, Dolidze. A place where Avda had told him much of their current troubles began; where the policeman, Burke, had entered their particular drama. Secure, limited points of entry. A good place for death.

So Tikhon would call and demand the old man be there. Then he and Avda would leave this apartment for the last time, never to return. He would leave Marina's body, wrapped in a rug and hauled to the bathroom, to be discovered in time. He would bring the kinjal dagger; and the Tokarev pistol he took from the idiots in the bar fight, what seemed like a lifetime ago. Volkov would die, and any men he brought. The mobster would never come alone, despite what Tikhon might demand.

And, finally, Tikhon would slaughter the KGB scum who, in America, called himself Kolya Slavin. As he should have done over a decade ago on the frozen slope of a mountain in Afghanistan.

Clack. Clack. Clack.

*

Avda remembered a cockroach in his own building. It would thread its way along the floor outside his room, big as a baby's hand, until he came near. Then the roach would freeze. Avda would freeze. They would stand locked in mutual terror until Avda stamped his foot and the monster fled to a crack in the wall.

Now he was the roach. But Tikhon had no fear of him.

He had been with many men in his job, but Tikhon was the only one he had felt made him a better version of himself. Avda had imagined he was Saint George, like the tattoo on his back, slaying whatever dragon troubled this strong, beautiful, haunted man.

Bullshit.

Avda needed his own Saint George now.

Would it be Maxim Volkov?

He had known about the old man who supplied Volkov with the drugs he pushed on the streets. The old man who Volkov seemed to respect, verging on fear. Then one night, Tikhon told him of the mountain in Afghanistan and the KGB officer who betrayed their patrol. Avda could see the pain in his lover, pain driven home with a traitor's bullet to his friend's head. So he had resolved to work as an agent for Tikhon. He fed the dirty cop working for Maxim Volkov whatever information suited the mobster; and he fed Tikhon tidbits to nip at Volkov's heels. The longer they could make life difficult for Volkov, the more the old man behind him would be driven to the fore, until Tikhon had his chance to strike. It would have happened at the bathhouse but for bad luck and the presence of the policeman, Burke.

Avda remembered seeing Burke at the project in Coney Island. How conceited Avda had been. The sneer, the brazen wink. How he wished Burke would crash through Tikhon's door now. Another Saint George.

More bullshit. More fanciful romance.

He had been used by Maxim Volkov.

Ultimately, by Tikhon as well.

And he was nothing to Burke. Nothing but a bug.

A cockroach.

Thirty-Eight

'Alright,' said Mike. 'Let's say the jigsaw holds together for now. A little ragged but I'll play. What next?'

'Avda Galkin,' said Callum. 'He's gone and the smart money says Tikhon's got him.'

'Or he's floatin' out there past Rockaway Park.'

'I think Tikhon needs him to draw Slavin out so he can take his old country revenge. If Slavin and Volkov are running a honeytrap for Russian intelligence, then I guess Avda's a star player.'

'And they're gonna want to protect their interests. Maybe they want him dead; maybe send him home.'

'Right,' said Callum. 'And why would Tikhon send me on a wild goose chase to Grove Court? Just maybe, so he could break into my apartment and leave the tape. That intimidates me, makes me feel vulnerable, and shakes things up: it forces Volkov to show his hand earlier – the cops got a honeytrap on film. Problem was, he didn't expect Trish to be there and give him a smack in the balls.'

Mike shook his head. 'So he's your friend now? Santa Claus come tiptoeing through the house to give you evidence?'

'Why not? He wants to ruin Slavin. Maybe I was insurance: if he couldn't kill Slavin, at least I could wreck his operation. Either way, Slavin and Volkov are gonna have to meet up with Tikhon.' Callum stabbed a finger at the ocean. 'That's when he'll carve Slavin up with that dagger of his.'

'And we got Georgie on Slavin; Gerry Martin sittin' on Volkov,' said Mike, dropping the Ivan One and Two designations. 'When the Russians move, we tail them and they lead us to Tikhon. But we got no evidence. And if Slavin really is an intelligence operative, he could have some kinda immunity anyhow. We're swimmin' in waters got a lot of sharks on the prowl.'

Callum nodded. 'But if we bust Tikhon, we got the dagger. We got Avda, who's a witness against Volkov. Maybe Volkov turns on Slavin, maybe not. But you got a shot at takin' down one Brighton Beach mob, at least, if we keep Avda alive – because I can't believe the only asset Tikhon's got right now ain't breathin'. And what're you gonna do, let Avda Galkin die? 'Cause that's behind door number one if we don't move on this.'

Callum lit a third cigarette. The cheap lighter threw an orange flame on his face, set hard against the breeze. Set hard against a lot more coming. He said, 'And I got another question for you. How come you haven't called OCID in on this – it's your unit? Or the Feds themselves? Why are you, me, Georgie and Gerry wingin' this ourselves?'

Mike checked his watch up close to his face. It was digital and the light lit his smile. His head looked like it was floating in the dark.

'When I'm done answerin', can we get off this sand? It's inside my shoes and Marcie'll bitch at me if I get any in the house.'

'Sure,' said Callum, blowing a stream of smoke heavenwards.

Mike said, 'Alright: what am I gonna take to OCI, or the Feds? We're here on your hunch and I still ain't convinced the pieces hold together so tight. We got jack shit on Tikhon. The guy's a fuckin' ghost. I take this to my boss, or the Feds, they're gonna think I'm ready for the rubber gun squad.'

They stood in silence for a moment.

Then Mike snickered and said, 'Whatever. I kinda like Avda. If this gives us a shot at pullin' him outta this alive, it's all good.'

Callum laughed. 'You jackass, O'Connell. You are so full of shit.'

'Oh yeah?'

'Here's how I figure,' said Callum. 'You hate workin' for the Feds – not with, *for*. This ain't like on the task force 'cause you ain't an equal partner this time. So you wanna bust someone by yourself just to piss them off so you don't get the office boy routine again. Maybe Organized Crime bores you compared to kickin' down doors with Narcotics, and you think you can send a "fuck you" with a bust on some Russian names. I dunno, but you ain't a fan of the Feds, which is why the black-suited cavalry ain't gonna ride in any time soon.'

Mike said, 'You cynical prick.'

Callum almost creased up at that one. 'Mike, you're my friend but, if I was feelin' *real* cynical, I might suspect you threw me into that bathhouse at the start of all this just to set off a reaction and get some kinda shit started.'

He watched the dark oval of his friend's face in the night.

'Cal, I'm only gonna say this once,' said Mike. 'You do what you want with it, then roll it up into a ball and kick it into the ocean.' He cleared his throat, shifted his feet a little. Then he said, 'I love you, man.'

Callum smiled. It came through in his voice. 'You don't get past first base, deserted beach or not.'

They walked back to the cars. The lights were on in the houses nearby. The clouds over Manhattan fifteen miles to the west soaked up the gleam from the City. They were parked next to one another, the only cars in the lot. The glow of street lights lit their faces.

Callum opened his door, stopped, turned to Mike. 'You think this is gonna work out?' he said.

'I asked myself that question every day I worked Narcotics. And almost every time, it might not have been a perfect result – but I figure we did some good, in our way.'

Callum would relieve Georgie on her watch over Slavin soon.

He wished he had a couple of bottles of beer in the trunk. Mike was way ahead of him. He went to his back seat and pulled a small cooler from the floor. He grabbed two Millers and handed one to Callum.

'You're gonna drink American beer with me for once, not that Canadian piss you like so much.'

Callum checked his watch. He had a little time. The radios were quiet. He popped the cap with a key and took a swig. Mike drank and checked his shirt, worried he might spill beer and piss off his wife.

The ocean whispered on the shore for a time.

Callum drained his beer.

He threw the empty bottle in his car and said, 'I gotta go.'

Thirty-Nine

The moon slipped behind a rag of cloud and Callum yawned.

0142.

The street stood wide, dark and silent.

He had left the parking lot on Manhattan Beach, driven to West End Avenue and radioed to Georgie that she could end her watch on Slavin's place. Then he'd called in with Gerry to check if he was OK to pull a double shift on Volkov. Gerry had said it was cool.

Now Callum sat in the rented Ford, parked in front of two red brick buildings on West End Avenue. Kolya Slavin was in a small house that stood alone, sandwiched between hulking modern condos a few yards down on the other side of the street.

He doubted Slavin lived there. More likely it was a safe house and calls were routed there somehow. Avda wouldn't know Slavin's address. He had no need to, within Volkov's operation. It must have been a major obstacle to hitting the old man. And if Kolya Slavin was former KGB, he'd know how to evade and cloak his movements. It would have been dumb luck if Tikhon had managed to locate and follow him. The task of slowly drawing him out must have required great patience, and a terrible hatred.

After a couple of hours, Gerry called in to say Volkov had split for a small house on a quiet residential street. A woman had answered the door in a robe. Probably a girlfriend.

Callum was bored.

He checked his cigarettes: half a pack left.

He'd need a piss soon. There was a space between the two buildings in front of which he'd parked where he could relieve himself and still keep an eye on Slavin's address. He looked forward to it. It got him out of the car for a couple of minutes.

*

By 0400 he was getting irritated with Gerry Martin. For the past two hours, each time Gerry checked in he hinted they should call it a night. Callum got that everyone was playing along on his supposition, but the condescension in Gerry's voice was starting to grate.

Callum was rationing his smokes now. Just four left in the pack. He'd have killed for a bottle of something for his dry throat, but he kept smoking his cigarettes and his mouth got hotter and more foul. He jumped at the tap on the window.

'Fuck!'

Bull-Neck stood next to his car with another heavy. Both held revolvers. Across the street, a light came on in Kolya Slavin's house.

A spark lit in Callum's chest.

He rolled down the window and worked at keeping his breathing even.

Bull-Neck said, 'License and registration, sir.' He rested his gun on the window, barrel pointed at Callum. His grin could have lit up Astroland. 'Or, make that gun and badge.'

Callum unclipped his holster and handed the Glock through the window real slow. He was sweating like a cardinal in a brothel. He glanced at Slavin's place but couldn't see any movement. He slipped his badge from his pocket, fumbled with it, dropped it on the floor of the car. He grabbed it and passed it to Bull-Neck. The hood laughed at his butterfinger-nerves and gave the badge and gun to his partner standing a few feet back.

'Out,' said Bull-Neck.

Callum opened the door and clambered onto the street. His legs were tingling with fear and anger. He fought down the adrenaline. He could smell tobacco, booze and body odor. Bull-Neck threw him hard against the Ford and frisked him, playing cop and loving it. When he spun him around again, another light had come on in Slavin's place.

'If only your partner, Ruiz, was here to see this,' said Bull-Neck. 'She'd want what I got even more, huh?'

He grabbed his crotch with his free hand.

Callum slashed the Russian's gun hand with the razor blade he'd slipped out of his badge on the floor and drove his right boot into Bull-Neck's crotch. He threw a fast combination to the body and yanked the thug's skull back before the other heavy had his head in the game. Callum held Bull-Neck between himself and the muzzle of the second revolver. Bull-Neck's gun lay on the ground where he'd dropped it. The razor blade drew blood from his throat. Callum could have sworn he could smell it. It gave him a thrill.

Both hoods growled in Russian.

Callum rode his adrenaline surge and slapped Bull-Neck hard on the ear.

He said to the second hood, 'You, shithead, empty your gun.'

One of the lights went out in Slavin's house.

Callum pressed the razor blade hard into leathery skin. Bull-Neck grunted.

Callum said, 'Empty your fuckin' gun or this asshole'll never sing Kalinka again.'

The second hood opened the chamber on the revolver. The rounds hit the asphalt and rolled.

'Toss my gun and badge over here.'

The hood pulled both from his pockets and threw them at Callum's feet.

'Now strip.'

The second light went out in Slavin's place.

'Fuckin' strip, now!'

The second hood said, 'Fuck you.'

Callum glanced at Slavin's. Was the old man getting ready to move? How long until he drove off and Callum lost him? Callum's skin itched; he felt a pure impulse to scream, lash out, hurt someone, anyone.

'Strip,' he snarled, 'or you'll be up on a manslaughter charge next to assaulting a police officer. 'Cause when I slash this dickhead's throat, it'll be on you.'

Bull-Neck spat Russian. The second hood began undressing.

A car started up somewhere. It could have been in the shadows up the side of Slavin's place.

White-hot rage surged from Callum's belly up to his throat. His heart went hell-for-leather against his ribcage.

'Faster!'

The second hood got down to his boxer shorts.

'Now get the fuck out of here!'

The hood started walking. Callum drew the blade across Bull-Neck's skin a little. Bull-Neck gave a strangled cry. The second hood looked back.

Callum spat, 'Fuckin' run!'

The hood jogged away.

A car appeared from the side of Slavin's place. It turned right and drove away toward Shore Blvd. Callum hooked a leg around Bull-Neck's ankle and got him down on his belly on the ground. Sitting on top of him, he watched Slavin turn right onto the Boulevard.

Jimmy Gilliland was in Callum's head, old man Fogelman too. It felt like they were crowding his skull, pressing against the bone. He closed his eyes for a second. Took a breath. Then he stood and kicked Bull-Neck once in the head, once in the ribs and twice in the balls. He heard a snap when he drove his boot into the ribcage.

'I ain't got time for you,' he said.

Bull-Neck rolled slow on his back, his knees together like he wanted to piss. His face was mincemeat on one side where it scraped the asphalt. He moaned.

Callum grabbed the thug's revolver from where it lay, gathered up his Glock and badge and got in his car. Then he gunned the engine and took off up the street in pursuit of Slavin, leaving the Russian gangster lying in his wake.

Forty

Callum saw the car take a left onto Neptune Avenue from Cass Place. It had looked like a Japanese make, small and boxy. As he followed, he saw it was a Toyota. He'd missed the plate, though, thanks to Bull-Neck and friend; and he couldn't get close enough now to read it without blowing the tail.

He followed under the el-train tracks. There were few other vehicles on the streets. Callum wished they had more bodies, that he could leapfrog on and off the tail with a couple of other cars.

They continued east on Neptune, passing dark, low rise car washes, grocery stores and seven-story chunks of Brooklyn tenement: buildings seemed scattered along the roadside, jumbled in size and style.

They drew up to a stop light.

Callum pulled up a few feet behind the car. The street lights couldn't reach so far into his Ford – his face would be in shadow. He waited.

The light changed to green.

The Toyota stayed put.

Then the passenger door opened.

A man in cargo pants and a Nets top clambered out. Leaving his door open, he jogged over to Callum's window. Callum was out before the man reached him.

The man stopped and looked scared. He spread his arms in surrender and said, 'Excuse me, but are you following me?'

He was black.

He wasn't Kolya Slavin.

*

Slavin eased his tired limbs from the black Mercedes. He felt the ache in his side where a bullet had razed a seam of skin from his body back in Afghanistan. His hand went to the wound in his chest where a mine had taken a pound of flesh; the wound Callum Burke had shown such interest in earlier today.

Slavin's Honda was parked back at the Brooklyn Beltway where he'd rendezvoused with Maxim Volkov, then travelled on in the Russian gangster's car. Now Volkov clambered out the other side of the Mercedes.

They had arrived at the location of the meet and were standing behind a massive, twenty-story high building in a housing project in Coney Island. From the air, the building would have looked like a huge capital "T". The street was empty, as were the lawns around the building. The residents would be sleeping before they rose early to work. Lovers would be lying in embrace.

It could have been Soviet housing in Moscow or Leningrad, thought Slavin.

His real name was Sergei Zykov – he had tossed it when he reinvented himself on entry to the United States. He had come to prefer his adopted moniker, Kolya Slavin. As far as he was concerned, Sergei Zykov had died in the mountains of Afghanistan. Only his handlers in the FSB knew his real name. Them and, perhaps, the mysterious psychopath who had demanded this meeting.

The man had called Volkov and claimed to have Avda Galkin. The FSB wanted Galkin back, breathing or otherwise. They wanted the honeytrap tied up before the Americans had a chance to get involved, and were willing to explore further avenues of possible business with Volkov once this had been achieved. Should Volkov fail, he and the men here tonight were deniable.

Slavin watched the mob boss shift from foot to foot. The gangster had ordered a couple of professional killers to eliminate two black drug dealers here earlier this month, then set up the killers for arrest. Now he was back at the scene of the crime.

'Fan out,' said Volkov.

His voice was strong as he barked the command in Russian but his eyes had a hunted look.

The FSB hadn't given them any men. The intelligence service preferred to avoid any such operation on US soil and had delegated instead to the Russian mobster. Volkov had brought three goons. Another two had been dispatched to Slavin's safehouse where, they knew, the Irish policeman Burke was sitting in wait. They had moved on Burke as Slavin left the safehouse a short while ago. Slavin liked the Irishman; he hoped Burke would walk again when those animals had finished with him. Burke could have been a good soldier in Afghanistan: he had the look of a resilient and loyal man.

Loyal. Like those boys on the patrol in the mountains. Like the soldier that Slavin had shot in the face the night he sold his soul. He had run to the Mujahadeen, seduced by the promise of money from their drugs and disillusioned by the pointless conflict. They had tended to him after the bullet grazed his side in the firefight. He had lived with the enemy for months in exchange for information and safe passage out of country. They had nursed him when he had been wounded by shrapnel in the chest, when one of their number had stepped on a landmine on the journey to the border. A brutal tribesman had pulled his skin tight like the top of a sack and sewn him up. They had fed him and watched as his fever eased and his strength returned. Finally, he had slipped into Pakistan. He had drugs from the Mujahideen, and money to bribe and forge his way to the United States. His plan had been to go west and settle but New York had seduced him and he stayed in Brooklyn. He had opened the bathhouse.

Then Volkov and his animals had forced their way into his business and pushed him out.

Volkov had connections in the Diplomatic Mission in New York and they came knocking. So he cut a deal with the new Russia – the prodigal son returned. He had contacts from his run from Afghanistan, a supply line for prime heroin. He would use them, and be used, in the service of the new Russia in exchange for a pardon from the inevitable punishment given a traitor: execution. He supplied Volkov, who could sell the heroin to keep money rolling into the intelligence boys' coffers. Then the honeytrap was knit to the drugs – and the next thing Slavin knew, he was up to his neck in filth and corruption.

Then Callum Burke appeared.

Volkov took Slavin's arm and they walked toward the apartment building. The terrain was shit, thought Slavin. No cover until they were in the building. This mystery caller had demanded they go to the roof, twenty storeys up, on the wing protruding from the rear of the main block: the stem of the "T". Smart. There were limited entry points on the roof and the caller had designated a particular staircase from which they should emerge. The location was a good choice. Perhaps Galkin had told his captor about the hit on the black dealers here, about the NYPD catching the killers cold.

The NYPD. Burke. It had been a simple slip of the tongue when he mistranslated the word *voronoy* for the policeman. His mind had been elsewhere; he found his thoughts drifting more and more these days. But today, at Coney Island, when Burke had asked him about Osobist: he had said it was Polish. Despite his shock and panic, he had been tempted to claim it translated as traitor – that's what he was and would be as long as he led this miserable existence. And he was so fucking tired of lying – to those around him, to himself, to the boys he saw in the nightscape of his dreams, still fighting and dying on that godforsaken mountain in Afghanistan, their death masks lit by the muzzle flash of his pistol as he shoots the young paratrooper in the face.

He wasn't religious, had seen precious little evidence of God in his time, but he knew he existed in a purgatory. Living in America, never to be American; working for Russia, never to be a true Russian again. God, he was tired.

He and Volkov entered the building flanked by two of the gangster's thugs, the third bringing up the rear. Volkov depended to a degree on contract criminals. With the men sent to occupy Burke, he had found just three thugs at such short notice to guard him at the meeting.

They reached the lobby. Of course, the elevator was stuck on a higher floor.

Volkov sighed and wiped his head with a handkerchief. He looked at Slavin with eyes that betrayed the fear of a predator turned prey.

'We take the stairs,' he said.

*

Callum sat back and took a long drag on his cigarette.

Goddamn Russian goons, buying time for Slavin to take off back on West End Avenue. He knew the old guy would have plenty smarts to stall a surveillance detail or shake off a tail. Now he was in the wind. Callum eased the smoke from his mouth like he was freeing pent up bad memories – Belfast, Hong Kong, Trish in the hospital looking broken. He shook his head as the smoke drifted into the Brooklyn night.

Fuck it, he thought at least I'm alive. Bull-Neck and his friend could've left him bleeding on the concrete back there. His hand hadn't stopped shaking after he stopped at the stoplight and saw the black guy. He'd bought a pack of Camels from a gas station and was on his third smoke to settle his nerves.

He smiled sad and thought what he would give for another of Mike's beers right now.

Callum cursed as his radio crackled and he dropped the smoke on his lap, sparks biting at his lap. He grabbed the radio and listened.

Then he heard a Coney Island address through the static and smiled a lot wider.

*

Wheezing, Volkov ushered the lead of his three bulls through the door to the roof to scout the area. They stood in a small hut at the top of a set of service stairs. The cramped space was hot and the air heavy, like a bathhouse. The only light came from a flashlight gripped in the last bull's thick hands. The first bodyguard, built like an athlete and holding an old Argentinian FMK-3 submachine gun, slipped through the door to the roof. As it closed behind him, there was a scuffling sound like an animal scrabbling through gravel, and the clatter of the weapon falling.

Nothing more.

The men inside were frozen.

Volkov, his face soaked with sweat, said, 'Should we go through?'

Slavin swallowed some acid bile and said, 'Do you like the alternative?'

The alternative was the wrath of the FSB.

They stared at one another for a few heartbeats. The two remaining bodyguards' faces were tight with confusion, their features rendered brutal and monstrous by the light of the torch.

'We throw the door wide,' whispered Volkov. 'No stealth. You through first,' he pointed to the bodyguard by the door with an Agram 2000 submachine gun, 'then us. You come through last and let the door close.' He nodded to the bodyguard standing behind them at the top of the stairwell, holding the flashlight and a Borz Chechen produced submachine gun. 'On three. One – two – three!'

The first bull lashed out and kicked the door open. He threw his body against the metal and pinned it back against the wall of the hut. The cool night air washed over Slavin and Volkov as they rushed outside. The lights of south Brooklyn spread wide before them like a panoramic constellation and their feet sounded huge and deafening as they scraped through the gravel. They whirled. Slavin saw the first bodyguard behind Volkov out on the roof. He saw the second make to join them. Then he saw the wraith appear from the dark of the stairwell behind the man, saw the slim pale shaft of the blade, the bone white hand close around the bodyguard's mouth. He made to yell as the killer's face, black in the dark, moved close to his prey and the dagger moved to the throat and –

The door swung shut.

Volkov moaned.

On the roof, there was no trace of the first man who had burst through the door or his weapon.

Slavin rasped to the last bodyguard standing, 'Go around the side of the hut – check the top! There must be a hatch somewhere!'

Volkov's eyes flashed as the old man ordered his own subordinate. They flashed again when his bull obeyed without first seeking Volkov's approval.

The bodyguard moved with care but the gravel surface and his heavy boots made stealth difficult. He disappeared around the side of the hut. Slavin saw the vast black void of the Atlantic to the south. He saw a cluster of flashing lights where the boardwalk would run past Brighton Beach. A crime scene, occupying a good proportion of the local police.

A sudden, guttural cry dissolved in a bubbling wheeze, then died on the sea breeze. The last of the bodyguards was gone. Volkov drew a pistol.

Slavin whispered, 'When's the last time you fired that at a man?'

Before the gangster could answer, there was a sharp crack. Volkov groaned and fell on his side. His pistol clattered to the gravel and lay still.

Forty-One

Callum heard the sharp snap of the shot. After the radio call he had driven to the project and taken the service elevator as far as it ran on the north wing of the apartment house, then run the last five stories to the top. Hot breath seared his throat. He was just stepping onto the roof when he heard the gunfire.

Shit! he thought. It's started.

He looked for any muzzle flash around the center point of the roof where the three wings met. Nothing. It was almost thirty yards away, crowned by two huge white water towers. A superintendent's hut was near the towers, just like the one from which Callum had come. Another hut was at the extremity of the southern wing.

He began running and saw another figure coming from the south. His radio crackled.

'I see you,' said Mike. His voice was shaky as he ran.

'Spot anyone in the center yet?'

'No. Stay sharp.'

Callum said, 'Ten-Four,' and pulled his gun.

*

Volkov whined on the gravel where he lay. Slavin felt his bladder loosen and took a gulp of air. He hadn't been this afraid since combat in the war. A boy came tumbling from behind the far side of the superintendent's hut. His hands were tied and he was gagged. Avda Galkin.

After Galkin came a man. For a moment, Slavin thought it was Callum Burke – similar height, similar build – but this man held a dagger in his left hand that had drawn the blood of three Russian thugs moments ago.

The blade was tarnished black in the night. In his right hand he held a handgun that looked like a Tokarev. He walked closer and somehow Slavin knew – he *knew* – before the words were out of the tight, hard mouth.

*

Tikhon said, 'You killed my friend, Dolidze, on a mountain in Afghanistan.'

Part of his mind was on the slope again; part on this rooftop in New York City. He felt the cold in the ground back on the mountain, the chill in his soul. He looked at the old man and saw a mental newsreel of a traitorous KGB bastard firing four shots at his friend's head. Dolidze, there one moment and gone the next.

The old man said, 'The 345th.'

Tikhon nodded and shot the old man in the right leg. The pistol cracked and flashed. Avda yelped. The old man stumbled back to the waist-high wall surrounding the rooftop.

Tikhon felt a surge of pure, white-hot fury rush from his balls up through his core and toward his chest. It erupted from his throat in a roar as he shoved the Tokarev pistol in the front of his waistband and switched hands with the kinjal dagger. The rollercoaster car was hurtling toward the crest, the climb almost as fast as the inevitable plunge.

He stood on Volkov's hand and crushed it as he passed him, ready to gut the old man above the streets of Brooklyn.

*

Kolya Slavin knew and he remembered.

He saw the young faces wrenched in terror and a blind,

animal anger. Saw the Mujahideen slaughter the youth of the Soviet Union. The Airborne troops fought with desperation and skill but the Dukhi were remorseless. Slavin had tried not to engage. But the callous Afghan bastards had thrown him toward a position where a soldier with an AKM assault rifle had just cut one of theirs in half. The soldier had seen Slavin; he had frozen in shock at the Russian face among the fierce features of the Afghan fighters; and Slavin had shot him four times in the head.

Now a man approached on this Brooklyn rooftop with the dagger in his hand.

The soldier Slavin killed had been in a foxhole. He must have had a companion, unseen, who watched the murder. No one else would have realised Slavin was a Russian in the chaos of a night firefight at close quarters.

I welcome him, thought Slavin. *This end is long due.*

He was tired and hollow with shame and putrid memories.

And then the police appeared.

*

'NYPD! Don't fuckin' move!'

Gerry Martin edged forward with his Glock in a two-handed grip, held far from his body like he was scared of the weapon.

Tikhon stopped his approach to the old man, his back to the cop.

Gerry said, 'Jesus, there are three dead men around the service door over there.'

Tikhon said in English, 'You can arrest me when I finish number four.'

His hand hovered near the grip of the gun in the front of his waistband. He saw the old man look at it. Tikhon wanted to take his time with the KGB scum – but that option was gone unless he could draw fast and put the cop down.

'You took your fucking time!'

The voice cut the night like the roar of a rocket. Maxim Volkov was indignant with fear. He looked up at the cop with hate and disgust. 'What the fuck do I pay you for? Kill him!'

Gerry moved closer. Shit! This was it, time to earn his wage. He'd sat down in his car on the street way too long, way too frightened to make his way up here. It was like he was outside his parents' bedroom, his dad waiting inside with the belt; or in the corridor outside the teachers' room in Holy Trinity, Sister Katherine waiting on the other side of the door with the rod. Just a scared little boy. Now it was time to grow up.

He'd never fired his gun in anger, didn't trust himself to hit the target unless he was a couple of feet away. He never thought he'd shoot a man in the back, no matter what the Russians paid him. It had all been tips on drug busts, a little security work at the illegal casinos; the money had been good and they'd even got him laid once in a while. But murder? Jesus Christ!

But he was in too deep – they knew too much about him – to step back now.

Pressure on the trigger, he thought. Remember the range. Time to grow a pair and put this cocksucker down. He'd done plenty bad since he went dirty for Volkov. Fuckin' Angel Patrosi, pullin' him into this shit. He'd imagine this Russian shithead here was Angel and drill him for draggin' him so far down.

Just an ounce more pressure on the trigger –

'Put the fuckin' gun down, Gerry! Put it down now or I'll shoot you dead!'

Georgie Ruiz appeared behind him and he pissed in his pants.

*

Callum saw Georgie behind Gerry Martin. He saw Kolya Slavin leaning back against the low wall surrounding the roof. He saw

Mike run under the water towers to join the fray. Callum was about twenty yards away. He tried to sort the thoughts in his head, bouncing around like atoms.

He'd pulled a switch on Gerry Martin, asked Georgie to watch Gerry while the cop watched Volkov's movements. Like Callum had suspected: the fucker was dirty. Mike had sat in the wings near Georgie's position.

Callum had figured Volkov would get the call for the meet, figured Tikhon wouldn't have a contact number for Slavin and would have to go through the gangster. Georgie and Mike radioed in the location of the meet after tailing Volkov; after Callum lost Slavin.

The fucking projects where the whole shitstorm kicked off.

Callum was ten yards away from the fracas now. He heard yelling, Mike's voice bawling above the rest. Then he saw Tikhon. Large as life and just as lean and tough as that day in the bathhouse.

He watched Tikhon pull a gun as Gerry Martin turned at the sound of Mike running in.

Callum yelled. It was like everything was at a crawl, underwater, his tongue heavy as bathhouse air.

'Gun! Mike! Georgie! Gun!'

Each syllable lagged behind a fraction of Tikhon's movement as the Russian pulled the pistol from his waistband, turned like a Bolshoi dancer, found targets with the speed of a computer.

Callum raised his gun. His arm seemed impossibly slow – bad dream slow. He fought through the mud of confusion in his head, cursed and threatened his legs until they picked up speed.

Tikhon got off four shots machine-fast. Then a fifth.

Six yards away, Callum saw Gerry Martin and Georgie drop. Then Mike.

Something cold plunged through his chest.

He saw Tikhon pivot toward him and now – finally – Callum's

arm was up and he fired fast and crazy, each muzzle flash an exploding star. Tikhon ducked and weaved. Callum's rounds bit into the super's hut, sending chips flying, sparked off an air vent, went sailing into the Brooklyn air. He closed the distance and bellowed.

Tikhon was gone, into the hut and down the stairs.

Volkov was lying on the roof, alive but shot.

Gerry Martin was lying with Georgie on top of him. She was already snapping cuffs on his wrists, unhurt.

There was Avda Galkin, still breathing.

No sign of the woman, Marina.

Mike was hit. It looked like his shoulder. He was swearing and growling and rolling a little on the gravel.

Kolya Slavin was still leaning against the low wall. He'd been shot in the leg and was bent a little, one hand on the wound. The old man had done better than Fogelman on meeting Tikhon. The dagger was lying on the roof, stained with blood. At least one more body around somewhere, Callum figured. He looked at Slavin. The old man looked like he was in agony. Callum figured he was hurting from a lot more than the leg wound now he'd met up with his past again in the flesh.

Callum said, 'Looks like your lucky night, Kolya. You get to live.'

'The luck of the Irish, Burke?'

'More bullshit stereotypes.'

'I thought so,' said Slavin.

He smiled and it was saddest thing Callum had seen in a long time. Then Kolya Slavin leaned back and pitched over the edge of the roof to drop twenty storeys to the concrete below.

Callum didn't sprint to the edge to watch. He didn't wait to hear the soft, wet crunch. He didn't say a word.

But he ran to the door to hit the stairs and catch the murderous bastard who'd put all this in motion.

Forty-Two

He heard the slap of footsteps a couple of flights below. Callum had lost count in the fug of the shootout but he figured he had over eight shots left in the Glock's magazine. How many rounds did Tikhon have?

Callum started leaping down four and five stairs at a time. He passed the eighth floor, the number painted on the wall. Everything was racing: his heart, his blood, his mind. He felt shit scared and crazy angry. Ghosts shoved him on – old man Fogelman, Jimmy in Belfast, victims he'd seen on three continents. Now Kolya Slavin, too. The angel on his shoulder was long gone. The devil was giving him his wind now.

So much noise, anger, terror in his head he didn't notice the footsteps had stopped below. The shot was deafening when he hit the fifth floor. He heard but didn't see the pistol fire. The wall by his face spat chips of concrete and then he was sailing through the air. Tikhon had got under him, used his own weight and momentum to throw him over the Russian's shoulder. Callum saw the stairs rush up to meet him and something snapped in his left shoulder when he hit the steps. He dropped his gun and the Glock clattered over the edge into the darkness below.

No more shots from Tikhon. The Russian was out.

Then Tikhon was on him. Callum was lying on the steps, head downwards toward the fourth floor. Tikhon straddled him and began pummelling. He landed a left across Callum's face. Callum felt the snap of knuckle against cheekbone. He bit the side of his mouth. His arms were trapped under Tikhon's legs. Another left and Callum tasted iron. He struggled, spat blood, swore. The devil inside him was still raging. If he was gonna join Kolya Slavin, Jimmy Gilliland and the rest, he'd go with fire in his belly.

He took another hard left and thought maybe this was it. Then he felt the metal of the empty pistol crack his head and an image of the guy he'd beaten senseless with his Glock in the alleyway flashed through his mind – the other guy who slapped Trish around. He had a crazy snapshot in his battered skull of the guy panicking with the catheter. He laughed and it sounded scary to his own ears.

Tikhon paused for a second at the insanity of the cackle.

Callum made a move. He bucked and kicked. He found leverage, heaved and Tikhon tipped over his head and rolled down the steps to the flat concrete square at the door to the fourth floor.

Callum struggled up. His face hurt; his head was pounding where the gun had cracked him. His shoulder throbbed but he didn't care. He'd had worse in the ring. He thought, this asshole hit me with three lefts. Where was the right?

Then he saw that Tikhon's hand was a bloody mess and he thanked the good Lord above. One of his haywire shots on the roof must have hit. Callum came at him. He swung with his right and the Russian ducked under, got his arms around him. Callum threw hard shots into the fucker's sides but the bastard lifted and threw him. He hit the steps and rolled. Now he felt a searing pain in the shoulder he'd landed on. It started hurting like someone had shoved a red-hot poker through the joint. He took a boot to the ribs, driving the wind from him.

He realised he could die here. This guy was ex-elite military. Tikhon dropped on Callum knee first and a bomb went off in his right hip. He could smell the sweat of the man now, a trace of booze. Blood too. It was smeared on the stairwell. He caught another kick and drove his foot up under it. Pure luck, he connected with something soft between the legs and heard a grunt. He scrambled to his knees and threw up a guard.

Tikhon took a swing and Callum went in under it, grabbing at his body. He hooked his arm around the Russian's waist and drove his own body up. Flailing with his free hand, he caught something wet and slick. It took him a second to realise it was Tikhon's wounded right hand.

Callum twisted it, dug his fingers into a small, soft hole soaked with blood. He heard a gasp. He got the asshole on his back on the stairs, drove his skull into the Russian's nose. He heard a pop and did it again. His shoulder was on fire, like it was tearing free but he fed on the pain.

Tikhon was crazy-strong, throwing wild punches with his free hand, but Callum grabbed the wounded hand with both of his and chomped down. He yanked the arm. Wanted it to snap. Didn't have the strength. Then he let go and went to work. Combinations on the motherfucker's face. Tight, hard body shots, then more punches to the ruined nose. He felt the punches to his own body slow and lose their sting. Callum grabbed Tikhon's head with his hands and smashed it off the stairwell.

Again.

And again.

It didn't drive any of it away: the death in Belfast; the hurt in his marriage; the violence of policework; the sight of a battered Trish in the hospital. But he couldn't stop. He didn't wanna fucking stop – because why shouldn't this psychotic, murdering fucker take all that pain? Why shouldn't he be battered so bad he couldn't hurt anyone ever again?

He was losing his grip on the head slick with blood, beginning to float as he moved beyond the pain in his own shoulder, when he felt hands hauling at him. He yelled, cursed, kicked. He was an animal and this bastard on the stairs was an animal, and this was what they did. This was the dance.

Then he heard Trish. Her scream reached inside and pierced all the savagery and the shit and darkness of his life – his cop life – and he couldn't breathe. He was smothered. Suffocating in a swamp of so much twisted, wicked wrong. But he heard Trish and he struck out for the surface. Struck out for the real Callum Burke up above all the darkness, who loved his daughter; who dug his churchin' on a Sunday; who felt something starting with the woman he now saw stood at the bottom of the flight of stairs. Trish.

He started to put faces together with names like a high school yearbook. Sarge, Billy Hutchinson. Some uniformed guys from the 60th Precinct.

He let go of the killer, Tikhon. Let go of the rage and felt the cops around him lift him, support him and carry him. He stumbled down the stairs to Trish. She went with him, and the guys holding him up.

Down the stairwell and out into the cool dawn air of another day.

Forty-Three

'So the bartender, he says, *Has that goddamn nun been hangin' around outside my place again?'*

The cops in the Chrysler minivan broke up at the joke.

They were waiting for the word from the boss to go sweep up a buy and bust operation near Chinatown and the Bowery. It was hot and humid outside. Inside the minivan, with the aircon broken, the air was thick enough to taste and rank with sweat. Kwan, the joke-teller, stole a glance at Callum. Goldblatt gazed out the window and Rubino went back to his paperback.

Callum knew the guys were wary of him, and had been for the two months he'd been in Manhattan South Narcotics Division. He was the fast-track golden boy all over again, the cop with the super-rabbi in Bochinni; he was the man who beat a Russian mafia ex-military spree killer senseless in a Brooklyn project, a couple of years after busting the Irish mob and a Chinatown Tong; and he was one of the three who exposed a couple of dirty cops in Brooklyn South – one of whom was being dragged over the coals by IAB. The other was six feet under in Calvary Cemetery.

It was partly Angel Patrosi who had made Callum suspect Gerry Martin was dirty. When Callum visited Patrosi's place, he'd checked out the photographs dotted around the room. Patrosi at a Christmas party with Sarge, Gerry and Trish. On a bust with the team. Fishing with Gerry. It had made Callum wonder: the only shot that didn't have a couple or more cops in was that photograph. It was candid, private. Patrosi and Gerry weren't buddy-buddy on the clock, but they shared downtime. Sure, Callum didn't like Gerry Martin much, and that colored his opinion of the guy. Still, he had wondered: birds of a feather?

And something Patrosi had said when Callum asked if he'd fed his Greenwich Village address to Volkov: that Angel wouldn't go there, even if he had a beef with someone. Well, Gerry had had a beef with Callum. He'd hated and feared him. Like the old soak Danny O'Neill had said the night of Patrosi's racket, *"We know where you live, right Gerry?"*

After Trish took her licks from Tikhon, Callum had agonised over how Tikhon knew his address. But Gerry had turned up a changed man and suddenly they were best buddies and working together to bring down the big bad. It had seemed a little too convenient, even then. And Callum got to thinking about that first bust on Beresford and Mayhew that started the whole Tikhon-Volkov-Slavin shitshow. Back then, Martin corrected Sarge on the killers being Russian rather than Romanian. He'd recognised the Russian pistol. In the heat of the bust it passed Callum by – but it came back to him after Tikhon broke into his place. Why the hell would Gerry Martin know the difference in an accent, or even a gun that didn't turn up much on New York drug busts?

So he had set Gerry up.

First he'd given him the job of checking phone records that led to the Russian Diplomatic Compound in the Bronx. It was a test. Mike had the records checked through the Feds, then Callum compared the results with Gerry's to see if he would play it straight. The results tallied. At the time it seemed a plus for Gerry; now, Callum thought either Gerry couldn't figure out how to fudge the results, or he hadn't even known about Kolya Slavin at that point.

Then Callum had given him surveillance on Volkov the night he figured Tikhon was close to calling out his targets. Lo and behold, two Russian thugs had mysteriously appeared at Callum's car window to work him over and stop him tailing Slavin. That was when Callum knew. No other way Volkov could have had knowledge Callum was sitting on the old KGB man.

Georgie and Mike confirmed it. Callum had asked them to sit on Gerry. Volkov had received a call. He'd run out of the place he'd been shacked up with a girlfriend and had a talk with Gerry at his car. Volkov had left for the meet. Gerry had followed. Georgie and Mike had leapfrog-tailed them and radioed the location – the Coney Island project – to Callum so he could come join the party. Then Gerry Martin was busted.

The asshole spat it right out to IAB, to avoid a conspiracy to murder charge for Trish's beating at Callum's place: Maxim Volkov had demanded Callum's address. Martin didn't know it so he went to Danny O'Neill and had the old desk jockey pull it. Back then, said Martin, he hadn't known Kolya Slavin existed – Callum could believe that one. From there, the math was simple. After the bathhouse confrontation, Callum had told Kolya Slavin he was a cop; Slavin had informed Maxim Volkov; and Maxim Volkov had gone to Gerry Martin and got the lowdown on Callum Burke, including an address. Avda Galkin got Callum's address from Volkov and Tikhon coerced him into sharing. The rest was history; and Trish was lucky she wasn't.

The night it all went down with Tikhon, Mike had done it right. He notified Communications that his team were hitting the location in 60th Precinct territory. They'd informed the 60th and, on Georgie's request, Sarge, Billy Hutchinson and Trish. The desk sergeant at the Six-oh had sent a couple of RMPs to the location and ESU was notified. It was all on the hoof and the tactical cavalry hadn't arrived until the show was almost over, but the rest of the team got there fast. They – especially Trish – stopped Callum giving Tikhon brain damage.

Then there was Maxim Volkov. A terrified and grateful Avda Galkin had ensured they had a real crack at Volkov and his crew by giving everything he had on them.

Tikhon was going down for the murders of Fogelman and Marina. For now, his history was still a mystery. He had no real

ID. But people above Callum's paygrade were talking to people in Russia's bureaucracy and military to put meat on the bones. Through Tikhon, if they could get him to talk in sentences of more than one or two words, they could even have a shot at Arkady Kuznetsov.

The FSB and Russian Diplomatic Mission were silent on any suggestion a Brighton Beach Russian mobster and former Soviet Intelligence Agent had been running a honeytrap operation for them in New York. Several staff at various western UN Missions had been recalled.

Callum had been off the Job for a couple of days with his shoulder. The injury wasn't serious and he enjoyed spending time in Brighton Beach afterwards, buzzing on the feeling he'd taken a couple of dangerous psychopaths off the street. But things had soured at Brooklyn South and the Six-oh. Gerry Martin was a shithead dirty cop, for sure, but he was still a cop. Some of the knuckle-draggers in the Job round those parts weren't shy about making it known they didn't welcome those responsible for him spending time with IAB in their neighborhood. The fact Angel Patrosi ate his own gun a week after word got out he was another cop on Volkov's payroll didn't help.

Callum hadn't told anyone but Mike about Angel, and Mike would never have gone to the rat squad. But Gerry Martin had rolled on Patrosi. Angel had asked his wife to make him a sandwich and kissed his daughter, then gone to his study in his Staten Island home and shot himself through the roof of his mouth. There was no Inspector's Funeral. Callum couldn't face attending the small affair that did take place. Not after looking Patrosi's kid in the eye at the door of the family home. Always the kids that suffered. Instead, Callum had booked an Amtrak ticket for Ohio, leaving next week. He'd go and hold his daughter and talk to his estranged wife and try to work out something better for all of them. He was gonna shovel a lot of the shit out of his head so there'd be way more room in there for his family.

And finally, he had been transferred. Manhattan South.

He was sad to leave Brighton Beach. He enjoyed the neighborhood, liked the people there, especially the first generation Russians and those not long off the boat. They were a people of warmth and passion. They could be quick to anger, loved their booze and tended toward romantic nostalgia or maudlin moods when in their cups.

A little like the Irish. Maybe old man Slavin had something with all that bullshit he used to spout.

Callum smiled. The other cops were talking about the Howard Stern movie and the chick with the speaker. Goldblatt was sure she went to his gym in Hoboken.

Georgie Ruiz turned from the driver's seat of the Chrysler and said, 'You okay, Cal?'

'Yeah. Hey, we still on for dinner Friday?'

'Sure. Trish eats shellfish, right?'

'Loves it.'

She nodded and smiled.

Georgie's husband Arthur was doing okay. Turned out someone in Trish's church was a specialist and Arthur had been to see them a couple of times. He was going in for surgery in a couple of weeks. Georgie was terrifed. She'd followed Callum to Manhattan South and worked reduced hours for now. It would be what it would be, but Arthur was getting the best care and he had a lot to live for.

Callum still went to church in Harlem. He prayed.

Sometimes, you just have to believe in happy endings.

Mike O'Connell got his.

The Feds were furious he stole their thunder. Once he recovered from the gunshot wound, a nick to his right arm, they kicked him into touch, figured they got rid of a bad apple. Mike was a pig in shit. He got out of Organized Crime Investigation.

The radio squawked to life. Word came in from the sergeant. They were good to go and the boss was coming along.

'I don't get it,' said Rubino, 'what kinda boss wants to kick down shitty doors and get his hands dirty with fuckin' skells when he could be ridin' in an airconditioned car listenin' to WAXQ all day?'

He jumped as a fist banged on the door like a gunshot.

Kwan opened it.

'Hey, lieutenant,' he said.

Mike stood in jeans and t-shirt, his shield clipped to his belt by his holstered Glock. He looked in at the cops in the minivan and gave each a nod. Callum almost missed the wink he gave Georgie. Then he looked at Callum. A couple of years' memories were swimming around in his eyes.

Still looking at his friend, he said, 'You ladies ready to go or are you still tellin' bad Irish jokes?' and ducked around the side of the van.

THE END

Acknowledgements

The Sky Turned Black was written during lockdown. It could never have happened without the patience, support and love of my wife and daughter, Tomoe and Hana. Hana, one day I promise there'll be an edition of my last crime novel, *Rat Island*, with a cartoon rat on the cover. Tomoe, you keep me sane through my trips into New York's underworld.

Thanks again go to former NYPD detective Neil Nappi – my time spent with him in New York is the gift that keeps on giving. Thanks, also, to Vic Ferrari, writer and former NYPD detective, whose replies to my queries, and whose own writing, have been a great resource. As with my previous book, the authenticity within the pages of *The Sky Turned Black* is thanks to them; all the inaccuracies are solely down to me.

Inna Marina, Alla Mitkaleva, Ludmila Lace and Nina Loginova showed me the best of the Russian people with their warmth and generosity. *The Sky Turned Black* seemed a less daunting task thanks to them.

David Cameron once again gave of his time in reading an early draft – looking forward to sipping a whiskey with him sometime soon in County Down.

My editor, Humfrey Hunter, has consistently believed in me and given me the opportunity to get my work out there. For that, I am always grateful. Ollie Ray did another great job in creating an atmospheric and evocative cover: thank you for giving the novel such a vivid face.

Finally, thanks to David Albertyn, Thomas Mullen and T.J. English, for taking the time to read my work. They are some of the best crime writers in the world, and to have them find positives in my work helped push me on.